Praise for Morgan Llywelyn's
Pride of Lions

"An old Irish proverb maintains that 'a good story fills the belly.' *Pride of Lions* does more than that, it totally fills the mind and soul. Morgan Llywelyn once again displays all the talents found in century-old traditions of revered Celtic bards. . . . Llywelyn, the consummate storyteller, smoothly weaves many threads into the rich tapestry of this novel that continues her Irish saga begun with *Bard*."

—*Rocky Mountain News*

"The remarkable author has released the sequel to her most successful historical novel, *Lion of Ireland*, and it captivates, educates, and stimulates just as *Lion* did. . . . Let the masterful guide take you through the gates of Kincora, walk with her to the grass covered banks of Holy Island, and see the panorama of eleventh century Ireland. . . . It is a journey you won't want to end."

—*Florida Irish American*

PRIDE OF LIONS

Morgan Llywelyn

TOR ®

A Tom Doherty Associates Book
New York

This is a work of fiction. All the characters and events portrayed in this book are either products of the author's imagination or are used fictitiously.

PRIDE OF LIONS

Cover art by Larry Selman
Map by Ellisa Mitchell

A Tor Book
Published by Tom Doherty Associates, Inc.
175 Fifth Avenue
New York, N.Y. 10010

Tor® is a registered trademark of Tom Doherty Associates, Inc.

ISBN: 0-812-53650-9
Library of Congress Card Catalog Number: 95-42566

First edition: March 1996
First mass market edition: March 1997

Printed in the United States of America

0 9 8 7 6 5 4 3 2 1

For MICHAEL

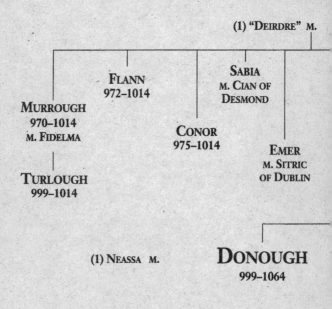

The Dynasty of the Dalcassians

(1) "DEIRDRE" M.

MURROUGH
970–1014
M. FIDELMA

FLANN
972–1014

CONOR
975–1014

SABIA
M. CIAN OF
DESMOND

EMER
M. SITRIC
OF DUBLIN

TURLOUGH
999–1014

(1) NEASSA M.

DONOUGH
999–1064

MURCHAD
D. 1068

*The second daughter of Blanaid and Malcolm, Doada, was the mother of Macbeth. Through Blanaid the blood of Brian Boru entered the family of Scotland and thence England.

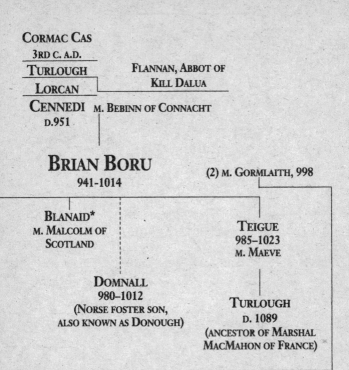

CORMAC CAS
3RD C. A.D.
TURLOUGH
LORCAN   FLANNAN, ABBOT OF KILL DALUA
CENNEDI M. BEBINN OF CONNACHT
D.951

BRIAN BORU
941–1014   (2) M. GORMLAITH, 998

BLANAID*
M. MALCOLM OF
SCOTLAND

TEIGUE
985–1023
M. MAEVE

DOMNALL
980–1012
(NORSE FOSTER SON,
ALSO KNOWN AS DONOUGH)

TURLOUGH
D. 1089
(ANCESTOR OF MARSHAL
MACMAHON OF FRANCE)

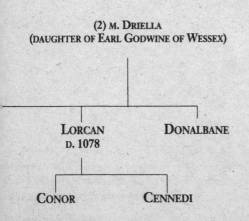

(2) M. DRIELLA
(DAUGHTER OF EARL GODWINE OF WESSEX)

LORCAN
D. 1078   DONALBANE

CONOR   CENNEDI

North Channel

kingdom
of
Ulster

•Armagh

Irish Sea

kingdom
of
Connacht

kingdom
of
Meath

•tara

•Clontarf
Dublin

LOUGH REE

•Clonmacnois

galway
bay
corcomrua
thomond

kingdom
of
Leinster

•Kincora
kill dálua

ossory

Shannon
Estuary

Limerick
(norse)

•Cashel

kingdom
of
Munster

Wexford;
norse territory

Waterford;
norse stronghold

desmond

•Cork

Atlantic Ocean

FOREWORD

by the Rt. Hon. Conor O'Brien, the Lord Inchiquin

In *Pride of Lions* Morgan Llywelyn has again produced a brilliant novel that is both fascinating from the historical perspective and eminently readable. By following the destinies of the surviving children of Brian Boru, particularly his troubled and troublesome son Donough, she has created a worthy sequel to her most highly praised novel, *Lion of Ireland*. Her Celtic gift with words and an extraordinary ability to bring the past to life are hallmarks of her literary excellence.

Morgan Llywelyn's uncanny knack of sweeping the reader back through the centuries comes from a deep, almost intuitive understanding of other eras. As a writer, she is always searching for the human reality behind both history and folklore. Thus the few fictitious characters she introduces in her books are absolutely true to their time. In *Pride of Lions* they play vivid supporting roles to the many historic characters, illuminating the society in which they lived.

The famous family descended from Brian Boru, the greatest of Ireland's High Kings, has played a major part in the history of these islands over the centuries. The dynastic marriages arranged for his children have had long-lasting repercussions. Brian himself certainly came closer to unifying Ireland than anyone up to the present time. His son Donough is much less famous, but presents a fascinating character study. Upon him fell the obligation of trying to live up to an almost superhuman father. He undertook the task with passion, as he lived all his life, but fate was to take a hand in shaping both his future and that of Ireland.

One wonders how different Irish history might have been if Donough had achieved his ambitions.

In *Pride of Lions* we have the rare opportunity to see what happens *after* an earth-shattering event: how people get on with their lives, what adjustments they must make, and what choices. Donough is a thought-provoking hero. Looking back across nine hundred years, the reader must judge for himself if he would have made the same choices. There is a fine irony—and the Irish have always appreciated irony—in the fact that for all his efforts to emulate his father, Donough took with him to Rome the physical symbols of his father's kingship. Brian Boru's crown and sceptre have never to this day come back to Ireland.

Factually, Donough's story as told in *Pride of Lions* is accurate. As a direct descendant of Brian Boru and Chief of the Name, I believe we O'Briens are lucky indeed to have Morgan Llywelyn as our modern-day Bard, telling the story of our race with such eloquence and passion.

The O'Brien,
Prince of Thomond,
18th Baron Inchiquin
County Clare, Ireland
June 1995

Rome, 1064

The road to Rome is very long, they say. My way has been longer and harder than most. I came here an old man, knowing I may never live to see Ireland again.

I came here because I must; because it was expected of me. The final pilgrimage to ask for remission of sin.

Have my sins been so great that I must cross the sea and use the last of my strength to seek forgiveness? There are many who would say so.

In youth, my sin was pride. We were proud, the cubs of the Lion. Passion and ambition were bred into us and we attacked life with a hunger that was hard to satisfy. I wanted everything my father had; everything he had been. At the time I thought I wanted them for myself.

Then I thought I wanted them because my achievements would make him proud of me, although he was dead.

He was not dead to me. He stood behind me, rode beside me, saw the world through my eyes and I tried my best to shape it to suit his vision.

His desire.

As I grew older I learned the meaning of desire. Firstly I desired the most magnificent palace in Ireland and would have done anything—literally anything—to make it mine. Kincora! It rises in my memory as splendid as ever it stood, with gray stone walls defying time itself and the summer sun turning the thatched roofs to gold.

I desired the power that had been my father's. With such power I thought I could have everything I wanted, and to that end I sought the kingship that had been his life's work. Placing myself in the gap of danger I swung the sword that had been his and took the blows. Took the wounds, bled the blood, paid a terrible price.

I desired women; the rampant pleasure, the boiling-blood madness, the explosion which shakes the pillars of the soul and assuages grief and pain. Then I desired one very special woman and secretly hated the Church that stood between us.

Such a long life . . . two wives, children sired, enemies made by my pride and because of my desire. And so much lost!

Kincora is not mine. The kingship I coveted was never mine either. Though I was called a king I did not bear the title my father bore. What little power I achieved was whittled away by conspiring enemies and well-meaning friends.

Wealth is lost, honor lost, I am an exile in an unfamiliar land.

I came to beg forgiveness for fratricide. That sin more than any other drove me to seek mercy from Rome, not for myself but for my posterity. I would not have my children think I died with such a stain on my soul, so I have made this very public gesture. One last duty fulfilled.

If you meet me on the road to Bolsano, where the Pope has granted me a few acres bordering on the lake, you will see, and perhaps pity, an old man with snowy hair and stooped shoulders. Once those shoulders were broad and I thought them capable of bearing any burden. Once I thought I would be young and strong forever, immortal as my father had become immortal, with a shining future before me.

I was wrong; wrong about everything.

And I am the happiest man alive.

From
The Annals of the Kingdom of Ireland
by the Four Masters

VOLUME II

"Aoṁ Cṙıoṫ, mıle a ceṫṙıe ɒecc.

... hı cCluaṁ ṫaṙḃ, ṙın aoıne ṙıa cCaıncc ɒo ṙoṁṙaɒ."

Coṙcaṁ ṙın ccaṫ ṙın bṙıan mac Cıɒeiṫ́ıꞬ, aṙoṙı eṙınn,

auꞬuiṫ ıaṙṫaṁ €oṙṙa uıle eṙıɒe ..."

Translation:
"The Age of Christ, 1014.

. . . at Clontarf, on the Friday before Easter precisely. In this battle were slain Brian, son of Kennedy, monarch of Ireland, who was the Augustus of all the West of Europe. . . ."

Chapter One

The tall boy on the gray horse cast an apprehensive look at the sky.

He could hear his men behind him grumbling as they rode. They resented his command of their company, considering it an undeserved appointment forced upon them by his father. Still more they resented being sent south for skirmish duty while Brian Boru was assembling the main army at Dublin for the battle to determine the future of Ireland.

Young Donough was as frustrated as his men, though in his case it was compounded by a growing sense of foreboding. The sky to the north, in the direction of Dublin, was filled with black clouds that had been boiling in eerie configurations since first light. It was now late in the day on Good Friday in the Year of Our Lord 1014, and the clouds looked more ominous than ever.

Donough tried to reassure himself. *My father would never initiate battle on a Holy Day,* he thought. *But what if his enemies forced a confrontation? Pagan Northmen have no respect for the Christian calendar.*

Watching the demoniac sky, Donough was increasingly certain that Brian Boru had already faced his enemies on the field of battle. The writhing clouds were witness.

He turned his horse's head toward Dublin and lashed its flanks with his horse-goad.

Chapter Two

As darkness fell, members of Brian Boru's combined forces began trying to identify their dead. The gruesome task was accomplished with little conversation. Most were too shocked to speak. They were seasoned warriors accustomed to the aftermath of battle, but none of them had seen thousands of corpses piled five and six deep until today.

Twilight was splintered by the shrieks and curses of the wounded, the prayers and moans of the dying.

Many of the Irish chieftains who had brought their personal armies to join the High King against the invaders had been killed in the battle. Their surviving followers wandered, dazed and leaderless, through the gloom. Malachi Mor began gathering up these strays and adding them to his own Meathmen.

Malachi had no idea where Brian Boru was. He had not seen the Ard Ri, the High King of Ireland, as he had held his Meathmen apart from the conflict until its outcome was certain. Only then had he led his army down from the high ground to fight beside Brian's other allies.

Now he was gathering for himself the remnants of a massive assemblage, warriors who had been willing to follow Brian Boru's banner wherever it led, even to death.

The irony was not lost on Malachi.

Litter bearers approached from the direction of the weir at Clontarf, carrying a body. A scrap torn from a saffron linen tunic covered its face. Malachi signaled the bearers to halt. Recognizing the man who had been Ard Ri before Brian Boru, they obeyed.

Malachi flicked the covering aside. The sightless eyes of a fifteen-year-old boy stared past him toward a canceled future.

"That's Prince Murrough's son," one of the bearers said. "The Ard Ri's first grandson." The man's voice was thick in his throat. "We found him floating facedown in the weir with his fingers still tangled in the hair of the last Viking he killed."

Malachi ran his fingers through his own thin gray hair. He found himself recalling that Brian Boru's mane retained a faint gleam of red-gold in spite of the passage of time, and appeared as thick as it had ever been. Such comparisons tormented Malachi, but he could not prevent them, any more than one could prevent one's tongue from tormenting a sore tooth.

Brian is a decade older than me, Malachi thought. *He's seventy-three this month. Can it be possible? Where have the years gone? And both of us still fighting.*

He shook his head ruefully, dragging his thoughts back to this time and place. He covered the dead boy's face and asked one of the bearers, "Where's Prince Murrough?"

"They're bringing him now," volunteered a Dalcassian warrior, limping past them in the twilight.

Murrough's litter bearers were Dalcassian heroes famed for their strength, yet they were tottering like old men as they approached. Both they and the litter were bathed in blood.

Malachi stepped forward to intercept them. "What

happened to him?" he asked, staring down. The face of the corpse was uncovered, but masses of clotted gore obscured the features.

"That blood's not from his wounds," a bearer said. "We carried him here through Tomar's Wood, where the worst of the axe fighting was. Blood's still dripping from the branches of the trees."

In spite of himself, Malachi shuddered.

With the hem of his own tunic he wiped the blood from the dead man's eye sockets. The lids, he was thankful to find, were closed. The face which he had so often seen contorted with anger was peaceful now, all quarrels forgotten.

Including ours, Malachi told Murrough silently. *Forgotten and forgiven.*

He laid the palm of his hand on the bloody forehead in benediction, then motioned the bearers to move on. The depth of his grief surprised him. He and Brian Boru's eldest son had never liked one another.

The collecting of the dead continued. It would go on for days.

The night smelled of death and excrement.

Somewhere down near the bay someone was chanting wildly. "Boru! Boru! Boru!"

Chapter Three

The gray horse had been bred for endurance on the limestone-rich plains of Kildare, but it was tired now. Men and horses alike were tired, yet Donough drove them on. "The Ard Ri needs me," he insisted.

As usual, Ronan, his second in command and the senior

member of the company, contradicted him. "The Ard Ri does not need you. I myself heard him say he does not expect us to join him until after Easter. Those were his precise orders."

Ignoring Ronan, Donough pushed on. Saturday evening found his band in the Wicklow mountains, the men wearied to the point of revolt. When they paused to water their horses at an icy stream, Ronan tried again. "You have to have some consideration for your men," he told Donough. "You're being reckless, forcing such a pace when there is no need for it. I must protest, Donnchad."

The youngster's gray eyes flashed. "I told you before. Call me Donough from now on." He pronounced the name *Donno* in his Munster accent. He despised the name Donnchad, which his mother had given him, and with which she prefaced her constant criticisms of him. He considered himself a man now, entitled to a new name to reflect his new status. Had not Brian Mac Cennedi become Brian Boru?

"Och, I forgot," Ronan replied with a shrug, as if it did not matter. "But listen to the voice of experience, lad. What you're doing is dangerous. Weary horses are likely to stumble and break their legs or our necks. It could happen to you as easily as to one of us, and then there would be trouble. We have orders to . . ."

"To what?" snapped Donough, instantly suspicious. "You have orders to what?"

"To keep you safe," Ronan admitted. "That's why the Ard Ri assigned us to come south with you while the rest of them went to Dublin."

"I thought so!" Donough exploded. "And I tell you, no one is needed to keep me safe. I can take care of myself! Am I not the same age my father was when he began fighting the Vikings? And am I not in command of this company? We're riding on to Dublin now, Ronan, and if that means we keep going throughout the night, so be it!"

Below a flowing russet moustache, Ronan thrust forward

a clean-shaven jaw. "If the Ard Ri were here right now," he said, "he would tear strips off you. He's famous for taking care of his warriors."

Donough felt a momentary empathy with his oldest half-brother. Murrough frequently complained of having Brian Boru held up to him, an unattainable standard of perfection. The burden of such a father weighed heavily on his sons, particularly the eldest.

Donough, the youngest, tried to imagine what his father would do in the same situation. Compromise, he decided. Compromise was one of the Ard Ri's most effective weapons, a lesson Murrough had never learned. But Donough would learn. He idolized Brian. It was his ambition to be just like him.

"I'll strike a bargain with you, Ronan," he offered. "You and the others ride on with me now until the wind changes. Whenever that happens, we will set up camp and have a rest before we go any farther."

Ronan looked dubious. "What if the wind doesn't change?"

"Surely it will, it's been shifting almost constantly for days. You yourself said you had never known it to be so unpredictable. Have we an agreement?"

The veteran hesitated, to make it look as if he had a choice. "We do," he said at last.

They mounted and rode on in gathering darkness, a weary band in saffron-dyed tunics and woolen mantles, bare-legged, cold, hungry.

One of the warriors remarked, low-voiced, to Ronan, "You were afraid he'd go off without us and report us as deserters to his father."

"I'm not afraid of Brian Boru," came the swift reply. "I tell you something for nothing—that lad's mother is the one to be feared."

At the mention of Gormlaith a ripple of coarse laughter ran though the company. "If we let her baby ride off by himself and anything happened to him," Ronan elaborated, "she would put a fearful curse on the lot of us."

"That Gormlaith is a curse all by herself," another man said.

No one disagreed.

The night was bitterly black; the wind was icy. Neither moon nor stars lit the way. The sky was opaque with cloud.

Sooner than he would have liked, Donough felt the wind shift, swinging around to blow straight out of the north. It had gained him a little more time, at least, and for that he was thankful. He signaled a halt and his men were sliding off their horses almost before he gave the order.

They made camp in the lee of a massive stony outcropping that shielded them from the worst of the wind. With flints, one of the warriors struck sparks and made a fire of dry gorse and winter-killed bracken. They were too tired to forage, so contented themselves with eating bread and stringy dried venison from their supplies, then settled down to sleep.

But Donough could not rest. He wandered around the perimeter of the campsite, listening to the snores of his men and the chewing of the hobbled horses as they grazed on mountain grass. The bitter wind tugged at the edges of the brat he wore, the heavy knee-length mantle fastened at the shoulder with a massive bronze brooch.

Although he was angry with his father for putting him in what he considered to be a humiliating position, denied a part in the real fighting, most of his anger was reserved for his mother. If it were not for Gormlaith there would be no invasion to threaten an aging High King who should have been allowed to live out his remaining years in peace.

Donough wanted to share those years with Brian Boru. He had not been allowed much time with his father while Brian and Gormlaith were married, for she had deliberately contrived to keep her son away from his sire so she could demand Brian's attention for herself. But when at last the

Ard Ri divorced Gormlaith under Brehon Law and sent her from Kincora, he had kept Donough with him.

The youngster had taken this as a sign of special affection, and began imagining himself someday supplanting Murrough as Brian's favorite, the son being groomed to succeed his father.

But now Murrough, who had spent his life trying to step out of Brian's shadow and be his own man, was with the Ard Ri at Dublin, while Donough was being held at arm's length. To keep him *safe.*

He ground his teeth in the darkness.

With no one watching, Donough did not have to keep up the façade of maturity he assumed by daylight. He could be what he was, a sixteen-year-old boy . . . well, to be honest, sixteen in two months . . . in unfamiliar country in the middle of the night, assailed by the fears that worry most youngsters at some time.

What would I do, he asked himself, *if anything happened to my father?*

The mere idea made his stomach churn.

Without Brian behind him, Donough was nothing more than Gormlaith's son; the son of the Princess of Leinster, the most hated woman in Ireland.

Surely, he thought, concentrating with desperate intensity, *God will not let anyone harm the Ard Ri!*

He pictured his father as he had last seen him at Kincora—tall, regal, looking far younger than his years.

But old nevertheless. Brian had been old for all of Donough's lifetime.

The boy recalled his father's voice, that deep, slow voice which dropped each word as if it were a jewel, compelling people to listen. Donough had strained his throat trying to force his own voice into a lower register, and when someone eventually commented that he was beginning to sound like the Ard Ri he had glowed like a beeswax candle.

He knew he looked somewhat like Brian. In his mother's

many mirrors he had studied his face, searching out similarities. He had the same broad brow and long, straight nose. To his regret he had also inherited his mother's curving mouth, but as soon as he could grow the drooping moustache of a warrior he would hide that flaw. Unfortunately he lacked Brian's famous red-gold mane, for his own hair was an auburn so dark it looked almost black unless he stood in the sunlight. But at least he was tall. Someday he might be as tall as the Lion of Ireland. Someday . . .

He tensed abruptly. He thought he heard a woman cry out—but what woman would be in these mountains at night when wolves might be hunting? Perhaps it was a wolf he heard. He dropped a cautious hand to his sword hilt.

The sound came again, raising the hackles on his neck. That was no wolf. Now Donough was certain it was a female voice, one with an unnameable quality at once familiar and frightening.

The wail drifted on the wind. And all at once, he knew.

"Ban shee!" he hissed in horror.

"Whassay?" mumbled a warrior lying near him on the ground, wrapped in a voluminous shaggy cloak.

Donough stood transfixed as the sound rose in volume, shrilling upward into an inhuman ululation as much a part of Ireland as her fields and forests.

"Mother of God!" gasped the warrior on the ground, trying to scramble out of the enveloping folds of his cloak so he could get to his feet. "What was that?"

"The guardian spirit of the Dal Cais," Donough told him with sudden, absolute certainty. His blood and bones identified the sound. "She who lives on Crag Liath, the Grey Crag above Kincora. But she's not there now. She's somewhere on this side of the country, and she's keening for the Dalcassian dead!"

"Jesus, Mary, and Joseph protect us!" cried the warrior, fervently signing the Cross on his breast.

The others were waking in spite of their weariness, the

very mention of the ban shee enough to cut through the fog of sleep. Their priests claimed that the ban shees— fairies, Little People, supernatural relics of a vanished race—were but myths and legends preying on superstitious minds. But when her next cry came with chilling clarity, they all heard it.

She screamed like a hare being torn apart by hounds. In that despairing shriek was all the grief and pain in the world.

"I told you my father needs me!" Donough sobbed in anguish.

In a matter of minutes camp was broken. The company set off at a hasty trot along narrow mountain trails, impelled by the memory of the ban shee's scream.

The first light of a gray, bitterly cold Easter morning found them descending from the mountains toward Dublin. The veteran warriors said little to one another. Fear and superstition rode with them, embedded in their bones.

Donough was also silent. His jaws were clamped tight on his anxiety, but his thoughts raced feverishly inside his skull.

His father, his half-brothers by Brian's various women, his Dalcassian cousins—all the men who represented stability in his life—were in Dublin to fight the invaders.

His mother was in Dublin too. Gormlaith, the antithesis of stability.

Once they left the mountains, their route joined with the Slighe Cualann, one of the five major roads developed by King Cormac Mac Airt in the third century of the Christian era to bring commerce and tribute from every part of Ireland to his stronghold at Tara. The island had countless small roads composed of foot-beaten earth, called bothars, or cow roads, because they were the width of two cows, one lengthwise and one athwart. But these casual trails were hardly sufficient for the traffic Cormac had envisioned— hence the slighe.

Originally constructed of oak logs laid down across timber supports, a slighe was designed to accommodate, two abreast, the war chariots once used by Gaelic champions. The passage of centuries had seen the disappearance of war chariots, although similar carts of wickerwork were still used for personal transportation by the nobility. Meanwhile wooden-wheeled traders' wagons had combined with the Irish weather to erode the slighe. Stones had been added to its bed from time to time so it would continue to provide a stable surface over mud and bogland, but it was very diffi- cult footing for weary horses.

Unthinkingly, Donough guided his horse onto the slighe. Ronan, directly behind him, reined his animal to one side and rode beside the slighe rather than upon it. The others followed his example. Donough noticed, but continued as he had begun, refusing to be instructed by his second-in-command.

Ronan grinned to himself. Proud and stubborn; not surprising.

As they drew closer to Dublin, the company began encountering refugees, big-boned, fair-haired people typical of the Scandinavian population of the city. The first ones they met were not prosperous Viking sea rovers, however, but three men and two women whose clothing identified them as members of the laboring class. The men wore tat- tered woolen coats and leggings that had been many times patched. The women, who might have been mother and daughter, were clothed in unfitted ankle-length gowns of coarse wool over shifts of equally coarse linen. Neither gown was ornamented with embroidery. Like all Vikings they wore shoes, but these were in bits and bound to their feet with string.

They straggled to a halt and peered up at the horsemen, fear in their eyes. The two women held hands.

"Are you from Dublin?" Donough demanded to know in an awkward mixture of aristocratic Irish and the Norse spoken by the inhabitants of Limerick, the only Vikings he knew. "What happened on Good Friday?" he asked urgently, leaning forward on his horse.

The refugees gaped at him, slack-mouthed.

Ronan, who was familiar with Dublin and its people, inquired in their own dialect, "Was there fighting on Freya's Day?"

A scrawny man with soot ground into every pore had been staring openly at Donough's torc, the gold neck ring that identified him as a member of the chieftainly class. Now the man transferred his gaze to Ronan. "Yah, yah, fighting," he affirmed. He waved his arms. "Big battle at the Meadow of the Bull!"

"Clontarf?"

"Yah yah."

Donough, following the exchange as best he could, said impatiently, "Ask him who won, Ronan. Ask him what he knows of my . . . of the Ard Ri."

Ronan repeated the questions but got no reply other than a blank stare. To emphasize his demand he drew his short-sword from the scabbard affixed to his belt, which reduced the Dubliner to near hysteria and made the women shriek and throw their arms around one another.

"I am a charcoal burner, I know nothing about anything!" the sooty man cried. "I know nothing!" His eyes skittered in their sockets like frightened insects.

A second man managed to say, "We were frightened so we hid. It is always people like us who suffer. No matter who wins, the victors burn and rape. We hid for a long time. Then this morning we came out when they opened the gates."

"When who opened the gates? Brian Boru's men, or Sitric Silkbeard's?"

The refugee shrugged. "Men with spears."

Men with spears were all the same to him, whatever their army.

Ronan turned to Donough. "We won't get anything from

this lot. They were probably cowering in a cellar the whole time."

"Let them go, then. We may have better luck farther along."

Ronan sheathed his sword and the company rode off, leaving the refugees huddled together like sheep, staring after them.

The next group was better dressed and was pushing a hand barrow piled with household goods. One of the women was leading a goat by a length of rope. When she saw the horsemen bearing down on them she tried to conceal the goat with her body.

A thickset man with a face like a red moon stepped forward warily. Donough let Ronan question him.

"I'm a shoemaker," the man said, "with a shop in Fishamble Street. I hope it's still there when we return," he added wistfully.

"What do you know about a battle? At Clontarf?"

"Not just Clontarf, but everywhere!" was the reply. "It was terrible, like the end of the world. People fighting all around the city and the plains beyond.

"We had been hearing rumors for weeks that King Sitric had summoned a great hosting from the north to challenge the High King of the Irish and take control of the country away from him. Everything would have been ours, then: the riches of this rich island . . . " He sighed as if they had been snatched out of his own hands.

"Go on," Ronan urged.

"For days, ships had been sailing into Dublin Bay bringing warriors from Scandinavia, the Orkneys, the Hebrides. Even King Amlaff of Denmark himself, someone said.

"Then Brian Boru came marching east with a great army gathered from throughout Ireland. He was even said to have Norse traitors from Limerick with him, come to fight against their own countrymen.

"When he reached the coast he put the torch to the land from Fingal to Howth, trying to intimidate Sitric. The smoke was so black we in Dublin had to light lamps in the middle of the day.

"My wife wanted to leave the city then, but I was not prepared to abandon my shop. So we stayed. On the morning of Freya's Day the Irish army swept toward the sea, and the longships sent another army ashore to meet them, and the battle began. There was such clashing and banging and screaming we could hear it even inside the walls of Dublin, though in the beginning the fighting was well north of the Liffey."

"The noise frightened the children," said a tall woman with a number of missing teeth. "They screamed and clapped their hands over their ears. I knew then we should have left." She cast a dark look at the shoemaker. "I warned my husband I would be raped if we did not leave at once."

"Make that man tell you about the battle," Donough instructed Ronan, but the narrative had been taken away from the shoemaker. His wife continued, with evident relish at being the center of attention, "I saw her, you know. With these two eyes I saw Kormlada." She gave Gormlaith's name its Viking pronunciation. "She was watching the battle from atop the walls of the city with her son, King Sitric. Her son by the old King of Dublin, him they called Olaf Cuaran."

At the mention of his mother's name Donough had fixed his eyes on the woman's face with fierce intensity.

"Olaf was Kormlada's first husband," she was saying, obviously preferring gossip to descriptions of battle. "She is Irish, you know, a princess of Leinster or so she claims, but she married a Viking king. After he died she married Malachi Mor, High King of the Irish. Then when Brian Boru took the kingship away from Malachi, did she not change her gown and marry *him*? And have another son by him, though she was old enough to be a grandmother!" The woman lowered her voice to a confidential murmur. "They say King Sitric offered his mother in the marriage bed to any foreign lord who could succeed in killing Brian Boru."

Abruptly, Donough exclaimed, "We have to go now!" He lashed his weary horse so savagely with the goad that it leaped forward into full gallop, its hooves skidding on the stones of the slighe.

Ronan shouted after him, "But I thought you wanted me to question . . ."

Donough was already out of earshot. Ronan glanced around at the other horsemen and shrugged. They set off after Donough.

The refugees watched them go. "What do you make of that?" asked the woman with the goat, which was chewing unnoticed on the embroidery of her sleeve.

"It was the mention of Kormlada that did it," said the shoemaker. "Did you mark how the beardless one went white around the mouth? The Irish hate her."

"She is not much loved in Dublin either," commented an older man leaning on a walking stick. "Swanning around the city, criticizing our customs. Her son may be King of Dublin but she is just an old Irish woman."

"*Just* an old Irish woman?" The shoemaker raised an eyebrow. "I myself have seen Kormlada striding down Fishamble Street with sunlight flaming her hair and the sea in her green eyes, and there is no Viking woman the equal of her, no matter how old she is."

His wife rounded on him. "You would say that, you man! Just because she has a big body and a disgusting amount of red hair you think she is a marvel. But she was born with those things, they are none of her doing. You know what people say of her: 'Kormlada of Leinster is most gifted in that over which she has no control, but works evil in all those things over which she has any power.' Did we not see the proof of the saying on Freya's Day?"

The shoemaker replied mildly, "Surely one woman could not cause a war."

His wife sniffed. "Consider this. Brian Boru had kept peace in Ireland for ten years. He even married one of his daughters to King Sitric to build an alliance with the Dublin Vikings. Then he divorced Kormlada, and suddenly there is war.

"Where would you lay the blame?"

Chapter Four

Lashed by intermittent rain, Donough's company hurried on toward the city. Though it was Easter Sunday, the celebration of the Feast of the Resurrection was the furthest thing from their minds.

Only by courtesy could Dublin be called a city. Compared to Rome or Constantinople it was a primitive town, a Viking trading port whose narrow, twisting laneways ran between cramped houses and shops of post-and-wattle construction, daubed with mud and manure to keep out the weather. Some of the more prosperous sea raiders had built themselves two-roomed houses of timber planking, but thatch made of river reeds was the ubiquitous roofing material. Goats and geese were penned in filthy yards, and half-wild swine rooted in midden heaps, adding to the pervasive effluvium of fishmarkets and smoky fires and wet wool and rotting seaweed and scabrous hounds and tidal mudflats and running sewage.

Dublin was a city you could smell, on a warm day when the wind was off the river, before you could see it.

Its origins could be traced to a small support settlement

that had grown up around several Christian churches on the south bank of the river Liffey at a place known as Ath Cliath—the Ford of the Hurdles. The Irish staked sheep hurdles—panels of woven wattles used to make temporary sheep pens—in the bed of the shallow river at this point, to provide a ford across the Liffey. While it did not keep their feet dry, at least it kept them from becoming mired in mud and silt.

Scandinavian sea rovers had first discovered the site in 837, when Norse longships explored the bay and the mouth of the Liffey. They returned in force in 841, when the full terror of Viking raids descended upon peaceful, dreaming Ath Cliath.

The Norse settled in to spend the winter at a nearby locale called Dubh Linn—the Black Pool—which was a tidal basin where the river Poddle joined the estuary of the Liffey. The Northmen busied themselves repairing their ships, gloating over their plunder, and enjoying a climate that was positively balmy by comparison with their homeland. They constructed what they called a longport, a camp that enclosed their beached longships inside a protective palisade.

Within a few years Dublin would be the principal Viking colony in Ireland.

In the beginning the Irish did not fully comprehend the ramifications. They had lived unmolested by invaders for over a thousand years. Even Caesar had not extended his campaign so far west. The Irish, who with the Scots comprised the Gaelic branch of the Celtic race, were a totally pastoral people. The resources of their island were so extensive they needed not take to the sea to support themselves, so they did not appreciate that the sea was a highway which could bring ever-increasing numbers of raiders to their shores. At first they considered the Vikings in their longships only a temporary hazard.

But when more and more Norsemen arrived—raiding,

pillaging, and, inevitably, beginning to form colonies wherever they found good harborage—the Irish took alarm. Then
the Danes followed the Norse, to vie for control of a lucrative
export trade in Irish gold, timber, leather, slaves, sacred
vessels, and secular ornaments of unmatched craftsmanship.
As the Viking presence grew, the Irish fought back.

Meanwhile, Norse trading centers were established at
such places as Waterford, Wexford, and Limerick. The
Vikings introduced the concept of settled towns to a land
whose inhabitants had gloried in the freedom of unfettered
herding and hunting for countless generations.

During the next two centuries Ireland was torn by almost
constant warfare between Gael and Viking. The Northmen
were as fierce at fighting as they were dedicated to trade, but
the Irish were ruled by a warrior aristocracy that defined
itself through combat. In the bitter struggle for control of the
island's riches, neither side managed a decisive victory.

To confuse the issue, as time passed the distinction
between native and foreigner grew blurred. Some of the
Vikings brought their own women with them, but others
married Irish women and sired half-breed families. Their
sons became mercenaries, fighting for both sides.

Some Irish chieftains formed alliances of convenience
with the Vikings to further their own burgeoning interest in
trade, or to add Viking warriors to their personal armies
when carrying on ancient feuds with other Irish chieftains.

Warfare ceased to be a simple matter of Gael against
Viking.

Nor was it merely Christian against pagan. Some Vikings
converted to the teachings of Christ, while some Irish
eschewed Christianity and continued to follow the Druid
way, to the profound displeasure of the Church.

This was the Ireland to which, against all odds, Brian
Boru had brought a decade of peace.

Now that peace was shattered.

In the uncertain aftermath, Donough and his men made

their way toward Dublin. When they met Vikings driving twenty-eight good oxen across the slighe, they fell on the startled herders and relieved them of their animals. "Spoils of war," Donough claimed. ,

The addition of plodding oxen to their company slowed him down, but he did not complain as his men expected. As they drew nearer the city, Donough was increasingly apprehensive about what he might find there, and willing to put off the moment as long as he comfortably could.

Soon enough the walls of Dublin loomed ahead. As a result of countless assaults and sieges over the years, the city was heavily fortified, protected by timber palisades and guarded gateways.

Close to the house of Vespers the horsemen crossed the Slighe Dala as it approached Dublin from the west. There they saw their first bodies. Irish warriors in saffron-dyed linen tunics and foreigners in chain mail lay twisted together in the dance of death, their blood stiff and black upon them.

Lowering their heads, the oxen stared popeyed at the corpses and gave them a wide berth.

One of Donough's men pointed toward the city. "I see figures moving on the walls."

"Guards on the palisades, no doubt," Ronan responded. "The question is, are they our men, or theirs?"

Donough narrowed his eyes. "It looks like they're wearing cones on their heads."

Ronan swore under his breath. "You have the eyes of an eagle. Vikings wear conical iron helmets, we don't, so those are Sitric's men."

Donough gnawed on his lip. If the Ard Ri had not captured Dublin, it must mean that for the first time in years Brian Boru had been defeated in battle. "I want to join my father right away," he told Ronan. "He needs my support."

For once Ronan was disinclined to argue. "He's probably still north of the Liffey," the veteran surmised, "supervising the gathering of the bodies and the digging of mass graves.

The best place for us to cross the river would be at the Ford of the Hurdles, which is beyond spear range from the walls. That way," he indicated with a nod.

The company rode along the west side of Dublin in the direction of the ford. Sitric's men watched in ominous silence from the walls.

"Why don't they yell at us, curse us, something?" one of the horsemen wondered aloud.

As they approached Fair Green they found a haphazard military encampment sprawled across the meadowland. Recognizing banners, Donough gave a glad whoop. "Dalcassians!" He rode forward eagerly. "Abu Dal gCais!"

No one returned the ancient shout of victory. It was met with a thunderous silence, and as he drew nearer Donough could see that these were men with nothing left to give, either physically or emotionally. Bloody, battered, as dispirited as the sodden banners that dripped from poles beside their officers' leather tents, they sat or sprawled on wet earth.

The faces they turned toward Donough as he rode up were the faces of men who had seen hell.

Defeat then, Donough thought. *Defeat confirmed.* He braced himself as for a physical blow.

A sandy-haired man with a luxurious moustache emerged from one of the tents. Over his knee-length leine was a brat of woven wool dyed a brilliant Munster blue and trimmed with wolf fur.

"Fergal!" Donough shouted to his cousin. "Fergal Mac Anluan."

The son of Anluan glanced up and frowned. "Oh. It's you."

Donough was taken aback. "Of course it's me."

"We could have used you on Good Friday."

"I'm here now!" the boy bristled. "Where's my father?"

Fergal gazed at him thoughtfully, started to say something, changed his mind, waved his arm toward the north.

Donough shouted over his shoulder to his men, "You lot stay here and mind the oxen. I'll be back to you when I've seen the Ard Ri." He galloped away before anyone could protest, including a second man who emerged from the tent to join Fergal.

"Could you not stop him?" the second man asked Ronan, who was dismounting.

"I can't do anything with him, Cian. His head is pure rock. Is it too dangerous for him to go off alone like that? I can go after him and . . ."

"I doubt if there is much danger to him right now," replied Cian, who wore a mantle even richer than that of Fergal. "But he'll be wanting someone with him."

"I don't understand," Ronan said.

Cian turned to Fergal. "Did you not tell them?"

"I hadn't the heart."

Ronan felt suddenly chilled. "Tell us what?"

Donough galloped on toward the Ford of the Hurdles, following a trackway of hoof-scarred mud. A party was coming up from the river toward him; a funeral party, marching to the beat of a bodhran, the goatskin-covered war drum. There was a guard of honor, fully armed, and solemn-faced bearers who carried two litters. The first of these was draped in the personal banner of Murrough Mac Brian.

Donough drew rein in dismay. "That can't be Murrough!" His darkest imaginings had never included the death of one of his siblings. Men claimed, "The cubs of the Lion are as unkillable as their sire."

The captain of the honor guard, who wore the distinctive blue and gold of the Dal Cais, signaled the cortège to halt. "It is Prince Murrough," he affirmed. "Slain in battle by a foreigner called Anrad."

Donough's mind struggled to catch up with his eyes and

ears. How could sturdy, aggressive, contentious Murrough be dead? *Dead?*

"Where are you taking him?" he asked numbly.

"To a place not far from here, called Kilmainham. We camped there before the battle, in some woods above the Liffey. Prince Murrough remarked that Kilmainham had a pleasant aspect, and said he would like to rest there again when the fighting was over. So . . . "—the Dalcassian paused, fighting for control—" . . . and so he shall."

Donough rolled his eyes toward the second litter. "And who is that?"

"Prince Murrough's son, Turlough. He fought as bravely as his father and they shall sleep together under the same stone."

"But Turlough's only a boy!" Donough protested as if that could somehow make a difference.

"He was your age," said the Dalcassian. "Old enough to die."

· Donough found himself torn by conflicting emotions. First was relief; the ban shee had not wailed for Brian Boru, but for Murrough and Turlough. He also felt a guilty pleasure in the realization that Murrough's place as Brian's chosen successor was now vacant.

But even as the thought crossed Donough's mind it was swept away by genuine grief. Murrough, although separated from him by more than a generation, had been part of the familial network so important to the Gael. And though he had always been antagonistic toward Gormlaith, Murrough had seemed to like her son, to the extent of engaging in good-humored horseplay with the boy when they happened to meet at Kincora.

Once, a number of years ago, Murrough had even given Donough a whistle carved from the wood of a thorn tree that grew on the slopes of Crag Liath.

Donough still had that whistle someplace.

Suddenly he wanted very much to go and find it.

The beat of the bodhran resumed, setting the cadence of a dirge for the marchers to follow. Honor guard and litter bearers prepared to move off. Rousing himself, Donough cried, "But what of my father? Does the Ard Ri not mean to attend his son's burial?"

The captain of the guard paused long enough to give him a level, measuring look. "The Ard Ri is on his way to Swords," he said in a strange voice as if the words hurt him.

"The Sword of St. Colmcille? Why would he be going to a monastery now?"

There was no way, the Dalcassian captain decided, to shield the boy from the blow. Best get it done. Harsh and quick and over. "Brian Boru's corpse has been taken to Colmcille's chapel to wait for the Bishop of Armagh to arrive and escort it north to Ulster for burial. I am sorry, lad. Sorry for us all."

Donough did not hear the last words.

He could only hear the ban shee scream on a rising wind.

Chapter Five

Some battles are destined to be remembered. Some are best forgotten.

It was enough to have survived Clontarf.

Of the thousands who had fought out of anger or avarice, the majority were dead.

Courage and cowardice had contested together, often within the same person. Memories would haunt the survivors for the rest of their lives. They had only to murmur, "Clontarf," and it would all come back again: the leap of loyalty, the slash of swords, the hiss of spears, the grunting and screaming and sudden stench as bowels opened in death or terror, the skirling of the war pipes, the thunder of fist-beaten shields. And worst of all, the sickening, unforgettable thud of the axe.

Used by warriors on both sides, the battle axe had turned the meadows between the Tolka and the Liffey into a bloody quagmire and made a nightmare of Tomar's Wood.

When the battle was over a few men were so appalled by the slaughter in which they had taken part that they hurled their weapons into the sea. Most, however, kept them to pass down from father to son, encrusted with legend. Someday old men would boast, "I was at Clontarf with Brian Boru," and those words alone would be enough to draw an audience.

But that was in the future. On Easter Sunday 1014 it was enough to have survived.

What remained of the Irish combined forces waited in dazed disarray for someone, anyone, to tell them what to do next. But their surviving officers were incapable of leadership. The loss of the Ard Ri had unmanned them.

In life, Brian Boru had dominated Ireland as no man before him. He was more than the High King, an over-lord claiming tribute from five provincial kings and two hundred tribal kings. He was a lover and Ireland was his grand passion. Throughout his life he had courted her with all the talents he possessed, including ferocious energy and a questing, complex intellect.

Although in his youth he tried to slaughter every Viking he could, in time he had recognized the permanence of the Scandinavian presence in Ireland. After two hundred years, Viking colonists simply could not be plucked out like a sore tooth. When he accepted this truth, Brian changed his approach and set out to win the allegiance of Norse and Dane and incorporate them fully into Irish life.

The breadth of his vision and the audacity of his ambition shocked some and infuriated others.

He entered into political negotiations with various tribal chieftains who had long enjoyed warring upon one another, forcing peace upon them with a canny mixture of bribery and intimidation. He encouraged alliances between Viking and Gael through trade, marriage, and the fostering of orphans. Through his own children he developed a network of dynastic marriage that extended beyond the shores of Ireland to intertwine with foreign royalty. To win ecclesiastical support for his schemes he rebuilt churches and endowed monasteries. With an unprecedented grasp of military strategy—stimulated by an education in monastic schools that included studying the careers of Caesar and Charlemagne—he built a navy, trained a cavalry, and planned perimeter defenses for the island to be a deterrent to any other foreigners attracted by Ireland's riches.

Those defenses were not yet in place at the time of his death, however. Murrough had been entrusted with their realization . . . in the future.

The influence of Brian Boru permeated every aspect of

Irish life. He had overthrown traditions, reinterpreted laws, reformed society, and reshaped the people's image of themselves. In so doing he had become the Irish Charlemagne.

His enemies, and they were many, accused him of being an opportunist and a usurper.

In the Book of Armagh he called himself Emperor of the Irish.

The Ireland of 1014 was a dream Brian Boru had dreamed and brought into being. His death was beyond comprehension.

Particularly to his son; to me.

Chapter Six

✠

The captain of the honor guard gazed up at Donough's pale face, in which the freckles stood out alarmingly. The youngster was swaying on his horse.

"Are you all right?" the Dalcassian wanted to know.

Donough could not answer him; could not even hear him. All he heard was the wind. The ban shee wind. Cold, so cold, with himself in its vortex and nothing beyond but a vast and terrible emptiness.

The Dalcassian stepped forward and seized Donough's horse by the bridle. *Thank God at least one of them is alive!* he thought to himself.

"This has been a shock for you," he said aloud. "Had no one told you anything?"

Donough stared over his head, silent.

The Dalcassian tried again. "Have you just arrived from the south? Are there men with you, shall I take you to them? Prince Murrough will wait, he has all eternity."

Donough managed to say something, he would never remember what, and the Dalcassian barked orders to his men. The cold wind blew. Donough sat on his horse. After a while he was aware that it was being led somewhere.

He rode above the pain, listening to the wind.

Then he was back at Fair Green. Someone took him into a tent, out of the wind.

But he could still hear it.

Inside the tent was Cian the Owenacht, Prince of Desmond, who had married Brian Boru's daughter, Sabia, in a union encouraged by Brian to establish an alliance between the Dalcassians and their ancient enemies, the Owenacht tribe. In his middle years, Cian was still handsome, though now he had the same exhausted look as the rest of them. He was slumped on a wooden camp stool, but at the sight of Donough he rose and pressed a cup into the youngster's hand. "Take this, nephew. You look as if you need it."

Donough drained the Danish ale without tasting it. Then he let himself sink to the ground, sitting crosslegged and gazing blankly into the empty cup.

Ronan and Fergal were also in the tent, together with the Dalcassian officer who had brought Donough. They began talking above his head. From time to time he heard his name spoken, but he could not summon the will to respond.

"I know I was taking a lot on myself," the Dalcassian captain was saying, "but I was doing what Prince Murrough would have wanted, I'm convinced of it. Can you see that, Prince Donnchad?"

"Donough," Ronan corrected him. "He wants to be known as Donough now."

"Eh? Er . . . of course, of course. Prince . . . Donough," the officer amended. "Anyway, the Ard Ri's men insisted his favorite son should be taken to Armagh and buried with him there, but those of us who had been closest to Prince Murrough knew he would want to rest in a place of his own, not his father's. So we wrapped another body in one of his cloaks and sewed it closed with leather thongs. We gave this to the Ard Ri's attendants, while we brought the real Murrough with us to bury at Kilmainham. Let the scribes write that he is entombed at Armagh if they want to."

As he listened, Donough's lips curled into the ghost of a smile. This was the sort of trickery Brian Boru might have employed.

The Dalcassian interpreted the smile as approval. "I may go, then? I may bury my prince at Kilmainham?"

The deference in his voice surprised Donough. He nodded assent, then sank back into the gray void where pain was kept at a distance by the simple expedient of feeling nothing.

The others resumed talking among themselves, but Donough no longer heard them.

Eventually, however, he became aware that he was shivering. With physical awareness aural comprehension returned. Fergal was saying, "I know he's too young, but he's all we have left. I don't think the Dalcassians would take orders from anyone else right now. We must have Brian's son take command or they will simply sit there until Sitric recovers from his defeat and comes roaring out of Dublin. If we give him time he could destroy us, weakened as we are."

Cian said, with a chill in his voice, "I am married to the Ard Ri's daughter. They should accept my command."

"You're an Owenacht, not a Dalcassian," Fergal pointed out. "They would never follow you; it's Donough they'll accept. And who knows? He may prove to be as much of a man as his father was at the same age."

"From your mouth to God's ear!" Ronan interjected.

With an effort, Donough broke his silence. "Did you say 'Sitric's defeat'? I thought he won."

Cian snorted. "Sitric win? Not likely! The battle was hard fought and there were times it might have gone either way, I admit. Many of our leaders were slain, chieftains and princes dying left, right, and center. But all the leaders of the invading force were killed, every last man of them. At the end of the day their army was shattered like ice on a pond."

Fergal said, "The Ard Ri had so arranged his battle lines that his enemies were trapped no matter which way they went. When the foreigners tried to escape to the ships that had brought them, the tide had turned. The ships were far out in the bay beyond their reach. Hundreds of them drowned in the sea and we killed hundreds more on the beaches, not to mention the slaughter that took place clear across Fingal. A few may have found safety inside the walls of Dublin, but when the battle was over, only a handful of the invaders was left alive. The Ard Ri gave the Vikings the worst defeat they've ever suffered," he added with ringing pride. "It was a great victory for him."

"Victory?" said Donough, unable to comprehend. "But he's dead."

"He is dead. But he died triumphant. What more could a warrior want?"

The words hung on the air, defining Brian's ultimate achievement. In silence, they considered it.

At last Donough spoke again. "What about Sitric? You said all the enemy leaders were killed."

"Not Sitric," Cian told him in contemptuous tones. "He never came out of the city. He's still in there—with your mother."

"And Maelmordha, my mother's brother?"

"The treacherous Prince of Leinster led Sitric's Vikings against Brian Boru and got killed for his pains," Fergal said smugly. "I know. I killed him. He died squealing like the vermin he was."

"My father?" Donough made himself ask. "How did my father die?"

"At the end of the day he was in his tent, praying. Prince Murrough had talked him out of taking part in the fighting by convincing him, not that he was too old, but that he was too valuable to risk. We were relieved, we thought he was safe. If the day went against us we would need him more than ever.

"A bodyguard was with him, of course, but late in the fighting he sent them away. Then a Viking called Brodir, the last surviving leader of the invasion force, was running for his life through the woods when he came upon the Ard Ri's tent. He attacked the old man he found inside and cleaved his skull with an axe."

Donough flinched. His face was the color of buttermilk.

"But Brian had kept his sword with him," Fergal continued. "Even as he was struck he sliced through Brodir's leg. It was a mighty blow, the blow of a young man. Brodir bled to death beside the Ard Ri. We found their bodies almost touching.

"The next day—yesterday—some prisoners that were brought to us tried to claim that Brodir survived. They were saying the Irish had caught him later and tortured him to death, but that was a lie they were hoping to spread. The Irish never resort to torture; the Vikings do it all the time. Those of us who had seen the two bodies in Brian's tent knew the truth."

Donough clung to what seemed to him to be the most important fact. "My father died fighting."

"He died winning," Fergal stressed.

Though his knees threatened to buckle under him, Donough struggled to his feet. "Have someone bring my horse. I must go to him. I must go to Swords."

"You aren't going anywhere just yet," Ronan said sternly. He put one big hand on Donough's breastbone and pushed him back down into a sitting position.

"We need you here now," Cian explained, and Fergal added, "This is where your father would want you to be, taking care of his Dalcassians for him. We need his son to take up where he left off."

"Then get Flann. Or Conor."

"They both died in the battle. And Teigue was left behind to guard Kincora, you will recall. Of all the sons, only you are alive and here."

Donough felt a great weight about to descend on him. He opened his eyes very wide, looking more than ever like a frightened boy. "But . . . "

"You've been crowing about being ready for command," Ronan said mercilessly. "Now's your chance to prove it. Take command of the Dalcassians. Or are you not able for it? Are you all mouth and no muscle?"

Donough squirmed inwardly, forced to confront a truth about himself. He saw now that he had merely been playing; playing at being a warrior. He could pretend to command a small company of cavalry because the grown-ups, Ronan and the other veterans assigned to him, were there to keep him from getting into too much trouble. They were a net held beneath him while he tried his wings.

But suddenly everything had changed. He was being asked to take charge of the Dalcassians, the personal army that had served his father so devotedly and which comprised the largest part of the army of the province of Munster.

It was a massive responsibility with no one to protect him from the consequences of his mistakes.

The mantle he had childishly coveted was his without warning or preparation. The only man who could have pre-pared him had trained Murrough instead, and now they were both dead.

Donough began shivering again, uncontrollably. *I don't want this! Make it not be happening!*

But it was happening. The other men were looking at him, waiting.

Waiting for Donough, through some miracle, to replace Brian Boru.

Chapter Seven

The corpse of the Ard Ri was borne aloft on nine shields lashed together, as was necessary to carry one who had been, in life, the tallest man in Ireland.

The procession carrying him to the monastery at Swords trudged to the solemn beat of the bodhran and the wild wail of the war pipe. "Brian Boru's March," someone said, giving name to the dirge.

Defying the gloom of a rainy evening, men carried torches to form a moving rectangle of light around the body. Icy drizzle made the torches sputter.

Brian Boru was wrapped in a crimson mantle and draped with his banner of three lions, modeled after the stylized Celtic lions in the *Book of Kells*. The priests had wanted to put his crucifix in his hands; his warriors had argued for his sword. In the end they compromised and gave him both.

Malachi Mor walked at the front of the procession with a deliberate space kept between himself and Brian's personal entourage. He could feel their resentment. From time to time he glanced covertly around to reassure himself that his Meathmen were within hailing distance.

The bulk of the procession was made up of warriors, but a number of priests accompanied them. The men of God kept their eyes averted from the horrific guard of honor that surrounded the body on its bier.

About this, Brian's warriors had been unwilling to compromise.

In a Celtic tradition much older than Christianity, the heads of the heroes who had given their lives fighting for

Brian had been arranged on his bier so they encircled his corpse, glassy eyes staring outward, vigilant in death.

Conaing. Duvlann. Niall of clan Cuinn, captain of the High King's bodyguard. Mothla of Oriel. Scandal Mac Cathal. Donall, a prince of the Scots, whose cousin Malcolm was married to one of Brian's daughters. Princes of Connacht and of Munster.

Flann Mac Brian.

Conor Mac Brian.

The intact body believed to be that of Murrough Mac Brian was carried separately, a few paces behind the Ard Ri. The plump little man walking beside it would have preferred walking beside Brian, but the warriors had elbowed him out of the way. Brian was theirs now, their fallen chieftain, and they had no patience with a mere historian.

Carroll did not take offense. He was accustomed to the warrior mentality.

From his vantage point to the rear he was busily committing every detail of the procession to memory, to be scribed in his leisure as Brian would have wanted.

Laiten, who had been Brian's personal attendant, dropped out of the procession for a moment to relieve himself. Taking advantage of the opportunity, Carroll waited and fell into step beside him. "I've been wanting to speak to you," the historian explained.

Laiten was short and slender, with dark wiry hair and a narrow face aged by grief. Little more than a lad, in recent days he had seen more of death than most men would ever know. "What do you want of me?" he asked. His voice was husky with weeping.

"Just conversation. We got such a late start that we won't reach Swords until after dark. Talk will shorten the journey."

Laiten was not deceived. Carroll's plump cheeks and pouched eyes gave an impression of guilelessness, but as everyone knew he had been the Ard Ri's confidant, learning the arts of manipulation from a master.

"I have nothing to talk about," the young man said shortly.

"Oh surely you must! You were in the eye of the storm. You could tell me so much from your own point of view about what happened on Friday. Who was where, that sort of thing. You don't know what a help it would be to me."

"You mean to write it down, I suppose?"

"One of the porters has my little folding writing desk and my parchments and inks. I can write tonight at Swords if the good brothers are not too mean with their candles."

"If you need more light ask Malachi for a lamp," Laiten said. "I should think he'll do all he can for us now."

Carroll's amiable expression faded. "Malachi didn't do much for us on Friday though, did he? He stood off until he was certain the battle was won before he came swooping in to claim a share of the glory."

"I don't think that's entirely fair."

"Are you taking his side, Laiten?"

"How dare you say that! Everyone knows I was devoted to the Ard Ri."

"Yet you left him defenseless."

"The Ard Ri was never in his life defenseless, even at the end of it. Besides, he sent us all away. As captain of his bodyguard, Niall tried to argue with him, but no one ever won an argument with Brian Boru. He insisted we join in the final fighting. Said we deserved a share of the victory. Obeying that order cost Niall his life, as things turned out. He was almost the last man to die . . . except for the Ard Ri himself."

"Exactly when did Brian send you away, Laiten?"

"After I reported to him that Prince Murrough had fallen."

"And were you not concerned, knowing he must be in despair over his son's death? How could you leave him?"

"I told you, he ordered it. Could you have refused a direct order from the Ard Ri? I could not. Besides, he didn't seem to be despairing. He was surprisingly calm. Almost . . . at peace." Laiten's voice dropped, became a whisper. "Looking back, Carroll, I think he knew what was going to happen to him. Knew, and welcomed it."

"How could he possibly have known Brodir would stumble across his tent by accident and kill him?"

Laiten hesitated. "He was warned."

The historian stopped walking. "By whom?"

The two men stood facing each other as the last of the cortège moved past them. Laiten did not want to speak, but Carroll's attentive gaze drew the words out of him. "On the night before the battle a woman came to the Ard Ri's tent."

Carroll's eyebrows shot up. "What woman?"

"I never actually saw her. I had been in the tent, adjusting the cushion on his prayer stool and lighting the lamp for him on his map table. The commander said he wanted to be alone, so I went outside and took my place by the tent flap as usual. Then suddenly I saw a woman's shadow as she passed between the wall of the tent and the lamp."

"Are you sure it was a woman?"

Laiten was indignant. "I know the hills and valleys of a woman's form! And it was a woman's voice I heard, but . . . strange, whispery as leaves. The very sound of it made my belly go cold. Even remembering . . . I don't want to talk about this."

"You must," Carroll persisted gently. "I'm sure he would want you to tell me. He wanted everything chronicled you know; that was his way. So tell me, Laiten—did you get a look at her when she left?"

"That's the strangest part. I never moved away from the tent flap, not for one moment. But after a while the Ard Ri called for me and I went into him . . . and he was alone."

"What do you mean he was alone?"

"I mean no one was with him. No woman, no living

being." A recollective shiver ran through Laiten's body.
"Yet I had been just outside the entire time and I swear she
never left."

Carroll's eyebrows tried to crawl into his receding hair-
line. "Did you ask Brian about her?"

"I did ask him. He smiled and said, 'My guardian spirit.'
Then he turned away and I was afraid to question him further, Carroll. You know how he was about people . . .
prying.

"But I swear to you on my mother's grave that I overheard the woman tell the Ard Ri he would die the next day.
When the battle was over. It would be the price of his victory, she said.

"So I don't think our leaving him made any difference. I
am convinced he sent us away so we would not try to save
him."

The evening seemed very dark.

The drizzle turned into a relentless bitter downpour. The
drums beat, the pipes wailed. Torchlight flickered and
flared.

On overlapping shields the corpse lay, hands folded over
crucifix and sword. Around it twelve decapitated heads
glared balefully outward, daring anyone or anything to
interfere.

Chapter Eight

Donough spent the remainder of Easter Sunday in the
Dalcassian camp. His band of horsemen mingled with the
remnants of Brian's army and listened enviously to their

descriptions of the battle. In a matter of days such stories would begin to assume mythic proportions, but now, recounted by weary men whose clothes still stank of the blood they had shed, the events of Good Friday were repeated in the crude terms of the foot warrior, embellished only with profanity.

Sometime during the night Donough fell asleep in Cian's tent with his head pillowed on his arm. His rest was disturbed by a jumble of swirling images compounded out of what he had seen and imagined.

Meanwhile the surviving senior officers had crowded into the tent. Sleeping at their feet, Donough heard them in some level of his mind below conscious thought. Heard them and entered into the stories they told until it seemed he was wading through the bloody weir; he was striding across the gory meadows. He was in Tomar's Wood with something red and sticky dripping down on him from the trees.

Axes swung in his mind.

His fists clenched in his sleep. He groaned and twitched.

Murrough fell a second time, and Donough seized his banner and ran forward, howling for vengeance.

Against a background of flashing swords, Brian Boru was cut down like a great tree, as an agonized Donough watched from a distance. When he tried to go to his father's aid, his feet seemed rooted to the earth.

In his sleep tears slipped from beneath his closed eyelids and ran down his cheeks.

"Wake up, lad. Wake up now." A hand shook his shoulder.

Donough muttered and pulled away. One moment more! One moment in which to fight off the paralysis, find a weapon, get to his father's side in time to . . .

"Wake up now! It's dawn."

As Donough struggled to reach Brian the shreds of dream dissolved into reality and he found himself lying on the floor of Cian's tent, beneath a shaggy mantle someone had thrown over him. He tried to shake off the hand tugging at his shoulder. "Ronan? Go away, leave me alone."

"It is not Ronan," a voice informed him, "and I will not go away. We must have our orders, Commander."

Commander? But Brian Boru was the commander.

Donough came awake with a startled leap as if he had been hurled from a height.

Cian of Desmond was bending over him. "We must have your orders." He snatched the mantle away.

"I'm cold," Donough complained.

"And am I not cold? It's a desperate bitter day, no fit weather for Easter Monday, but what difference does that make? Be up now. You can warm yourself at the fire outside. The officers will be gathering soon for your orders."

"My orders," Donough repeated blankly. *This is still the dream*, he thought. *Or some other dream.*

He was ushered out of the tent into a cold dawn. Streaks of pale light were appearing above the Irish Sea. For the first time in days the morning promised to be clear, but the smoke of numerous campfires hung thick enough in the damp air to make him cough.

The world was too tangible; this was no dream.

I am supposed to lead my father's army!

The years of childhood. Toy swords. Shields made from basket bottoms, and javelins that were broken broom handles. Himself strutting up and down, pretending to be a commander of warriors.

Suddenly the play was real.

He had never been so afraid in his life.

Swallowing hard, he swept his eyes across the camp and tried to think like Brian Boru. But the only thought that came into his head was a vague dismay at the number of men now looking to him for leadership.

An army. My army. What do I do with them?

He turned around as if the answer might be behind him.

There, to the east, the dark bulk of Dublin's walls rose in silhouette against the dawn.

Sitric's stronghold. If my father were still alive he would be planning to capture Dublin now. Seize the city, punish Sitric, do . . . something . . . about Gormlaith.

At the thought of his mother, Donough's thoughts twisted into a tangle.

A small group of officers was coming toward him across the camp ground, talking among themselves. Most of them were Dalcassian, but some were Cian's Owenachts.

Donough must command them as the Ard Ri would have done.

But he suffered a massive disadvantage. While Murrough had—reluctantly—trained at Brian's elbow, Donough had been kept away from his father most of the time. As a result he knew Brian more through reputation than personal experience. In his eyes his father was the consummate hero, all knowing, utterly fearless.

The deliberate construction of that image by Brian himself had been well concealed from his youngest son.

Never having had access to the man behind the image, Donough could only give a superficial imitation of Brian Boru.

But he tried. Uncertain, grief-stricken, on that cold Easter Monday he swallowed his fear as best he could and prepared for the day to come.

"Cian," he told the Owenacht prince, "your tent will be my command post from now on, as it seems the largest one here." He did not bother to ask permission. He had never heard his father ask anyone for permission to do anything.

Cian was outraged that a mere boy, no matter whose son, would appropriate his tent—an Owenacht tent, not Dalcassian—so arrogantly. *Usurper!* he thought. *Ignoring rank and custom!* Brian Boru had been called a usurper when he took Malachi Mor's kingship from him. Now here was his son setting out on the same path.

But Cian said nothing aloud. He smiled a fraction too

broadly and relinquished his quarters with a courteous bow. This is the way princes should behave, his attitude said to Donough—who did not notice.

The youthful commander placed himself in front of the tent, and the officers arranged themselves in a semicircle around him. They were tired past the point of weariness, and there was not one among them who was not bruised and sore at the very least. Their faces were old beyond their years as they waited for a boy to give them orders.

Donough stood as tall as he could and prepared to pitch his voice as deep as it would go, mindful that it had only changed during the last year and might not be totally trust-worthy. It was one more thing to worry about.

Under his breath he whispered a single word, like a prayer. *Father.*

Then he filled his lungs and addressed the officers. "We shall finish the campaign the Ard Ri began! This means we capture Dublin and punish Sitric Silkbeard for his treachery in breaking his truce with the Ard Ri."

"But we haven't finished burying our dead," one of the officers protested. "And we have more wounded men than able-bodied ones; what about them?"

Donough realized his error. Caring for the dead and wounded first had been one of the tenets of his father's mili-tary philosophy. "We must take care of them before we do anything else, of course," he said hastily. "Then we can challenge Sitric."

The officers exchanged glances. They knew, better than he, how depleted their troops were. Such battered men were in no condition to take up arms again so soon.

Donough sensed their hesitation, and in that moment it seemed as if someone standing at his back pressed hard against him. Reflexively, he stepped away from the tent. The rising sun promptly haloed his auburn hair with cop-pery fire. Seen thus, his features were in shadow.

"We can succeed!" he assured the men.

His youthful lankiness was concealed by clothing, but his height was obvious. It was, almost, Brian Boru's height. And surely that deep voice was Brian's voice?

It was the season of Resurrection and they desperately wanted to believe.

Fergal Mac Anluan began to smile. "Yes," he whispered to himself. "Yes."

"As long as the Vikings cower behind the walls of the city they're safe," Donough went on, "since we don't have enough healthy men to storm the gates and go in after them. But what if we lure them out? We have a herd of their oxen, fine strong beasts, valuable. I propose to begin slaughtering those oxen one at a time on Fair Green, in plain sight of the palisades. That should bring Sitric's men out to try to stop us, and we can attack them as they come."

The cleverness of the stratagem was as familiar as the deep voice. A couple of the captains shouted their enthusiasm.

While burial parties dug graves for foot warriors, other men built sledges to transport the wounded and carry dead chieftains back to their own people. When these preparations were complete, Donough ordered every man capable of wielding a weapon to the Fair Green and gave the order to begin slaughtering the oxen.

Sitric's men watched from the catwalk atop the palisade.

Donough gave the signal. A two-handed sword blow to the neck cut halfway through the spine of the first ox, and the animal fell to its knees. As it toppled onto its side the Dalcassians shouted defiance toward Dublin.

Sitric's men responded with a hail of spears that fell short, and a thunder of curses. They vowed to torture every Dalcassian to death and rip out their lungs to leave atop their torsos, forming the Viking "blood eagle."

"They'll have to come out here to do it," Ronan remarked, grinning with anticipation. He took his short-sword from its leather sheath and tested the blade with a practiced thumb. The other Dalcassians were similarly preparing for battle, finding that the prospect eased the stiff-ness from their joints and the soreness from their muscles.

But Cian of Desmond was unhappy. "Those oxen are spoils of war," he complained. "They should have been divided among us, not wasted like this. The Vikings may not even come out after them."

"They will," said Ronan confidently.

He was wrong. Some pragmatic mind within the city ordered the Viking warriors to stay where they were, safe within the walls.

With Sitric Silkbeard. And Gormlaith.

Chapter Nine

When a battle was over, no matter which side won, the local women scavenged the battlefield in search of valuables. It was a time-honored tradition to strip the dead of their ornaments and weapons before their fellow warriors could retrieve them.

In the peaceful latter years of Brian Boru's reign, how-ever, this profitable pastime had been seriously curtailed.

But Clontarf made up for the privations of the previous decade. Dead men littered the ground for miles and the scavengers swarmed over them like bees at the hive. They were still at work on the last unclaimed bodies when Donough ordered the oxen slaughtered.

From where he stood, waiting with fading hope for the Vikings to emerge from the city, he could see some women in the distance. The loyal Irish had all been claimed by then; they were now working on Viking dead, or some of Maelmordha's followers. As Donough watched they bent to their task like harvesters in a field, stooping over one corpse after another and picking it clean. They were country women; they did not flinch.

"That was a fine idea you had," Ronan said abruptly beside him, startling Donough from his reverie. "Pity it didn't work. What are you going to do now?"

"Any suggestions?"

"Me? I should say not, you're the commander now," Ronan replied cheerfully. He was enjoying seeing the lad under pressure; it might make a man of him.

Donough gave him a cold stare. "I didn't say I would take your suggestions, I just asked if you had any." He meant to deflate the man. Ronan's lack of respect could prove disastrous if it were communicated to the other warriors. Leading them would be impossible then.

Turning on his heel, Donough strode across Fair Green with no clear destination in mind, although he walked as purposefully as if he had someplace important to go. He paused once to gaze regretfully at the pile of cooling meat that had been twenty-eight fine oxen.

The scheme had not worked. Nothing to do about it.

He bit his lip and went on, feeling the men's eyes on him, wondering if they were beginning to lose faith in him.

Fergal Mac Anluan, who had killed the last ox, came toward him, wiping his weapon clean.

"Fergal," Donough greeted him, "tell me—how many of my father's officers are still alive, do you know?"

Fergal stopped to think. "Not enough. Why?"

"I was thinking about appointing a new second-in-command. Ronan's a good man, but sometimes I don't think he . . . has enough respect for me."

"Fair enough. Well, there are several members of clan Cuinn who were part of Brian's personal bodyguard."

"Where are they?"

"Gone north with Brian's body, I imagine."

"Will they return to Thomond? Afterward?"

"I should think so, their clanhold is not far from Kincora."

"Who else knew my father's ways?"

Fergal began ticking off his fingers. "There's Carroll, of course. The historian. Brian rarely went anywhere without him, not since together they rewrote the *Book of Rights*. He had great respect for Carroll's knowledge of the law. I would say if any man knew the shape of Brian Boru's mind, it would be Carroll."

"I know Carroll. He's too old and too fat, and he's a scholar not a warrior. No use to me."

"Perhaps you will find someone when we return to Kincora," Fergal said hopefully. "We could leave at dawn tomorrow and . . . "

Donough's gray eyes flashed. "I'll decide when we are going to leave. And that won't be until we've taken Dublin."

Fergal was disappointed. It had become obvious to him that they were not going to be able to capture Dublin. Any further effort to do so would be a waste of time and energy. He wanted to go home.

The battle was over.

He started to say as much, then realized Donough was not paying any attention. The youngster's gaze was fixed beyond him, on something in the distance. "Who's that over there, Fergal?"

"Where?" Fergal turned to look. "I don't see anyone."

Donough pointed across an expanse of meadowland. "There, beyond that ditch. Where the women are scavenging. Do you not see that slim girl in the red skirt?"

Fergal shaded his eyes with his hand. "They're nothing more than tiny black figures to me. You take after your father; he always could see a bedsome woman."

Donough reddened. "I wasn't . . . "

"Of course you were, and why not? If you want her, go get her. You're the commander now, that's better than being a chieftain when it comes to women. They love a man with a long spear and a hard sword." Fergal winked.

"I have no intention of . . . "

The wink was replaced with a knowing look. "You've never had a woman, is that it? Do they frighten you? If I had a mother like yours I would be terrified of the creatures myself, but . . . "

Fergal was talking to empty air. Donough was walking briskly away.

He imagined himself storming the gates of the city and breaking them down through sheer force of will. He saw himself seizing Gormlaith by her red hair and dragging her through the streets screaming for mercy, though no man in Ireland had ever heard her plead for mercy.

Exciting images boiled up in him, heating his blood. He paid no attention to the direction his legs were carrying him. In his mind he was in Dublin.

When the girl in the red skirt stepped in front of him he almost ran into her.

Donough halted in astonishment. Where had she come from so suddenly?

Seen close up she was not really a girl. She had a slim body and youthful posture, but fine lines filigreed the skin around her huge, dark eyes.

Donough's gaze swept down her body. In spite of the coolness of the day, she was clad only in a simple smock of bleached linen and a heavy skirt of red wool. Her high-arched feet were bare. Though she stood on muddy ground they looked white and clean.

Puzzled, he looked back to her face.

"You cannot take Dublin," she said. "Do not try."

"What do you know about it?"

"More than you."

"You live near here? You're one of the women I saw picking over the corpses?"

"You cannot take Dublin now," she reiterated. "Take the Dalcassians back to Kincora."

Her eyes locked with his. He tried to look away but could not.

She raised one hand and extended her fingers toward him. When she flexed her wrist, her fingers trailed through the air in a flowing gesture as if beckoning Donough to follow.

His feet stepped forward of their own accord.

Alarmed, he tried to grab her wrist. She ducked under his arm and ran past him. When he turned to follow her he found himself staring directly into the blazing sun.

He blinked furiously. Patterns of crimson and gold swirled on the inside of his eyelids until he pressed the heels of his hands against his eyes and forced a soothing darkness.

When he opened his eyes, the woman was gone.

A thoughtful and troubled Donough returned to the camp. He longed to discuss his experience with someone but he dare not.

One thing was certain. He would not attempt to capture Dublin now. Whether he had seen a supernatural vision or a real person hardly mattered; the omen was too compelling to ignore.

When he reached the command tent he found Cian there, meticulously combing his hair in front of a polished metal mirror. "Leave me, I need to think," Donough ordered.

Cian's knuckles whitened on the comb. "This is my tent."

"I need it now."

The Owenacht stiffened. "Very well." His eyes were icy. "Whatever you want, Dalcassian. For now." He left, his shoulders rigid with outrage.

Donough tardily realized his mistake. It was wrong to antagonize Cian. Brian Boru had worked long and hard to replace the ancient feud between Owenacht and Dalcassian with amicable relations.

I'll apologize to him later. But . . . would my father have apolo-

gized? I never heard him apologize to anyone. Perhaps I should just let it go . . .

When he issued the order, there was a general air of relief. "We're going home," one man passed word on to another.

"Home to Munster."

They set out in midweek. As they moved away from the city they were aware of the Dubliners on the walls, watching them go. They forced themselves to walk proudly, as a victorious army should, though many of them had painful injuries and had to struggle not to limp.

Donough glanced back just once. If his mother was among the watchers on the walls, he did not see her.

They made their laborious way west and south, stopping frequently to rest the wounded. Herders and smallholders they met along the way were generally indifferent to them. Some had heard of the battle as news was shouted in the customary way from one hilltop to another, but their life was the land. Princes and chieftains fighting for sovereignty had little significance for them.

"I'll have to pay tribute to whoever's in charge anyway," one smallholder told Donough. "One sheep in twenty. To one king or another. It's all the same to me as long as I have enough lambs in the spring. You say we won a great victory, but I didn't fight. I had no reason to fight."

"For your sake the Ard Ri gave battle to Sitric Silkbeard and the invaders from the north."

"Vikings, you mean? He fought Vikings?"

"He did. And some Leinstermen who allied with them."

"The Vikings buy my fleeces and pay well for them. Why would I want anyone to fight the Vikings?"

"They wanted to take Ireland for themselves," Donough tried to explain.

"They are here anyway, are they not? Have been for years. And how could they take Ireland? Could they tie it to their longships and tow it away? I don't understand."

Musing on the vagaries of chieftains, the smallholder returned to his home.

Women the Dalcassians encountered responded differently. Some of the younger ones licked their lips or shifted their hips and smiled at the warriors, making a great point of bringing water and medicaments to the wounded. Older women enquired anxiously over relatives who might have been at Clontarf, and threw their skirts over their faces to keen for the dead.

There was ribald talk of women in the camp at night.

Donough listened, half-enviously.

Fergal had guessed correctly, he was afraid of women. Gormlaith was his principal example of the female sex: volatile, sensual, jealous, manipulative Gormlaith, who made trouble for the pleasure of it and had kept the men of Kincora at one another's throats until Brian at last sent her away.

Gormlaith was a storm Donough did not care to repeat in his own life.

So he looked at women and listened as other men talked about them. From time to time he found himself thinking of the woman in the red skirt; of her high-arched feet.

But he kept himself to himself.

In spite of opportunity, his men did the same. Many of them were too wounded to be interested in any woman, and those who were able-bodied still felt the memory of Clontarf oppressing them. They were not ready for pleasure.

Weary and depressed, they marched on through the province of Leinster toward that of Munster, which contained the kingdom of Thomond, tribeland of the Dal Cais.

At Athy they camped beside the river Barrow to rest and tend the wounded. Willows lined the riverbank, trailing their fingers in the water. As Donough broke off a willow twig to scrub the pastiness from his teeth, he found himself recalling a dark-eyed woman trailing her fingers through the air, beckoning him . . .

"Abu Gillapatrick!" rent the air. A dozen armed warriors screaming their war cry came bursting through the willows, holding up shields and brandishing spears.

Donough dropped the twig and grabbed for his sword. Other Dalcassians in various states of undress scrambled for their weapons while the wounded lay helpless and watched.

"It's not an attack," Ronan advised Donough. "Not with so few men. It's a delegation of some sort, talk to them."

Nodding, Donough stepped forward, relieved to feel Ronan move into place behind him.

The foremost of the strangers asked in a hostile tone, "Are you Dalcassians?"

"We are. And you?"

"Men of Ossory."

Donough turned his head to enquire over his shoulder, "Ronan, are we in the kingdom of Ossory?"

"We are, I believe."

"You trespass in our territory," announced the leader of the delegation.

Donough assured him, "We mean no trespass. We're returning to our homes after the battle."

"What battle?"

"The war against the Northmen at Dublin. The Ard Ri won in all our names," Donough could not resist adding.

The Ossorian sneered. "Did he now? I don't recall asking that Dalcassian to fight for me."

"If he had not, by this time next season you would be subject to Sitric Silkbeard and sending a sizable portion of your corn and cattle to Dublin as tribute."

"Not me. I'll never pay tribute to anyone but Mac Gillapatrick, Prince of Ossory. He sends me to tell you that no Dalcassian is welcome in his kingdom. He is but an hour's march behind us, coming to give you battle."

"We're in no condition to fight!" Donough protested. "Can't you see? We have a number of wounded men.

Surely your prince would not attack wounded men who are only trying to get home."

The Ossorian replied coldly, "In an hour you will be punished for your trespass, Dalcassian." He gave his spear a final menacing flourish, then he and his companions trotted back the way they had come.

Fergal was appalled. "This is outrageous! Ossory spits in the teeth of the rules Brian Boru laid down for warfare."

"Brian is dead," said Cian succinctly.

"And Mac Gillapatrick knows it," Ronan added. "He was an old enemy of the Ard Ri, who once wiped his face in the mud and forced him to submit. He would never dare this if he thought the Ard Ri was still alive."

"I won't let him!" cried Donough, clenching his hands into fists.

Cian asked, "Just what do you think you can do about it?"

"I have a plan," Donough lied.

"It better be more clever than your last plan. Look at these men of yours. They can't fight a fresh army. And who do you think you are—Cuchulain? Will you try to stand off Mac Gillapatrick all by yourself?"

Cian wants to see me humiliated, Donough realized. *Probably they all want to see Gormlaith's son humiliated.*

"If you don't want to stand with me, Cian, you're free to go, you and the men you brought with you. You're not Dalcassian, Mac Gillapatrick has no quarrel with you."

Cian glowered at Donough. "I have never run from a fight in my life," he grated through clenched teeth. "But I don't owe any loyalty to an unweaned puppy who can suggest I might. The strength of the Dalcassians is broken, killed with Brian Boru. Perhaps it is time for Desmond to ally with Ossory." The Owenacht prince promptly signaled his men to fold his leather tent, and without further discussion he and his fellow tribesmen left the camp.

Donough stood with folded arms, watching them go. There seemed nothing to say. Gradually he became aware of something like a presence—less substantial than a presence—standing with him. Or inside his skull, watching. Something . . . male. Strong . . . confident . . .

At that moment a wounded warrior on a sledge lifted one feeble arm into the sky, fist clenched, and cried with all his strength, "Abu Dal gCais!"

Donough smiled. "Cuchulain, is it?" he said softly.

He began issuing orders.

The men of Ossory came marching through shafts of sunlight, chanting fighting songs. The Dalcassians had been supreme in Ireland long enough. Defeating them would establish the Ossorians as the new champions—for a time.

At their head rode Mac Gillapatrick, a grizzled prince cloaked in speckled green. The news of Clontarf had been shouted across Ireland in the time-honored tradition, exciting the interest of the nobility if not the common people. Mac Gillapatrick had rejoiced in the death of his old enemy while Brian Boru's body was still on its way to Swords.

As they drew near Athy, the Prince of Ossory could almost feel Dalcassian blood on his sword. An old grudge was about to be settled. Brian's hard-won peace had died at Clontarf; the good old days, the days of battle and glory and the tribal warfare by which Gaelic chieftains defined themselves, were about to return.

Mac Gillapatrick was actually grinning when he caught his first glimpse of the Dalcassians. Sitting on his horse, he saw them before his foot warriors could. His jaw dropped, pulling the grin out of shape.

In another moment his followers had seen what he saw. The warriors slowed to an astonished halt.

Facing them was a phalanx of timber stakes cut from nearby trees and driven deep into the earth. A wounded man was bound to each of these stakes, standing upright as the dying Ulster hero Cuchulain had bound himself up-right to a standing stone, so he could meet his enemies on his feet.

A few of the men were actually already dead, bodies of the nobility being returned home for burial. But every figure had a weapon in its hand, though in some cases swords had been bound to stiffened fingers with leather thongs.

Beside the stakes stood the remaining able-bodied Dalcassians. The courage of their wounded comrades heartened them as nothing else could. Every last one of them was prepared to fight to the death, and it showed in their haggard faces.

The terrible army waited for the Ossorian attack.

Mac Gillapatrick's men were dismayed.

"What are you waiting for!" he shouted at them when he had recovered from his own surprise. "There is our enemy; attack!"

His men did not move.

As they watched, the head of a gravely wounded Dalcassian slumped forward in death. But the sword remained in his hand.

Several Ossorians signed the Cross on their breasts. "A bad thing, this," said one of them nervously.

The Prince of Ossory was infuriated. "Attack them!" he screamed as another Dalcassian sagged in his bonds and died.

One of Mac Gillapatrick's officers said, "What good will it do us to attack dead men? There's no glory in it."

"You disobey my order?"

The officer glanced back toward his men, reading their faces. In the hierarchy of Gaelic warfare every army was composed of individual bands of men who had sworn loyalty to a leader from their own tribe. Should one of these leaders leave, his men would go with him. Their allegiance was to him, not to the prince he followed.

A second officer spoke up. "We cannot attack such desperate and resolute men," he told Mac Gillapatrick flatly. "It would bring shame upon us."

"But they are Dalcassians! I order you to cut them down as they stand!"

The men looked from him to Donough's army. They had taken up arms during the reign of Brian Boru, when the proudest boast a man could utter was, "I am an Irish man." They had been proud of themselves in those days. They would not set that pride aside now.

Leaving Mac Gillapatrick raging, they turned and marched away.

Chapter Ten

The walls of Dublin were not enough to contain Gormlaith's passion. While remnants of Brian Boru's army were in the area she dare not leave the city, but time and again she climbed up the ladder to the catwalk just inside the palisade and stared out across the Liffey, toward the nine hills and slightly sloping plain of Fingal. The area where Fingal met the sea was called the Meadow of the Bull because there the sea roared like a bull, as charging waves beat themselves to a froth against the sand dunes.

Clontarf. Gormlaith's lips shaped the word silently.

Overnight her legendary beauty had faded. Her mirror, which only days before had reflected a vital, desirable creature still glowing with the fires that had captivated three kings in turn, now revealed a woman suddenly catapulted into old age.

No worthy man, she reflected bitterly, would fight for her favors now. The northern warlords who had been lured to Ireland to kill Brian Boru and claim her as their reward were all dead. Every noble chieftain who ever wanted

Gormlaith was dead—except for Malachi Mor. And having possessed her once, no power on heaven or earth would induce him to take her again.

She walked alone on the walls of Dublin and shook her fists at the sky.

Eventually Sitric lost patience with her. He knew as well as she did that his mother's value was gone.

He sent an attendant to bring her to his hall, a smoky, timbered chamber resembling an overturned longship. It was as close as Sitric Silkbeard cared to get to ships. The Viking King of Dublin was, to his chagrin, subject to uncontrollable seasickness, a weakness he was at great pains to conceal.

As he waited for his mother to join him, Sitric considered the situation. He still held Dublin, but only because his opponents lacked the strength to claim the final prize. They would probably go home, lick their wounds, and return in the spring. Brian Boru had taught the Irish tribes to unite, and against such a union Sitric had no chance.

But who would lead them now?

While he awaited Gormlaith's appearance—she was habitually late—he was to his surprise joined by his wife: a daughter of Brian Boru.

Emer had made her loyalty plain during the recent battle, cheering for her father's forces and disparaging the Northmen. On the night of Good Friday she refused to join her husband in the marriage bed and had avoided him since. She joined him now merely because she was hungry and expected a meal to be served in the hall.

When she entered, Sitric smiled as affably as if they were on the best of terms. It was not hard to smile at Emer; she was a pretty woman, with a round sweet face and wide-spaced eyes.

But now the sweetness was gone from her face, and her eyes were the color of winter.

"Emer, wife! I have missed you. Were you ill?" Sitric enquired solicitously.

"I am mourning my father."

"Of course, of course. A brave man he was; it was a shock to hear of his death."

She laughed mirthlessly. "I'm sure. Especially since you had assembled ten thousand men to try to kill him."

"You exaggerate. We had less than half that many. The Ard Ri's forces were twice the size of ours. That's the only reason they won."

"That's your version, is it? You forget that I was there, from the walls we could see how large both armies were."

"You misinterpreted what you saw," he replied blandly. "How could a woman understand a battle?"

Her lips narrowed to a thin line. "You forget again—I was raised at Kincora. All my life I watched warriors train and listened to their talk. I could probably lead an army as well as you—better, for I'm no coward."

Sitric drew back his hand to hit her but stopped himself with an effort. He must not make more of an enemy of Emer than she already was. He had plenty of enemies. What he needed now were allies. There would be few enough of those after his recent defeat.

Forcing himself to stay calm, he said, "You think I wanted to avoid the fighting? Not at all, I ached for it; my fingers itched to hold the axe. But I am King of Dublin and it was my responsibility to stay with my city and look after my people."

"How convenient for you." Emer studied her fingernails rather than Sitric's face. She wondered how she could ever have agreed to marry him. She had only done so to please her father. In those early days of marriage, had she ever enjoyed looking at Sitric? she wondered idly. He was a big blond Viking with Gormlaith's proud profile and broad hands not averse to hitting women. Ugly hands with gnarled knuckles.

Years of living with Sitric had magnified his faults in Emer's eyes and diminished his virtues. She could tick off the former on her fingertips: he was brutal, he snored, he farted, he lied. He was petty and greedy and scheming, his toes were crooked, and he was getting a bald patch on the crown of his head.

Gormlaith swept into the hall, distracting Sitric's attention and consigning Emer to the role of fly on the wall. Whenever she appeared she drew the focus of attention to herself and held it there. Gormlaith took up all the air in a room.

Emer felt invisible when she was around.

Gormlaith was as tall as her son, great-limbed and great-spirited, and even at sixty she had a straight spine and an arrogant carriage. Her famous mane was still red, though a succession of servants spitefully claimed it was dyed, and her heavy-lidded eyes were still green, though not the startling emerald of her youth. In their depths something stirred lazily, like a predator swimming below the surface.

"How dare you send for me like some servant!" was her greeting to Sitric.

He was instantly defensive. "I didn't send for you, I requested the pleasure of your company."

Gormlaith stalked past him to the nearest cushioned bench—the only one in the hall, his—and sat down, stretching her long legs before her in a curiously masculine gesture. "As the pig requests the pleasure of the butcher," she retorted. "What do you want, Sitric? You always want something."

"Why is everything you say to me some sort of accusation?" He busied himself with his drinking horn, but could not resist a covert glance in her direction to assess her mood.

"Stop looking at me," Gormlaith demanded. "*He* looked at me like that when he thought I wasn't watching." She need not identify whom she meant. There was only one *he* in Gormlaith's vocabulary.

Sitric cleared his throat nervously. She was the only person who could reduce him to awkward self-consciousness. "Mother, I need to talk to you about your, ah, habits."

"Habits? I have no habits. I do what I like when I like, and never the same twice."

"I mean going up on the palisade and shaking your fists at the sky. It's making my men uncomfortable."

She shrugged one shoulder. "They are easily upset, then. But we knew that already. Look how they ran away from *him* on Good Friday."

Sitric gritted his teeth. She was deliberately goading him, trying to make him lose his temper, but he was determined she would not manipulate him this time. "They did not run from Brian Boru. My men fought as Vikings should, unflinchingly and to the death."

Gormlaith's reply was scornful. "They ran like hares, the cowards." She turned toward Emer, the first indication she had given of being aware of the other woman. "You saw them, too, didn't you?"

"I did see them. When I remarked on it, your son hit me." In spite of herself, Emer felt a flush of gratitude to Gormlaith for including her in the conversation, for acknowledging and validating her presence as if bestowing a gift. Having the uncanny ability to center attention on herself, Gormlaith occasionally enlarged her sphere to include others. They invariably felt flattered. Even those who most disliked her could not help responding. This was one of her gifts, and she used it to telling advantage.

Now she gave Emer the sympathetic look of one abused woman to another, creating a sisterhood in the presence of the tyrannical male. Then she smiled; a slow, conspiratorial smile. She turned back toward Sitric.

"You hit your wife but you won't hit me, will you?" she asked her son in a low, deadly voice. Rising from the bench, she took a stride toward him with a fluid grace that belied her years.

Against his every intention, Sitric backed away from her.

Gormlaith laughed.

But there was no mirth in the sound. No amusement left in her. She was hollow. She would spend the rest of her life with a howling void at her center.

Until he set her aside, she had adored Brian Boru with all the excess of her flamboyant nature. She had flaunted her sex to excite his jealousy and played political games out of an ambition the equal of his own. When he divorced her, she had sought a fearsome revenge.

When it came it cracked her heart down the middle.

I am wreckage, she thought. *I am alone in the world without* him, *who was my only equal.*

I am alone.

Her huge eyes stared at Sitric out of cavernous sockets. "Hit me," she invited. If he hit her perhaps she would feel something again.

Shaking his head, Sitric took another step backward.

"Coward." With another shrug that dismissed the King of Dublin and all his works, Gormlaith turned to leave the hall.

"Wait!" Sitric cried.

"Why? Is there the remotest possibility you might say anything worth hearing?" she asked over her shoulder.

"I need your advice," he admitted.

She waited where she was. Her back was eloquent.

Sitric said, "You of all people understand the politics of high kingship. You've been married to two of them and you know every possible claimant. Tell me who I shall have to deal with now."

She turned halfway toward him. "Why should I?"

"Mother!" Sitric heard the pleading in his voice and knew it was a mistake, it would only make her more contemptuous.

But Gormlaith merely yawned. "Very well, I have nothing better to do anyway. And aren't those wretched servants of yours going to bring us some food sometime or other?" Radiating boredom, she sauntered back to the cushioned bench and sat down. "Let's look at the situation, Sitric. Malachi Mor is the most obvious claimant; he was Ard Ri before. Remember that until the rise of the Dalcassians, the High King was always a member of either the northern or the southern Ui Neill.

"But *he* destroyed the tradition of alternate kingship. Malachi might well attempt to reestablish it now that *he's* gone."

Sitric pointed out, "Brian Boru put an end to the alternate kingship not only so he could be Ard Ri, but also so he could establish a dynasty of his own, with one of his sons succeeding him. Of course, what he wanted no longer matters."

"Are you so sure?" Gormlaith asked softly. "Remember— one of his sons is my own Donnchad."

"That boy? He's not High King material."

Gormlaith drew in her breath with a hiss. "Who are you to judge?"

"I am also your son," Sitric reminded her.

"You are a proven loser," she retorted. "You had enough allies to conquer the world and you still couldn't defeat *him*. To think I gave birth to you! But I would like to be proud of at least one of my sons—perhaps I will help Donnchad succeed his father as Ard Ri so he can punish you as you deserve."

Sitric was taken aback. "You wouldn't," he said faintly.

"Would I not?" Her eyes glittered. Whatever had been languishing in their depths rose toward the surface, scenting an easy kill.

Chapter Eleven

The return of the army to Kincora should have been a triumphal progress, but an unrelenting melancholy accompanied them every step of the way. The horsemen rode at a weary walk for the most part, only stirring their animals into a trot when they had a hill to climb. Dragging the sledges carrying the wounded and dead, the foot warriors slouched along in no particular order, the discipline Brian Boru had enforced now abandoned.

A lantern-jawed man in a badly torn saffron tunic growled, "We won, but what did we win? The Ard Ri's dead. That maggot Sitric still holds Dublin. The invaders have gone back to where they came from, but they may return next spring, or the year after."

"They always do," commented another, whose bloody axe was thrust uncleaned through his belt, rusting.

A third man added, "As long as we have fat cattle and yellow gold and fair women, some foreigner will try to plunder us. It's as certain as fleas in your bedding."

"I won't let anyone plunder us," Donough wanted to say. "I can defend Ireland just as my father did."

But he kept silent, half afraid they would laugh at him.

Beltaine—May in the Christian calendar—lay sweetly across the land, fragrant with the bloom of whitethorn. After a cold, wet spring the sun shone almost every day as if trying to make up for past omissions. Mud dried, making marching easier.

But the Dalcassians remained haunted by Clontarf.

As they drew near the Shannon, however, Donough felt

his spirits rise. He began sitting taller on his horse and craning his neck as if he could glimpse Kincora through the dense woods east of the river. In his mind Kincora represented prestige and security in a world where both were hard come by. He loved the sprawling fort as his father had loved it, inordinately proud of every stone and timber.

He was, however, uncomfortably aware that Brian had left Teigue in charge. Donough had the army of Munster with him, at least its largest, Dalcassian component, but Teigue held the royal stronghold.

While the army was still some distance away, scouts observed its approach and hurried to Kincora to report to Teigue.

They found him in the great hall, which crowned a hill south of the eel weir on the Shannon that gave Kincora—Ceann Coradh, Head of the Weir—its name. The immense rectangular hall served a dual purpose. Brian Boru had used it as his audience chamber as well as his banqueting hall, calculatedly awing visitors with an ostentatious display of gold cups and bejeweled goblets on every table in the room.

The Ard Ri's private apartments had been built of stone, but his great hall was made of wattle-and-timber paneled with fragrant cedar, its shingled roof supported by pillars made from tree trunks adzed to a uniform size, then inlaid with silver and copper. Brightly colored woolen wall hangings suspended from bronze rods deflected draughts. The hall boasted not one but two stone hearths, each a third of the way down the center, and blazed with an extravagance of beeswax candles.

The Ard Ri's carved bench sat on a raised dais to the right of the main doorway. In his father's absence, Teigue had not presumed to occupy the royal seat, but he did take his meals in the hall. He enjoyed watching the scurry of servants using the twin corridors leading to the kitchens, a design of Brian's that allowed one set of servitors to carry in fresh food while others removed the emptied platters, without getting in each other's way.

Teigue was licking roast mutton fat off his fingers when the scouts were brought to him with a message that would not wait. "The Dalcassians are only a few miles from the Shannon," they reported breathlessly.

"Who leads them?"

"The Ard Ri's youngest son."

Teigue abruptly stopped licking his fingers and wiped them on one of the linen napkins which were among the luxuries of Kincora. A tall, slim man, he had his dead mother's colouring. His hair was dark brown, his eyes a soft blue screened by thick eyelashes.

"You can't mean *Donough's* in command of the army?" he asked as if not certain he had heard correctly.

"Apparently he is. He rides in the lead and the banner of clan Dal Cais is carried beside his horse."

Teigue immediately told the nearest servant, "Run; find Mac Liag for me if he is anywhere in Kincora. Tell him I need him in a hurry!"

The servant trotted away, soon returning with a puffing and panting Mac Liag at his heels. The man who had for so many years been Brian Boru's chief poet was past the age when running was possible, but he scurried as fast as he could. As he entered the hall he complained, "You have no reason to put such strain on an old man, Teigue! You know I'm not well. I was just about to go to my own house for a little rest and to work some more on the lament for . . . "

"I sent for you because I need an honest answer," Teigue interrupted, knowing the spate of Mac Liag's words would continue indefinitely if unchecked. "I need the truth and I know I can hear it from you."

The poet smiled. A praise singer by profession, he was as amenable to flattery as the nobility he served. "Poets are not always concerned with facts, but they are scrupulous about the truth," he replied.

"Then tell me truly—you've observed my half-brother Donough throughout his life; is he tainted by his mother's blood?"

Mac Liag was puzzled. "Why ask me about him? He could hardly be less important in the . . . "

"He could hardly be more important," Teigue contradicted. "According to the news we have received, Murrough, Flann, and Conor are all dead, which means that of my father's sons by noble mothers, only Donough and I still live."

As Teigue spoke of the slain princes, Mac Liag's eyes misted and his mouth began working; eulogies were shaping themselves on his tongue.

Before the poet could launch into them, Teigue asked him bluntly, "If only we two survive, which of us is best equipped by character and disposition to succeed our father?"

Mac Liag looked distressed. "I can hardly answer you. I know you well and I've known young Donough all his life, and you are very different from one another. Frankly, I never envisioned either of you wearing Brian's mantle."

"Neither did I, Mac Liag. But our father's titles are now vacant, and Donough is bringing the Dalcassians home even as we speak. Gormlaith's son is leading Brian Boru's personal army, do you understand?

"This is what I need you to tell me: Is there enough of his mother in Donough to make him dangerous?"

"I honestly don't know," the poet replied.

As Donough and the warriors approached the east bank of the Shannon, Fergal Mac Anluan recalled, "Years ago Brian had a big wine cellar built someplace around here, did he not? To store the three hundred casks of imported wine the Limerick Vikings paid him in tribute every year?"

Donough was too young to have remembered the construction of the cellar, but several of the officers grinned.

"It's in this general area," one of them affirmed. "He hid it on this side of the river so the warriors garrisoned at Kincora would be less likely to raid it. But we might as well find it and bend our elbows; it's the least we deserve after what we've been through."

Without even glancing toward Donough for permission, a score of men plunged into the undergrowth, searching for the path that would lead them to the cellar.

"Halt!" Donough shouted after them. "We have no time for that now!"

Ronan promptly challenged him. "And why not? What else do we have to do?"

"You have to follow me," said Donough, summoning all the authority he could muster. Here was the real challenge to his leadership; not at Athy, facing the Ossorians, but here in Thomond with the lure of drink tempting weary warriors. He would have liked to find the wine cellar himself; he felt as if he could drain a cask without help from anyone.

Then Ronan said patronizingly, "Go on without us. Too much red wine makes boys ill."

Some of the other men sniggered.

Now, a voice within himself told Donough. *Now or never.*

He was startled; the words were spoken in a deep, calm voice not recognizably his own. But in one smooth motion he found himself drawing his sword, pivoting on his horse, and leaning forward to press the sword point against Ronan's throat.

"We're going to Kincora," said Donough. "The wine can wait."

For a long, long moment no one moved. The foot warriors were watching him; the horsemen kept their eyes on Ronan.

The balance shifted one way and then the other. Both men felt it as they read one another's eyes.

Then Ronan drew back an infinitesimal distance and said in a carrying voice, "On to Kincora it is, Commander."

Donough lowered his sword.

He said nothing and kept his face impassive.

But he was astonished and not a little relieved that Ronan had backed down. Perhaps he would not need to name a new second-in-command after all.

They splashed through the shallows, fording the river where for centuries thousands of cattle had crossed to be paid as grudging tribute by Leinstermen to the King of Munster. Brian's birthplace, a seventh-century ring-fort which he had assimilated into the northern ramparts of Kincora, was known as Beal Boru—The Fort of the Cattle Tribute. The enforced tribute had long been a cause of bitterness between Leinster and Munster.

Gazing up at the timber palisades and countless outbuildings of Kincora sprawling along the west bank of the Shannon, Fergal Mac Anluan wondered if the cattle tribute would be paid this year, now that Maelmordha of Leinster and Brian of Munster were dead.

A sound like the voices of angels drifted to them, clearly audible above the roar of the falls below the ford. Members of the nearby monastery of Kill Dalua were chanting the *Pater* and the *Alleluia*.

Donough was the first to canter his horse up the incline from the river. He did not even wait for the man carrying the Dalcassian banner to precede him as convention dictated.

With a broad smile on his weary face, Donough came home.

Chapter Twelve

For the construction of his stronghold thirty years earlier, my father had employed the most skilled craftsmen in Munster. The massive oak gates were carved with the heads of saints intermingled with zoomorphic figures from a more pagan age; the iron hinges that held them were elaborately wrought. Even the smallest nailheads were engraved. Timber ceiling posts and rafters were both carved and ornamented with copper and silver. Wattle-and-timber walls were coated with dazzlingly white limewash. The stone used in the construction of private chambers, and the chapel, was precisely cut and fitted so tightly a knife blade could not be inserted.

Brian Boru's own restless mind had designed numerous innovations to add to Kincora's magnificence. Uniquely among Irish strongholds, his fortress was filled with light. Every chamber boasted small windows set just below the eaves, so that any stray sunbeam—or moonbeam—might find its way inside.

The late Ard Ri had with justification called Kincora his palace, a testimony to that Irish artistry which created incomparable goldwork and illuminated gospels unequaled in Christendom. Viking Dublin seemed offensively crude by comparison.

As I entered the stronghold I felt again a sense of timeless familiarity. It was as if I had always known this place, always been a part of hopes and dreams and events unfolding within its walls. Long before I was born, some essential element of myself had existed at Kincora. With birth I had begun to take an active part in a life I had previously been observing from the shadows.

Chapter Thirteen

From the watchtower over the gate a sentry was signaling to someone inside, informing them of the size of the contingent approaching. Kincora was accustomed to armies. As many as three thousand warriors had been garrisoned there at one time, and on occasion three hundred boats moored on the banks of the Shannon.

When the gates creaked open, Brian's youngest son rode forward without looking to left or right, as he thought a conquering hero should.

Teigue was waiting for him inside.

Donough was filthy from the journey, and when he saw his brother he regretted that he had not taken time to bathe at the river. By contrast Teigue's face glowed from a vigorous scrubbing and every item of clothing he wore was fresh; his silk-lined blue mantle with its marten fur trimming was fit for a king.

His wife Maeve claimed it heightened the color of his eyes.

Teigue welcomed the returning heroes of Clontarf effusively, and his greeting for Donough contained all the cordiality of one loving brother for another. He insisted everything must wait until the weary men had been given a chance to bathe and refresh themselves. "Then I shall meet you in the great hall and hear all about it," he told Donough. "You will be using your old apartments, of course?" he added innocently.

Gormlaith's old apartments.

Donough hesitated. "They hold unpleasant memories."

It was Teigue's turn to hesitate. Then, "Of course, of course, we can find somewhere better for you. For now you may use my chamber. There's a fire in the brazier and I'll send servants to you with heated water and a change of clothing."

"Something like you're wearing?"

Teigue glanced down at himself and his lips twitched, fighting back a smile. "I don't always dress this grandly," he admitted.

"So I recall."

"My wife chose these for me."

Donough made no comment.

He was ushered into Teigue's private chamber, a circular room carpeted with freshly gathered rushes. A woman's touch was obvious in its appointments.

It had been a long time since Donough had seen much luxury. Gormlaith had always surrounded herself with costly things, but her taste was florid, excessive. She insisted on dyes vivid to the point of garishness, and never satisfied herself with one of any item if she could get three or four.

In Teigue's chamber, his wife Maeve had exerted more subtle taste. A gilded book shrine sat on one small trestle table in isolated splendor. Another table displayed Maeve's copper-alloy toilet implements decorated with bird-head motifs against a field of red enamel; works of art in their own right.

Cushions were piled on a linen-covered mattress plump with goose down and sweet herbs. Donough glanced at it; looked away. He felt like a child invading the closed world of adults.

He almost expected to hear Gormlaith shout at him to go away.

A gray-haired bondwoman brought him a copper ewer of heated water and a basin. She stood patiently waiting, staring into space, while Donough washed himself, then she carried the dirty water away as another bondwoman entered the chamber with a pile of clothing in her arms.

Mindful of Teigue's costume, he selected a leine with bell-shaped, pleated sleeves. He drew the finely woven bleached linen garment up through his belt until it hung just above his knees, to show off the muscles of his legs. Over this he wore an embroidered green and gold mantle, which he fastened at the shoulder with a penannular brooch set with amber. Because he was a prince in his own palace he did not go barefoot, but donned leather shoes ornamented with scrollwork of silver wire.

His saffron-dyed warrior's leine and muddy brat were left abandoned on the floor.

When Donough finished dressing he picked up a mirror from among the collection of women's toilet articles. The face that looked back at him was older than he remembered, beginning to be stamped by experience; to his joy there was a definite moustache growing and his jaws needed a razor. He was fumbling among the various implements in hopes of finding one when a woman cleared her throat behind him.

He swung round.

Teigue's wife was only a few years older than Donough; a dimpled woman with fair hair dressed in curls and plaits. She wore a long smock of silky linen bound with a blue girdle. Her fingertips were rouged with ruam, but the red of her lips was natural.

Donough found himself staring at those lips. They made him think of ripe fruit.

Since his marriage, Teigue had rarely returned to Kincora, having a fort of his own beyond Crag Liath in a broad valley embraced by mountains. And he had never brought Maeve with him; this was the first time Donough had seen her.

Or she him. She did not remember him as a boy. She was looking at a man.

She smiled. "Donnchad? Or is it Donough now? I seem to recall hearing my husband mention you had changed your name."

"It is Donough," he replied with an answering smile. "How did you know me?"

"Because of your resemblance to the Ard Ri."

From that moment Donough was devoted to Maeve.

She accompanied him to the great hall, listening with flattering interest to whatever he said. She could not help noticing when he reached out to touch a carving on a post with appreciative fingers, or paused to take an admiring look at the elaborate ironwork of a torch holder.

He saw her watching. "Home," he said softly.

Maeve understood. She loved her own home in the valley beyond the hills.

The hall was crowded when they arrived. Members of the hand-picked company of warriors Brian Boru had left behind to guard Kincora were stationed around the walls, every man holding a spear upright.

With a broad smile, Teigue came forward to greet his brother. The smile faded when Donough's first words to him were, "My father never allowed weapons in the banqueting hall."

"He did on occasion," Teigue countered. "You were probably too young to remember."

The reference to his age irritated Donough. It was exactly the sort of remark his mother might have made to put him in his place; he assumed it was deliberate, as he assumed Teigue's regal attire was a deliberate attempt to intimidate him.

His face hardened. "Why are all these people here?"

"Surely you know many of them," Teigue replied. "There stands Cathal Mac Maine, Abbot of Kill Dalua since the death of your uncle Marcan. Beside him is Eamonn, chieftain of clan Cuinn, and over there is your cousin Fergal. And Enda, my chief steward, and Conor, a cattle lord from Corcomrua, and . . ."

Donough responded to each face with a nod of acknowledgment. But his eyes kept returning to a small cluster of men who stood apart. They wore heavily embroidered triangular mantles, and ankle-length tunics innocent of girdling.

"And those men over there, Teigue?"

For the first time, a note of wariness crept into Teigue's voice. "Brehons," he said.

"Why are there so many judges here? I can't recall my father having more than one or two at Kincora."

"That would have been the usual complement," Teigue agreed. "But under the circumstances we need the advice and counsel of every expert in the law."

"Under what circumstances?"

Teigue looked at his brother blankly. "Why . . . the fact that both our father and Murrough, his tanist, his chosen successor, died at the same time. The Dalcassians have lost their chieftain and brehons must preside over the election of another."

But tribal chieftainship, as both men were aware, was the least of the titles so abruptly vacated. Thomond was the tribeland of the Dal Cais, but only one of many tribelands tributary to the larger province of Munster.

Brian Boru had also held the title of King of Munster, the first major step he had taken on his way to becoming High King of the Irish.

Ard Ri.

In the days since news of Clontarf reached him, Teigue had accepted that he would follow his father as chieftain of the Dal Cais. He had even conceded he might claim the crown of Munster as well. But no mention of the high kingship had crossed his lips. Teigue was basically a simple man who would rather stay with his herds and his family than slog through deep mud to wave a sword in the face of some rebellious under-king.

Only Maeve knew how dismayed he had been to find himself the senior prince of his clan.

Upon receiving the news, Teigue had sent for every brehon he could gather. Whatever decisions were taken now must have the support of the practitioners of the ancient Brehon Law.

Brian Boru had overthrown tradition but not the law itself; he had, however, reinterpreted various laws to support his own ambitions. Traditionally the kingship of Munster had been held alternately by a prince elected from the senior branch of the Dalcassian tribe and one from the Owenachts, just as the high kingship had been held alternately by a chieftain from the northern tribe of the Ui Neill and one from the southern branch.

Until Brian Boru had wiped away alternate succession, and the divisiveness it engendered, with sword and strategy.

Now he was dead. In the vacuum of power following Clontarf, leadership might be redefined.

The timing of Donough's arrival was fortuitous; the two surviving sons could now hear the brehons' pronouncements together.

Chapter Fourteen

The great hall of Kincora was abuzz with conversation: the low, angry rasp of a swarm of bees about to attack.

"Why didn't you bring the Ard Ri home?" the patriarch of a Dalcassian family challenged Donough as he and Teigue were making their way to the top of the hall. "You brought other dead princes with you for their people to bury; surely you could have returned the Ard Ri to us."

"He should be entombed here, in the chapel of Saint Flannan!" insisted the sonorous voice of Cathal Mac Maine. The portly, tonsured abbot bore little resemblance to the late Ard Ri, though his father had been Brian's first cousin. Only his ambitious eyes and the stubborn set of his jaw revealed their kinship. "Is there any place in Ireland so suitable for the tomb of Brian Boru as the chapel where he said his prayers?"

Another man stepped forward to shake his fist in Donough's face. "We demand to know why you left the King of Munster to sleep among strangers in Ulster!"

Donough was taken aback. "It wasn't my decision. By the time I got there they had already taken him away."

"Why?!!!" a dozen voices roared.

Although Teigue had not spoken, Donough directed his reply to his brother. "It seemed to be an arrangement the priests made."

"Did you not question it?"

Donough had no answer. Too much had happened too fast; he was now aware that a lot of loose ends had been left dangling. A more mature man might have behaved differently, might have been less dazed, more . . .

"You don't know what it was like," he said, "trying to think clearly in the middle of so much confusion. I did what everyone demanded of me, I brought the Dalcassians home. If you want an explanation about our father's burial you should ask those who took his body to Armagh."

"They haven't returned yet. But we'll get an explanation, I promise you," Teigue said loudly enough for all to hear. "For now, we need to be reminded of the law pertaining to elections."

The angry buzz subsided but remained an undercurrent in the hall.

Standing to one side, Maeve listened enthralled as the brehons recited laws embedded in poetry to facilitate memorization; laws hammered out over many centuries, long before Christian monks brought literacy to Ireland. Every aspect of Irish life was addressed by Brehon Law. In spite of herself she was moved by the beauty and precision of language, a living tongue defining the structure by which a people consented to be governed.

Once women numbered among the brehons, but it had been five centuries since there was a female judge in Ireland. Under the patriarchal influence of the Church, women were no longer allowed to be part of the professional class. The brehons summoned to Kincora were all men in their middle or late years, with faces of seamed sobriety.

The chief brehon of Munster, whom custom dictated must belong to the tribe of the Deisi, began by intoning, "As people go by many roads to a royal residence, so they come to the law of the Senchus Mor, the Ancient Great Knowledge, by many covenants."

Behind his hand, Fergal Mac Anluan remarked to Ruadri of Ara, "They have to say that now. Brian Boru changed a lot of the old customs, didn't he?"

Ruadri said with a grin, "Brian Boru didn't wait to be

elected. He took what he wanted and then proved he was the best man to have it." Ruadri was but a year older than Donough Mac Brian and audacity attracted him.

Choosing his words carefully, the chief brehon continued, "The Dal Cais of Thomond mourn their fallen chieftain, but he must be replaced swiftly; a tribe cannot be without a head. As is . . . usually . . . the custom, in the absence of a tanist a tribe selects as its chieftain the best qualified man from the preeminent clan. Teigue Mac Brian is now the senior prince of that family, and furthermore a man of good health and sound judgment.

"If none of his close cousins challenge him, and the principal men of the Dal Cais assembled here today agree, we can proceed to the election and announce his chieftaincy."

Seeing the pain on her husband's face, Maeve knew he was thinking of his older brothers, those who should have stood between Teigue and the leadership he had never sought. Her heart went out to him.

Then she looked at Donough and saw the light leaping in his eyes as he raised his right arm, requesting to be allowed to speak.

The chief brehon nodded permission.

"Will the chieftaincy include Kincora?" Donough wanted to know.

The brehons exchanged glances. Property was a major source of contention, necessitating hundreds of tracts in Brehon Law. The judges did not want the tribal succession to descend into an interfamily wrangle over Kincora.

The chief brehon cleared his throat. "As the royal residence Kincora will . . ."

"It's always been my home," Donough interrupted—an almost unprecedented breach of decorum that caused a ripple of shock to spread through the hall. "Teigue has his own fort; he doesn't need this one. Nor does he love it as I do. Let him be chieftain if he wants, but give me Kincora."

On the faces of the brehons he read their unanimous

intention to refuse, which only strengthened his determination. He would fight; had not Brian Boru always fought for what he wanted?

"My father willed Kincora to me!" Donough blurted. "He made me heir to his holding!"

There was a momentary shocked silence.

"When did he do that?" asked a cadaverously thin brehon from Nenagh.

"On the evening before he sent me south with my cavalry. We were feasting here in the hall—I was sitting below the Ard Ri's seat—when he leaned forward and told me I was to be his heir if anything happened to him."

Teigue was staring at him. "I didn't hear him say that."

"He wasn't talking to you, he was talking to me. Flann was sitting right beside me, though, and he heard him. Flann told me he had no objection. He had his own fort. They all did. Murrough the tanist had a great stronghold. I was the only one with no home but these walls."

"Flann Mac Brian is dead," the chief brehon pointed out. "Who else have you as witness?"

After a moment's pause during which his brain was racing, Fergal Mac Anluan raised his arm. "I was in the hall that night, sitting with my kinsmen. I happened to overhear Brian's words to Donough, so I can testify to the truth of his claim."

Even Donough was surprised. Flashing his cousin a grateful smile, he said, "You see? I have a witness, a noble of the Dal Cais whose word must be accepted. As my father's chosen heir, I inherit his principal residence."

"If you were to have Kincora," interjected yet another brehon, speaking slowly and thoughtfully, "why was your brother Teigue left in charge here?"

"Because my father knew I wanted military experience. Teigue prefers being a cattle lord to bearing arms; I'm the one who takes after Brian Boru."

Maeve hurled her silent thoughts at her husband with all

the strength she possessed. *Leave it!* she urged him. Let Donough have this great sprawling pile, then you and I will be free to go home to our children and our valley.

But Teigue could not leave it, his sense of duty overrode his desire for a quiet life. Gormlaith had been a consummate liar and her son might be the same; what he was claiming might run counter to Brian Boru's intention, and that Teigue could not allow. "I'm sorry," he said, "but I cannot accept this without more proof. If my father left such a will surely it was committed to writing. We must wait until Carroll returns and ask him, for he kept all the Ard Ri's records."

Donough glared at Teigue. "Are you accusing me of making a false claim?"

"And me?" Fergal interjected angrily.

"I would never question the honor of either of you," Teigue replied. "I simply feel it would be better to wait until we've had a chance to talk with Carroll."

Donough flung out his hands to the brehons. "What are my rights?"

From the depths of a capacious memory trained through twenty years of study, the chief brehon recited, "Under the law, on the death of a father each son is entitled to an equal share of the land he held and the cattle fed upon it, but one of the sons, in addition to his equal share, also inherits the father's residence. Whether this favored son is the eldest or a younger son depends upon the discretion of the father.

"However," he added, looking sternly from Donough to Teigue and back again, "the son who claims the residential inheritance is thereafter responsible for guardianship of the unmarried women of the family, is bound to provide hospitality for all those who have a claim upon his tribe, and is obligated to succor and defend any of his own who are in need and distress.

"Think upon this, both of you. Kincora is large and its

dependents are many; the responsibility for Kincora is a
heavy burden requiring strong shoulders and a wise head."

Donough felt the massed weight of eyes turning toward
him, accusing him of a youth and inexperience he could not
deny. "You have no wife, no children," challenged Cathal
Mac Maine. "What do you know of caring for women? You
don't even have the care of your own mother."

Someone at the back of the hall laughed. "Gormlaith
needs no one to take care of her."

"Except in bed," chimed in another voice. "Half the men
here have taken care of her in bed at one time or another."
The laughter billowed into a wave.

Donough balled his fists. His brother felt the leaping tension in him. "Go easy," Teigue advised out of the corner of
his mouth. "You have to expect such talk."

"No one speaks of your mother this way," Donough
replied bitterly. "You're lucky; your mother's dead."

Teigue went white. At that moment something hardened
in him against his brother, a stone in his heart that would
never dissolve.

But Donough, who had spoken out of an excess of emotion, did not notice.

Maeve did, however. Suddenly she had the strange sensation that the ground had shifted under her, under all of
them, and she wanted to run to her husband and feel his
arms around her. With an effort she restrained herself.

Teigue turned toward the chief brehon. "I do not accept
my brother's claim of a will in his favor," he announced in a
voice stiff with formality. "Unless and until such a claim is
proved, I intend to retain the control of Kincora, which my
father gave into my hands for safekeeping."

Donough whirled on him. "Do you claim all else that was
his as well? Do you mean to be King of Munster too, and
possess the fortress of Cashel?" He started to say more but
common sense finally caught up with him and he refrained
from asking if Teigue wanted to be Ard Ri.

What he had already said was enough to constitute a challenge, however. Teigue's pride forced him to respond, "I will serve my people in whatever way they decide."

"The Owenachts may fight you for the kingship of Munster," warned a prince from the Slieve Aughty mountains.

"Then I'll fight," Teigue replied grimly.

In spite of himself Donough laughed aloud. "Teigue Mac Brian, fight? The closest you ever came to emulating our father was when you made canoes out of bark and sailed them on the Shannon. And then you let them get away from you."

Maeve hurled her thoughts at her husband with all the strength she possessed. *Leave it be!* she shouted at him silently. *Stop now before this goes any further!*

But he did not hear. Addressing Donough, but speaking for the benefit of everyone in the hall, Teigue announced, "In the absence of evidence to the contrary, I must consider myself Brian Boru's heir. Donough, I invite you to remain as my guest at Kincora until Carroll and the others return from Armagh. If at that time your claim to our father's stronghold is confirmed, I will of course surrender it to you. In the meantime I ask those present to vote on the chieftaincy of the Dal Cais."

"And what of Munster?" someone called.

No! Maeve shouted silently.

With shadows in his eyes Teigue said, "If I become chief of the Dal Cais, I am willing to hold the kingship of Munster for my tribe."

Chapter Fifteen

For a man who was chief poet of Munster, a rank second in status to that of the king, Mac Liag had a very modest home. Built of timber planking, it was rectangular in shape with a sod roof and only two chambers. But Mac Liag loved his house by the lake. It had, he rhapsodized, "An ash tree on one side of the doorway and a hazel on the other. A row of pines behind, singing with the wind. Salmon and pike and perch and Gillaroo trout for my supper, and the song of the lark to wake me in the morning."

In the poet's old age his widowed son Cumara lived with him and tended his simple needs. It was Cumara who answered Donough's knock on the doorframe—the door itself was hardly ever closed—and made no effort to hide his surprise. "No one calls on my father here," he told the unexpected visitor. "The Ard Ri was the only exception. This is father's private place; those who wish to see the chief poet attend him at Kincora."

"I want to see him, but I don't want to talk to him inside Kincora," Donough told the round-shouldered, brown-haired Cumara, who in spite of being a widower was but a decade older than himself.

"I'll send him out to you if he's willing," the other man replied.

As Donough waited he gazed out across the lake. Lough Derg, the Red Lake. Sometimes carmined by sunset, sometimes flushed with tides of roseate plankton that appeared and vanished inexplicably.

Sometimes stained with blood.

"You sought me, Prince Donough?" inquired a mellifluous voice behind him.

Donough turned and looked down at Mac Liag. He had last seen the poet in the hall at Kincora three months earlier, but in those three months Mac Liag had aged years. His subcutaneous fat had melted away, leaving his flesh sagging from his bones like a garment borrowed from a much larger man.

Donough said, "You were my father's friend, and I need a friend now."

Inclining his head in the direction of Kincora, Mac Liag replied, "Surely you have many friends inside."

"Do I? And who would they be? Friends of my mother's, perhaps?"

"Perhaps."

"Come now, Mac Liag, you know she had no friends here."

"That was her own doing. Brian gave her every opportunity to have a good life with him. Had she made him happy, his friends would have been hers."

It was the first time Donough had ever heard anyone refer to his father's happiness—or lack of it. Such a possibility had never crossed his mind. He was so young that the emotions of others were still abstractions to him, Brian's most of all. "Isn't being a king enough to make any man happy?" he asked.

Mac Liag gave him a long look. "Walk with me, lad. Walk with me and we shall talk of kingship. And other things." Over his shoulder he called, "We'll be back by sundown."

The poet's son appeared in the doorway. Cumara had the face of the perpetually anxious, with deep frown lines scoring his brow, and pale blue eyes that anticipated bad news. "Don't you need me to come with you?"

"Not necessary. If I require an arm to lean on I'm sure I can rely on my young friend here," Mac Liag replied.

They strolled away from the house by the lake, following a winding path among the murmurous pines. Donough waited for Mac Liag to begin the conversation, but the poet, for once, was silent. Even their footfalls were hushed by the centuries-deep carpet of pine needles.

When Donough cleared his throat to speak, Mac Liag put a restraining hand on his arm. "Smell."

"*Smell?*"

"The fragrance of the pines. My feet press out perfumed oils as I walk, and the blackbird on the high branch sings to me. And I am happy, do you understand?"

Donough was plainly puzzled. "Not really. I thought we were going to talk about kingship."

"We are," said the poet. "I know what happened in the hall yesterday, even though I was not present. There are no secrets at Kincora. You were foolhardy to challenge Teigue for your father's palace."

"I have as much right to it as he has."

"But you are . . ."

"Don't tell me I'm too young!" Donough flared. "I'm a man by every law, including that of nature."

"I was going to say you are inexperienced," Mac Liag replied smoothly. "What do you know of managing a vast strongholding?"

"I've spent my life at Kincora, watching Brian Boru. Surely that's enough experience."

"You've spent your life at Kincora, but not watching Brian Boru. Until he threw her out, your mother kept you as far away from him as possible. You weren't trained at his elbow, you were hidden behind her skirts. And I never noticed you rebelling," Mac Liag added.

"I did rebel! Every chance I got. But she was always . . ."

"I know. Gormlaith did everything she could to keep you a child. You were an ornament to be taken out and paraded when she wanted to boast of her motherhood at an age when other women are boasting of their grandchildren."

Donough turned and faced the poet squarely. "Do you hate Gormlaith the way everyone else does?"

"Hate?" Mac Liag considered the word. "I never hated her. Do you hate the storm that blows down your trees?"

"Then will you be my friend although I am Gormlaith's son?"

Pity moved the old man to say, "Of course I will be your friend, lad. For your father's sake. He used to come here, you know. To my little house." The trained voice, which age had not destroyed, grew reminiscent. "We would sit for hours at my hearthside, talking. Sometimes he played his harp for me here. Or he would summon me to a banquet at Kincora and give me the first drink of red wine from his own cup." The faded eyes misted.

Donough was too impatient for the future to be enthralled with the past. "As my friend, you must support my claim to Kincora."

Mac Liag's eyes opened wide. "I did not say . . ."

"When Kincora is mine, you shall come to every feast and always have the first drink from my cup," the young man promised.

"Listen to me, Donough, while I give you a friend's advice. The possession of a palace will not make you happy. Your father had Kincora but there was always a hunger in him, a longing for something else; something more. Don't I know? I, who was with him?

"He was a lonely man; to the very end he was a lonely man. Murrough's mother died in his arms, other women were never enough for him, and then finally Gormlaith . . .

"Even with all his power, the Ard Ri was not happy. I don't think there was one day when he experienced the contentment I know in my little house by the lake. Out of a lifetime of experience I tell you: that feeling is more to be desired than all the noble strongholds in Ireland."

"Your 'little house by the lake,'" Donough quoted. "Your

own place. Well, Kincora is my own place. And I depend upon you to help me get it!"

Later, as he sat brooding by his hearthside, Mac Liag said to his son, "How do I find myself in such a patch of nettles? Teigue has been elected chieftain of the Dal Cais and will no doubt become King of Munster. When that happens, he intends to rule from Kincora as his father did before him.

"As chief poet of Munster, my loyalty is to the king.

"But now I've told . . . worse than that, I've promised . . . young Donough that I would be his friend. For a moment there, in the shadows of the trees, he looked so much like his father . . . I'm a sick man, Cumara, I'm not able for this," the poet moaned. "Being caught between Brian's sons will destroy me entirely. I've heard my last cuckoo sing from the whitethorn."

For as long as he could remember, Cumara had heard his father complaining about various ailments. Brian Boru's death had unquestionably hit Mac Liag very hard, but Cumara privately believed the old poet had the constitution of bog oak. In spite of that he was worried; it was his nature to worry. Patting Mac Liag's hand, he said, "Put it out of your mind, father. Let Teigue and Donough sort it out between them and you stay clear."

"I want to be waked for six days," Mac Liag said. "Six; it is an honor I deserve."

"You aren't going to die, you won't need a wake."

"Six days, with candles lit 'round my bier. And Cathal Mac Maine to pray over me, no one else. Do you understand? Bury me at Cashel, the royal seat of Munster. Though, mind you, I would rather be buried here beside the lake. But we must think of my station."

"Yes, father." Cumara sighed.

"And one more thing—be sure to tell me as soon as Carroll gets back, will you? I need most urgently to talk with him."

Chapter Sixteen

As Kincora waited for the late Ard Ri's retinue to return from Armagh, Donough busied himself mustering support. One he was relying upon was his cousin, Fergal Mac Anluan. He found Fergal in the low stone building Brian had constructed as an armory. Together with Odar the smith, Fergal was counting the various weapons the Dalcassians had reclaimed from the dead and brought back to Kincora; weapons that gave mute evidence of the ferocity of the battle. The light of smoking fat burning in bronze lamps revealed substantial damage.

"Some of these blades are beyond repair," Odar was saying as Donough ducked his head under the lintel and entered the building. "The best thing to do is melt them down and re-forge them. We can still use most of the old hilts, though; particularly for the short-swords. The great-swords are another problem. Being two-handed, they need to be shaped to the wielder's grip, so we'll have to assess them individually.

"Now these axes are a different matter; they're made to stand more battering. A hammering here, a new edge there, and they're ready to kill a man tomorrow." Odar squinted at Fergal. "You know the test of an expert axeman? Cut a man in three pieces, first with a forehand blow and then with a backhand, before his dead body can hit the ground?"

"I not only know it," retorted Fergal, "I can do it."

"Can you now?" Odar did not sound convinced. "It's an achievement rarely seen. Why, the last time I saw . . ."

"You probably saw my father do it," said Donough,

stepping forward into the lamplight, which threw the bones of his maturing face into stark relief.

"I believe I did. In the battle of Glenmama."

"Could you teach me?"

"Did the Ard Ri not teach you?"

Donough busied himself with pawing through the pile of damaged weaponry and did not answer.

"You can do something for me," Odar said to him. "When you next talk with your brother, tell him he'll get as many as three hundred usable weapons out of this lot."

Donough swung around to glare at the smith. "*He'll* get? These are mine; I brought them back."

"Of course you did, and fair play to you, but the chief will have the distributing of them among his Dalcassians."

"*My* Dalcassians. I brought them back, too."

Odar took a long, slow look at Donough. The smith had not lived in the heart of a warrior society all his life without being sensitive to shifts in the wind. He stole a glance at Fergal, but the son of Anluan was keeping his face studiously blank.

"I had best get to work," said Odar in a tone that made plain they were both expected to leave him to his craft.

Outside the armory, Donough caught his cousin by the arm. "You know the Dalcassians are mine, they followed my banner home."

"They aren't your private army," Fergal pointed out. "The chief of the tribe is their ultimate commander."

"Are you not on my side? What about the will?"

"That was different."

"How?"

"I thought you made a good argument; you should have Kincora. Besides, I like you and it's always a good idea to have a prince owing one a favor. That's worth a small lie."

"A lie? Are you saying you didn't hear my father make me his heir?"

Fergal narrowed his eyes. "Are you saying he did?"

"You didn't hear him?"

"No, of course not. But it doesn't matter, I . . ."

His words went unheard. Biting his lip, Donough walked rapidly away.

As she crossed the paved courtyard between the private sleeping chambers and the grianan, the women's sunny-room, Maeve noticed him sitting slumped on the ground with his knees drawn up to his chest and his back against a wall. He looked so dejected she could not resist going over to him.

He looked up gratefully. "Is there any news of Carroll's return?"

"Not yet. You should not pin all your hopes on him, Donough. So much has happened; if there was a written will, it may have been lost in the confusion. Or Brian might have intended to dictate it to Carroll as they marched to Dublin, then been overtaken by events and forgot about it."

"My father never forgot anything," Donough said stubbornly.

Maeve laughed. "Och, everyone forgets."

"Not my father."

"Have you nothing to cling to but your memories of him and your desire for Kincora?"

The gray eyes that looked up at her were bleak.

Impulsively, she bent down to him. "I have a sister visiting me," she said. "Younger than me, not yet betrothed, and very pretty. If you're old enough to bear arms you're old enough to marry, and if you have a family to shelter and support it would strengthen your claim to Kincora. Though why you would want a place this large and all the headaches that go with it is quite beyond me," she added.

"A wife? Your sister?"

"And why not? Neassa has all the virtues required of a woman of high rank, she has a lovely voice, she can embroider and make mead and command servants. I'll introduce you, shall I? Who knows, you might like each other."

Donough found himself gazing into the square neck of Maeve's gown, at her full round bosom. "I suppose there's no harm," he replied.

That night, as the main meal of the day was being served in the banqueting hall, Maeve and a young woman approached Donough. They had to thread their way around long benches and small trestle tables, trying not to trip over outstretched legs, for almost the length of the hall. The strained relations within the clan of Brian had resulted in a change in seating arrangements.

Enda the chief steward had been plainly embarrassed when he led Donough to his new bench. "Here, with your own table and a stool for your feet, will this do?" he had asked hopefully.

"But my brothers and I always sat in the center of the hall between the two hearths," Donough protested. "Where Teigue is sitting now."

Enda would not meet his eyes. "There is a new order of precedence now, set by Prince Teigue. I can only obey."

Donough said nothing, merely seated himself on the bench.

But he gazed across the hall at his brother with such intensity he was unaware when Maeve stood beside him. She had to tap his shoulder to gain his attention.

"Prince Donough, I want you to meet my sister, Neassa. Is she not as lovely as I promised?"

The woman who stood beside Maeve was very like her: the same sweetly rounded form, the same fair coloring. Seen by the light of a hundred candles, she had a tempting glow.

A wife, Donough thought with sudden fierce determination. *When I have a wife I have to have a fort. And it's going to be this fort.*

He could see it so clearly in his own mind, every detail a replication of his father's life—except, of course, for Gormlaith—that he was almost surprised to find himself still seated far from the center of the hall, with the girl called Neassa looking at him as if he were a stranger.

He forced his mind back to the present. "Sit here beside me," he invited, "and share my cup."

Neassa raised her eyebrows and cast an interrogatory glance at her sister. Maeve hastily informed Donough, "An unmarried woman of our rank cannot share a cup with a man unless he has offered her father a bride-price. You know that."

"I know that," he echoed, a dull red flush creeping across his cheeks. Then he said brusquely, "So what would be a satisfactory bride-price? Would your father accept five cows? And what sort of dowry will come with her?"

Teigue's wife was taken aback. "Both dowry and bride-price are usually arranged through an intermediary with no close personal interest," she informed him. Women often knew more about these things than unmarried men. "A distant cousin, a priest, a brehon . . . someone who can negotiate between the two parties over a period of weeks or months."

Donough made an impatient gesture. "Too long. We could be dead tomorrow; I've seen plenty of dead men recently, enough to make me want to do my living while I can. Your family lives just up the river, so send word to your father immediately that I offer him five cows, and I shall settle another five cows on Neassa the day we marry. If that is not enough, ask him what he will accept."

Maeve could not resist asking, "Do you actually have ten cows?"

"I do of course, didn't you hear the brehons? Teigue and I will share equally all the cattle our father fed on his land-holdings. I have hundreds of cows," he elaborated, throwing his arms wide in an expansive gesture that swept the cup from the table nearest him and splashed its contents over Neassa's gown.

She drew back with a startled cry and began mopping furiously at herself.

By the next day everyone in Kincora—and much of the surrounding countryside—had heard the news. "Prince Donough has chosen a wife!"

"The woman is Maeve's sister," an understeward informed a kitchen servant.

"But she has not agreed to the marriage," the kitchen servant told a porter.

The porter assured his wife in bed that night, "They will marry, of course. Even if the girl's against it, I should say her family will prevail upon her. A prince of Thomond, and all those cows!"

"Her family has already married a daughter to a prince of Thomond," the wife reminded him. "Teigue Mac Brian. And him with the chieftainship and Kincora as well."

"Kincora is not so certain," said her husband. "Young Donough's disputing his claim. He says there's a will."

"Is there?"

"And how would I know? All this talk. . . . Turn around here, woman, and put your head on my belly."

Arranging a marriage was not as swiftly done as Donough would have liked. It seemed to him that Brian Boru had only to snap his fingers and his wishes were fulfilled at once, but people appeared determined to thwart and frustrate his youngest son.

Once Neassa told Maeve she was willing to consider his proposal—an admission she made in response to her sister's urging, and with some reluctance—the girl was promptly returned to her father's house to remain there until all negotiations between the two clans were concluded. Runners would be sent back and forth, brehons consulted and then consulted again. An accurate current count of the late Ard Ri's cattle must be made, for under the law Donough could not give away a single cow until the size of the various herds in their various meadows was known and the cattle were evenly divided between himself and Teigue.

"But we know I shall have more than ten!" he protested vehemently. "Why can't I just take ten now?"

There was, however, no arguing with the law.

Yet had not his father successfully manipulated the law?

Donough stormed to the house on the lake to complain to Mac Liag, "Why is everything being made so hard for me?"

"It is not. It just seems that way because you're young."

"I merely want to marry quickly. Is that so unreasonable?"

"Not at all. People have been doing it for years. I myself . . ." Mac Liag paused, a reminiscent smile spreading over his face like the last glow of sunset. "I did not have a prince's marriage, with complicated property settlements," he continued dreamily. "I am a poet. I kidnapped my wife; I carried her away into a sea full of stars and . . ."

"Kidnapped?" Donough's eyes were very bright.

"I did of course, an ancient and honorable tradition. She was delighted, though she essayed one small shriek of protest just to observe the conventions. But . . ."

Mac Liag found he was talking to himself. Donough had gone.

"Ah, to be young again," the poet wistfully observed to his son. "Young and impetuous, thinking all things are possible."

Staring into his own future as sole caretaker of an elderly, crotchety parent, Cumara, who liked to think of himself as still young, commented glumly, "Nothing is possible."

The banner of the Ard Ri, its golden field and three red lions stained with blood, was carried through the main gates of Kincora. The entire population of the great fort turned out to greet it in reverent silence.

Behind the flagbearer came Brian's retinue, exhausted, hollow-eyed; men who had survived the end of the world.

After the entombment in Armagh they had stayed on for some days as guests of Bishop Maelmuire. When they finally

left Ulster, Malachi Mor had insisted they stop at his stronghold in Meath for more hospitality. There he had entertained his old rival's followers so lavishly that Carroll was
moved to remark, "Malachi dreams of being High King
again."

"Not a dream," replied a member of clan Cuinn. "Who
else is there to succeed Brian but a man who already knows
the office?"

Carroll thought of arguing, but somehow it did not seem
worth the effort.

Nothing seemed worth the effort anymore.

And so Brian's men came home to Munster, and the
gates of Kincora opened to receive them.

An interrogation similar to that which had greeted
Donough awaited them, but Carroll had the answers.

"The Ard Ri was entombed in Armagh at his own
request," he explained to Teigue even before going inside to
wash his feet and face. "It was an arrangement Brian made
years ago; I was with him when he made it. In challenging
Malachi Mor for the high kingship he needed all the allies
he could get, particularly the Church. So we made a
journey to Armagh and he left twenty ounces of gold on the
altar there while confirming Armagh as the principal ecclesiastical city in Ireland. In the clerical record he titled himself 'Emperor of the Irish'—a designation the Church let
stand.

"Then he paid the supreme compliment to Ulster. He
willed his body to be buried at Armagh so his flesh would
become one with the north.

"The flattery was successful. When he challenged
Malachi, the northern clergy—while they did not actively
support Brian—did not support Malachi either. Thus Ulster
was instrumental in Brian's becoming Ard Ri, and now they
have given him a funeral more splendid than any ever seen
in Ireland. He was waked for twelve nights and twelve days,
and masses said in every chapel and monastery for the

repose of his soul. His body rests in solitary honor in a great
stone tomb on the north side of the church at Armagh; his
debt is paid, as he willed."

"As he willed," Teigue echoed. "So shall it be. But . . .
speaking of wills, have you seen my brother?"

"Dead," Carroll replied dolefully. "Murrough, Conor,
Flann—all dead."

"I mean Donnchad; Donough, as he calls himself now.
He claims there was a will, and we need you to verify it, if
you can . . . where *is* that boy?" he interrupted himself irritably, looking around. "I would have thought he'd be
among the first to greet you."

But no one knew where Donough was, until one of the
horseboys came forward to say, in a rather nervous voice,
"Prince Donough galloped away from Kincora at first light
on his best horse, and leading another."

Teigue stared at him. "Another?"

"For his wife to ride, he said."

Chapter Seventeen

Beyond the earthen embankment which encircled her
father's stronghold was a tree-fringed meadow Neassa
visited at sunrise on May mornings. Beltaine dew was prized
for its ability to improve a woman's complexion. It was most
efficacious on the first day of the month, but Neassa was a
young woman who liked to be certain; she collected the dew
each dawn as long as Beltaine lasted.

On the last day of May she lingered in the meadow
longer than usual. In a household crowded with parents,
siblings, servants, and an occasional sick cow, it was the only

place where she could be alone with her thoughts. Neassa was of a passive rather than a contemplative nature, but she had several things on her mind this morning.

Under Brehon Law, a woman could not be forced to marry against her wishes. Brehon Law did not preclude relatives from bringing considerable pressure to bear, however. Neassa's father Gadhra was a cattle lord with a sizable holding, but he was always eager to enlarge his herd. Upon learning that Donough wanted to marry Neassa he had begun making plans at once.

"The Ard Ri's son Teigue gave me that spotted bull as part of the bride-price for Maeve," he recalled. "Best bull I ever had. Every heifer he covered produced a calf. A number of them even had twins," he added with a gleam in his eye.

"I don't know that I want to marry Donough," Neassa had protested. "He's a stranger to me. And he's clumsy. And he doesn't even have a full moustache yet."

"He's old enough to lead an army, so he's old enough to marry," her father replied. "How large a bride-gift did you say he was willing to offer for you?"

"Maeve sends word that he is a fine young man, more comely than her own husband and with strong white legs," Neassa's mother added. "Few men have his advantages; you'll grow thin and gray waiting for another."

Neassa was not convinced. She had not had one glimpse of Donough's white legs before he spilled red wine over her, ruining the new gown she had so painstakingly embroidered for her first visit to Kincora. At that one brief meeting he had seemed abrupt, distracted, paying hardly any attention to her, and she could not imagine spending the rest of her life with him.

He was probably very dull, she decided. Something better would come along.

Now she meandered dreamily across the meadow, swinging a small glass phial hanging from a leather thong and thinking in a vague way about the future. About marriage. About curling her hair in a different style. She began toying with the idea of entering a convent and imagined herself garbed in bleached linen—which was very becoming—and doing good works. She might even one day be a saint like Princess Brigit of Kildare and . . .

Neassa's reverie was interrupted by the cadence of galloping hooves. Startled, she dropped her little phial of dew just as Donough burst out of the woods, riding one horse and leading another. He reined to a hasty stop and they stared at one another.

Neassa recovered first. "What are you doing here?"

He took a deep breath. "I've come . . ." His voice cracked; his face turned a fiery red. He tried again. "I've come to kidnap you."

Teigue was astonished. "He's done what?"

"Kidnapped Gadhra's daughter, Neassa. Rode right into her father's holding, the runner says, and carried her away with him."

Teigue's face was as stormy as a March morning. "That proves it. He's too impetuous to be entrusted with any responsibility, never mind letting him have Kincora. What am I going to say to Gadhra? He's my father-in-law and I've always had good relations with him, but he won't take this well. No proper negotiations, no bride-price . . . unless I offer him one in my brother's name. Should I? *Damn* Donough! I don't even know what one does in these situations. Send me a brehon!"

While Teigue struggled with the formalities and cursed his half-brother, Donough and his stolen woman were galloping across Thomond.

Galloping is not an altogether accurate description. They had begun at the gallop, with Neassa, who had never ridden a horse in her life and refused to mount the one Donough had brought for her, slung across the withers of his mount like a sack of corn. In this uncomfortable position she had protested so loudly that he was forced to slow to a more sedate pace.

So he kidnapped his wife at the walk, once they were out of sight of her father's landholding. Trusting the superfluous horse to find its way back to the stables at Kincora, he knotted the reins on the animal's neck and turned it loose.

Then he allowed Neassa to sit up in front of him, and tried to make her comfortable straddling his horse's shoulders with his arms around her, one hand holding the reins. He could smell her hair and feel the warmth of her body, and when he glanced down he could see the swell of her breasts, and her skirt hiked up to her thighs.

She busied herself smoothing the front of her gown. Had she known she was going to be carried off she would have worn something more suitable, like the flowing draperies of Irish princesses in the ancient legends. Instead she was clothed in a plain ankle-length dress of brown wool over a bodice of very crumpled linen. No jewelry, even. And her exposed thighs looked too fat.

To keep him from paying attention to them she tapped his arm and remarked brightly, "Sitting on a horse puts one up very high, doesn't it?"

"It does." Donough waited for her to say something else but she did not. His mother had a fund of intelligent conversation for any occasion, he recalled, and even at her worst Gormlaith was entertaining. Perhaps Neassa was too frightened to be charming. Perhaps when she got to know him better she would be a good companion.

For her part, Neassa had changed her mind about Donough. Obviously he was not dull. When he announced he was going to kidnap her she had been startled, then willing. On a radiant spring morning the idea was delightful.

But as the day progressed and she grew increasingly tired

of sitting on the horse—and increasingly sore in her female parts—delight faded.

"Stop squirming," said Donough. "You're upsetting the horse, he isn't used to carrying double."

Neassa protested, "And I'm not used to riding! Can't I get down and walk?"

"How would that look if anyone saw us—me mounted and you afoot?"

"We could both walk and lead the horse."

"That would look even odder. Besides, why should I walk when I have a perfectly good mount? Now sit still and enjoy the ride."

Neassa tried to think of a persuasive argument, but none occurred to her. She shifted her body as delicately as she could to ease the most sensitive portions of her anatomy off the horse's bony withers. "Where are we going and how soon will we be there?" she demanded to know.

Donough was asking himself the same question. Caught up in the excitement of putting his idea to practice, he had not thought farther ahead than the actual seizure of Neassa. He assumed that a man who kidnapped a woman usually took her back to his own stronghold, but he had none. The purpose of this undertaking was the acquisition of Kincora. Under the circumstances he could hardly take her there and beg Teigue to give them shelter. Teigue would probably order him to take her home again and then give him a tongue-lashing for being impetuous.

Which he had been. He knew it. But that did not help now.

He must make Neassa physically his; then Teigue could not force him to give her back to her father. But where? If she was to be the wife of a prince of Thomond she should not be ravished in the open like a herder's daughter. She was entitled to a roof, walls, a proper chamber and nuptial bed.

Instead they had a sunny sky beginning to cloud over,

and rolling grassland furnished with bracken and occasional briars.

Neassa was squirming again and the horse flattened its ears with annoyance. Donough could feel the hump forming in its back; in another moment the beast would start bucking and ignominiously dump them both.

A quick decision was imperative.

Donough reined his horse to a halt in the lee of a low hill, which offered a sheltered grassy hollow with a scattering of daisies. By a stretch of poetic imagination, one might call it a sea full of stars.

Would enough ardor, he wondered, persuade Neassa to overlook the shortcomings of the place as a wedding chamber?

He pushed back onto the horse's rump to give himself room to swing a leg over behind the girl, then slid off. Holding up his arms to her he invited, "Come down to me."

She was instantly suspicious. "Why?"

"So I can hold you properly."

"You were holding me on the horse. Why did you get off? Is he going to run away with me?" Her voice rose.

"He's not going anywhere; he's well trained. Come down."

For a woman who had been anxious to get off the horse, she seemed curiously reluctant. "Why?" she repeated.

There was a light in her eyes Donough would have recognized as flirtatious if he had been a more experienced man.

"Because I want you to!" he replied in exasperation. He seized Neassa by the waist and tried to pull her off and she shrieked—not too loudly—and struck out at him—not too hard.

Donough had never fought with a woman. Unsure how to react, he tried to fend her off while still managing to get her onto the ground with him. In the struggle he lost his balance and the two of them fell, hard. His efforts to twist his body so he would cushion her fall went awry, thanks to her wild struggles, and when they hit the ground he somehow found himself on top.

The wind was knocked out of her, but not for long. Before Donough could gather his thoughts, Neassa shrieked in earnest. "You clumsy maggot, you've hurt me!"

Her voice was sharp enough to pierce holes in earlobes. Such a cry from a woman would bring anyone within hearing to her aid; Donough had no desire to be caught in such an embarrassing position. "Be quiet," he hissed at her. "You're not hurt."

"I am hurt! You owe me compensation, you owe me at the least an amber pendant and an ivory comb and . . ." She went rattling on, listing the sort of rewards with which her long-suffering father purchased peace in his own home. Appalled, Donough responded by clamping his hand over her mouth and one long leg across her body, pinning her down.

Above his hand her furious eyes glared at him.

There was only one thing he knew to do. He must possess her here and now so he would have a claim to her as wife. If he let her get away she would probably never allow him a second chance.

When he first thought of kidnapping Neassa, Donough had allowed his healthy young imagination to run riot with images of her body and the things they would do together. A woman of his own! He would be gentle with her, he promised himself; gentle and considerate but so passionate he would awaken desire in her and they would . . .

Reality was different. Fumbling with his clothes while simultaneously trying to hold down the struggling girl, he discovered that ardor was not always available on demand.

"What are you doing?" she asked unnecessarily. What he was attempting to do was perfectly obvious.

Donough did not answer. Clutching her in mounting desperation, he shifted his body and tried to come at the problem from a different angle.

Her skirt was in the way. Had she been cooperative the

matter would have been quickly resolved, but as it was he had to try to push her clothing aside with his knee since he already had both hands occupied.

Neassa wailed, "You're ruining my gown!"

"I'll give you a new one," he panted.

She was not inclined to be reasonable. "I don't want a new one, I want this one, and I want you to let go of me!"

But by now Donough was grappling with her in grim earnest, feeling both his future and his manhood at stake. He dare not stop no matter how much he wished he could.

He had listened to warriors boasting of conquest and rape, and like many youths felt a certain vicarious excitement. But when the opportunity came it was the last thing he wanted to do.

He was disgusted by the struggle, which embarrassed rather than inflamed him and demeaned them both. At the start of the day he had only the best and most noble intentions toward Neassa. How could matters have disintegrated into this sweaty scuffle among the weeds?

Then Neassa squirmed under him in a different way, and he felt the moist opening heat of her against his naked flesh. He gasped as his body took over, freeing him of conscious thought, his penis swelling and thrusting as if it had a mind of its own.

"No," she said with her mouth against the side of his face, but the word had no meaning. It was just a sound. When she repeated, "No no no no no," her half-hearted protest was lost in the plunging rhythm of his body.

He felt a barrier; he pushed, something gave and the girl gasped with pain but he could not stop.

He experienced a peculiar sense of ascension as if he were running up a mountain while the air became thinner and thinner and his breathing more and more labored. He was desperately eager to reach the top, where someone or something wonderful waited for him, yet he did not want to get there. He wanted to go on climbing and climbing with the oxygen-starved rapture growing in him until . . .

The climax when it came caught him by surprise. A violent shudder swept through his body at the summit of the climb and he cried out a name, but he was not aware he cried out.

He was aware of nothing but the intensity of the pulsing spasm that shook him, tearing his soul loose from its moorings.

To her credit, Neassa lay quiet under him while passion subsided. The passion had been his, not hers, but she had enough generosity to allow him the full experience. Only when he was quiet and his breathing began to slow did she say, in an aggrieved voice, "You're crushing me."

Donough sat up hastily. His heart was still pounding, but he was in control of himself again—more or less. In control, and contrite. He did not want to look at her. He did not know where to look nor what to do. What to say. Of course he could not apologize, he was Brian Boru's son.

Out of the corner of his eye he saw Neassa slowly sit up, raising her hands to her hair in a timeless womanly gesture of repairing the damage. Her skirt foamed around her thighs; another foam was mixed there, streaked with blood. When she caught him looking she thrust out her lower lip. "You've made me very sore."

Late in the day, a sentry on the gates called down to those inside, "Someone's coming. A single horse." He squinted into the twilight, then grinned. "With two riders."

A flushed and defiant Donough rode through the gates as soon as they creaked open, looking neither left nor right. In his arms, Neassa was swiveling her head on her neck as if she had never seen Kincora before.

Her lips were curved in a smug little smile.

As soon as Maeve saw her sister's smile, she knew everything. But Donough insisted on spelling it out for Teigue when he met with his brother in Teigue's private chamber.

"I consummated a marriage with this woman, I made her a wife to me under Brehon Law. I know the contracts hadn't been agreed, and there was no priest on hand to call down God's blessing on us, either. But she is my wife and I need a home for her."

Teigue's arms were folded across his chest and his face was set in hard lines. "You behaved very badly. Her father and kinsmen are furious with us, and I don't blame them."

"She's my wife," Donough reiterated doggedly. "I need a home for her."

"You can stay here until a fort can be built for you on your share of our father's landholdings."

"I don't want some other fort. I want this one, the one he willed to me!"

Teigue sighed. "Send for Carroll," he said over his shoulder to a servant.

The confrontation was brief and unpleasant.

"Brian left no written will," Carroll told Donough with certainty.

Carroll was fresh from a discussion with Mac Liag on this very subject, in which they had agreed that the boy was intelligent and full of spirit, but unready to assume major responsibility. "Remember he's Gormlaith's son," Carroll had stressed, "and a more irresponsible woman never lived. We must protect her son from himself."

"I agree," Mac Liag responded. "But tell me—in confidence, mind you—was there a will?"

Carroll hesitated. "Never a written one. Although . . ."

"Although?"

"Before the battle got underway Brian did send for me, to remind me of his promise to bequeath his body to Armagh should he die. And during that conversation he also specifically bequeathed his blessing to his youngest son. Not to Teigue or any of the others, but to Gormlaith's child. I wondered about that since."

"Could he have meant to single out Donough for special privilege, even above his brothers?"

"Possibly," Carroll conceded. "It was hard to know what was on Brian's mind at the time. He was old and tired and a terrible battle was just ahead. Had he been thinking clearly, I cannot believe he would have bestowed favors on the child of the woman who caused the battle. Surely Brian never loved Gormlaith!"

Mac Liag allowed himself the faintest of smiles. "Do you remember how she looked when they were first wed? The sight of her was enough to stop your heart." With an effort, the old poet dragged his thoughts back to the present. "But you're right of course; it would be a dreadful mistake for the boy to inherit Kincora. It could only do him harm."

"There was no will," Carroll reiterated now. "I'm sorry."

Donough looked astonished. "But there must have been! He told me his intentions!"

"I cannot deny what he may have said to you, but I assure you he left no written will with me, nor did he dictate one to me."

Donough glared at Teigue. "Did you order him to say this?"

"Not at all," was the honest reply. "Try to be reasonable, lad. You and your, ah, your Neassa are welcome to live at Kincora as my guests while we make the appropriate arrangements to celebrate your marriage and placate her father's tribe."

The mention of Neassa reminded Donough that on the ride back to Kincora, he had promised her the palace would be hers to command. This was going to make her unhappy, and he already knew her well enough to know she was not a woman to suffer in silence.

Chapter Eighteen

News traveled rapidly across Ireland when it concerned the marriages of kings and princes, involving the complicated network of tribal alliances. In Dublin, Gormlaith listened to the tidings from Munster with growing anger.

"My son marrying a mere cattle lord's daughter? He can't!" Her eyes flashed with a trace of their old fire. "Did he learn nothing from me? A marriage must enhance status or enrich the clan. *He* understood that. He married one of his daughters to my son Sitric and another to a prince of the Scots. And married his other sons into the most noble families of Ireland . . . except for that foolish Teigue, of course, who never did have sufficient ambition." Gormlaith snorted with contempt. "What can a cattle lord's daughters offer to the clan of an Ard Ri? My son is young and foolish and they are taking advantage of him in Thomond. A cow-eyed girl has wrapped her plaits around him, obviously. Or her thighs. Well. I'll soon put a stop to her gallop."

When his mother came storming into the hall to announce that she must leave Dublin at once, Sitric felt a powerful desire to fall to his knees and offer sacrifices of thanksgiving to Odin. With an effort he restrained himself. He knew Gormlaith too well to agree with her; that would only make her change her mind.

"Leave the lad alone," Sitric said, combing his beard with his fingers. "You're out of it now, away from Kincora and all its unpleasant associations. I thought you never wanted to see the place again."

"I do not. But he is my son and I have an obligation to him."

"I need you here, Mother," Sitric replied, straight-faced.

"You certainly do, you're not capable on your own of minding mice at a crossroads. But I am going to Kincora to stop this ill-advised alliance, so I insist you provide me with a cart appropriate to my station. And a guard of honor."

In all of Dublin, Sitric knew, there was no cart which Gormlaith would consider fine enough for her, but he commandeered the best vehicle available and had it further fitted out with cushions and fur robes. A pair of swift horses were put into harness, another pair provided for a change of team, and a guard of sturdy Dublin Danes hastily assembled.

Sitric's instructions to them were cryptic. "Do not let my mother out of your sight," he said. "But should some misadventure befall her, take your time about rescuing her."

Although he did not explain, his men understood.

Like a storm blown inland from the Irish Sea, Gormlaith swept toward Kincora.

During the reign of Brian Boru a woman could travel unmolested from one end of the island to the other wearing all her jewels, but Brian was dead, and already outlaws were gathering in the forests. An elderly woman swathed in furs and glittering with gold should have been a prime target. Yet no one bothered Gormlaith.

"Doom rides with her," people whispered to one another, regarding her with the superstitious fear usually reserved for druid stones and fairy trees.

She took the reins of the team away from the appointed charioteer and drove the horses along the Slighe Dala herself, lashing them unmercifully with the long whip. Her guard on horseback was hard-pressed to keep up with the careening wicker cart. "She'll overturn herself and be killed," one of them remarked to another.

"Not that one," was the reply. "You couldn't kill Gormlaith with an axe."

Throughout the journey she complained continually about everyone and everything, including the accommodations provided each nightfall by chieftains through whose territory they passed. None wanted to put a roof over Gormlaith's head, but none dared turn her away.

They offered only minimal hospitality, however.

In return Gormlaith insulted the proud Irish chieftains to their faces.

One of her embarrassed escort commented, "Now I understand why Sitric Silkbeard has turned as gray as a badger. That woman lives under his roof."

"And his wife is a daughter of Brian Boru," a companion pointed out. "Can you imagine what life must be like for Sitric, caught between those two women?"

"Better for him if he had swung an axe at Clontarf and let the Ard Ri kill him," said a third.

The others nodded agreement.

For the men assigned to accompany Gormlaith the trip seemed interminable, but she was even more impatient. With each turn of the wheels she grew increasingly worried that her foolish son might be married before she could get to him.

Her fears were well-founded. Teigue had urged a speedy wedding to mollify Neassa's kinsmen, and Donough did not argue. Once the formalities were observed, he intended to reassert his claim to Kincora.

Neassa wanted to invite everyone she knew to watch her wed the Ard Ri's son.

"We are not going to offer hospitality to every playmate of your childhood," Maeve informed her sister.

"Why not? Brian Boru entertained hundreds of people all the time, he . . ."

"My husband has a very different temperament, and I

assure you he does not want some huge crowd devouring his stores and lingering for weeks in his hall."

Neassa pouted. Maeve ignored her.

There was to be no huge crowd invited, but Donough had insisted that his father's closest friends attend the wedding. From Mac Liag he begged a list of Brian's favorites known to be still alive.

They sat together beside the hearth in Mac Liag's house, squinting at the names by firelight while an early summer storm lashed the waters of Lough Derg to a froth.

"Who's this?" Donough queried, pointing.

Mac Liag bent closer. "Och. Padraic, of course."

"Padraic?" Donough did not recognize the name.

"He was your father's spear carrier originally, when Brian was still a young man. In time he became a trusted confidante. At the Battle of Glenmama he suffered an injury that cost him his eyesight and Brian pensioned him off.

"No man ever loved Brian Boru more—or was more loved by him," Mac Liag added wistfully.

"I'm surprised he wasn't kept at Kincora to end his days in comfort with my father."

"Bit of politics there," Mac Liag explained. "You see, Padraic had become, ah, involved with a woman who was not a Christian. A druid, a follower of the old ways."

"A druid?"

"Indeed. A woman called Niamh. Padraic was very fond of her and I always thought Brian encouraged it, because he had a certain sympathy with the druids himself. Not that he would ever admit it, what with trying to keep the support of the Church for his various policies. But I knew what was in his heart. Did I not see him sneaking out in the dawn to carry little gifts to *herself* on Crag Liath?"

Cumara, tending the fire, stiffened at the mention of Crag Liath, and Donough threw Mac Liag a startled glance, but the old man did not notice.

"In time the woman called Niamh left Padraic," the poet went on. "No one knew where she went, only that her mother came for her and took her away. Padraic grieved for a long time. I personally think that's why he was careless in battle and got himself blinded.

"He never stopped yearning for her, and Brian assured him she would return one day. And so she did. But Brian could hardly invite a druid woman to stay around Kincora what with bishops and abbots coming and going like changes in the weather, so he gave Padraic a holding near his birthplace, somewhere beyond Ennis."

Donough was intrigued. "He lived there with a druid?"

"Indeed. When she came back to him she brought a child who was the very image of him, and they had more children after, who were raised in the Old Faith." The poet chuckled. "Padraic's eyesight was all he had lost. Everything else worked just fine."

"So they married?" Donough had marrying on the mind.

Mac Liag paused to rub the bridge of his nose with thumb and forefinger. "I wouldn't say they married, exactly. Druid rituals are rather . . . different. But they were devoted to one another. When Niamh died Padraic requested permission from Brian to raise a great cairn in her honor, and Brian himself placed the last stone.

"You should have heard the lament I composed, one of my best efforts." The old man's voice trembled. "Everyone wept. We came back here afterward and Brian sat right there where you sit now and we talked . . ." He drifted off into his memories.

Cumara touched Donough's shoulder. "There's a break in the weather for the moment, so you had better go now. I'll put him to bed before he begins to cry."

When Donough left Mac Liag's house and set out upon the muddy, well-worn footpath leading back to the gates of

Kincora, he found himself glancing off to his right toward the forested heights of Crag Liath.

Lowering clouds hid the summit. The already-saturated air was charged with the certain return of the storm. Donough stopped; stared toward the brooding crag.

He had always accepted without question that the guardian spirit of the Dal Cais was a ban shee, a disembodied relic of the race of sorcerers called the Tuatha de Danann who had been defeated by his own Gaelic ancestors fifteen hundred years earlier. The ban shee had warned him of Clontarf.

But now he found himself wondering. Who—or what— dwelled on Crag Liath? To whom had his father carried "little gifts"?

A ban shee from the pagan past? Or someone more substantial? How could Brian have known the druid woman would return to Padraic?

Donough suddenly found himself wondering how much he really knew about Brian Boru.

The marriage of Donough Mac Brian to Neassa Ni Gadhra would encompass several components. First Donough and Neassa would agree to the provisions of a marriage contract in front of a brehon, as Irish nobility had done since before the coming of Christianity. This contract dictated the terms upon which the relationship would be conducted. Afterward the guests would assemble to hear the ranking cleric, Cathal Mac Maine, deliver the blessings of the Christian faith.

The servants were gossiping in the kitchens as they prepared the banquet that would follow. "The Ard Ri would have sent hunters out to fetch every wild boar and red deer in Thomond for the feast," they told one another. "What sort of a princely celebration serves common mutton and pike from the river?"

Teigue's steward Enda silenced them. "My master does not want to give young Donough ideas above his station.

This is not the marriage of a king, but merely of a younger
son. It is to be festive but restrained."

Restrained. The servants looked at one another.

"Alas, Kincora," one muttered under his breath, repeat-
ing the refrain from Mac Liag's lament for Brian Boru.

Chapter Nineteen

At Clontarf Brian Boru had broken the power of the
Vikings, but as he had foreseen they were not to be driven
out of Ireland. A string of traders' wagons belonging to
Norse merchants based in Limerick encountered Gormlaith
as she turned onto the road to Kincora.

The Norse merchants of Limerick were only peripherally
aware of the great battle that had taken place on the other
side of the island, although warriors from that city had
marched with Brian Boru. Limerick's principal interest was
in trade. Using the sea lanes, a constant stream of goods
poured into and out of Ireland no matter what battles were
being fought. Irish gold and leather were much valued
abroad, while Irish chieftains were a reliable market for luxuries the Vikings imported from as far away as the shores of
the Caspian.

At the sight of the traders Gormlaith signaled a halt. She
stepped down from her cart and with her cloak billowing
behind her strode toward the Norse wagons.

Sitting on their horses, her escort watched impassively.

Gormlaith demanded of the burly blond man walking
beside the first team of oxen, "Where do you think you're
going?"

The Norseman gaped at her. He was young; this was his

first venture in charge of his father's wagons. He had hardly expected to be challenged by an aging Irishwoman wearing more gold jewelry than he had ever seen on one person in his life.

Resting one hand on the broad, warm back of the nearest ox, he said, "We are on our way to Kincora, mother," automatically using the Norse term of respect applied to any female out of childhood.

Gormlaith glared at him. "I'm not your mother. And who invited you?"

The woman's tone was deliberately rude. His spine stiffened with indignation but he refrained from looking back at the other drivers to see how they were reacting. He was in charge now.

"We are traders," he said. "Traders are welcome everywhere. As it happens, we are taking ale and silks and cinnamon to Kincora for a marriage celebration."

Gormlaith raised her eyebrows. "Cinnamon, you say? Real cinnamon, not shaved tree bark you're trying to pass off on the ignorant Irish? Let me see." Shoving past the startled man, she leaned over the side of his cart and threw back the hide covering.

"Now wait here . . ." The Norseman reached for her just as a spear interposed itself between him and the woman. He looked up to see a Danish warrior on a horse glaring down at him.

He was not to be intimidated. "This is my wagon and these are my goods!" he protested. "Some strange woman can't just . . ."

"She is the Princess Gormlaith," the mounted man informed him.

"I don't care if she's the Goddess Freya, she has no right to paw through my goods!" The Norseman had started to say something else when, tardily, he recognized the name of Gormlaith. When accompanying his father to Kincora as a youngster he had never met the woman, but he knew who she was.

Everyone knew who she was.

He hesitated, unable to believe that the harridan rummaging through his trade goods like an avaricious badger could possibly have been the most beautiful woman in Ireland and wife to three kings in turn.

Gormlaith extracted a muslin bag and held it to her nose, sniffing suspiciously. "It is real cinnamon," she conceded at last. But as she tossed the bag back into the wagon she told the Norseman, "Of course you could be planning to cheat them some other way."

The young merchant glowered at her. "I don't cheat anyone. I give honest value for honest coin."

Her green eyes suddenly sparkled. "Coin? Did you know that my son Sitric ordered the first coinage ever to be struck in Ireland? You probably have some. His profile is on them. He wanted to use mine, of course, but I convinced him his own face would be more appropriate."

At this Gormlaith's escort exchanged glances and bit their lips. It was well known in Dublin that Gormlaith had campaigned vigorously to have her face reproduced on the coin, and made Sitric's life hell for months afterward because he used his own image instead.

She continued, "If you're going to Kincora, it must be to try to sell your rubbish to my other son. But he won't buy it. He has excellent taste; he learned it from me." She cast a final contemptuous look at the contents of the wagon and went back to her cart. With one foot on the step she paused. "Do you know this woman he's supposed to be marrying?" she called to the Norseman.

The encounter was so bizarre he was not certain whether he should answer, but the warrior on horseback prodded him gently with the tip of his spear.

"I know her. Know of her, that is. She is sister to the wife of Teigue Mac Brian."

"How many cattle does her father have? You trade with him for his leathers?"

"We don't trade with him; his cattle have poor-quality hides."

"Hah!" Gormlaith exulted, springing into her cart with surprising agility. She snatched up the whip and curled it over her horses' backs and they leaped forward. In a moment the cart was whirling away with its escort in hot pursuit, leaving the Norse traders in their dust.

The leader of the traders gazed after her thoughtfully, wondering if it might not be more prudent to bypass Kincora altogether and sell his goods to the chieftains beyond Nenagh instead.

Most of the invited guests had already arrived at Kincora and been shown to their accommodations, in private chambers if they had sufficient status or in one of the large wattle-and-timber guesting houses.

While awaiting the formalization of their marriage, Donough and Neassa had been assigned an apartment once reserved for Murrough. It would have been unthinkable to return Neassa to her father before the wedding; such an insult would have meant a clan war. With or without contracts and blessings, she was now wife to Donough and his responsibility.

Already that responsibility was beginning to chafe slightly. At night among the furs and blankets he enjoyed her, but during the day he wanted to put her out of his mind and devote himself to solidifying alliances. Yet no sooner had he found an out-of-the-way corner where he could discuss politics in private than Neassa would appear at his elbow.

"Ah here you are, Donough! I was looking for you. Tell me, do you think I should wear these beads my sister gave me for our wedding? Or are these better?" She pirouetted for his inspection, oblivious of the other men with him, destroying a mood Donough had been at pains to create. No matter how he tried to get rid of her she would linger, talking about trivia as if it were the most important thing in the world, until the men whose support Donough had been wooing abandoned him to her.

Fergal summed it up. "Neassa chatters constantly and says nothing."

"She's just young and excited," Donough defended her. He must be loyal to her in front of others; that was part of the marriage contract under Brehon Law.

His cousin scoffed, "You say that now, when she has you by the balls, but wait until she's older. She won't improve."

Donough did not want to believe him. He determined to find admirable hidden qualities in Neassa that no one but himself could appreciate.

They must be there. He wanted to love her.

He wanted to be happy.

Surely all it required was an effort of will.

The wedding was to take place on the first day of the new moon. A few guests were late in arriving, and a messenger had brought a chillingly curt response from the prince of Desmond to the effect that he and his wife did not care to attend any festivities honoring Donough Mac Brian.

"Trouble there," Teigue remarked to his wife. He promptly summoned Donough for an explanation.

"Father married our sister Sabia to Cian of Desmond for the express purpose of making peace between the Dal Cais and the Owenachts," Teigue reminded his brother. "Yet now there seems to be a new grudge developing. What happened?"

"We quarreled, but it was nothing."

"Nothing? If it's cost me the support of the Owenachts it could mean serious trouble for my kingship."

Donough folded his arms. "You're determined to be King of Munster, then?"

"Father held that title until he died and I'm his oldest surviving son."

"According to the tradition of tanistry, any of our close cousins might make an equal claim to the title," Donough pointed out.

With a wave of his hand, Teigue dismissed tradition. "But none of them has, out of respect for our father. In case you have forgotten, Donough, it was Brian Boru's plan to found a ruling dynasty based on direct succession, father to son, like the royal families of the Britons and the Gauls."

"I'm not arguing that point. I'm just questioning whether you are the best man to follow Brian Boru as king."

Teigue gave his younger brother a hard stare. "I am the *only* man," he said in a stern voice. He had not wanted kingship, but now, angered at Donough's reaction, he began to feel some of Brian Boru's ambition surfacing in himself after all.

Donough checked a scathing retort. Further alienating his brother would serve no purpose. Besides, Teigue was the closest kin he had left, other than sisters he never saw and a mother he did not want to see.

With an effort he admitted, "I made a mistake in quarreling with Cian. But the Owenacht tribe has always been contentious. Had you been there, the same thing might have happened. Cian is easily offended."

"I don't want you blaming this on Cian. You have to take responsibility for what you do yourself."

"That's what I was trying to do!"

Teigue gave a tired sigh. "Leave it then, Donough. When this wedding is over I shall attempt to reestablish friendly relations with the prince of Desmond."

Donough replied, "That should be my task if I'm responsible for the problem."

"I don't want you muddying the waters any further," his brother said sternly.

* * *

"I feel like a spancelled horse," Donough complained to Mac Liag later. He found himself journeying to the old poet's house by the lake almost every day, seeking . . . he knew not what.

"Spancelled horses accept their hobbles and are obedient," Mac Liag replied.

"But it was I who brought the army of Munster back from Clontarf! I even won a victory of sorts on the way. Surely I deserve better than to be treated like a child now."

The old man's eyes twinkled. "Your brother Murrough voiced the same complaints right up until the time he died. Brian would never let him run."

"At least he let Murrough die with him," Donough said bitterly.

"It is not easy to be one who survives. I know. Every day of my life I regret that I did not die with the flower of the Dalcassians."

"That's exactly what I mean!" the young man cried. "You talk like everyone else, as if all that was finest and most noble is dead! But *I'm* alive. Look at me. I'm flesh and blood standing here before you."

"Be patient, lad," counseled Mac Liag. "What is for you will not pass by you."

As Donough was leaving the poet's house he said out of the side of his mouth to Cumara, "It's all very well for him to talk, he's lived his life and had his honors. But what about me?"

Cumara looked sympathetic.

The day of the wedding dawned overcast. A curtain of soft gray rain hung in the sky north of the lake.

Brooding above Kincora, Crag Liath was lost in cloud.

Teigue's steward Torcan had offered Donough an attendant to help him prepare for the occasion, but he had asked Fergal to be with him instead.

"I want an ally at my elbow," he explained to his cousin.

"Why? Are you nervous? It's only a marriage and you've already lain with the woman."

"I want you with me," Donough repeated. Fergal's common sense did not seem to help with the knot in his belly.

He dressed in a new leine and a mantle large enough to wrap four times around his body. So much woven wool was indicative of his wealth as a prince. The mantle was crimson speckled with gray and black, and decorated with huge horsehair tassels.

Standing in front of him, Fergal held up a mirror so Donough could examine the effect. In the polished metal surface he thought he looked rather like his father. "Do I remind you of anyone?" he asked Fergal.

"You remind me of a scared boy afraid someone's going to give him a whipping," his cousin remarked unfeelingly. "Are you ready to go?"

The first event of the day was the recitation of the agreed marriage contract before the senior brehon. This was a private and sober ceremony as befitted legal arrangements concerning property. Only Teigue and Gadhra accompanied the young couple as their two clans would be bound by the settlements made. Once the contract had been formally accepted by both sides and tokens exchanged—gilded leathers representing the bride-price of cattle, ceremonial knives representing a strengthened alliance with Gadhra's clan—the festivities could begin.

The blessing of the Church would be delivered by the Abbot of Kill Dalua in the chapel of Saint Flannan, and would mark the beginning of three days of celebration. Priestly participation was not customary for ordinary marriages, but had become increasingly a part of weddings involving noble clans as Christianity consolidated its hold on Ireland.

When the wedding party left the private chamber

where the marriage contract had been formally accepted, they crossed the main courtyard of Kincora to the gray stone chapel. Kinspeople and dependents now crowded around them.

Servants had lined the way with newly cut rushes and strewn their path with fragrant hawthorn blossoms, the last of the season. The poets claimed hawthorn bloomed longer around Kincora than anywhere else in Ireland.

"I feel like a queen," enthused Neassa, beaming left and right. She was resplendent in a sleeveless coat of loosely woven wool over a semifitted linen gown lavishly embroidered with silk thread. Imported glass beads were sewn onto her slippers. She waggled her fingers at the spectators as if they were her subjects. Once or twice she giggled.

Donough was both elated and embarrassed. This was only the second ritual of his life in which he had played a central part, and he did not remember the first, his baptism. He paced forward self-consciously, trying to look dignified.

Neassa matched her stride to his, but one step behind. Under Brehon Law theirs was a marriage of the second degree, as they were not equal in status and property; her position in the procession was ordained by custom.

Among the crowd forming a line on either side of their passage was a bony, elderly man whose faded hair still retained a hint of red. By the sunken hollows of his blind eyes Donough identified him as Padraic, former spear carrier. Several young people clustered protectively around him.

One of them was a slender, dark-haired girl.

Donough had almost walked past her when something captured his attention and he turned to look.

Alone of all the wedding guests, she wore no shoes. Her high-arched white feet were bare, and the skirt she wore over her linen smock was red.

Donough lifted his gaze to her face. Her nose was very straight, almost Grecian; the modeling of her rather stubborn chin would do honor to a queen. Beneath level eyebrows, stars welled from fathomless pupils, setting dark eyes aglow.

It was a face he would have recognized anywhere, though he could have put his hand on his heart and sworn he had never met her before.

While they stared at each other a silent conversation took place between them. Its intensity left him shaken.

Donough forgot the crowd around him, forgot his new wife at his shoulder, the abbot waiting for them. He was surrounded by gray cloud pierced by a single beam of light, and in that light stood the girl in the red skirt smiling at him as if she had known him a thousand years.

Chapter Twenty

I could never afterward remember entering the chapel, nor the prayers Cathal Mac Maine intoned before the altar. Although my eyes remained fixed on the abbot, some deeper sense was searching the dim interior for the girl's presence.

When I realized she had not entered the chapel I was upset. I wanted Cathal to stop droning on and on so I could go outside again and see where she was.

Neassa elbowed me in the ribs. "The responses," she hissed.

"The . . . ah. Indeed." I dragged my mind back to the present and mouthed the expected Latin. Cathal signed the Cross over us, more prayers were offered, the ceremony was over.

I almost ran from the chapel.

The girl in the red skirt was gone.

Chapter Twenty-one

In honor of the occasion, Mac Liag had worn all six colors to which a poet was entitled. His leine extended to his ankles in pleated folds; his long, semicircular mantle was striped in yellow, green, black, red, gray, and blue-purple. Even Teigue, who was not yet King of Munster, was not so gaudily attired. Mac Liag stood out from the throng in the courtyard like a rainbow.

Donough went straight to him. "That blind man who was here a while ago, that was Padraic, was it not?"

"It was. I was glad to see him; it's been a long time."

"Who was that with him? The young woman in the red skirt?"

Mac Liag searched his memory. "I didn't notice her, but I suppose she was one of his daughters. He is a widower like myself, you know, and he—"

"Why didn't they come into the chapel?" Donough interrupted impatiently.

"Ah, Padraic would never be guilty of such an impropriety."

"What do you mean?"

"Don't you remember what I told you? His wife followed the Old Faith and her children do the same. Pagans are not welcome in Saint Flannan's, and Padraic would never enter without them."

Donough's temper flared. "Who says they would not be welcome? It's my marriage, I can have whoever I want, and I wanted Padraic and his family in the chapel!"

Cathal Mac Maine appeared at his elbow, the abbot's heavy features set in folds of disapproval. "You have just come from the House of God," he reminded Donough. "I expect a certain decorum from you with the blessing still crowning your brow. Instead you are willfully making trouble."

"You overheard what we were saying?"

"Of course I did. Your voice is deep and it carries. You wanted to bring pagans into the House of God."

Mac Liag tried to smooth things over. "I was just explaining to him, Cathal. He didn't know."

"I knew," Donough contradicted him. "You told me before. But I wanted my father's old friend and his family too. In light of Padraic's service to the Ard Ri, no one can deny them Kincora."

"Kincora, no," the abbot agreed. "But I would stand in the doorway of Saint Flannan's and bar them from its sacred precincts with my own body if necessary. Do you hear me?"

Teigue excused himself from a conversation he was having with Gadhra and strode across the courtyard toward them. "What's wrong here?"

Donough tried to bite back anger. "Why do you always assume there's something wrong when I'm involved?"

Cathal Mac Maine promptly launched into an explanation, complete with expressions of clerical outrage. Donough began defending his position, Mac Liag tried to outtalk them both, and Teigue struggled futilely to take charge of the situation.

Voices snarled into a knot.

* * *

"Look at those men over there!" Neassa protested to Maeve. "It's my wedding day and they're quarreling, trying to ruin it for me."

Her sister cast an experienced eye over the group in question. "They are men of the Gael," she commented. "They love to argue. They aren't doing it to ruin your feast day, I assure you. Irish princes are warriors, that's how they became nobility in the first place, by fighting and winning. You cannot tame them; you would destroy them."

"Your Teigue's no warrior," Neassa replied thoughtlessly. "Everyone know's he's as gentle as an ox."

Maeve rounded on her sister. "My Teigue can fight as well as any! You are a stupid, ignorant girl."

"Don't shout at me!" Neassa flared. Her face turned red, her eyes filled with angry tears.

Within moments people were taking sides. A fight was as good as a wedding; better, in the opinion of many. Raised voices echoed through the stronghold of the Dalcassians.

By late in the day, the great hall was given over to feasting. A constant stream of servants moved in and out of the kitchens, bearing food and drink and taking away empty platters, while tactfully ignoring arguments that waxed or waned on every side. Guests discussing Donough's marriage later would boast that it was the most contentious they had ever attended. Three fights had turned serious and Ferchar the physician was kept busy tending injuries.

After she had drunk too much mead in the women's gallery, Neassa began sobbing and demanding to go home with her father.

Gadhra suggested to Teigue that the property arrangements might be forfeit if his daughter was dissatisfied.

Fergal Mac Anluan hit one of Gadhra's kinsmen over the head with a three-legged stool.

Ruadri of Ara found himself involved in a violent argument over which of the Dalcassians had acquitted themselves most bravely at Clontarf, and soon that battle was being refought by torchlight in the courtyard, with the wolfhounds of Kincora adding to the confusion as they tried to join in.

Only the storm center, Donough Mac Brian, did not take part.

His brother was angry with him, the abbot was angry with him, his wife was crying . . . he slipped out of the hall almost unnoticed and walked through the mist to the main gates of Kincora.

"Did the blind man, Padraic, leave by this way earlier?" he asked the sentry.

"I just came on duty. Wait here; I'll ask around if anyone saw him."

As Donough waited, a fresh wind sprang up off the lake, blowing the mist away. Shreds seemed to drift toward the rising moon and form a circle there, until one pale face peered from a pastel halo.

The moon was gazing toward the summit of Crag Liath.

Donough wandered out through the open gateway. His feet chose their path without his conscious thought, turning northwest.

One of the guards came trotting after him. "Prince Donough. Prince Donough! You were looking for the old blind man? His children have taken him home, back toward Ennis. They did not choose to spend the night in Kincora. They will seek hospitality from friends along the way."

Donough stood still on the path. Ennis lay to the north-west, across mountain and forest and bogland.

Reluctantly he turned to go back inside. But first he looked toward Crag Liath bathed in moonlight.

"Where are you now?" he asked the girl in the red skirt.

The wind blew off the lake. The night air smelled damp and sweet, like the earth.

Donough's keen ears heard distant sounds coming closer.

At once an armed guard stood beside him.

"There's horses coming down the road," the man affirmed, cupping one hand behind his ear. He shouted up to the sentry in the watchtower, "We're about to have company! Look sharp!"

"Late guests?" Donough wondered.

"Very late indeed, if they are guests. But that's why we keep the gates open. They're coming fast; must be someone who knows the road even in the dark."

Donough lingered to see who the new arrivals might be. Soon a wicker cart came careening into view, followed by an escort on horseback. Gormlaith stood bolt upright in the cart with her feet braced against its swaying as she drove the exhausted horses toward Kincora.

Chapter Twenty-two

Three large torches set in iron holders as high as a man could reach burned on either side of the gateway. They shed a golden light that illuminated the road as far as the nearest stand of trees. In that glow Gormlaith's face appeared haggard, the lines deeply scored, the famous eyes sunken. Yet her posture was as arrogant as ever. Whatever her failings, men would always say of her that she had the walk of a young queen.

As she stepped from the cart, Donough gazed at her in dismay. He could almost feel the bonds he had thought broken tightening around him again. "What are you doing here?"

"I came to prevent your making a dreadful mistake," Gormlaith replied.

"What mistake?"

"Marrying someone who is not good enough for you, of course. Now show me to—"

With great satisfaction Donough announced, "If you mean Neassa Ni Gadhra, I've already married her." It was the first time in memory that he had been able to thwart his mother.

Gormlaith folded her arms across her breasts. "You can't. You simply cannot have done."

"I have, this very day."

"A *contract* marriage?"

"Of the second degree. Sworn to before the chief brehon of Munster. Gadhra and Teigue were—"

"Then you can just go back to the chief brehon and tell him you divorce the woman," Gormlaith demanded. "Tell him you made a mistake."

From the moment Donough saw the girl in the red skirt he had known marrying Neassa was a mistake. Suddenly Gadhra's daughter seemed . . . ordinary, no different from any number of other females.

Yet she was his wife, by agreed contract. His choice. If Gormlaith ordered him to set Neassa aside, he would keep her no matter what.

When he set his jaw he looked, in the flickering torchlight, more like his father than he knew.

"No, Gormlaith." He did not call her Mother. He had never called her Mother.

The tall, haggard woman drew a deep breath. Sitting on their horses behind her, her mounted escort watched silently. No one could predict what she might do.

The sentries at the gates were just as uncertain. They remembered Gormlaith from the old days; remembered her all too well. She could explode like a pine knot in the fire and ignite everything within reach.

The chief sentry said over his shoulder to the man nearest him, "Run, don't walk, to Prince Teigue and tell him she's here."

The guard ran.

Gormlaith paid no attention. Tall in the torchlight, she challenged her son with her eyes. "Who put you up to this? Your weakling brother? Let me speak to him!"

Throughout his life Donough had accepted his mother's tyranny because he had no options. When he was a child she controlled him totally, and had continued to do so until the day Brian Boru sent her from Kincora.

Since then, however, Donough had taken up arms, seen battle, and led an army.

He would not let Gormlaith tyrannize him now.

He opened his mouth to tell her so—just as she put one hand on his chest and shoved him aside like a servant. With head held high she stalked through the gates of Kincora for the first time since her banishment.

The sentries tried to stop her but she pushed past them as well. They did not dare turn their weapons against a woman, even this one. In Brian Boru's Ireland no man raised his hand against a woman.

They had no such compunction when it came to her male companions, however. These were Dublin Vikings, all too recently the enemy. When Gormlaith's escort tried to ride through the gate they found their way barred by crossed spears.

The captain appealed to Donough. "We aren't supposed to leave her."

The young man sighed. "I'll take care of her," he said with obvious reluctance. He turned to the chief sentry. "Find someplace for my mother's bodyguard to spend the night. She'll want them to accompany her back to Dublin tomorrow."

As Donough followed his mother into the fort, two sets of armed men were left facing each other in the torchlight. Dalcassian eyed Viking. "I would be happier myself," commented the chief sentry at last, "if you took her away right now."

His opposite number frowned. "I cannot. Surely your prince would not deny hospitality for the night to a woman."

"That woman?" The sentry squinted up at the man on horseback. "The Devil himself would deny her hospitality. But I suppose you might as well come inside until this is sorted out. There's plenty of food and fodder, and you can sleep in the guards' quarters. I like that horse of yours, by the way," he added conversationally, to show there were no hard feelings. "Kildare horse, is he?"

Meanwhile the sentry who carried news of Gormlaith's arrival to Teigue in the hall was getting a sample of the welcome she could expect. "Stone her before she puts one foot inside the gate!" cried a Dalcassian.

There was a shout of agreement from among the assembled guests.

"That woman is to blame for all the ills of Ireland!" cried a chieftain's wife.

Mac Liag braced the palms of his hands on the trestle table in front of him and pushed himself to his feet. "Honesty compels me to disagree," he said, his speech slightly slurred by an excess of red wine. "I feel no more affection for her than you do, but trouble has many parents. Surely on the occasion of her son's wedding feast we can put aside our animosity and—"

"Don't make any special effort for me!" cried a voice from the doorway. Heads swiveled as Gormlaith swept into the room as if she belonged there. "And I don't need you to champion me, Mac Liag," she added. "I can take care of myself. And of my son, come to that."

Her son was close on her heels. He tried to lay a restraining hand on her arm but Gormlaith shook him off. "Teigue! Are you to blame for this absurdity?"

Teigue had risen from his seat and started toward her with his arm outstretched and his hand raised, palm outward, to bar her way. "You are not welcome here," he told her.

"Nonsense. When could a mother not come to her son's wedding?" She turned to Donough. "Would you disgrace yourself in front of your tribe by such cruelty to your own mother?"

"I—"

"I thought not. There, you see, Teigue? He wants me."

Donough tried to step between them. "I never said that, I was going to—"

"Be quiet now and let me handle this. You are in enough trouble, and I haven't arrived a moment too soon. Where's this wretched girl you purport to have married? Let me have a look at her."

From the moment of Gormlaith's entry Neassa had been staring at her, slack-jawed. Now she tried to slump lower on her bench, but the older woman's unerring gaze sought her out in her place of brief honor at the front of the women's gallery.

"You there! Stand up, if you aren't a cripple!"

At Gormlaith's command Neassa rose, trembling, to her feet. Maeve hissed at her, "Sit down, ignore her," but the girl did not seem to hear.

Gormlaith raked Neassa with her eyes, then turned to her son. "You married this, Donnchad? I am astonished. Look at that face, she has no more brain than a gosling. How can you possibly expect to get brilliant children from a stupid woman? This is no second-degree marriage. At best it's a union of the tenth degree because one partner is simple-minded."

Gadhra's face turned black with fury. Kicking back his bench, he hurled himself at Gormlaith. "You insult my daughter! I demand compensation under Brehon Law! I'll fast on your doorstep, I'll have a third of everything you own, I'll demand the poets strike your name from the histories!"

Teigue was at a momentary loss for words. Donough seized the first thought that came into his head. "Gormlaith,

I am called Donough now, not Donnchad. And you are insulting my wife as well as Gadhra's daughter. You are—"

Recovering, Teigue interrupted, "You insult us all with your foul presence, woman. You persuaded your brother Maelmordha to rebel against my father and you enticed your son Sitric and his Viking allies to join him just to see Brian Boru dead. You have bathed Ireland in blood, and if I were not a Christian man I would—"

"If you were not as meek as a woodmouse you would have fought beside your father at Clontarf," Gormlaith replied. "At least my Donnchad is—"

"Donough!" the young man cried.

One of Gormlaith's gifts was the ability to think on several layers at once. Tonight was the first time she had heard his new name, yet the urgency in his voice told her it was important to him. She saw at once an advantage to herself, a way of winning some degree of gratitude if not affection. "My Donough," she amended with no perceptible hesitation, "is a warrior. And a warrior prince has no business lumbering himself with a dreary cow who will bear sons with no shine on them."

The hall was in uproar. Gormlaith's last words were drowned in shouts and babble.

But Donough heard them. Some part of his brain registered agreement.

Neassa was staring at Gormlaith exactly like a heifer waiting for the butcher's axe.

The girl in the red skirt would not respond in that fashion. Without ever having exchanged a word with her, Donough knew she would stand toe to toe with Gormlaith and give as good as she got.

Her face was stamped on his mind like the imprint left on the retina after staring at the sun; a fine-boned, intelligent face.

When and how would he see her again?

Meanwhile there was a tangle to be sorted out in the

great hall of Kincora. Amid noise and drink and anger Donough must juggle his mother, his new wife, his ambitions—and the image of the girl in the red skirt.

For a moment he felt overwhelmed.

Then from some unguessed well within him, a voice spoke. A voice as curiously familiar to him as Padraic's daughter.

Be cold, it instructed. *Suppress all emotion so you can think clearly.*

Donough stood immobile, his attention captured. An unseen but powerful presence stood beside him, invisibly filling space.

Be cold, the voice repeated.

Obeying, he began consciously distancing himself from his feelings.

Think. There are opportunities here. Find them and use them. One step at a time.

Donough drew himself to his fullest height. Looking down at his older brother, he said sternly, "Teigue, I will not allow you to insult my mother."

"What about the insult to my daughter?" cried the furious Gadhra.

"I married Neassa and paid a good bride-price for her," Donough reminded him. "That hardly constitutes an insult."

"This woman insulted my Neassa," snarled Gadhra, stabbing a forefinger at Gormlaith. "Disavow her. I demand it!"

Her eyes locked on Donough's. "Would you repudiate your own mother? What would your father say?"

"Our father set you aside!" Teigue all but shouted at her.

Donough stood as if listening for a moment. Then he said, "But Brian Boru never insulted my mother in public, nor allowed anyone else to do so. And I would not be less a man than he.

"If my mother is not welcome here, neither am I. The shame is on your beard, Teigue, if you drive a son of Brian

Boru from Kincora on his wedding day. Is this the method you choose to steal my patrimony from me?"

"Steal!" cried Teigue. He could hardly believe such a charge had been leveled against him. A more physical man would have struck Donough without hestitation, but Teigue merely stood with his eyes starting from his head. "*Steal!*" he repeated imprudently.

Those who had not heard the word the first time heard it clearly the second.

The hall was thrown into confusion. The name of Brian Boru had been invoked not once, but repeatedly.

Men who a moment before had been ready to stone Gormlaith glanced uneasily at one another.

"When the old Ard Ri was here . . ."

"Brian would never have . . ."

Their eyes rolled toward Teigue.

"Perhaps he lacks his father's . . ."

"Perhaps," suggested Fergal Mac Anluan, "Prince Teigue is not the right man to have Kincora. Prince Donough's claim may be the more valid, in the light of his character. He holds a shield in front of his mother as a son should, and he has not lost his temper under provocation."

Someone else added, "See how young Donough resembles his father!"

The poet Mac Liag looked from one of Brian's sons to the other and stroked his beard.

Many in the hall were looking from one to the other. Donough exuded an unexpected dignity beyond his years; Teigue, off-balance, was red-faced and sputtering.

Deciding the time had come for clerical intervention, Cathal Mac Maine raised his arms to attract attention. "Our Lord who took part in the wedding feast at Cana would be grieved to see this occasion becoming one of discord! Put aside your disputes and let us celebrate together."

But he might as well have tried to stop ripples spreading across the surface of Lough Derg.

The day had been studded with quarrels. As if each were one step on a stair, they had led inexorably to this moment when men must choose sides.

Gormlaith was aware of the change of mood before anyone else in the hall. She took note of the subtle way men began to range themselves on one side of the room or the other, closer to Teigue or to Donough.

More of them chose Teigue. But the young ones drifted toward Donough.

She wondered how Donough could have known that his father never insulted her in public. He had hardly ever been with the pair of them in public. A good guess, no doubt.

Obviously he was a clever young man. Gormlaith smiled. Donough was the future.

Chapter Twenty-three

In the abbot's chambers at Kill Dalua the next morning, Cathal Mac Maine sat brooding.

The room was more comfortably furnished than the usual monastic cell. Cathal had a bench with arms, a personal prayer stool, a small desk for his scribe's use, and—in direct contravention of the Rule of Maelruain—a mattress of feathers. Around his neck he wore a gold chain given him by his kinsman, the late Ard Ri.

Yet he was not a happy man.

Staring out through the single small window the chamber boasted, he could catch a glimpse of the tree-fringed shore of Lough Derg. Beyond those trees lay Kincora.

Rising heavily to his feet, Cathal began pacing the flagstoned floor. Five steps one way, four steps the other. Once he could have crossed the room in three strides. Long ago, before his cousin Brian Boru stood atop Tara Hill and was proclaimed High King of the Irish.

A lifetime ago, it seemed.

Twelve years.

Now the old lion's cubs were fighting over the spoils.

The abbot sighed and tugged at his lower lip with thumb and forefinger.

Quiet as a mouse in a corner, his scribe sat and waited. He had put down the quill and plugged the silver ink pot with a lump of beeswax. The morning should have been devoted to making annalistic entries, but little would be accomplished while Cathal was in this mood.

The abbot sighed again. "The life of man," he announced portentiously, "is an endless burden."

"Father Abbot?"

"A burden, Brother Declan. A cross to bear. Do you not agree?"

"Oh I do most emphatically agree, Father Abbot!" The monk leaned forward to emphasize his perfect accord with his superior.

"Then why did you not say so?" Cathal snapped.

Brother Declan blinked. Trying to keep up with the abbot was his personal cross. "I was just going to say so, Father Abbot."

"Hunh." Cathal resumed pacing. "What can you know of burdens, of the weight of responsibility I bear?" He waved an arm to include the monastery and undefined regions beyond. "To whom can I look for aid in doing God's work?"

He gazed out the window again. "The late Ard Ri was a most generous patron to this monastery, you know. We wanted for nothing during his reign. He was an exceptionally devout man."

"He was an exceptionally clever . . ." Declan stopped,

realizing the words he was about to say would get him into trouble.

But Cathal snatched them unspoken from his mind. He glared at his scribe. "What calumny were you going to repeat? That Brian gave gifts to the Church merely to further his own interests? Have you forgot that according to the Rule of Maelruain of Tallaght, we are not allowed to accept gifts from sinful men but must pass all such on to the poor? I tell you, the late Ard Ri was the holiest of men and a credit to our tribe. Anything else is a lie put about by his enemies."

Declan lowered his eyes contritely. "Indeed, Father Abbot."

"There are even those who claim he maintained, ah, druid connections, but that is also a lie."

"A lie. A malicious slander."

"No more Christian prince ever walked the earth than my late cousin," Cathal insisted. "His death was a tragic loss, but I have taken comfort in the knowledge that his son Teigue is an equally pious and obedient man who will continue his father's good works.

"But I must say I have serious misgivings about his younger brother. Yesterday at his wedding—his own wedding, mind you!—Donough disgraced himself. He began by wanting his father's old spear carrier and his pagan children to be made welcome in Saint Flannan's chapel."

"Shocking," murmured Declan with downcast eyes.

"Then the Princess Gormlaith arrived, and that put the cat among the pigeons I can tell you. There was a frightful row. Donough claimed his brother was trying to steal his patrimony, and Teigue claimed Donough was trying to take Kincora away from him.

"Not content with quarreling under a roof, the brothers and their followers went outside and fought in the courtyard. They seized the weapons they had left at the door of the hall and attacked one another in spite of all I could do to separate them. Once they had weapons in their hands, the blows they rained on one another became deadly. Poor young Ruadri of Ara was killed, and several others may die of their injuries."

Brother Declan interjected, "Fights between brothers can be savage. My own brothers and I, for example . . ."

"Indeed." Cathal was not interested in a recitation of his scribe's family squabbles. "I thought Teigue would unleash the entire force of his army upon Donough, but before that could happen, fortunately the youngster came to his senses and realized how badly outnumbered he was. He left Kincora and took his surviving supporters with him. And his wife and mother," Cathal added.

"His mother? Princess Gormlaith?"

"The very woman. As if he needed to bring down any more curses upon his head."

"Where did they go?"

"I have no idea, but they left a shambles behind them. I don't mind telling you, Brother Declan, that I am deeply worried. This could mean a serious split in the Dal Cais. Should Donough and his supporters gain the ascendancy, I fear for our monastery. This is a young man who has sympathies with the Old Faith. He might not be as generous with us as Teigue."

Declan scratched the bald top of his tonsured head above its circular fringe of hair. "What will you do?"

"Support Teigue, of course!" snapped the abbot. "But I'm not happy about this. To be perceived as siding with one of Brian's sons against the other is to invite trouble. Bear in mind, Declan, that more Irish chieftains have raided and looted Irish monasteries than ever Vikings have. Under Brian's rule such crimes ceased, but in this new age . . ."

Cathal Mac Maine left the thought unfinished. He resumed pacing his chamber, five steps one way, four the other. Meanwhile his scribe occupied himself by pursuing an itch that made its way from the top of his head to the small of his back, settling maddeningly where he could not quite reach it no matter how he squirmed.

His woolen robe only made the itch worse.

Donough's departure from Kincora had been bitter for all concerned. He was coldly angry, Teigue was hot with rage, Neassa was crying, and Gormlaith was protesting at the top of her lungs and threatening everyone in sight with reprisals.

"My son Sitric and his Vikings will burn this miserable heap of timber around your ears!" she shouted to the sentries on the gate as she left.

But it was an empty promise and she knew it.

Following Clontarf, Sitric's warriors were in short supply. The few who now accompanied Gormlaith scarcely constituted a threat.

Donough regretted he did not have enough men to settle the issue then and there. Even if they had sided with him, however, most of the battle-weary veterans he had led back from Clontarf had long since departed for their own homes. Of the few Dalcassian officers who had attended the wedding, a majority proved loyal to Teigue.

A few left with Donough, however, including Fergal and Ronan—and also Conor of Corcomrua, who had a small band of his own warriors with him. "We'll see more excitement by going with Prince Donough than we will if we take Teigue's side and stay here polishing our shields," Fergal assured Conor.

"I agree with you. I know a man meant for trouble when I see one. Donough's not going to have a quiet life, whatever happens."

To their surprise, Mac Liag and his son joined them. "My father wishes to offer you hospitality for a few nights, until you decide what you want to do next," Cumara told Donough.

Donough was reluctant to accept. "This will not endear you to my brother," he warned the poet.

Mac Liag shrugged. "I'm too old to worry about such things. Besides, who would harass a dying man?"

"You aren't dying, Father," Cumara responded automatically, as he had done at least once a day for as long as he could remember.

"Of course I am. It's a miracle I've lived this long, and I have no desire to live longer. The house will be yours when I'm gone and you can take another wife to look after you, instead of yourself tending a sick old man."

In an aside to Fergal, Cumara remarked, "I've tended that sick old man for so long I've forgot what to do with a woman."

"You will remember soon enough when you have the chance," Fergal replied with a wink and a nudge. "Your parts fit hers, and the rest is obvious."

Seasoned warriors all, the Dalcassians would sleep on the ground outside Mac Liag's house, but the poet ushered Donough and the two women inside. "You may have my bed," he told the newly married couple. "It's a real bed-box, carved oak, with a feather mattress." His faded eyes twinkled with unforgotten fire.

For some reason an image flashed through Donough's mind of Crag Liath, brooding above them. "I'll sleep outside with my men," he decided. "They expect it."

Neassa thrust out her lower lip. "They do not expect it. I expect you to sleep with me."

"If anyone requires a feather mattress, I do," Gormlaith announced. "You can squabble over sleeping arrangements all you like, Donough. But Mac Liag will show me to his bed."

The old poet looked so horrified even Gormlaith had to laugh. "Where I shall sleep alone," she added, then laughed again at the relief on his face.

"What about me?" wailed Neassa.

"I'll fix you a pallet by the hearth," Cumara promised.

She would not be mollified. "Am I to surrender the only

good bed to that woman? I'm the one who just married a prince!"

Cumara exchanged glances with his father. As gently as he could, Mac Liag took Neassa by the elbow and drew her aside. "I suggest you take what's offered and say nothing, little flower. There is trouble enough already, and no one has ever profited from arguing with Gormlaith—quite the reverse."

Neassa turned with arms outstretched in supplication toward her husband. But Donough had already left the house.

He wrapped himself in his cloak and lay down on the ground with the other men, to sleep for what little remained of the night.

Dawn found him still wide awake, lying on his back with his arms crossed behind his head. The night had turned cold but clear; the dawn was a glory. Salmon-colored light blazed across the sky, silhouetting the mountains east of the Shannon.

Donough sat up and glanced toward the house. All quiet.

Perhaps too quiet, he thought, remembering that both his mother and his wife were under the same roof. After Gorm-laith had left Kincora and moved in with her son Sitric in Dublin, there had been much amused speculation as to what Sitric's home life was like, with Gormlaith and Brian's daughter under the one roof.

What am I going to do with her? Donough asked himself. *Send her back to Sitric? Will he take her? What if he refuses?* He rolled over on his stomach and reached out to touch the shoulder of the sleeping Fergal. "Fergal! Are you awake?"

"I am now," came the growl from within a fold of woolen cloak. "But I did not want to be."

"Listen here to me. Your mother and father ended their marriage, did they not?"

Fergal sighed, groaned, tossed the cloak aside, and

propped himself on one elbow. "They did. Why? Are you tired of the fair Neassa already?"

Donough chose to ignore the question. "Where did your mother go—after?"

"Under Brehon Law she was given back all the property she had brought to the marriage, of course, plus her share of the bride-gift. She had a fine house built for herself in the Arra mountains. Why?"

"I wonder if my mother got her dowry back."

"From which marriage?"

"Any of them. My father."

"If she did," Fergal replied, getting up to go relieve his bladder into the lake, "it's gone now. Spent on jewels and silks, I'd say from the look of her. There's a woman who denies herself nothing."

Donough rolled over and gazed up at the sky once more. Already its clarity was marred by the first threads of dark cloud.

Chapter Twenty-four

Embosomed among the oaks in a stone-and-turf cabin smothered by ivy, Padraic sat dreaming. Behind his sightless eyes old wars were fought anew. Bronze battle trumpets blared. The bodhran thundered its relentless beat. A giant with red-gold hair strode among his enemies swinging a two-handed sword no ordinary man could brandish.

"I wonder who has Brian's sword now," Padraic murmured.

A soft voice replied, "Don't you remember, Father? You

asked, and that historian, Carroll, told you. They carried the sword to Armagh with the Ard Ri's body."

"I heard," the blind man said, "but I'm more interested in what I didn't hear. Carroll never said they put the sword in the tomb with him. Brian Boru's sword? I'll wager it came back to Munster under someone's cloak, Cera."

"You have a suspicious mind." His daughter laughed.

"I learned from the Ard Ri."

Humming as she worked, Cera busied herself about the house. They had been away for a time and there was much to do. According to the custom of the country, in their absence they had left the house open, with food and drink and blankets set out for any passing traveler who might need them. Someone had obviously availed himself of the hospitality, but had taken only a portion of the food and left the blankets neatly refolded.

The hearth needed to be swept and the fire relaid, however, and fresh water fetched from the nearby spring. More bread must be baked in the round stone oven behind the house, using wheat ground in the mill at Ennis. There were goose eggs to gather and spinning to be done, the last of the previous year's wool transformed into cloaks for the next winter.

Cera's three brothers had departed shortly after dawn to work the fields of their holding, while their sister Failenn searched out medicinal plants among the hedgerows. None of them would return until dark. Only Padraic's youngest daughter would spend the day with him, but he was not lonely.

He had the past.

He tried to recall the exact words his Niamh had said about the past, the druid wisdom she had shared with him.

"The past is the future" . . . was that it? "Life is a spiral; we come the same way repeatedly, but each time we have a different view."

"Please God," Padraic murmured to himself. "Please

God." He saw no contradiction in calling on his Christian god to verify druid faith.

"The Great Fire of Life shines on Christians the same as it does on druids," Niamh had often said.

His reverie was interrupted by Cera's hands tucking a blanket around him.

He tried to push her away. "I'm not cold, pet; I'm a warrior."

"Of course. But I'm cold, though I've put another stick on the fire. The weather will change soon."

He did not ask how she knew. Druids always knew.

By midday a ferocious storm was lashing the kingdom of Thomond from the rim of the ocean to the grasslands of Tipperary.

As she worked at her spinning wheel, Cera patted her foot in time to the music in her head. Occasionally the music broke out in the form of a melodious whistle, a sweet, slow air as haunting as the scent of hawthorn.

Her father cocked his head to listen. "I swear your mother used to delight me with that same song," he remarked. "Her that died when you were a tiny wee mite. How can you know her music?"

But Cera only smiled.

The fire on the hearth crackled and snapped its own music. From time to time the young woman arose to feed it a bit of wood. Once, passing close to her father, she paused to look down at him. "Where do you go behind your closed eyes?" she wondered aloud.

"Here and there. Here and there."

"With Brian Boru?"

"Aye."

Aside from the fire and the drumming of rain on the thatch, the house was very quiet. Cera and her father were alone together within a globe of being. It was a time when one might ask the deeper questions.

"Are you never bitter, Father? About your eyes?"

"Why should I be? Did I not have the use of them for many years, more years than a lot of warriors live?"

"You gave all those years to the king and kept nothing for yourself."

He turned his face up toward her. "I'm not a wise man, not like Carroll or Mac Liag. But this I know. If you are blessed with strength, other people rely on it, and you give gladly because a gift is meant to be shared." He paused and drew a deep breath. Cera thought his hands trembled a little, resting on his thighs.

"Then one day," Padraic went on, "you find yourself alone. Those with whom you shared yourself have gone off with the strength you gave them, leaving none behind for you.

"There is only the empty sea and the empty sky then, if you have eyes to look at them. But I have no eyes, so I look at the past instead. And it is bright and shining, Cera. Like your name. Bright and shining."

"Cera means bright red, Father," she reminded him gently.

"Aye."

"My hair is not red."

"Is it not? Come here to me, pet."

She bent down. The freckled hand, its fingers gnarled and nobbled with age, stroked her dark brown hair.

"It feels red," said Padraic.

Later, when he had fallen asleep by the fire, Cera went to stand in the doorway of the house and watch the last of the storm blowing away eastward.

The storms off the ocean always blow eastward, she mused, her eyes following the curtains of rain now sweeping the distant Shannon.

Kincora.

Padraic's blind eyes saw only the past, but his daughter stood in a doorway facing eastward and looked to the future.

* * *

Mac Liag's hospitality was exemplary, but it was obvious from the first night that the arrangement must be short-lived. The house was too small and the proximity to Kincora made everyone uncomfortable. They were very aware of Teigue's guards passing daily on the road a spear's throw away.

"They're spying on us," Gormlaith told the captain of her escort. "Teigue hates me, I'm sure he's much angrier with me than he is with my son."

"We can go back to Dublin," he suggested hopefully. He was not comfortable being heavily outnumbered in hostile territory.

Gormlaith rewarded him with a frosty stare. "Go, then."

"We can't go without you; we have orders to stay with you."

"I am with my son now. I don't need you any longer. I insist you go." Her eyes were like chips of green stone.

The big Viking hesitated.

"GO!" she screamed at him. Her fingers hooked into talons; her face became a mask of fury.

As they were riding back toward Dublin at a brisk trot he told his men, "I had rather face Sitric Silkbeard any day than argue with that woman!"

Waiting until they had been gone for quite some time, Gormlaith casually informed Donough that her guard had abandoned her. "I don't know where they went," she said innocently. "They just took off."

Donough had a sinking feeling in the pit of his stomach.

When he began soliciting offers of accommodation for the immediate future, Conor offered him the hospitality of his own clanholding at Corcomrua.

Donough's expression brightened.

"In the Burren? North of Ennis?"

"It is. At a place called the Fertile Rock," Conor added with obvious pride.

"That's a long way to take these women," Cumara remarked as the party was preparing to leave Mac Liag's house, but Donough would not be dissuaded.

"The farther I am from my brother right now, the better for both of us," he said grimly.

And so Donough Mac Brian and his followers set out across Thomond in the direction of the Burren. In spite of all he could do to dissuade her, Gormlaith was determined to accompany them. "I am abandoned—what else can I do?" she argued.

"That woman is going to be like a burr tangled in his hair," Fergal prophesied to Ronan.

Though she had dispensed with her bodyguard, Gormlaith had kept her cart. She made the journey in style, driving the horses herself—with Neassa, at Donough's insistence, beside her.

Neither woman was happy about the arrangement.

Each expressed her dissatisfaction to Donough at every opportunity.

The trip to the Burren seemed to take a very long time.

"That cart slows us up," Conor told Fergal. "It's less than two days on a good horse."

The other replied, "I suspect Donough would gladly leave the cart behind if he could—contents and all."

For the most part, however, Donough managed to ignore the complaining women. Their voices became magpie-screeches in his ears, as much a part of the background as the thud of hooves or the creak of cartwheels or the rustle of summer-wind through summer-leaves. Donough rode with his men, beside first one and then another, talking or being silent as the mood took them.

They traveled west from Lough Derg through mountainous land dotted with lakes that gradually gave way to bog and grassland in the valley of the Fergus. As they rode Donough questioned Conor about various landmarks—and distances.

"Have you never been in the west of Thomond before?" the lord of Corcomrua wondered.

Donough shrugged. "I had no reason to be."

"Yet you seem most interested in it now."

"Some of my inherited landholdings are here. Besides, this is Dal Cais country. Should I not familiarize myself with every meadow and mountain?"

Conor grinned. He was a stocky, merry man with a permanently wind-chapped face and very white teeth. "Why? Do you envision yourself being chief of the tribe some day? Your brother Teigue looks to be in good health to me."

Changing the subject, Donough extended an arm and pointed. "Does Ennis lie off that way?"

"There's nothing of interest in Ennis," Conor assured him.

"No important forts?"

"Not really, no. Some minor cattle lords have holdings, and there's a mill on the river, but not much else. Even the nearest crossroads fair is at Spancil Hill."

"I thought my father's old spear carrier lived near Ennis."

"Blind Padraic? He's a bit farther on, somewhere around Drumcullaun Lough."

"Will we pass his holding?"

"Not at all. It will be much easier, since we have the cart, if we swing north soon. There's a road of sorts, that way."

The landscape changed again; became a moonscape. Great slabs of gray limestone lay like paving upon the earth, with a profusion of rare and delicate flowers thrusting up between them. "The Fertile Rock," Conor pointed out.

Donough looked around appreciatively. "None of my new holdings are in the Burren, but I might like to have a fort here myself."

At once Conor's cheerful face turned sour. "This is *my* land," he stressed.

Conor's wife made the party welcome when they arrived at his stronghold, and sent her women scurrying for heated water and cool wine. "I don't know how she tolerates living here," commented Gormlaith as she bathed her face and feet. "This isn't a palace, it's a pile of rocks."

Fortunately Conor, Lord of Corcomrua, did not hear these disparaging remarks. After greeting his wife and introducing his guests he had promptly set off for Galway Bay, just north of his holding, to conduct some trade. The unforeseen influx of so many guests meant arranging for additional supplies; he would exchange promises of hides and butter for smoked cod and barrels of herring.

Despite Gormlaith's criticism, Corcomrua was a stronghold worthy of a chieftain. A circular cashel, or stone-built fort, its construction was dictated by its location. In the Burren stone was the most common material. Within buttressed stone walls stood several round stone houses as well as a capacious kitchen. Beyond this central ring-fort, secondary walls protected outbuildings and penned livestock. Burren limestone provided rich pasturage even in winter, and the lord of Corcomrua was known for the quality of his cattle.

When she insisted that she have "accomodation befitting my rank," Gormlaith was given sleeping space in the grianan, the women's sunny-chamber. Donough, Neassa, and the other ranking members of the party were put in the guesting house.

At night the men sat around the central hearth in Conor's house and drank mead and discussed the situation. Burren mead was delicious, a potent honey-apple wine that sang through the veins. A few goblets were enough to make a man optimistic.

"When the rest of the Dalcassians learn how Teigue has treated me, they'll take my side," Donough said.

Conor extended his goblet to his wife for a refill. "In what way? Become your army instead of his? Do you hope to gain Kincora by force?"

"I just want what is mine."

"But if you can't prove it . . ."

"Teigue has the title," Fergal Mac Anluan interjected. "He's chief of the Dal Cais now, no one can displace him from Kincora."

"The King of Munster could," said a voice from the shadows.

Gormlaith had entered the room.

Chapter Twenty-five

Women did not customarily break into the conversation of men, but Gormlaith had never been one to follow custom. She walked straight to the hearth and seated herself on a bench, then unabashedly hiked her skirts around her knees and stretched her long legs toward the fire.

Donough could not help noticing that his mother still had fine legs.

They all noticed.

After a long moment the cattle lord of Corcomrua inquired, "What did you say?"

"Something that should be perfectly obvious, even to men. As chief of the Dal Cais, Teigue cannot be forced from Kincora—except by his overlord, the King of Munster."

"But Teigue's going to be King of Munster."

Gormlaith's green eyes widened. "Is he? First he has to be elected, which can't happen until the chieftains of the tribes convene. We're in high summer and I know you Munstermen. Everyone is busy with their herds, or tilling the fields. There will be no convening at Cashel until the cattle are brought in after harvest." Turning toward Donough, she said, "And by then you can have enough supporters to claim the kingship for yourself."

He stared at his mother.

"Close your mouth," she smilingly advised him. "A gaping mouth is an invitation for a demon to enter."

Having planted the seed, she appeared to devote her total concentration to warming herself by the fire.

King of Munster. Claiming tribute in the form of cattle and produce from every tribal king in the south of Ireland.

The thought hung on the smoky air and they studied it; all except Gormlaith, who gazed into the flames. As she knew full well, firelight flattered her skin and burnished her faded hair.

At last Fergal remarked, "Donough would make a better king than Teigue. He has more spirit."

From under their eyebrows the assembled men darted glances at one another, each of them considering the advantages to be gained by supporting an ambitious prince on the rise. Their fathers and grandfathers had grown wealthy supporting Brian Boru.

Conor named the blight on the fruit. "It would undoubtedly cause a major split in the Dal Cais. Teigue may not be the timber kings are made of, but he's convinced his duty lies in that direction. He won't surrender kingship easily."

"He doesn't have it, not yet," Gormlaith reminded them, keeping her eyes on the fire. "If someone else is elected, he would abide by the decision. He is . . ."—her lip curled—". . . a basically docile man. Anything for a quiet life, that's Teigue."

Now they were all looking at the fire as if it contained an oracle about to tell them the future.

Before long, Gormlaith felt the atmosphere change. Enthusiasm had the men by the throat. They began talking in rapid, eager voices, making plans.

Only Donough remained silent.

But she knew how to reach inside him.

Turning toward her son, she said softly, "Your father would be so proud of you. There are outlaws on the roads already, did you know that? Just since he died. He devoted himself to making travel safe. But now . . . I myself was stopped, right here in Thomond." She neglected to explain that she had stopped of her own volition to interrogate a trader, not surrender her jewels to an outlaw.

Donough regarded his mother somberly. *I wonder if I have a choice*, he asked himself. Already he could hear the other men beginning to make plans, discussing the numbers of warriors each could rally, the various pressures they could bring to bear on chieftains they knew. The noble network was considerably entangled. There was not a man in the room who was not related by marriage or fosterage, or both, to some powerful Munster clan.

By the time Gormlaith finally retired to her bed in the gri-anan, there to rest as smug as a cat in the sun, the next few years of Donough's life were being mapped out for him.

Still, she could not be sure of him. He had not leaped at the suggestion as she had hoped; he had sat back, listening to the others as they strove to convince him. He might need more pressure, Gormlaith decided as she pulled her wolf-fur robe up to her chin against the chill of a Burren night.

Early in the morning she intercepted Neassa as the young woman made her way to the latrine trench. In the most casual of voices, Gormlaith remarked, "This isn't much of a place, but I know a cashel much finer."

Neassa glanced at her suspiciously. "What are you talking about?"

"The real Cashel, the ancient stronghold of the kings of Munster. You have never seen it, I suppose. But you will when your husband goes there for his inauguration."

Neassa forgot the pressure in her bladder. "Inauguration?"

Gormlaith stifled her contempt. The fool girl could only mimic what others said, she had not a thought of her own. "As King of Munster, of course. Did you not know? Did he not mention it last night on your pillow? We are all encouraging him to make a claim; he's as entitled to be king as his fool brother."

Smiling, Gormlaith sauntered off.

Neassa ran to find Donough.

Cathal Mac Maine was upset. The four years since he succeeded the late Marcan Mac Cennedi as Abbot of Kill Dalua had been years of ecclesiastical success and personal satisfaction—until Good Friday, 1014. After that, disaster followed disaster. First there was that fight at Kincora, brother against brother and good men dead. Then the summer turned wetter than any in living memory. Cattle stopped giving milk, geese stopped laying eggs, bees sulked in the hives. Chieftains who had made peace with one another were suddenly quarreling again.

The change of seasons did not improve matters. Autumn was early and bitter, with pellets of ice blowing down from the mountains. Shortly before Christmas had come news of a shocking murder in the great monastic school at Clonmacnois—and now, early in the new year, this.

"Why am I being punished, Lord?" Cathal demanded of the sullen heavens.

It was too much.

"Brother Declan, enter in the annals that Domnall, son of Donohue of Desmond, is undertaking a hosting of his followers for the purpose of sacking and looting Limerick."

Declan almost dropped his quill. "Brother Abbot? I thought Domnall fought on King Brian's side at Clontarf, as did the Vikings of Limerick. Why would he attack his former allies?"

"This is a deliberate Owenacht provocation to test the new Dalcassian King of Munster."

"But surely," protested the scribe, "Teigue Mac Brian can break the Owenacht's spear."

Cathal scowled. "That's the problem. He proposes to

take no action. 'Perhaps the plunder of Limerick will satisfy the Owenachts and there will be no further trouble,' he says.

"Who knows what may happen next? If he gets away with this, Domnall might pillage Kill Dalua just to heighten the insult. I cannot understand why God is allowing this to happen!" Cathal added in a rising moan.

Word of an army on the move traveled faster than the shadows of clouds racing before the wind. From small-holding to ring-fort, news was shouted that Owenacht warriors were marching across the countryside toward Limerick.

And Teigue was gathering no army to stop them.

Within the stone walls of Corcomrua, Gormlaith blazed with triumph. "I knew that wretched Teigue was inadequate! Now's your chance," she told her son. "Seize the kingship of Munster and fight Domnall yourself!"

It had been a long, hard winter for all of them. Gormlaith and Neassa were like chalk and cheese; any room with both women in it at the same time was soon icy with hostility. Donough had sent an urgent message to Sitric, his half-brother and erstwhile enemy, asking him to supply an escort to take Gormlaith back to Dublin. But no reply came.

At night, Donough put his arms around Neassa and allowed youthful lust to take its course, but the coupling was curiously unsatisfying. She talked too much, for one thing. Even when he lay atop her she prattled about living in a palace, and blamed him for having one. "If you were King of Munster . . . ," her monologues invariably began.

Donough closed his ears.

He knew what was happening. His mother was trying to manipulate him, using his poor silly wife as one of her tools. Rebelling, he put all thought of the kingship from his mind and refused to talk about it with the other men.

On the day he learned Teigue had been inaugurated King of Munster at Cashel, Donough had thought of mounting his horse and riding off alone in search of Drum-cullaun Lough. But fear held him back. He could not say what he was afraid of; perhaps that he would not find the girl in the red skirt after all.

And if he did, what then?

Time dragged by and the stone walls of Corcomrua seemed to close in. They were getting on one another's nerves; every day brought a quarrel or a fistfight. Finally Donough offered to take his party and leave; go anywhere, just get out from underfoot. But Conor would not hear of it. "Surely I can offer hospitality to my friends," he insisted, mentally adding up the favors he would one day be owed. "Once spring returns, you can think of finding a home of your own."

Spring seemed a long time away.

Then the Owenachts set out to plunder Limerick, and once more Gormlaith urged Donough to seize the kingship. For one moment wild excitement thundered through him. She was old, but there was still a power in her when she was excited. She infected him with her dream, so he saw himself wearing the gold circlet on his brow . . .

Reality set in. "Even if I was willing to challenge my brother I don't have enough men," he told his mother bluntly.

"But Conor and Fergal and these others . . ."

"Not enough."

"The Dalcassians would stand with you. You led them before."

He shook his head. "They follow Teigue now. As they should," he added, fighting back his bitterness. They had been, so briefly, his—but he remembered how it felt to have an army at his back.

Gormlaith had started him thinking, however. That night by the fire he remarked to Conor, "This is not just about looting Limerick. Unless I am very much mistaken, this is the Owenachts wanting to reclaim the kingship of Munster.

Before my father, Owenacht and Dalcassian held the kingship alternately, you know. I suspect they want to see if Teigue is strong enough to retain it now. If they decide he is not, an Owenacht prince—probably Cian—will try to overthrow him."

"Do you care?"

Donough considered the question. He was still angry at Teigue, yet . . .

When he told Fergal what he intended to do, his cousin was taken aback. "You're returning to Kincora? After your brother threw you out? Why, in the name of the Sweet Virgin . . ."

"He's my brother," said Donough.

When Donough set out for Kincora, Conor of Corcomrua joined him, rallying other warriors from the Burren to accompany them. Conor felt he had by this time a sizable stake in Donough's future.

They refused to take Gormlaith, however. She was left with Neassa at Corcomrua "to keep you safe." No matter how she raged, her son was adamant, although Conor's own womenfolk were not too happy at the prospect.

As Donough rode away, the January air smelled crisp and clean, sweeping the smoke of too many late-night fires from his nostrils.

He did not see the woman who stood in the gateway, watching him go.

While Donough was on his way to Kincora, Domnall Mac Donohue gradually approached Limerick, the Norse trading town at the mouth of the Shannon. Teigue was making no move to intercept him, so he took his time. His men were marching through rich countryside, and plundering was good. The Owenacht felt no responsibility toward the smaller, weaker tribes of Munster. Brian Boru had been the mortar that held them all together, but he was gone.

If this raid was successful, Domnall was considering challenging Cian for leadership of their tribe. And that might be just a steppingstone. Anyone, no matter how obscure, could rise to the highest honors in Ireland—had Brian Boru not proved it?

No one was more surprised than Teigue when Donough arrived at Kincora with a small army at his back. At first he refused them admittance. But at his wife's urging, he finally met with Donough in the great hall.

Donough's followers were kept outside the stronghold, however, and their weapons taken from them while the two brothers talked. Conor and Fergal and some of the others wandered down to the river to throw stones across the water and wager who could hurl a missile the farthest.

Teigue faced his younger brother in an atmosphere sparking with tension. The timbers of the hall still seemed to echo with their anger of the preceding summer.

The older man would not bring himself to apologize for the argument between them, and it never occurred to Donough to apologize. But he did say, "We lost a lot of Dalcassians at Clontarf, and you might not feel you have enough men to confront Domnall. So I brought you as many as I could gather."

"You brought warriors for *me*?"

"Of course."

"Who said I was going to fight Domnall?"

"You are, aren't you? This march on Limerick is just the first step in a campaign, anyone can see that. Stop him now, or fight him and Cian and their whole tribe before next winter."

Teigue scowled. "Who told you to say this to me? That scheming mother of yours?"

The skin around Donough's eyes tightened but he held

his temper. "Gormlaith isn't with me now. I don't need anyone to do my thinking for me. I'm trying to think like my father—and so should you, if his kingdom means anything to you."

"You brought this on us, quarreling with Cian."

"It isn't Cian," Donough pointed out, "who's attacking Limerick. You have to stop him."

The Abbot of Kill Dalua kept making the same argument. After considerable soul-searching, Teigue had been about to give in when Donough arrived. His unexpected appearance was like an omen. Still, Teigue could not surrender without a struggle—not to Gormlaith's son.

"Perhaps I'll think about it," he said grudgingly.

"Think fast. I expect Domnall's at the gates of Limerick by now."

Domnall Mac Donohue was not at the gates of Limerick—not quite. He and his men were still some miles south when they learned an army was rushing toward them from Kincora.

Domnall was frankly surprised. "I didn't think he'd fight!" Dispatching runners to collect his scattered, pillaging warriors, he prepared for battle.

Teigue's Dalcassians were not scattered. As they had learned to do under the late Ard Ri, they formed into a tight battle formation and marched with grim purpose. Donough rode with the other officers, glancing back from time to time to be certain his personal followers stayed close behind him.

All his being was concentrated on the battle to come. He no longer thought of his mother, or Neassa—or even the girl in the red skirt. Whatever importance they had in his life would be in abeyance while man met man to fight to the death.

He felt both weightless and intensely alive.

Soon he would be in battle. Not simple skirmishing, but

war as Brian Boru had known it, roaring overwhelming war, hundreds of men running at one another in white anger, wielding their weapons with singleminded ferocity. War that defined a man, showed him his own strengths and weaknesses, exalted his courage or laid bare his cowardice.

How could a man know himself until he experienced war?

All his life, it seemed, Donough had been waiting for this day. It did not matter that he followed Teigue's banner. What mattered was having the opportunity to prove himself to himself.

He wondered if he would be sufficiently courageous. Before his very first skirmish he had been nervous and excited but not fearful, because he did not know what to expect. Now he knew. He had seen and heard and smelled death and he knew that most men were afraid, though they did not admit it to one another. Admitting fear weakened a man, somehow.

Marching to face the Owenacht, Donough knew he was afraid—not so much of death, as of a failure of nerve.

Or worse—of failing to live up to what he expected of himself.

Chapter Twenty-six

Domnall Mac Donohue veered away from Limerick and led his warriors along the east bank of the Shannon, looking for a battleground that would give him the advantage. He decided to await Teigue at a rocky ford above a series of falls, a place where men of the Uaithne tribe built small boats for fishing. Coming down the west bank of the Shannon from Kincora, the Dalcassians would have to cross the river to attack. Armies were always vulnerable while fording. A barrage of well-thrown spears could reduce Teigue's force by as much as half before they ever gained the riverbank.

Domnall gave the order to pitch camp. His Owenachts erected barricades of loot covered with leather hides; their recently acquired plunder included everything from chests of clothing and casks of wine to farming tools and sacks of corn. They settled down behind this makeshift stockade in anticipation of their next success.

They did not have to wait long.

Brazen trumpet and goatskin-covered bodhran announced the approach of the Dalcassians. As so often that spring the day was cold and wet, with a numbing wind that carried the sound.

Domnall of Desmond, a tall, dark man with blue eyes as hard as polished stones, surveyed his warriors with approval. Behind their barricades they waited to hurl javelins at the Dalcassians as soon as they reached the midpoint of the river. Those who survived the first onslaught could be expected to form a broad line and charge the Owenacht emplacement, but a second barrage should complete their destruction.

A broad line no more than two or three men deep had characterized Celtic warfare since the days when the Gauls fought Caesar. Having studied Caesar's campaign strategies, Brian Boru had attempted to introduce new tactics to his own warriors. Abandoning the frontal assault that risked everything on a wild charge, he had developed more complex and subtle formations, varying them to suit the terrain and situation.

With his death, however, the warriors of Ireland had quickly reverted to their old familiar battle style. Not enough time had passed to turn Brian's innovations into tradition. So Domnall was confident that the Dalcassians, like his Owenachts, would fight as their ancestors had fought; as their grandsons would fight.

Brian Boru was dead and nothing had really changed in Ireland after all, Domnall thought, grinning mirthlessly as the first Dalcassians emerged from the trees on the far side of the river. "Get ready, lads," he called to his waiting men.

They shifted behind their barricades; peered cautiously over; hefted their throwing spears.

On the far side of the river, Teigue looked first to the left and then the right, gathering the eyes of his officers. He was not a warrior by inclination or disposition, but the men with him were what remained of the army Brian had forged.

"Now," he said.

They flowed forward to take the shape of a spearhead, each man half-shielded by the man in front of him. Meanwhile flankers moved wide to circle above and below the falls, closing in on the Owenacht camp from the rear.

There would be no expected broad frontal charge.

The point of the spear, as they began fording the river, was Teigue himself, riding a stocky bay horse with a black mane, descendant of the Norse horses imported two centuries earlier by the Vikings. His two largest captains rode behind him, and behind them were four almost as large. Instead of the traditional round shield, all carried shields specifically shaped to protect the upper body while on horseback. The shields were worn on the arm of the hand that held the rein, leaving the other hand free for weaponry. The warriors' heads were protected by fitted leather helmets reinforced with metal plates, lighter than the old bronze Celtic helmet, more comfortable than iron Viking headgear.

As the leaders splashed through the shallows they formed an almost invulnerable wedge. Close behind them more Dalcassians maintained a tight formation. Ronan was among them, and Fergal. They had fought this way before, they knew exactly what to do. They roared across the river and hurled their human spearhead straight at the heart of the enemy.

A few Owenacht javelins found their targets, but the Dalcassians were so tightly packed and thoroughly shielded that for the most part they shed the missiles as a turtle sheds rain.

Donough rode in the third rank of the spearhead. From the moment his horse entered the river his fears were submerged beneath a wave of exhilaration. "Now," Teigue had commanded. Now and now! Gallop forward now, scream now, hurl oneself at the enemy with the high, hot battle-lust pouring through the veins like wine . . .

With a mighty effort Donough controlled himself. The men around him did the same, their natural impetuosity curbed by years of training. Instead of a rash headlong charge into sure death they held to the rhythm of martial music, the rain of spears glancing off their shields providing a counterpoint to the thunder of the bodhran.

Vercingetorix of Gaul had once watched Caesar advance on him thus; cold, determined, implacable.

As the Dalcassians emerged from the river, Teigue reined his horse off to one side. "I will lead you, but I won't personally kill an Owenacht," he had informed his men when they set out that morning. "When I stand on the Rock of Cashel to receive my father's crown as King of Munster, I don't want the men of Desmond to refuse me because Owenacht blood is fresh on my hands."

Out of the corner of his eye, Donough saw his brother ride clear of the action.

The position at the front was briefly vacated.

Before anyone else could fill it, Donough surged forward. Brandishing his short-sword he shouted, "Abu Dal gCais!" Then with sudden inspiration he bellowed his father's personal war cry, the unforgettable cry that had not been heard in Ireland since the Ard Ri died.

"Boru!" roared the old lion's youngest cub. "Boru! *Boru!* BORU!"

Behind him the full force of the living spearhead drove into the Owenacht barricade.

Order and discipline vanished in the wink of an eye. The mounted Dalcassians sent their horses plunging through the flimsy barriers. Within moments the muddy earth was littered with everything from pitchforks and torn hides to spilled flour and broken wine casks.

The foot warriors flooded through the breach.

Throwing down their spears, the Owenachts met them with swords and axes and bare fists, fighting a desperate defensive action, but the momentum was with the Dalcassians.

Owenacht nerve broke. First one and then another threw down his weapons.

Domnall screamed at them, but it was no good.

Brandishing his two-handed sword, the warlord from Desmond rushed forward to attack his enemy with all the mad bravado of a mythic hero, shrieking the war cry of his tribe.

Some of his men followed.

Many did not.

Without hesitation, the Dalcassians cut them down.

Watching from upstream, Teigue was aghast to realize his younger brother had so swiftly assumed leadership. But it was too late to ride back and try to wrest it from him; too late, and the maneuver would be too obvious.

Donough fought as he had long dreamed of fighting, with reckless abandon, adding to the energy of his youth the force of his pent-up frustrations. He leaned from his horse to strike one man after another. But that was not good enough; he wanted to be immersed in battle. So he slid from his mount and fought on foot amid the press of struggling bodies.

From his observation point Teigue glimpsed his younger brother's head towering above the others. Then it vanished.

In that moment Teigue forgot the friction between them and shouted "Donough!" When moments later Donough reappeared at the center of the melee, apparently unscathed, he felt limp with relief.

I'll let him have Kincora, he thought. *I'll let him have anything he wants, if only he survives this!*

Some instinct deep within him, however, prevented his making it a sacred vow.

Through the stink of sweat and the smell of blood, feet slipping on mud compounded by spilled wine, ears deafened by screams and shrieks and the clang of metal, Donough fought.

He had no sense of time passing.

A battle axe swung toward him like death's reaper. He ducked instinctively, lifting his shield, and felt the power behind the thwarted blow shiver into his bones. He lowered the shield just enough to counterattack and caught his opponent off-balance. With a lunging thrust Donough drove his short-sword into the man's exposed armpit.

As Teigue watched, regretting every decision he had made, the battle spilled out of the broken barricades and spread up and down the banks of the river. By this time the flankers had crossed successfully and were moving in from the rear. Screams of anger changed to howls of fear as the Owenacht warriors realized the hopelessness of their situation. Some tried to run.

Donough saw a tall man who appeared in a fleeting glimpse to be Domnall Mac Donohue, sprinting toward a stand of trees.

Coward. Donough ran after him.

The forest swallowed them.

* * *

Teigue, watching, could stand no more. He galloped back and joined the fighting.

As he ran through the woods in pursuit of the Owenacht, Donough thought of the Norseman Brodir, fleeing after the Battle of Clontarf. Running for his life until he came across a tent in Tomar's Wood where the aging High King waited and prayed for Irish victory.

Brodir had halted to kill Brian Boru.

Anger lent wings to Donough's feet. In his imagination he was not pursuing an Owenacht, an Irish man like himself, but his father's killer. "Boru!" he screamed into the darkness of the trees.

In the cabin smothered by ivy, Cera had been fretting for days. Padraic could feel her anxiety. Her knitted brow formed a pattern that disturbed the air around him.

"You need to be away from here for a while," he told her.

"Not at all! Have I not just been away? As far as Kincora, which is farther than I've ever traveled before."

"And you've not been the same since," her father pointed out. "What troubles you?"

"Nothing troubles me."

"You can tell me. Do I not always understand?"

"Nothing troubles me!" She did not like the feeling of mental fingers teasing at the edges of her mind, seeking a way in. Padraic had learned too much in his time with Niamh.

Cera plied her twig broom on the earthen floor so ferociously that she stirred up a cloud of dust, making her father cough. She burned the stirabout in its iron pot and the cabin reeked of scorched oatmeal. She put too much wood on the fire, until Padraic complained of the heat and went outside into the rain.

When his sons returned that evening he suggested to Torccan, the eldest, "Perhaps you might take some of our produce south to the market at Limerick. It's a bad year, we won't get anything for it around here, but the Vikings will always buy wool. And, ah, while you're about it, take Cera with you. I don't think I can survive another day in the house with her."

In the far distance, someone was playing music. For a time Donough was content to lie dreamily, listening. Harp music. A small bardic harp with brass strings, like the one his father had played occasionally in the hall at Kincora.

His senses sharpened. That was no harp, but the pounding of the bodhran. He felt a vague disappointment and tried to go back to sleep. But he could not. The pounding was not that of a drum, but his own head, throbbing agonizingly.

Keeping his eyes closed, he tried to assess the situation. He seemed to be lying on the ground—he could feel twigs beneath him. Yet his head was pillowed.

His pounding, aching head.

In spite of himself, he moaned.

Instantly a cool hand touched his forehead. "Sssshhh, that only makes it worse."

The hand moved and was joined by another hand, one on each side of his head, bracketing the tormented skull between them, pressing very gently as if to press out the pain.

Donough tensed, but the pain grew no worse. In fact, it lessened. Then he heard a sound like humming and a vibration passed through his body.

The pain eased more.

He was able to open his eyes.

Light stabbed his pupils; he closed his lids quickly, then opened them a hair's breadth at a time, peeping out.

At first everything was blurred. His vision slowly cleared to reveal a dark shape bending over him. He was lying with his head in someone's lap. Or so it seemed.

"Did we win?" he asked hoarsely.

"Win what?"

"The battle." His lips were dry, his tongue thick.

"I saw no battle. Only you and the other one, the one who hit you."

Donough tried to raise his head. "Where is he?" Before a blinding stab of pain lanced through his skull, forcing him to lie down again, he glimpsed a man lying on his face a few paces distant.

Donough closed his eyes, grateful for the touch of the soothing hands on his head again. "What happened to him?"

"He was trying to hurt you."

"Did you . . . ?" He left the thought unfinished. Talking, even thinking, was too painful. Closing his eyes, he let himself tumble down into some lovely soft gray wool that seemed to have gathered around him . . .

When next he opened his eyes, he saw the rotting litter of a forest floor. His cheek was not pillowed on a lap, but on the earth.

A man lay facedown a few paces away.

Experimentally, Donough raised his head. No pain. He got to his hands and knees and crept over to the other man.

When he turned the body over he was disappointed to discover it did not belong to Domnall Mac Donohue.

Nor was there a mark on it. No weapon had slain him, whoever he was.

Suddenly Donough was fully conscious, every sense alert. The memory of the previous conversation came back to him like an echo.

Who was with me? A woman?

"He was trying to hurt you," I thought my rescuer had said. But what was the voice like? Male . . . no. Surely it was female. My ears were ringing and I was groggy; I should have paid more attention.

But had the conversation ever taken place at all, or was it his imagination, the dream of an injured man? It was receding like the memory of harp music, fading into the blur of battle and excitement and chasing someone . . .

Donough returned to the body and examined it again. There were not even any bruises. A big, strong warrior with the unmistakable stamp of an Owenacht was dead of no apparent cause.

With tentative fingers, Donough examined himself. He found a sizable wound on the right side of his skull, above and slightly behind the ear, where the glancing blow of a blade had torn loose a flap of skin. His neck and shoulder were bathed with blood, which had already begun to form a crust.

His ears were still ringing. But there was no pain.

In its sheath, he found his short-sword.

The last he remembered it had been in his hand.

He began a systematic search of the surrounding forest. No one. Only the trail left by broken undergrowth where he had chased the Owenacht.

Returning to the dead warrior, Donough studied him thoughtfully for some time. Then he drew his short-sword and stabbed the man through the heart. The Owenacht's battle axe he thrust through his own belt.

Expecting pain, he crouched, wrestled the dead body onto his shoulders, stood up.

There was no pain.

Bemused, he set off through the woods carrying his dead enemy and looking for the rest of the Dalcassians.

Chapter Twenty-seven

✠

In the annals, Declan of Kill Dalua subsequently wrote, "A battle was fought at Annacotty, the Ford of Small Boats, between the sons of Brian Boru and Domnall of the Owenachts. A number of men were slain."

As Donough had discovered before he returned to the ford, the man he killed in the forest was not the Owenacht leader. That honor had gone to his cousin Fergal Mac Anluan, who endlessly recounted every detail of the death of Domnall Mac Donohue until no one would listen.

Teigue had also slain several men, but he did not talk about them. For a victorious warrior, he was in a far from celebratory mood.

"All-out war with the Owenachts, that's what this means," he predicted glumly to his officers as they made their way back to Kincora. "Cian was turned against us already, now the rest of his tribe share his enmity."

He shot a dark look toward his younger brother, riding off to one side. But Donough did not notice. His thoughts were far away.

He was trying to recall the voice of the person who had soothed his injured head in the forest—and perhaps saved his life. A conviction was slowly growing in him, based on no fact whatsoever, that he had been rescued by the girl in the red skirt.

Impossible, he knew.

And yet . . . and yet, he wanted to believe.

He rode bemused, letting his horse pick its own way.

From time to time he reached up absentmindedly to scratch at the dried blood crusted on his ear and jaw.

As soon as they reached Kincora, Teigue summoned his personal physician to examine his brother's head wound. Ferchar had Donough sit on a stool in the courtyard, in good light. "You say you were hit with an axe?"

"Only a glancing blow, fortunately. I brought the axe back with me."

Donough tried not to flinch as Ferchar lifted the partially dislodged flap of skin with a practiced thumb, bathed it gently with willow-water to free the clotted hair, then eased it into its proper place and affixed an herbal poultice of rib-wort and plantain. "For an axe wound this is remarkably clean," the physician commented. "Men who survive axe wounds usually die anyway of some latent poison that clings to the blades, but there is no sign of purulence here. Did you bathe your head in a magic spring? Or did the guardian spirit of the Dal Cais come down from her mountain to mend you?" he teased, chuckling.

Donough did not laugh. Instead something shifted behind his eyes.

He had told no one of his encounter in the forest, partly because it might be a figment of his imagination resulting from his head wound. Partly because, if real, it was a very private memory.

His response to Ferchar was simply, "The axe hasn't been forged that can kill me."

Perhaps it was true.

Once Teigue learned that his brother was going to be all right, he crisply informed Donough that his services were no longer required at Kincora.

He chose not to remember the promise he had made to himself in the ford.

Donough was genuinely taken aback. "Is this how you show your gratitude for my help in the battle?"

"There would have been no battle if you had not caused trouble between our tribe and the Owenachts."

"A quarrel! It was just a simple quarrel!"

"That's how wars start," Teigue told him. "Had it not been for your 'simple quarrel' I doubt if the Owenachts would ever have undertaken to march on Limerick."

"You can't know that! Don't you listen to the news your own messengers bring you? Battles are breaking out all over Ireland. Men who have been allies for years are turning on one another. The Ard Ri held them together, but those coalitions are falling apart now."

Teigue ignored him. "You alone are responsible for this problem," he insisted, "and I think the farther you stay from Kincora, the better. Perhaps with time resentments will die down."

"And you'll continue as King of Munster without opposition," Donough said darkly. "Or so you think."

"What does that mean?"

Donough shrugged. "Whatever you want it to mean."

Gathering his supporters, he informed them in terse monosyllables that they were leaving again. "We will go back to Corcomrua long enough to collect my women," he told Conor, "but then I must build a fort for myself. I don't have to have Kincora to survive."

But the jut of his jaw and the light in his eyes said otherwise.

Before they set out for the Burren once more, Donough called on Maeve. "Whatever happens between Teigue and myself," he told her, "I shall always be grateful to you for the kindness you have shown me."

She put out her hand to him. "I don't want the two of you quarreling. I don't think he does either, not really. But by now it's become a matter of pride with him; he's his father's son."

"So am I," said Donough.

* * *

He had one final visit to pay. Approaching Mac Liag's house by the lake, he found the poet standing in the doorway as if expecting him.

The old man's face was gray with fatigue.

"He's working too hard," Cumara told Donough. "He keeps insisting he will die soon and he's trying to complete a biography of Brian Boru first. Writing it all down himself, he won't even send for a scribe from the monastery."

"I have things to relate I would not want one of Cathal's monks to hear," said Mac Liag.

Donough asked, "Should not Carroll be compiling the history of my father's life and deeds?"

The poet's faded eyes twinkled. "There are some things even Carroll does not know. He would only tell facts; I know truth. Come inside with me, lad, and we can talk while I take a rest from my labors. But only briefly, mind you. There is much still to be done and I don't want my inks to dry up."

They seated themselves on either side of the hearth while Cumara served them with summer foods: berries and soft cheese, stewed cresses, a cake made of flour, curds, and eggs. He poured brimming goblets of mead from a jug and put some sticks on the fire, though the day was warm enough and the inside of the house was stifling.

As Donough studied Mac Liag's face, he realized the chief poet really was dying. Some integral spirit had collapsed.

"Before I leave Kincora for . . . for what may be a long time," Donough said, choosing his words carefully, "I would appreciate a little more of your truth."

Mac Liag stirred his bowl of cheese with his forefinger. "What can I tell you?" Aside from suckling his finger like an infant at the breast, Donough observed, the old man had little appetite.

Cumara hovered, watching him anxiously.

Donough said, "Talk to me about Crag Liath."

"You know what everyone knows."

"But you know more," Donough insisted. "You are a treasure-house, the repository of Dalcassian myth and legend."

"A treasure-house?" Mac Liag smiled, pleased. "Perhaps I am. For example, I can tell you that myth is often just a name for forgotten history." He interrupted himself to twist around on his stool and address his son. "Find some work to do outside. This does not concern you."

Grumbling under his breath, Cumara left the house.

Before he spoke again the poet took a long drink of mead and belched pleasurably, exhaling a fragrance of fermented honey and apples instead of an old man's sour stench. "The spirit of Crag Liath," he resumed in a murmurous voice, gazing up into the rafters as if he could see her there. "Her true name, the ancient name she bore as one of the Tuatha De Danann, is Eevin, the Danann word for 'beautiful.' Cathal's monks would probably spell that Aebhinn, in the way they have of contorting the language—if they wrote her name at all, which they would not. She and her kind are anathema to them."

"Is Eevin a ban shee?"

"A female fairy?" Mac Liag's lips twitched. "According to, ah, legend, what we call fairies are actually the undying spirits of the race that dwelt in Ireland when our ancestors arrived, many centuries before Christ was born. The Gael defeated the Tuatha De Danann with iron swords, but they could not drive them out. The Danann melted into the land itself, becoming such a part of it they could never be expelled.

"So the myth goes," Mac Liag added, emphasizing the word myth. "Then there is another opinion which holds that Eevin was but the first of a long line of druid women who have practiced their sacred rites on Crag Liath for centuries. Where the gray stone broods in the silent glen, Eevin's daughters pray to gods older than time. Or so some say." Mac Liag paused to slurp up another fingerful of cheese.

"Is that the real reason my father visited the mountain—to take offerings to druid ceremonies?"

Mac Liag pretended to be shocked. "A fine Christian king like Brian Boru?"

"I know enough about my father to know he sought allies wherever he could find them."

"He was not seeking political alliances on Crag Liath."

"What, then?"

"He never told me."

"But you have a suspicion."

"I do. I think he was looking for a woman."

Donough leaned forward. "A druid woman? A real flesh-and-blood person, not the guardian spirit of the Dal Cais?"

"Must she be one or the other? Why not both?"

"You're talking in riddles, Mac Liag."

"Do you think so? Let me tell you a real riddle; a mystery. All his life, at least for as long as I knew him, Brian Boru was haunted by a druid woman. He had known her when they were both very young. He told me that much one night when there was too much red wine taken. Fiona, her name was.

"He loved her, lost her, let her go. Became too busy hacking his way to kingship. But she was always just beyond his range of vision, somehow. Even in the days when Gormlaith lived here, there were times when Brian went alone to Crag Liath looking for the one he called Fiona."

"Did he find her?"

Mac Liag shook his head. "I cannot tell you. I honestly don't know."

The two men gazed together into the fire. Donough took a drink of his mead. Then suddenly he lifted his head. "Perhaps she found him. At Clontarf."

"What do you mean?"

"Carroll said there was a strange tale of some woman

who visited the Ard Ri in his tent the night before the battle, and then vanished."

"Ah, that could not have been Fiona. She would be too old, if she were still alive at all, to make such a journey."

"Would she?" Donough wondered. "You said she was a druid. Do the druids not have magical powers?"

The old man's expression stiffened. "Cathal claims magic is evil, the work of demons."

"Somehow I don't think you believe him. Tell me this, Mac Liag. Why does the Abbot of Kill Dalua hate the druids so?"

A twinkle returned to the poet's eyes. "Now that's an interesting question, especially since we were talking of Crag Liath. Get up and pour me some more mead, lad. This is not a story to be told with a dry throat."

Mac Liag waited while Donough refilled his goblet, then he emptied it in one draught. "Listen closely, I shall only say this once. There are those who wish it forgotten entirely. As you may know, Saint Da-Lua founded the abbey here late in the sixth century. He was a grandson of Eochaid, then King of Munster—an Owenacht. The next prominent abbot was Flannan Mac Turlough, for whom the chapel is named. His father was a king of the Dal Cais who reputedly rose to power through the aid of a demon.

"A demon is what they call her now, you understand. But in the legends of our tribe, Turlough's benefactress was none other than Eevin of Crag Liath. Through her magical influence the Dal Cais gained control of all Thomond and were able to demand alternate kingship of Munster. From her gray crag she watches over them yet, and when a Dalcassian dies, she keens.

"Once such alliances with ancient spirits were encouraged. It was their land before it was ours. Your kinsman Cathal Mac Maine, however, is filled with zeal and a desire for reform. He wants to stamp out every vestige of the Old Faith and replace it with Christianity—in which he holds an important position. He hates the druids because they still revere the spirits he wants to extirpate.

"As for Eevin, Cathal considers her a humiliating reminder of Dalcassian connections to paganism. He would put her entire mountain to the torch if he dared, burn down every tree she is said to love. But for all his self-righteousness he doesn't dare. He believes in her too, you see; he was Dalcassian long before he was abbot. He is torn between two faiths and hates the one he believes to be the source of his dilemma." Mac Liag yawned abruptly. "Talk wearies me these days, I'm afraid. And I still have writing to do before I sleep."

Donough took the hint and stood up. "I am tired myself," he lied, "and my men are waiting for me."

"Before we part, lad, answer one question for me. Did you ask these things out of simple curiosity, or something more?"

Donough felt he owed the old man an explanation. "It's not just curiosity. On Good Friday I heard the voice of the ban shee. Then after we reached Dublin a woman I had never seen before appeared and gave me good advice. At my own wedding I saw her again, only with a younger face. And when I was injured in this most recent battle, the same woman helped me—I think. Somehow I hoped you could . . . explain . . ."

Mac Liag's mouth was hanging open. "His heir," he said in an awed voice.

"What?"

"Brian is dead and now she's come to you. You are truly his heir, though not in the way you expected."

The two men stared at one another, locked in the same mystery.

At last Donough broke the silence. "But she's a real person! I mean, the girl at my wedding . . . she's real, I know she is."

"Fiona was real," Mac Liag told him flatly. The old man

sighed, fumbled for his cup and refilled it. "I fear for you, lad," he said at last. "I fear for you . . . and envy you."

Chapter Twenty-eight

When Donough and his men returned to Corcomrua, Gormlaith was quick to point out her son's mistakes to him. "I could have told you there's no point in trying to mollify Teigue. You won't persuade him to cede anything to you by doing him favors. Force is the only thing men respect. Once the Owenachts were defeated, you should have pointed out that the victory was your doing and appealed to the Dalcassians to follow your banner thereafter, instead of Teigue's. You could have won them in that moment, but you wasted your opportunity. Listen to me after this; profit from my knowledge of kings and chieftains."

Donough eyed her wearily. He was in no mood for a lecture from Gormlaith, but once she started talking nothing would stop her. If he walked away she would follow him, yapping on and on until he longed to strike her.

Yet he dare not, any more than Cathal Mac Maine dared put the torch to the trees on Crag Liath.

At night he bedded Neassa, who chattered constantly but with less purpose. He was soon deaf to her voice and merely lay with his arms around her, waiting for youth and lust to take over. When they did, he performed and she accepted, a fertility ritual older than time. But something was missing. He knew it if she did not. Afterward, unspent because he invariably held back a part of himself he simply could not give, he lay awake and stared into the darkness.

Sometimes he saw his mother's face.

Sometimes he saw Padraic's daughter.

On the day Neassa told him she was pregnant, Donough announced he was beginning the construction of a fort in a valley south of the Burren, using the labor of local clans tributary to the Dal Cais.

"I don't want to live in another lonely outpost in the wilderness like Corcomrua, days away from my father and clan," Neassa pouted. "I insist you provide me with a home more suitable to my rank."

Donough laughed. "Your rank? You want a home suitable for a cattle lord's daughter?"

"For a prince's wife," she countered. "Which I am."

"Then you and your children will live with this prince wherever he lives," her husband informed her.

Donough did not plan to restrict himself to western Thomond for the rest of his life. He still dreamed Kincora would be his someday. But in the meantime he determined to build a stronghold as much like Kincora as possible for his growing family.

And out of the various landholdings that were now his, he chose to build not far from Ennis, not far from Drumcullaun Lough. He explained his decision by claiming the site was conveniently equidistant from Corcomrua and Kincora.

Gormlaith was as indignant as Neassa. "I have no desire to vegetate in some nettle patch where nothing important ever happens!" she told her son.

"There are no nettles; the area is overrun with ivy instead. But if you don't like it, you can certainly go back to Dublin."

"You need me with you, you have no worthy advisors." Recognizing the stubborn set of his jaw, so like his father's, she softened her tone. "Besides, Donough, I had rather be with you. Sitric doesn't want me; he would turn out his own mother as Teigue turned you out of Kincora. We belong together, you and I." She ran her fingers lightly down the bare, muscular arm emerging from the sleeve of his linen tunic.

Gooseflesh rose in the wake of her touch.

Gormlaith smiled. "You don't really want me to go," she said. He was her son, but he was a man.

Gormlaith had always known her power over men.

Donough sped another urgent message to Dublin, imploring Sitric to send for Gormlaith. Offering cattle with her, like a dowry.

In time a small delegation arrived at Corcomrua with Sitric's refusal. They brought other bad news as well.

"There is plague in Dublin now," they said. "People are dying left, right, and center." Strong, sturdy Vikings, they feared no living man, but at the word "plague" they trembled. "Let us stay here with you," they pleaded.

Remembering that Brian Boru had incorporated Vikings into his army, Donough was happy to agree. "Swear loyalty to me and carry arms on my behalf," he stipulated, "and I'll treat you better than Sitric ever did."

It was a vague promise based on an uncertain future, but at least the fort in the ivied valley was tangible. And growing. As soon as he had arranged with Conor for food and sleeping space for his Vikings, Donough prepared to make one of his frequent journeys to check on the fort's rate of progress.

Gormlaith intercepted him before he could get away. "You see! I have to stay with you. I couldn't go back to Dublin if there's plague there."

"Are you not worried about Sitric?"

"Him? He's a survivor," she replied with a shrug. She had not forgiven Sitric for losing at Clontarf. Gormlaith never forgave losers.

Donough reminded her, "I have a half-sister married to your son, and I worry for her."

"You've never been close to her. She's much older than you."

"But she is my blood-kin."

Gormlaith raised a sarcastic eyebrow. "And so is dear Teigue. What a close and loving family you are, the clan O Brian."

He was relieved to put her behind him. Relieved to be away from Corcomrua, which was not his, and Neassa, who was.

Neassa, who complained constantly about her nausea and thickening waist, and wanted her husband with her every moment because no one else would tolerate her whining.

Donough rode south with a lifting heart, watching for the landmark bulk of the region's highest mountain.

His new fort was rising in a meadow beside a clear, peaty stream with Slieve Callan looming beyond. The local clans who were building the fort claimed that druid rites were performed on the summit at Altoir-na-Greine, the Altar of the Sun.

Donough had wanted a mountain overlooking his fort, even if it was not as near as Crag Liath was to Kincora. Still it was there; a mystical height, a reassuring presence.

He required a mountain in his landscape.

He often thought of Padraic's daughter, yet did not go in search of her. Strangely enough he was satisfied, for the moment, just knowing she was somewhere not far away. Like Kincora, she seemed a promise for the future, as tangible to him as the fragrance of the hawthorn that perfumed the air of Thomond.

The scent of magic.

With that perfume in his nostrils, Donough sat on a hummock and watched contentedly as his fort sprang from the soil like a cluster of stony plants. Its design was determined by a pattern in his head; he began to fancy it might resemble the shape of his own brain, if one could remove the top of his skull and peer inside.

His desire for Kincora began to fade.

Then he returned to Corcomrua late one evening to find Conor's stronghold in an uproar. Neassa was very ill.

"She was fine when I left," Donough protested to any who would listen, but little time was spared for him. The female population was frantically busy, either tending the sick woman or huddling in corners to discuss her condition with much muttering and arm-waving.

Donough could get no solid information from any of them.

Exasperated, he joined the men outside. "It's my wife in there, and they won't tell me anything."

The Corcomrua cattle lord gazed at him sympathetically. "You have a lot to learn about women. When one of their own is ill, they close around her and make us feel as useless as wings on a fish. It's a way the women have of exerting their power."

Donough remarked, "That isn't the way my mother exerts hers."

"Och, no." Conor laughed. "Your mother's different. None of the rules apply to Gormlaith."

Including, it seemed, a welcome into the society of the women tending Neassa. When Gormlaith tried to join them, Neassa protested until her mother-in-law was barred from the chamber.

She stood quivering with outrage in the courtyard, aware that the men were watching her. "I've never been so insulted!" she cried.

"Somehow I doubt that," murmured Fergal behind his hand to Ronan.

The night grew later; darker. Glimmers of light from bronze lamps filled with shark oil from Blacksod Bay shone through the cracks in the door, but no one emerged from the chamber where the sick woman lay. Once or twice Donough knocked on the door and called out, but the only response he received was a demand that he go away.

"Why don't you keep a physician here?" he demanded of Conor.

"I don't have enough rank to entitle me to a personal physician. But my women know herbs and potions, they'll take good care of her. Stop pacing back and forth, will you? You're wearing a groove in the courtyard."

Shortly before dawn, Conor's wife came out. Her face was drawn with fatigue. "I'm sorry," she murmured to Donough.

"Sorry? Sorry for what?"

"They're both dead, there was nothing we could do."

He felt suspended in space. "Both?" The word had no meaning.

She put a hand on his arm. "Your wife and child. Neassa burnt up with fever and slipped a tiny dead boy, then died shortly after. It was God's will."

Donough felt no earth beneath his feet, no air in his lungs.

In that moment Neassa became precious to him.

Her miscarried infant was equally precious. A boy; a son! A child Donough had thought of only as an abstraction, another reason for building the fort, suddenly became a flesh-and-blood person.

And dead.

My child, he thought, the reality sinking in. *My child!*

A spasm of agony convulsed him.

He did not know if he wept for Neassa or the dead infant or all the possible futures so cruelly extinguished. He sobbed like a child, though he was seventeen years old and a man.

Then two arms enfolded him and a hand at the back of his neck pressed his face into someone's shoulder.

Gormlaith held Donough locked in her arms while he wept, her eyes daring anyone else to try to comfort him.

* * *

When a messenger came to announce the fort on the peaty stream was almost finished, Donough showed no interest. "You can move down there now if you want," he told his mother with an air of indifference.

"I? Live by myself in the wilderness?"

"You can have servants."

She laughed harshly.

"What are you going to do?" people kept asking him, but he did not know. It was easiest to do nothing.

The fever that had claimed Neassa did not kill anyone else, though several in Conor's fort sickened for a time until the lord of Corcomrua sent for help to purify his stronghold.

"A priest could bless the place," he explained to Donough, "but the spirits that inhabit the Burren are older than Christianity. We need someone who knows how to placate them, so I'm sending runners for a druid."

Donough's eyes brightened for the first time in days.

Then he was angry with himself for hoping it might be Padraic's daughter who responded to the summons.

At night he lay on the bed he had shared with Neassa and endured the corroding pangs of guilt for the first time in his young life. He gnawed on his knuckles and writhed, sleepless, as he imagined the things he might have done differently; actions that could have led to a happier outcome.

If I had known she would die . . . if . . . if . . .

A druid arrived in due course, leading an ass piled high with sticks of ashwood and bags of herbs. He was a stooped graybeard with a feral face; no one could be less like Padraic's daughter. He built fires throughout the cashel, creating clouds of thick smoke scented with spratling poppy, borage, and trefoil. The smoke was driven into chamber and outbuilding by means of flapping blankets, while the druid chanted unintelligibly in a high, nasal voice; a song for elder gods.

When the old man had performed this ritual for three consecutive nights at the dark of the moon, he packed what remained of his wood and herbs and sat down to enjoy a feast prepared by Conor's women.

"Your home is safe now," he assured them. "Have you any ale to wash down this meat? It seems a little tough and my teeth are not what they were. I would not mind a few more stewed apples, while you're about it. And some honey-comb, perhaps, with a nice bit of oatcake?"

When he had gone, Conor called in Christian priests to bless his stronghold.

They wrinkled their noses at the smell of herb-scented smoke but wisely refrained from commenting. They were men of the Burren.

Chapter Twenty-nine

I rode south one more time to the fort in the ivy-girt valley. With Neassa and the child dead it was hard to imagine myself living there, but I needed to have another look at the place. Perhaps then I could make some decisions about what to do next.

Ronan and a small armed guard accompanied me, but I insisted they wait some distance from the fort. I wanted to be alone within the walls.

The men who had built the fort were gone. The

stronghold was completed, lacking only furnishing and provisioning. Oak gates yawned ajar, waiting.

Waiting for what? I wondered as I spancelled my horse and turned it loose to graze. The animal was used to the soft leather hobbles and knew exactly how long a step it could take as it drifted off across the meadow, sampling various grasses.

I just stood and watched it for a time, forestalling the moment. Then I turned and walked slowly through the gateway.

There should have been a welcoming ceremony with a symbolic burial beneath the lintel. Harp and pipe and timpan playing; people singing. The first fire kindled on the hearth, a whole ox roasting on the spit. Vats of ale and buttermilk. Men roistering, women laughing.

Instead there was . . . nothing.

In front of the round stone house I would have shared with Neassa, I cocked my head to listen.

Soft wind whispered across Thomond. In the meadow a cuckoo reiterated its two-syllable announcement of self. The air was heavy with summer; high summer, drowsy and warm. Cresses were green in the stream. Insects rustled through the ivy on the bank.

Within the fort, however, there was only stillness and silence. No life but my own.

Something seemed to stir at the edge of my vision; when I turned to look nothing was there.

Can a place that's never been lived in be haunted? The ghosts of a future that will not happen, perhaps.

Steeling myself, I peered inside the unoccupied house.

My imagination had long since furnished the chamber with a carved and painted bedbox, iron firedogs at the hearth, chests for clothing, a woman's loom, cauldrons and vats and pots, herbs suspended from the rafters, drying.

But when my eyes adjusted to the dimness they saw only empty shadows.

Something ached at the bottom of my throat.

Turning away, I wandered around the stronghold. Mine was a desultory examination; the enthusiasm I once felt was gone.

I had not re-created Kincora after all. The fort was too small and too ordinary and its very newness offended me, the skinned surfaces of the stone, the wounded wood still bleeding from axe and adze.

As if to add to my pain, everywhere I looked I found sloppy workmanship, not good enough for Brian Boru but obviously considered good enough for Donough Mac Brian. The Celtic carvings on pillar and post looked as if they had been hacked out of the wood by a malevolent child. Iron hinges that should have gleamed with grease were raw and dull, already dappled with rust.

Nothing was as I had dreamed.

Suddenly I froze.

This time I was certain I saw something out of the corner of my eye.

I spun around.

Shifting shadows on a stone wall briefly produced the effect of a full skirt brisking around a corner.

A trick of light made an arm seem to beckon from an open doorway.

My heart thudded. "Are you here?" I cried as I ran forward, hope and guilt struggling for supremacy.

Guilt won. My steps slowed.

If I had been with Neassa and the unborn child instead of here . . .

If I had not been lured by the vision of another woman and wanted to build my fort close to her . . .

Druids . . . Accursed . . . Cathal is right about them . . .

I stopped. Turned around, prepared to make my way back to the gate.

Then I heard a sound like a light foot pattering over beaten earth and my heart leaped again.

Someone was humming at the very edge of audibility.

Instinctively my hand dropped to my sword hilt.

But the voice was light and soft; a woman's.

The wife of one of the local laborers, I tried to tell myself, curious to see what her husband built.

But I did not believe it.

Without bothering to summon Ronan and his men, I undertook a thorough search of the fort.

While the sun moved through the sky I moved from chamber to outbuilding and back again, crossing and recrossing my tracks, peering into storerooms, clambering onto walls to see what was on the other side. I had the profound conviction that the fort contained another being who was always just a few steps ahead of me. Or a few steps behind.

Several times I whirled around to find only my shadow following me.

But I was not alone. Of that I was certain. And I wanted desperately to find her.

Until Neassa's death I had been a boy; now I was a man. Being a man was terribly lonely.

"Where are you?"

Only echoes answered.

"Who are you?"

The echoes mocked me.

At last, despairing, I stood in the center of the stronghold I had built and recalled the words of the poet Mac Liag: "The possession of a palace will not make you happy."

Chapter Thirty

The cold, sharp air of Alba did not smell like home, even after all these years. If she closed her eyes, Blanaid could still summon Ireland: lush grassy meadows fringed by fragrant, magical hawthorn; wet ferns glowing as if with inner light; holly guarding the approaches to primeval forests of oak and ash that rang in all seasons with birdsong. Her senses were starved for that wanton luxuriance.

On a day like this when the wind was blowing from the southwest, it was easy to surrender to melancholy. The Welsh princes who sometimes visited her husband's court had a word, *hiraeth*, that meant a deep yearning, and another word, *cynefin*, that referred to one's own place, one's native habitat. Blanaid understood both words, though she had learned little Welsh.

She did not speak of her feelings to Malcolm, of course. He had no patience with women's moods, the ephemera of emotion. His interests and energies were totally involved with being King of Alba, a title he had held since 1005.

King. Blanaid rolled the word on her tongue. *Ri,* in Gaelic; from the Latin, *Rix.*

Brian Boru's daughter, she had been educated as befitted her station.

"Ard Ri," she whispered to herself. "High King."

That would always and only mean Brian Boru to her. How strange to think that Malachi Mor had reclaimed the title, with no formality, but as his right. Stranger still that no one had bothered to oppose him.

"Who could?" Malcolm had commented when they learned the previous year of Malachi's accession. "Who else has the stature? Malachi has tradition behind him, being a prince of the Ui Neill, and he certainly knows the obligations of the office."

"He should by now," Blanaid had remarked bitterly. "He learned them by observing my father."

"I meant from his own experience. Before Brian."

Before Brian. Sometimes Blanaid felt that everything in life was divided in two parts, before Brian and after.

If she felt that way, how much more intensely must they feel it in Ireland?

Her mind far away across the sea, she paced slowly along the footpath leading down to the pond where she bathed in warm weather. The hardy Scots braved the water even in the dead of winter, but she came from a gentler land. She would not bathe this evening in late summer. There was already a hint of autumn in the air, a smell of woodsmoke. The wise woman predicted the winter of 1016 would be bitterly cold.

Blanaid shivered and drew her cloak more tightly around her body.

Behind her rose the stony mass of Malcolm's royal seat, looking almost like a natural outcropping of rock. A hill-fort had stood on the site since ancient times, he once told her; built and destroyed and rebuilt and expanded in that curious death and rebirth common to such places.

From what stronghold does Malachi Mor rule Ireland now? Blanaid wondered. Not Tara, surely. Tara had not been used as a primary royal residence for centuries. Newly inaugurated high kings occupied its decaying magnificence only as a symbol of possession, and soon left for sturdier, more comfortable abodes. Brian had ruled from Kincora, although he could have used Cashel, seat of the kingdom of Munster. Malachi probably held court in his family stronghold at Dun na Sciath—not as kingly a palace as Kincora, Blanaid thought smugly.

But as she knew, he was demonstrating his reestablished kingship in other ways. In January of 1015, together with his kinsman Flaherty, King of Aileach, Malachi had led a successful attack on Dublin. The two looted and burned Sitric's city in retaliation for the Easter rising against the Ard Ri, then turned southward and exacted revenge upon Leinster, taking many hostages. Gormlaith's brother Maelmordha had been prince of Leinster, had joined Sitric in the rebellion against Brian, had fought and died at Clontarf. So Leinster must pay.

As part of his punishment of the eastern province, Malachi had—ill advisedly, Blanaid thought—bestowed kingship of Leinster on Donncuan, the son of one of Brian's slain officers.

"A gesture of reconciliation," Malcolm had remarked when they heard the news. "Malachi's trying to mend his walls with the Dal Cais. He obviously has wit enough to realize he cannot retain the high kingship without the support of Munster."

The Leinstermen were predictably outraged at this arbitrary bestowal of their tribelands upon a Dalcassian prince. Defeated at Clontarf by the man they would always consider "that upstart from Munster," they were simmering, biding their time. They would rebel again; nothing was more certain.

The old pattern of reprisal, Blanaid thought wearily. My father tried to break that mold. But now . . .

Malachi as Ard Ri and everything the way it was, before Brian. The flower of the Dal Cais dead at Clontarf, and Malachi, apparently by general consent, presiding over an Ireland that was reverting to unbridled tribal warfare.

Sometimes Blanaid felt very old and tired.

A shrill whistle split the air behind her. She turned to see her maidservant standing at the top of the path with two fingers in her mouth. The woman called down, "Your husband summons you, lady. He says there's something you might like to hear. A messenger brings the latest tidings from Ireland!"

Blanaid was briefly startled, as if God had overheard her thoughts and sent a direct response. Taking her skirts in her two hands, she hurried up the path.

A yellow-haired, jug-eared messenger stood warming his backside by the fire in Malcolm's great hall while he regaled king and courtiers with a mixture of hard news and titillating gossip.

As Blanaid entered the hall, Malcolm threw an automatic glance in his wife's direction. His dark eyes gleamed like obsidian beneath their heavy black brows. The sight of her still pleased him after all these years, though he never told her so. Revealing affection to a woman was a sign of weakness.

But she was wearing well, he admitted to himself.

He had wanted an Irish wife because he had an Irish mother who wore well. When Brian Boru, who was then only King of Munster, was marrying his children into noble families wherever he could to extend his influence beyond provincial borders, Malcolm had agreed to have a look at one of his daughters.

One look at Blanaid had been all he needed. Twenty-six years later she was still good to look at, with a straight back, a relatively unlined brow, and large eyes the color of the sea off Montrose. In dim light she could be mistaken for one of her own daughters.

"I thought you'd be interested in hearing this," Malcolm said now as Blanaid paused just inside the low, arched doorway. "It's about Ossory."

Pressing her lips tightly together, Blanaid crossed the room to seat herself on a cushioned bench near the hearth. No matter how many times she told him, her husband still thought she came from Ossory.

"Tell us that part again," Malcolm instructed the messenger. "Take up where I stopped you before."

Dutifully the man recited, "When Maelfogarty of Ossory led a raiding party into Thomond recently, Prince Donough Mac Brian recruited an army to challenge him. The Ossorians defeated the Dalcassians and a number of Donough's followers were slain."

Malcolm turned to his wife. "What do you think of that? Your Ossorians must be good warriors."

"They are not my Ossorians," she reminded him patiently, as she had done many times before. "My mother was born in Ossory, but all her people came from Connacht. Those things matter in Ireland. I am connected with Donough Mac Brian, though; he's my half-brother."

Malcolm suppressed a smile. Teasing his wife gave him a small and secret pleasure because she never seemed to realize she was being teased. Long before she set foot on the shores of Alba, Blanaid had believed that all Scots were humorless. As Malcolm, until he met her, had assumed all Irish were emotional. Blanaid, however, was a deep pool, keeping her feelings to herself. She managed his household calmly and competently, eschewing extravagance, which pleased him. There had never been great passion between them—he believed she was incapable of passion—but her very serenity had proved a haven in his otherwise turbulent life.

And he did enjoy teasing her.

"I know about your half-brother," he said aloud. "And you have another who is now King of Munster. Should he not be the one to challenge raiders in his kingdom?"

Blanaid's thoughts ran back over the years, searching for brightly lit niches of memory along the dark passageway of time. "Teigue was always the least contentious of us," she said. "I recall him as a rather gentle boy, compared to the others."

"Gentle." Malcolm gave a dismissive snort. "Not a particularly desirable attribute in a king; kings have to be fighters. What about Donough? What's he like?"

"I don't know him. You and I were married and I was in Alba before he was born. He was the youngest of all Father's children."

"Your father certainly sired a number of sons," Malcolm remarked, his rasping voice tinged with envy. Though he was only thirteen years younger than the late Ard Ri of Ireland, his offspring were lamentably fewer: four daughters. His people blamed Blanaid, but in his inmost heart he suspected the seeds for sons withered and died in him before he could ever sow them in a woman. Punishment for his sins, if one believed in such things. But a king could ill afford a conscience.

"Prince Donough is a widower," volunteered the messenger in response to Malcolm's query. "His wife miscarried a son and died of a fever."

A frown stitched Blanaid's forehead. "A widower already, and he not twenty? That's a hard beginning."

The messenger nodded agreement. "Added to that, Prince Teigue has refused him part of the inheritance he claimed, and now this defeat; a defeat he did not deserve!" the man added, betraying his own sympathies in the family quarrel. "He's a fine warrior, Donough is."

Malcolm stroked his beard. "His mother is Gormlaith, is she not? We could hardly expect a son of the notorious Princess of Leinster to be . . . gentle." With a half-smile, he turned to Blanaid. "Perhaps we should invite this brother of yours to Glamis and get to know him."

Donough was astonished to receive an invitation from the King of Alba. Ostensibly it came from his sister Blanaid, but it would never have been issued, he knew, without her husband's approval.

When he mentioned the invitation to Gormlaith her face lit with enthusiasm. "Send him our acceptance this very day!"

"*Our* acceptance?"

"Well, of course, *our*. You know nothing of foreign courts. You will have to have someone at your side to explain the intricacies of knotted relationships, and who better than me? Who more sympathetic to your own cause?"

Donough gave his mother a look. "What is 'my own cause'?"

She smiled sweetly. "Whatever you want it to be, my son. You wish to emulate your father—do you think I don't know? To realize his unrealized dreams? A noble ambition and one of which I am sure he would approve. But if you are to succeed, you will require more than an army. You will need the support of foreign warlords. The world is much larger than Ireland. You saw how advantageous his foreign connections were to him at Clontarf, when Malcolm sent a great prince of the Scots to fight on your father's side.

"The time has come for you to expand your reach, my son; this invitation is an omen. And I shall be with you, helping you all the way. I desire for you everything you desire for yourself. You know that."

He knew no such thing. Gormlaith danced to her own music, and if she offered help, one could be certain it was only to further some scheme of her own.

He had never meant to keep her with him indefinitely. In an effort to discourage her, he had abandoned any idea of living in a fort and built himself a sort of camp in the valley of the Fergus, a cross between a military encampment and the seasonal dwellings thrown up by herdsmen. It had proved to be an excellent focal point for gathering disaffected Dalcassians to him, but the facilities were deliberately made uncomfortable for a woman.

Gormlaith, to his dismay, had chosen to see the whole thing as an adventure. "I'm tired of luxury," she had announced. "I get tired of anything after a while—a gown, a man, a way of life. This camp of yours will refresh my jaded palate, Donough; it's a fine idea."

To prove the point, she settled into a lean-to constructed of woven branches and thatch and made herself quite at home, as if she had grown up following the cattle from pasture to pasture. She dressed in unbleached linen, went barefoot, and swam nude in the river, scandalizing Donough, who thought she had already exhausted her capacity for shocking him.

"You're too old for such carry-on!" he protested.

"Nonsense, it's taking years off me. Are you afraid one of your men will look at my naked body and grow a spear of desire? That would make me younger still, I assure you!"

Gormlaith threw back her head and hooted with laughter at the look on her son's face.

But she proved unable to face a winter in the open. Having ascertained that the plague had ended, she finally returned to Dublin to impose herself on Sitric and his wife—an imposition they did everything to discourage. It took Malachi Mor's burning of the Viking port to drive Gormlaith out, however, and once more she made her way west to appear at Donough's camp, confidently expecting him to take her in. "I *am* your mother," she said as if no other argument were necessary.

That became her pattern. Summer with Donough, winter with Sitric; time divided between Gael and Viking. Neither man liked it, and Sitric's wife was almost manic in her hatred of Gormlaith, but no one could force Gormlaith into any other arrangement. When all else failed she fell back on motherhood, demanding the protection of her sons as her right.

Sitric Silkbeard was heard to mutter that the exposing of female infants at birth was probably not a bad idea.

But Donough had been glad enough to have Gormlaith waiting when he returned from his defeat at the hands of the Ossorians.

Old scores had been settled; many of his best men were dead. Yet to his surprise Gormlaith spoke no word of criticism. She briskly set about tending the wounded and making small jokes to boost their spirits. She even flirted with them; the more grievous a man's injuries, the more flagrant her behavior.

On some it worked wonders. Men who were given up for dying revived after having their heads pressed into Gormlaith's still capacious bosom.

Donough told Fergal, "I hate to admit it, but there are times the woman is an asset."

She would not be an asset in Alba, however; of that he was convinced. The prospect of traveling to the land of the Scots with Gormlaith was daunting.

But she busied herself with plans and preparations as if there was never any question of his leaving her behind. She made a point of telling his officers, "This will be the journey of a lifetime for me, and aren't I fortunate to have a son who will take me to foreign courts, to mingle with people of my own stature? What a memory to treasure in my old age!"

She clasped her hands over her breasts. She rhapsodized over Donough's kindness. At some point he realized he would have to take her or risk the profound disapproval of his men, all of whom had mothers.

Although she kept dropping tantalizing hints about the life and times of Malcolm the Second, she was careful not to reveal what she knew. "I shall tell you when we're underway," she promised. "It will make the voyage go faster, and be fresh in your mind when you actually set eyes on the man."

Donough knew she was manipulating him; recognized her tactics with a dark and bitter amusement and a certain reluctant admiration. But it was not worth arguing; there was too much to be done. Arrangements to be made, good-byes to be said.

Since his final frustrating visit to the fort he had built south of the Burren, Donough had tried not to think about Padraic's daughter. Like the abandoned fort, she was a symbol of youthful dreams and extravagant plans set aside. Neassa's death and the loss of his son had changed something inside him.

But he did not want to leave Ireland without informing Padraic's daughter. It was inexplicably important to him that she know where he was.

Taking a fast horse and no bodyguard, he set out to find her. He told no one, not even Fergal, where he was going.

A lashing rain was falling as he galloped through an endless sea of wet weather. His horse plunged beneath him like a ship breasting the waves; spume blew back from its open mouth to fleck his clothing.

Blind Padraic's holding was easy enough to find. A herder on a hillside gave him exact directions and he galloped on, the bulk of Slieve Callan looming ever nearer. The rain blew away; a watery sun shone.

At last Donough took pity of his blowing horse and drew rein on the shores of a lake to allow the animal to drink. While the horse sucked up water in grateful gulps, Donough looked around.

It occurred to him that this would have been a better site for his fort than the one he had chosen. Fish leaped in the shallows as if begging to be caught. A solitary islet in the middle of the lake was an ideal nesting site for wildfowl, and the sandy beach on which he stood was perfect for launching small boats. As for pasturage, on one side swelling hills climbed toward green uplands, on the other were sweeping meadows tufted with arbutus.

Aside from the sounds his horse made while drinking, the silence was absolute.

A peculiar light glittered on the surface of the lake.

The horse raised its head and snorted softly.

Donough tensed. His warrior's instincts told him he was not alone. Very slowly, he turned.

She was standing almost directly behind him at a distance of fifteen or twenty paces.

Today she was not wearing the red skirt, but a short apron that barely covered her knees. Her leine was open at the throat and her hair tumbled unbound around her shoulders. She hardly seemed clothed at all; he was intensely aware of her supple body beneath the veiling fabric.

"How long have you been standing there?" he asked.

She smiled and walked toward him. "Long enough."

"How did you know I was here?" It did not occur to him that this was an odd way to begin their conversation, as if they were old friends who had just found themselves in the same room.

She did not answer.

Donough dropped the horse's reins and walked forward to meet her. The words which had been coming so easily dried up on his tongue when he was close enough to touch her. He held out one hand instead.

Hesitantly, she reached to let her fingertips just brush his. Her fingers were warm and real. His hand closed over them, drawing her closer to him.

When she lowered her eyes her long lashes swept her cheeks.

"Have you been following me?" Donough asked in a choked voice.

She would not look up. "Why would I do that?"

"Was it you that day, in my fort?"

"What fort?" Still she kept her eyes down.

He tightened his grip on her hand. "Not far from Drumcullaun Lough. Surely you knew I built one there."

"Did I? What possible interest would I take in the building of a fort, Prince Donough?" Now she raised her eyes to his and he saw laughter in them.

"You know my name but I don't know yours."

"I am called Cera." She pronounced it with a soft, west-of-Ireland accent. *Karra.* "I was named for one of the wives of Nemed."

Donough told her, "I named myself."

She did not ask how this could be. She simply accepted, as she accepted his arm passing around her shoulders and drawing her closer.

Chapter Thirty-one

When Donough knelt on the earth, Cera knelt with him. Their faces were so close he could smell the sweetness of her breath. He felt there was something he should say, but she read the thought in his eyes and laid her fingertips across his lips.

Then she replaced her fingers with her mouth.

Her body from the knees up pressed against the length of his. He curved over her, striving to draw even closer. At first his mounting desire did not even seem sexual, but rather an overwhelming need for completion, for drawing her into him to fill a great aching hollow at the center of his being.

But when she moved against him and he felt the softness of her belly, he became aware of an erection so huge and hard it was painful. With a groan, he thrust blindly against her.

She responded by cupping her hands around his buttocks and trying to pull him yet closer.

"What do you want?" he whispered hoarsely.

"You."

"How?"

"In me."

Her words brought him to the brink of orgasm. Fighting for control, he turned his body so he could lie down and pull her down beside him. He dare not lie on top of her; he would surely spend himself then, before he could enter her.

He held her in his arms and studied her face with wonderment.

She was pagan, and he had only lain with a Christian woman, reproaches and whimperings and subtle refusals that must be overcome. Cera did not engage in such subterfuge. She astonished him by the openness of her response and the frankness of her caress. She celebrated his body as she celebrated the life force in the trees and the birds and the earth, with a joy that enfolded Donough in golden heat.

"I want to touch you," she said, her hands busy beneath his tunic. Her fingers closed around the swollen penis with infinite tenderness.

He gasped. If he felt so much as the pulse in her flesh he would come, but she realized this and kept still. Incredibly still.

He throbbed in her hand.

"You are beautiful," she said.

Never in his life had Donough exerted such an effort of will. He held the orgasm like a sun waiting to explode, while his eyes searched her face; his ears attuned themselves to the surrounding sounds; his skin felt the warm sun and the damp grass and the soft wind blowing. He was more intensely alive and aware than he had ever been, and he wanted the moment to last forever.

She knew. She smiled at him.

"Gently," she said. "Slowly," she said.

The urgency that had been cresting receded. He was able to run his hand over her body, freeing her from her clothing. Suddenly the idea of fabric separating them was obscene to him. But when bare flesh touched bare flesh he almost came again.

"The feel of you!" he exclaimed.

Cera made a sound in her throat, a soft little hum that vibrated through her skin and into his body.

He could not hold back any longer. Rolling over on top of her, he felt her thighs open to him as he sank down and in to a luscious wet welcoming. The muscles of her body gripped him and drew him deeper with no effort on his part.

She was very small, he realized tardily, and for a brief moment he was afraid of hurting her. Neassa had often complained that he hurt her. But even as the thought crossed his mind Cera's hands clutched his hips and pulled him even harder against her, demanding his full strength and passion.

He plunged and the sun exploded.

Some time after, he became aware that he was lying with her legs wrapped around him. It must be uncomfortable for her; he tried gently to disengage. But she moaned as if in pain and held him tighter. "Don't go."

"Just to be more comfortable . . ."

"Don't go!" she cried.

He relaxed into her embrace. And slowly, subtly, the rhythm began again, her interior muscles pulsing until they set up a matching pulse in himself. The sense of heightened awareness returned; he was aware of the flattened softness of her breasts against him and the contradictory firmness of her small nipples.

When he thought of her breasts she rotated smoothly on his impaling penis and sat up, riding him as he lay on his back. He gazed up at her breasts in fascination and she, looking down, laughed with delight at the expression in his eyes. Her pelvis thrust forward and back, simulating the motion of a rider on a galloping horse.

The sensation was overwhelming. They were free and naked together, galloping, galloping . . .

The second explosion was almost as intense as the first but different, a fresh discovery for nerve and muscle. He was instantly greedy for more and sat up, pulling her against him, twisting to find a new position, a new way of exploring the wonder that had befallen him.

She laughed—or he laughed—the sound bubbled up from their shared body and the source did not matter, they were one and the same.

He murmured a name into her hair—it did not sound like Cera.

She responded with a name for him as she buried her face in the hollow of his neck. The name was not Donough. They spoke older names in a forgotten language but they understood one another. All was remembered and resumed, the sweet happiness coming to them again, and they celebrated its return in the sunlight, laughing.

Chapter Thirty-two

Padraic heard the door creak open, felt the wind blow in on him. Fecund summer wind. He raised his head.

"Cera?"

"I am here, Father."

"Where were you?"

"In the next valley, collecting herbs."

"Is it herbs I smell?"

She did not answer.

"The next valley," Padraic mused. "The lake of the arbutus?"

Silence.

"The lake with the drowned city that only appears every hundred years?" he asking teasingly.

Uncharacteristically she snapped, "Don't make fun of an enchantment."

He was instantly contrite. "I learned that much from your mother. Is it there, then—the lost city? Have you seen it?"

But she had spoken all she could. She needed silence. She built up the fire and pounded his cushions and left him to go and stand in the open doorway, gazing out across her memories.

She had spent the entire afternoon with Donough, the two of them as free and thoughtless as mating deer on a meadow. No questions had been asked nor answers demanded. Being together was so natural, she somehow assumed it would be permanent. She expected him to lift her up before him on the horse and take her to . . . to wherever he was going.

It was as if a door had opened for Cera. Without hesitation she would step out of one life and into another. He had only to take her hand.

But when the sun began to sink and the shadows grew long on the lake, she felt a change in him. Some vital part withdrew. He wrapped her in a fine woolen cloak from the pack tied behind his saddle. He caressed her face and stared into her eyes and brushed her mouth with his, but he did not say, "Come with me."

He did not say, "Now you are mine," though she strained with every fiber of her being to hear the words. She who had been free all her life had given herself totally to him, and longed for the acknowledgment of that gift.

Instead he stroked her hair.

When he caught his horse by the mane and vaulted aboard, he did not hold down a hand to her.

"Where are you going?"

"To the land of the Scots—Alba," he replied. The word tasted strange in his mouth. He had almost forgotten about Alba and Malcolm during the long afternoon.

"Can I come with you?" She hated herself for asking; she should not have to ask.

He gazed down at her. Her eyes were so clear they sparkled, her mouth looked soft and bruised. For all the passion of the day, she seemed innocent in a way Donough could never remember being. He felt a sudden impulse to sweep her up into his arms and . . .

Be calm, he warned himself. *Think this through. Make no hasty decision you may regret later.*

He was obliged to be shrewd and pragmatic if he would imitate his father. Brian had been many things, but never, so far as Donough knew, impulsive.

Gazing down at Cera, he fought back his emotions and tried to assess the situation objectively. What could such a girl understand of political expedience? Could he make clear to her the importance of establishing a relationship with the King of Alba, who was surely as far outside her sphere as the stars? How could he clarify in a few words the complex machination his mother had taken a lifetime to learn, and by which kingdoms were achieved? Cera was a daughter of sun and wind; she had no need of such knowledge.

And there was the core of the problem. Not her ignorance, but her wisdom. Cera was a druid.

Even Brian Boru, Donough thought, had not dared offend the Church by marrying his druid woman.

The cold, hard facts of the situation shattered the magic as she looked up at him, waiting.

Anything he might say to her now would sound like an excuse, or, worse, a betrayal.

Yet how could he use her body and then just gallop away?

What had taken place between them was more than a sexual act; he knew that already. Had known it before he ever put his arms around her. Yet she belonged to a world that stood aside from his as if separated by a veil. She was— he passionately desired her to be—mystery and magic, ancient sorceries and youthful dreams.

She was more than he could afford.

Something seemed to be tearing inside him, like a piece of cloth being rent down the middle.

He mumbled a few words, claiming pressing obligations. She watched his face in silence. Her eyes were as limpid as lake water.

"I have to go," he insisted with increasing urgency, afraid if he did not leave now he would never leave. "But I'll come back for you. I will . . . as soon as I can . . . when I have accomplished . . ." Words failed. He waved one hand in the air, trying to define the indefinable.

He could not explain why he was leaving her behind, not without hurting her, and as he looked into those huge eyes he would rather anything than hurt her.

Baffled, angry with himself, he had finally turned his horse and ridden away.

Now Cera stood in the doorway of her father's house and gazed east, the direction he had taken. Then she spoke over her shoulder to her father. "How far away is Alba?"

"How far away is Alba?" Gormlaith asked. "Once we reach the coast and arrange for a vessel to carry us, will we be there in a day? Two days?"

Fergal Mac Anluan shrugged. "I'm no seaman. You lived with the Vikings all those years; surely you know more about the duration of voyages than I do."

Gormlaith hated admitting there was something she did not know, but in fact she had never been on the water. No man had been willing to entrust his life to the savage sea with Gormlaith in the boat beside him. In the days when her hair was like living flame, she had been denied on the grounds of superstition: a red-haired woman in a boat meant disaster.

The hair was faded now, but she was perfectly aware that boatmen would still like to refuse her. Donough would have to be forceful.

"I've been to sea a score of times," she told Fergal airily, trusting her words would get back to Donough. "When I was in the boat there always seemed to be calm weather, in fact. My first husband, Olaf Cuaran, called me a good-luck charm. But I just don't recall how long it takes to sail to the land of the Scots."

Her son, since returning from some brief, mysterious journey about which he would not speak, had been worrying Gormlaith. His mood was distracted; he seemed almost uninterested in the trip to Alba, whereas he had been enthusiastic before. Now he acted as if it were some unpleasant task which must be gotten out of the way.

She hammered at him. "If you can make an ally of Malcolm of Alba, you will have extended your reach beyond Ireland. The Dal Cais will be forced to recognize you as their true leader and give you enough support to overthrow Teigue."

"I don't want to overthrow him," Donough told her wearily, knowing she would not listen. "I just want what is rightfully mine. That's all I've ever wanted. That, and to make my father proud of me."

Her temper snapped. "Your father's dead! What about making me proud of you?"

Donough stared at Gormlaith. "Aren't you?"

Her eyes blazed, but for once she could think of no answer.

Accompanied by two score trusted warriors, including Fergal and Ronan, Donough would journey to the east coast to arrange passage on a boat for Alba. Since before the annals were written down, trading vessels and sea rovers had crisscrossed the Irish Sea, following routes established by leather coracles in the Bronze Age.

During the early centuries of the Christian era, Gaelic chieftains had sailed across those same waters from Ireland to settle permanently in the highlands of Alba. In time their new homeland had transformed the colonists, imbuing them with the characteristics necessary for surviving in a colder, more rugged land. They continued to refer to themselves as Scots, however, a reference to Scotia, one of the ancient names for Ireland.

Brian Boru had revived that ancient kinship by marrying a daughter into the clan descended from Kenneth Mac Alpin, who had been the first Gaelic chieftain to style himself king of both the Scots and the Picts, the indigenous Albans. By uniting these two peoples under one monarch in the middle of the ninth century, Mac Alpin had set a pattern

Brian subsequently followed with the Gael and the Viking in Ireland.

In the wake of Brian's death, however, the cohesion he had achieved took on an ugly form. As Donough and his party traveled across Ireland, they were several times set upon by bandits, roving gangs of Hiberno-Norse mercenaries owing allegiance to no one but their own greed.

The first band came roaring out of the forest near the crossroads know as Ros Cre, Cre's Wood, where the Slighe Dala was intersected by a market road. In deference to Gormlaith's cart, Donough had decided to follow the slighe almost as far as Dublin, then circle to avoid the city, and sail from one of the fishing villages to the north. He had no desire to try procuring a vessel in Sitric's city.

But they were still a long way from the eastern coast when the first attack took place.

"Outlaws!" screamed Gormlaith. She saw them first; they had waited until Donough's armed escort passed by, then ran out onto the roadway shouting threats and trying to seize her cart. The cart contained herself, a driver Donough had assigned to her, and all the personal baggage she could cram into it, including some items she had no intention of revealing or surrendering.

When the outlaws drew close Gormlaith snatched the whip from her driver and began lashing at them with it. Her cries were louder and more savage than theirs. "I'll eat the face off you!" she screamed at a lantern-jawed youth who wore a tunic of untanned skins.

"And you . . . I'll make you crawl back in the womb of the worm that bore you!" This to an older man who had succeeded in getting one foot inside the cart before she kicked him viciously. He fell back; Gormlaith leaned forward and spat on him as he writhed on the road clutching his private parts.

Meanwhile, Donough wheeled his horse and galloped back to defend his mother. Fergal and the warriors were close behind him. There were two score of them, trained and well-armed Dalcassians who could assess a combat situation at a glance and take appropriate action without waiting for orders. Swiftly they circled the outlaws, divided them, and proceeded to hack them down while Gormlaith shouted advice and encouragement from the cart.

At last she could restrain herself no longer. She leaped down, ran to the nearest fallen man, retrieved a short throwing spear from his dead hand, and hurled it at another bandit.

Her aim was surprisingly good, but her arm was not strong enough to drive a spearhead into living meat. The blow glanced off harmlessly. Her intended victim was surprised enough, however, to drop his guard, and in that moment one of Donough's men severed his neck with an axe.

Donough took no prisoners. When all the bandits were dead he surveyed the wreckage triumphantly, only to be disconcerted when Ronan remarked, "You should have left one alive to go back to wherever he came from and warn them not to attempt you again. Brian Boru always left a witness alive."

Next time, Donough promised himself. Next time.

Although he had a couple of injured men, which necessitated making camp for a few days until they were well enough to travel, Donough was exhilarated by the battle. The interlude with Cera sat more lightly on his conscience. Reality was here and now, fighting, winning, building—rebuilding?—a kingdom.

He stole a glance at his mother. Her color was high, her eyes sparkling. She looked a decade younger, and he understood what men had seen in Gormlaith.

That night she sat close beside him at the campfire. "We showed them, did we not?" she kept asking excitedly. "If I had a sword I could have killed a couple myself. Would have done."

"I suspect you would," Donough replied, amused.

She looked at him quizzically. "What happened to . . . to your father's sword? Do you have it?"

His jaw muscles tightened. "I do not have it. I don't know where it is. I suppose it was entombed with him."

Her eyes glinted. "The sword of Brian Boru?" It was the first time she had spoken that name in ages; it sounded sharp on her tongue. "I doubt if it went into the tomb to rust, and you know nothing about human nature if you think it did. At the last moment one of his devoted followers probably carried it off under his mantle." Gormlaith laid her hand on Donough's arm; softly, softly. "But it should be yours," she murmured.

Sitting upright and naked in his bed, Malcolm turned his sword over in his hands, testing the edge with his thumb in his nightly ritual. A sword, he mused, was a powerful symbol. More powerful than a crown. With the sword Swein, King of Denmark, had beaten the Anglo-Saxons into submission and put Wessex under Danelaw. After Swein's recent death, his son Canute had taken up his kingship together with his territorial ambitions, and Malcolm had little doubt that Canute would prove at least as formidable as his predecessor.

Malcolm did not intend for Alba to be included in the Danish grasp.

"I wish you would not keep your sword in the bed with you like a woman," Blanaid protested. She was sitting on a bench by the brazier, plaiting her hair for the night.

"If you object to sharing the bed with my sword, then go back to your own chamber."

"You sent for me," she reminded him calmly. "Are you dismissing me now?"

He grinned, a flash of white teeth within his gray-streaked black beard. "Of course not. I need you."

Blanaid went on plaiting her hair. They had been married too long for her to think he desired her sexually. "You need someone to talk to," she said. It was not a question.

Resting the sword across his knees, Malcolm scratched the grizzled mat of hair on his chest. "Who else can I talk to? This is Glamis; the stones themselves are steeped in treachery. A king remains king only until he makes the mistake of trusting someone, but even so I must have ears to hear my thoughts. No man can live alone inside his head without going mad."

Blanaid nodded. "This is Glamis," she echoed. "The stones are steeped in madness."

"Not mine. Nor splashed with my blood either, not while I keep my wits about me. And stay informed of Canute's actions." Malcolm picked up the sword again. "Canute is on my mind a lot these days. He's a rapacious man like all the Land Leapers, Blanaid, and now that he has established himself in Albion I expect him to be a threat to Alba. I need a strategy to forestall him."

Malcolm's wife tossed the heavy plait of hair over her shoulder and stood up. Firelight from the brazier silhouetted her form within her linen gown, but Malcolm did not notice. *How soon is eaten bread forgot!* she thought.

"After you defeated him in Moray, you married our daughter Thora to Sigurd the Stout to help insure he and his Orkneyites would not attack you again," she reminded her husband as she padded barefoot across the flagstoned floor and clambered into bed beside him. "That was a successful strategy . . . as far as it went. But." Her voice was bitter.

"But," Malcolm echoed. "Are you going to blame me for the fact that he attacked Ireland instead? Your father was able for him; Sigurd was slain."

"So was my father," Blanaid said huskily. Shivering, she

pulled the blankets up around her shoulders. Malcolm never seemed to feel the cold and slept naked summer and winter. The bed smelled of him: a male smell, a bear smell, heavy and musky.

"Your father was an old man," Malcolm reminded her. "He had an incredible life and a long one, but everyone must die sometime. In truth, I envy Brian Boru his death at the moment of his greatest victory. Few of us end on a mountaintop with the world at our feet."

She wanted to change the subject. "What do you plan to do about Canute?"

"I do not know—yet. He's a fierce young Dane with ambitions."

"Has he a wife who might have Alban sympathies?"

"He married the daughter of a wealthy Northumbrian soon after arriving in Albion, I was told. The Northumbrians are eager enough to stay in my good graces . . . for now. But I would say Canute is not the sort of man to be influenced by any woman. Do not overestimate your sex."

Eyes lowered, Blanaid replied, "My sex has more power than you credit. What of the Princess of Leinster? Was she not the lure that tempted Sigurd to his death—Sigurd and how many others?"

Malcolm bared his teeth again and stopped caressing his sword. "Gormlaith," he said thoughtfully, "is a trophy. Men are hunters; we appreciate trophies. A woman who has been wife to three kings and is famed for her beauty is surely the ultimate trophy."

In his voice was an undertone that made Blanaid bridle. "Gormlaith is an old woman," she told him as she twisted on the bed to punch up her pillow. "An old, raddled woman, withered and juiceless. And you will never see her in Alba."

Chapter Thirty-three

At Dun na Sciath, Malachi Mor was taking a rest. Well-earned, he felt. The year 1016 had been a difficult one. From the beginning, reasserting his authority as Ard Ri had not been easy; too many Gaelic princes remembered that he had relinquished the title to Brian Boru without a struggle. In their eyes his stature was diminished and they could not resist challenging him. When the King of Ossory murdered Donncuan, King of Leinster—whom Malachi had placed in that kingship—it became necessary to march an army into Ossory, kill the offending warlord, plunder his tribeland, and carry off a number of hostages.

Hostages of noble birth guaranteed the submission of Ossory—for as long as their captor held them.

Then a revolt arose among the Ui Kinnsellagh, who refused to pay tribute to the Ard Ri. That meant another battle and more hostages taken. The guesting houses at Dun na Sciath overflowed and Malachi ordered more built.

As his chief brehon reminded him, "Hostages must be treated at least as well as their captor treats himself; anything less would be a cause of dishonor." So whole roast oxen and tuns of ale disappeared into the bellies of Malachi's enforced guests, who were thoroughly enjoying themselves and showing no desire to go home.

"I suppose I should begin negotiations with their tribes for their return," he remarked to his son Ardgal, as he and another son, Congalach, joined their father for a day's hunting with hounds in the rolling meadowlands beyond Dun na Sciath.

But Malachi had not got around to negotiations. It was easier to let the matter be, for now, and join the hostages at their feast in the banqueting hall. Malachi Mor had always enjoyed presiding over banquets and entertainments. Among his friends he was called "Malachi of the Cups" for good reason.

He was not left in peace to play the genial host, however. Messengers kept arriving, even from the most remote corners of the land, to inform him of fights and feuds and banditry, of monasteries looted and women abducted and cattle raided.

"Why are you telling me this?" he complained to a wall-eyed messenger from Connacht who entered the banqueting hall dripping from the rain.

"The former Ard Ri wanted to be kept informed of everything that happened in Ireland," the man replied, surprised at the question. "So he could . . ."

"I know, I know. So he could interfere."

"So he could take action if necessary," the messenger corrected, his thoughts running back to the good old days of three years ago. "Now Prince Aed of the Ui Briuin requests the support of the Ard Ri in putting down a revolt among the clans of . . ."

"What has this to do with me?" Malachi asked with rising irritation, waving a half-eaten thigh of young pig in the air. "Are these clans rebelling against my authority? Do they refuse to pay their share of the tribute due Tara?"

"They do not, but . . ."

"But they are Aed's problem," Malachi said firmly. He resumed gnawing the sweet roast piglet.

"Soon they will be the problem of all Connacht if the fighting boils over and . . ."

"Should that happen, then I will deal with it. But until that time, return to Aed and tell him he is to sort out his own affairs and leave me to mine."

When the messenger, obviously disconcerted, had departed, Malachi remarked to Ardgal, "Brian Boru had a peculiar concept of kingship. He tried to control the entire land himself, like a charioteer with a team of hundreds of horses and all the reins in his hands. And where are his grand ideas now? In a tomb at Armagh, moldering.

"As for me, I have no intention of galloping off to Connacht to embroil myself in some local squabble. I shall reign as Ard Ri with all the generosity and justice at my command, but I must save myself for the big battles."

That there would be more big battles, he had no doubt. He would have liked to be able to say to Ardgal, "I'm getting too old for this," and enjoy a bit of sympathy. But he could not forget that Brian had been older.

Besides, the way he caught his sons looking at him from time to time made Malachi reluctant to admit the weight of the years. An ambitious son . . .

Perhaps, he thought, it would be wise to make a few gestures to encourage goodwill. To this end he announced that he would build new churches and repair others which had fallen into decay, and would also endow a school and maintain the students at his own expense.

When he learned of these undertakings, the Abbot of Killaloe was not impressed. "The attempts of a lesser man to emulate a greater," he commented with barely concealed contempt.

Cathal Mac Maine then visited his kinsman, Teigue, to urge him to consider putting forth a claim to the high kingship. "Malachi Mor means well and is a pious enough man," the abbot said, "but he is Ui Neill, and it seems a shame to let the rule of Ireland pass from Dalcassian hands."

Teigue had been dreading the moment when someone would openly press him to fight for his father's supreme title. He had his arguments ready.

"Ruling Munster," he informed Cathal, "is increasingly demanding. So many tribes, so many underkings, the Owenachts always sniffing for a weakness. . . . I am leaving this very afternoon for Cashel to spend the next month hearing an endless stream of complaints and petitions and trying to sort out various quarrels. Yet you want me to take on more? You said it yourself, Malachi is a pious man. Let him keep the high kingship. How much longer can he live, anyway?"

Returning to Kill Dalua, Cathal instructed Declan the scribe to write in the annals: "The Age of Christ, 1016. The second year of the second reign of Malachi Mor. New churches were built in Meath and Ulster, but none in Munster. Likewise a new fine monastery was endowed, but not in Munster. Teigue, son of Brian, ruled Munster but did not demand the beneficence the province was due."

As he took Cathal's dictation, Declan was aware of the abbot's anger. He was putting it in writing for the world to remember.

All the major monasteries compiled annals, and were in unspoken competition with one another for the most extensive and beautifully illumined. The Annals of Kill Dalua had been considered very fine in Brian Boru's day, but without the patronage of an Ard Ri behind them, their reputation would fade while the gilding and colored inks were still bright.

Two days later, Cathal was still turning over the problem of Teigue in his mind. On the one hand he wanted the man to be obedient and manageable; on the other hand, it might be better for Kill Dalua if he were of a more aggressive disposition.

As often when he had a problem, Cathal Mac Maine went out into the orchard beyond the refectory to be alone with his thoughts. He strolled among the well-tended apple trees with his hands tucked into the sleeves of his robe and a frown of concentration on his face, sufficient to deter anyone from interrupting him. From time to time he fingered the crucifix he wore. Occasionally he rubbed the bridge of his nose, or scratched his tonsured head.

The morning was still, with only a hint of a breeze. The abbot continued to pace up and down, ignoring the sweet song of a blackbird perched on the stone wall enclosing the orchard. Suddenly Cathal stopped walking; lifted his head; sniffed. Sniffed again.

His eyes opened wide.

Smoke!

In the distance he heard the first shouts and cries echoing across Lough Derg.

Cathal whirled and ran back inside.

In his little house on the lake, Mac Liag was resting from his labors. The detailed account of the life of Brian Boru was all but finished; nothing remained but to reread it, check the text for errors, and arrange for it to be copied out and bound.

"I shall send it to Kells, I think, for copying," he told Cumara. "The scriptorium there produces the finest handwriting in . . . What was that? Did you hear something?"

Cumara went to the door and stood listening. When he turned back toward his father, his face was drained of color.

"It sounds like Kincora's being attacked!"

In Connacht a series of small clan wars had exploded into tribal conflicts, and a chieftain on the edge of Thomond, anxious to enhance his reputation and thus intimidate his rivals, had seized upon the idea of attacking Brian Boru's old stronghold as one sure way of gaining glory. With Teigue away and the Dalcassians divided as a result of the split between the brothers, the raid was cleverly timed.

It was also well planned. One band of Connachtmen made a wide circle that brought them south of the great fortress, while the main army attacked from the north. Sentries who had lost their vigilance during the long years of peace were routed. Torches were put to the timber palisades, gates were burst open.

Meanwhile a separate company was dispatched to plunder the nearby monastery.

Cathal and his monks resisted, but they were not trained warriors. Out of deference to their calling the Connachtmen did not kill them, merely trussed them up like fowl and left them on the bank of the Shannon to watch helplessly as the roofs of Kill Dalua burned.

But the fires set at the monastery were nothing compared to the damage done to Kincora.

Mac Liag came pelting down the road with the skirts of his robe hiked up around his knees. He had not run in decades, but he ran now. Cumara sprinted beside him, pleading with him to go back, but his words were wasted on the wind.

"Kincora," Mac Liag panted over and over. "Kincora."

In his camp beyond Cre's Wood, Donough was just preparing to move out and resume his journey when he heard the sound of faraway shouting. Almost at once the shout was picked up by a woodcutter nearby and passed along.

"Kincora is attacked!"

Thunderstruck, for a moment Donough could not gather his thoughts. Then he bellowed a hasty succession of orders.

"You have no reason to go back there now," Gormlaith tried to argue with him. "It's Teigue's responsibility. You and I are going to Alba to . . ."

"You're staying here! Ronan, you and a dozen men stay with her and take care of her. The rest of you come with me—to Kincora."

They rode away at a gallop, leaving Gormlaith standing in the road, furious.

When Donough reached the east bank of the Shannon, the sky was stained with greasy smoke from the conflagration across the river. His company galloped headlong through the ford, sending up a spray whose individual droplets reflected the blazing thatch visible above the tops of the palisade. Men and women could be seen running down to the river for endless futile buckets of water, while others streamed away from the fortress, carrying salvaged property beyond the reach of the flames.

"Where's Teigue?" Donough shouted at the nearest man as he reached the west bank of the river.

The man, carrying a wine cask that had been pressed into service as a water bucket, was covered in soot. There was a smear of blood across his forehead and his eyes seemed unfocussed. "Gone to Cashel," he managed to say.

"And left Kincora undefended?"

"Och no, there were guards here . . . but they came so fast . . . so unexpected . . ." The dazed man struggled to organize his thoughts.

"Who came?"

"Connachtmen." The other drew a deep breath, steadied himself, declared vehemently, "This would never have happened if your father were still Ard Ri!"

Donough gave a groan of anguish.

The great gates gaped ajar. From inside came the crash of burning timbers.

Chapter Thirty-four

Leaving his wife and children at Cashel, Teigue sped to Kincora with his steward, Enda, and the historian Carroll. By the time they arrived the last ember had been extinguished, however.

A forlorn spectacle remained.

Most of the wooden parts of the fortress had been destroyed by the fire, including several sections of palisade. Stone walls still stood, but the mortar had been damaged by the heat and many stones were cracked. Extensive repairs would be needed before Kincora was usable again.

Teigue paced through the rubble, pausing from time to time to pick up a bit of debris. "They were very thorough," he remarked bitterly. "Look at this, Enda."

"One of the hinges from the watergate," the steward affirmed, examining the warped and twisted iron.

"Can Odar the smith repair it?"

"If not, he'll melt it down and reforge the piece. But I'd say it will take some time with the smithy working at white heat before all the metalwork is replaced. And as for the timber . . ."

Carroll interjected gloomily, "Gone. Gone forever, the timber that rose at Brian's command."

Teigue lifted his head. "You sound like Mac Liag. Where is he, by the way?"

Cathal Mac Maine supplied the answer. When the Abbot of Kill Dalua learned of Teigue's return, he hurried to Kincora from the sanctuary he and his monks had taken on Holy Island in Lough Derg.

Cathal was a coldly angry man. "You left us undefended," he accused Teigue with no pretense at pleasantries.

"I left an adequate garrison here. They . . ."

"They were fat and complacent and the Connachtmen
swept over them like the tide. At the end of the day they
were battered senseless, no more use than a cauldron made
of butter. The only real warriors we've seen in a fortnight
are the ones who came with your brother."

"My brother? Donough? What was he doing here?"
Teigue asked in surprise.

"He came faster than you. And when he saw what had
been done to Kill Dalua—and to this place, of course—he
set off at once to retaliate."

"Donough?"

"'Vengeance is mine, saith the Lord,'" Cathal intoned.
"Yet seeking revenge in this instance is a noble act and I do
not blame him for it. In this past year alone, the monasteries
of Clonmacnois and Clonfert and Kells have all been
attacked by looters. Ireland is going mad. Have you not
noticed?"

Aware that Carroll was listening to this exchange with
interest—and would undoubtedly memorize every word—
Teigue retorted with rising anger, "Of course I've noticed,
but I don't know what you expect me to do about it. I'm
King of Munster and those monasteries are in—"

"Kill Dalua is in Munster," Cathal interrupted him, "and
so is Kincora."

Teigue's thoughts returned to Donough. "What I don't
understand is my brother's plan. Is he attacking the Connachtmen on his own?"

"Not the Connachtmen. He has gone to seek reprisal
from Malachi Mor."

Teigue was dumbfounded. "Malachi Mor? Has Donough
lost his mind?"

But a fierce and joyful light had begun to burn in the eyes

of Carroll. "Yes!" the historian said under his breath, smacking his fist against his palm. "Yes, Donough!"

Teigue shot him a puzzled glance. "You approve of this? He is usurping the privilege that is mine."

"You weren't here," interjected Cathal Mac Maine.

Teigue fought to keep his temper by trying to change the subject. "Where is Mac Liag?" he inquired. "I expected to find him here composing another lament."

From somewhere behind them came a great crash as two men with a team of oxen pulled down what remained of a terminally damaged wall. Cathal started at the sound, then gathered himself and replied, "To our deep sorrow, Mac Liag has recited his last lament. When the fire began he came running as if it was his own home burning, but the effort was too much for him. He fell in the road and died, just outside the gates. May God be merciful."

"Dead?" Teigue could not imagine Mac Liag dead. The man had been a fixture of his world since boyhood.

Cathal nodded. "Though his son was with him, nothing could be done. His heart cracked, they said, as the stones cracked at Kincora."

There was a pained silence. The men stood in a little cluster in the center of the destroyed fortress, bowing their heads. One must be quiet and reverent in the hours after death, while a soul was standing in front of its Creator for judgment.

At last Carroll said, "Where is Mac Laig's son now? I would like to talk to him. The last words of the chief poet of Ireland should surely be commemorated."

"Cumara has gone north," was the reply. "Gone with Prince Donough in search of reprisal."

Donough raged up the Shannon as far as Lough Ree and attacked the Stony Island and the Island of the White Cow, where Malachi kept a small garrison and a fleet of boats for river transport. He and his warriors swooped down on the unsuspecting Meathmen, routed them completely, carried the boats away and took a number of hostages. The raid was a spectacular success in which they did not lose a man.

Chapter Thirty-five

✠

Every step of the way, I could feel my father looking over my shoulder. The idea of attacking Malachi's garrison on Lough Ree had come, I firmly believed, from the unseen spectator who not only guided my actions but had begun controlling my emotions as well.

As I lay wrapped in my cloak the night after our raid on the Island of the White Cow, I felt as if I need only put out my hand to touch an aged giant whose hair was frosted with silver. I was so convinced I whispered, "Are you there?" He did not answer, but an almost tangible sense of his presence reassured me.

He had come to me while I stood amid the appalling destruction at Kincora. Come with his fierce, proud spirit pouring over me, entering me to use as his instrument.

Brian would waste no tears weeping over what was done. He would act for the future.

As if I looked through his eyes, watching Ireland from some remote remove, I saw quite clearly the situation that now existed. The center had collapsed. The former Ard Ri had governed through an exercise of intellect and will, foreseeing problems, laying long-range plans that engendered a sense of confidence in the people. Malachi Mor, with all the goodwill in the world, could not fill his place. Malachi saw only what was in front of his nose. He did not act; never had. He only reacted.

The root cause of the destruction surrounding me was not the men of Connacht. They were, as was the rest of Ireland, simply responding to changed circumstance.

The real cause was Malachi Mor.

I could not challenge him; not yet. I had only a handful of warriors by comparison to the armies he could summon from the kings' tributary to him. Ulster and Leinster, Munster and Connacht were all obliged to supply warriors to the Ard Ri.

But I could issue a warning. Warn Malachi, then set about putting myself in position to make a formal challenge.

Suddenly I saw it all spread out in front of me like a map on a table.

In that moment all independence of action was taken from me. My father took command. My subsequent actions were dictated by him. I believed it then, and I believe it now.

My cousin Cathal Mac Maine would have said I was possessed, I suppose, and seen it was a device of the Devil.

Mac Liag had once told me my father was haunted by a druid woman. I, in my desire to emulate him, had imagined myself haunted by Padraic's daughter.

After Kincora burned, I was haunted by something very different.

Chapter Thirty-six

✠

Gormlaith approved.

When Donough returned to the camp near Ros Cre with the Meath warriors he had taken hostage, she would give him no peace until he recounted the event to the smallest detail. Then she gloated, "That's a fist in the eye for Malachi!"

As Fergal remarked sarcastically to Ronan, "Being a former husband of the Princess Gormlaith is a sure way to earn her undying enmity."

To Donough's grateful surprise, he did not have to explain his reasons for the raid on Lough Ree to his mother. She understood at once with an unfeminine political acumen. "Of course you had to take reprisal against Malachi; he is ultimately responsible for the disintegration of the kingdom. Such a successful raid into his own territory will carry a clear message. From now on he must see to it personally that your interests at least are protected, from Connachtmen or anyone else. Furthermore, you have made it plain that Kincora is one of *your* interests, thus outshouting your wretched brother."

At Dun na Sciath, Malachi indeed got the message. He was horrified. "I am no longer a young man," he protested to his sons. "How am I to cope with another fiery-eyed Dalcassian? Was not one in a lifetime enough?"

His sons were having the same worry. A repetition of their father's humiliating rivalry with Brian Boru was the last thing they wanted. "If this isn't an open revolt against your authority," counseled Ardgal, "don't blow it up into one. Make an offer for your hostages—one large enough to be tempting but not so large as to encourage a repeat of the incident—and when Donough accepts, make peace with him."

"But why did he do it?" wondered Conor, Malachi's youngest son.

The High King favored him with a morose stare. "Because he's a Dalcassian. I suspect this is his way of warning me that he is angry over the destruction of Kincora. The Dal Cais tend to think in twists and spirals, and act accordingly. I like things simple, straightforward. We of clan Colman are not such a devious breed."

Malachi's son Ardchu said nothing. But he thought to himself that perhaps being devious paid, if the success of the Dal Cais was any example.

Donough waited in his camp, and as he had expected, within a few days emissaries from Malachi, riding fast horses, arrived to make arrangements for the return of the hostages. They met with him in the privacy of his tent, where they were almost painfully formal. He was glad they had come promptly; feeding the two score warriors he had taken was straining the patience of his own warriors. On them fell the task of hunting and foraging, and the Meathmen were voracious eaters.

Gormlaith continually advised her son on how to treat them while they were in his custody. "Give them the best of everything, so they will have no cause to speak against you when they return to Malachi. Make them think you have unlimited resources at your disposal. That's what *he* always did."

But Donough did not need her advice.

In return for the freedom of the hostages, Malachi's emissaries brought Donough twelve horses, twelve fur-bordered cloaks, and, last but by no means least, a massive gold ring. Within their hearing Donough pretended to be dissatisfied. "The least he could have done was send us one horse for each man we are holding," he grumbled.

But secretly he was delighted. The horses would be useful for the rest of their journey to the coast, where they could be exchanged for passage to Alba. The cloaks would be handsome gifts for the court of Malcolm the Second.

As for the ring . . .

He took it to Cumara. "Have you seen this before?" he asked Mac Liag's son.

"I have. The last time I saw it, it was on the hand of the Ard Ri . . . the former Ard Ri, that is."

Donough nodded. "I thought so. How did Malachi get it?"

"He is an honorable man, whatever his faults," Cumara replied. "If you're thinking he may have stolen it from Brian's dead hand I'd say you are mistaken. Your father probably gave it to him before the battle at Clontarf. Perhaps they exchanged rings as a pledge of alliance."

"And now he has sent it to me. What am I to read into this, Cumara?"

"Whatever you wish, I suppose. My mind is not the sort that interprets the games chieftains play."

Donough smiled thinly. "Mine is."

He slipped the ring on the forefinger of his left hand, leaving the right hand unencumbered for the sword. It fitted perfectly.

After the Meathmen had departed with the hostages, Donough held a little celebration in the camp beyond Ros Cre. His men threw more sticks on the fire than necessary and one played a pipe, while another drummed the bodhran.

Donough sat with his back against an oak tree, listening. His seat was a pile of autumn leaves; his cup held clear water from a nearby spring. No poet entertained him, no servants shuttled to and fro carrying heaped platters, but he was content. Almost content . . .

Cera . . .

Resolutely, he pushed the thought of her from his mind. Yet like the smell of woodsmoke she lingered at the edge of his consciousness, sweet, haunting . . .

No!

Standing up abruptly, Donough brushed himself off like a man ridding himself of cobwebs. He caught his mother watching him.

"What's that ring on your finger?"

"Just a ring."

"Let me see," she demanded imperiously.

He held out his hand for her perusal. Gormlaith's eyes glittered. "This was your father's."

"It was."

"How did you come by it?"

His reply was studiedly careless. "He wanted me to have it. It's part of my inheritance."

Gormlaith raised her eyebrows.

When they were preparing to break camp and move on toward the coast and Alba, Cumara came to Donough's tent. His serious face was more serious than usual.

"Since you have your father's ring, I think you should have this too," he said, holding out a leather bag. "I brought it away with me from home, I did not think it wise to leave it there unattended."

For a moment Donough's heart leaped into his throat. The sword! The sword after all!

Then he realized the bag was the wrong size and shape. Strangely, however, his hands trembled as he reached for it.

"Your father left it with mine," explained Cumara, "before he marched away toward Dublin. My father believed he knew what fate would befall him, and was making his preparations. Like telling you of your inheritance."

Slowly, reverently, Donough reached into the bag and drew out a small bardic harp.

The instrument possessed a curved forepillar with a T-formation thickening, a relatively shallow soundbox, and an elegantly curved neck. Abstract Celtic and zoomorphic Scandinavian motifs were carved together into the polished willow wood. A ribbon of finest gold wire traced the curve of the neck, the pins were of silver, and the nine brass strings, though slightly tarnished, were sound.

The two men gazed at the harp in admiration. At last Cumara said, "Many's the time I've seen your father sitting in our house with this on his lap. He preferred the slow airs to the sprightly ones, and kept his eyes closed when he played; it was as if no one else was there, only himself and the harp. I thought it a strange thing for a warrior to do."

Donough said nothing. But that night, their last night before setting out once more, he lay wrapped in his cloak with the ring on his hand and the harp beside him. From time to time he reached out and gently stroked the strings. Although he lacked the long fingernails necessary for playing the harp properly, it rewarded him with a ripple of sweet, clear sound that was almost bell-like.

"How long would it take to learn to play you?" he whispered.

As they rode eastward the next morning, he moved his horse close to Fergal's. "Who do you suppose has my father's sword?"

"I have no idea."

"My mother has a theory; she doesn't believe it was put in his tomb in Armagh."

Fergal squinted between the pricked ears of his horse, assessing the road ahead. "She's probably right. King Brian's famous sword that knew how to win wars would be too much of a temptation."

"Who would take it? Can you guess?"

"I cannot, but I would say any of the warriors might have

done it. Or even Malachi Mor himself. There was magic in
that sword."

"Magic." Donough's eyes were briefly dreamy.

As he rode, he imagined the great sword in its scabbard,
belted around his waist. He could almost feel its weight
against his thigh. The blade was so long only a very tall man
could wield it, and the heavy, counterbalancing hilt was
designed for huge hands.

Huge hands. Donough looked at his own.

They were big enough.

The weather grew cold and bitter, and Donough began
forcing the pace. Once winter set in it would be hard to persuade a shipowner to transport his retinue across the Irish
Sea. Even the Vikings abandoned the northern seas during
the season of storms.

Twice more they were attacked by outlaws, but in both
instances, and with increasing anger, Donough repelled them.

When they neared Dublin they swung north, made a
wide circle around Sitric's stronghold, and angled toward
the coast. Their route took them past a tiny chapel dedicated to Saint Mobhi, where they stopped long enough to
drink from the saint's holy well. The water was curiously
bitter, yet left a sweet aftertaste on the tongue.

For some reason, that taste reminded Donough of Cera.

They reached the tiny fishing village of Skerries shortly
before sunset on an evening when sky and sea and air were
all a cold, stony blue. Beyond the curving arm of a sandy
beach, several islands were visible, the nearest only a short
distance away. A collection of currachs and coracles was
beached on the strand, upended so they resembled the black
carapaces of giant beetles entangled in a web of drying
fishing-nets.

"We shall make camp outside the village," Donough
decided, "and in the morning we'll inquire about passage to
Alba. I want to take Fergal and Cumara with me, and you,

Ronan, with four of your best men. And my mother, of course," he added unenthusiastically. "The rest of you can return to Thomond with my thanks."

His mother had surprisingly little to say. She stood in her cart staring at the expanse of open water with an unreadable expression.

Arranging transportation to Alba took several days, for none of the little fishing boats was capable of carrying a large party such a distance, even if their owners had been willing to undertake the journey with winter coming on. But at last a local man whose wife's brother had married the daughter of a Hiberno-Dane undertook a complicated negotiation on Donough's behalf, and succeeded·in hiring a battered Viking longship, replete with dragon-headed mast.

The vessel would be crewed by Danes and captained by the owner, a Dane called Ragnald, whose ship would otherwise be idle in the off-season. He considered a dozen horses an unexpected windfall and accepted them gladly to pay the fare, though when he realized his passengers would include a red-haired woman he upped the price.

"Red-haired women at sea are terrible bad luck," the Dane insisted.

When the time came for boarding, Donough's escort, none of whom had ever made a sea voyage before, stood aside to a man.

"You first," Fergal told him cheerfully.

Are you with me? Donough silently asked the unseen presence that had impelled him this far.

No discernible response.

When he stepped into the boat, the others followed.

Donough was surprised by the feel of the boat. The wooden planking beneath his feet seemed unexpectedly thin, so that he was aware of the sea below as if it were a living creature. The water moved, heaved, had a mind of its own, and he was about to ride on its back with only a timber shell to protect him from its whims and vagaries; its savagery.

But this is more than my father ever did, he reminded himself. Then, to that unseen presence, he added, *We take a great leap now*.

Chapter Thirty-seven

✠

Writing in the annals of Kill Dalua at the end of the year, Declan recorded, "The Age of Christ, 1017. The third year of the second reign of Malachi Mor. In this year died a number of abbots, and a number of princes were slain, often by their own kinsmen. The son of the King of Leinster was blinded through treachery by Sitric of Dublin, and his brother likewise murdered. Malachi undertook predatory excursions into various kingdoms and many men were killed, including his son Congalach and his chief brehon. Teigue, King of Munster, undertook the rebuilding of Kill Dalua, but a great wind arose off the lake and three times stripped the roof from the chapel."

To supervise the reconstruction, Cathal Mac Maine left Holy Island and, with half a dozen monks, resettled himself rather uncomfortably in the damaged monastery. He quickly grew suspicious that Teigue's men were retaining the best building materials for Kincora while providing flawed stone and green timber for repairs to Kill Dalua. Swathed in righteous indignation, he set off to the fort to complain. None of his monks were asked to accompany him; he did not want them to witness their abbot in a display of temper.

As he approached the main gateway, Cathal met a party

of four headed in the same direction, three young men and a barefoot woman who was swathed in a hooded cloak. The leader was a freckled, angular man with red hair and a strangely familiar face, but Cathal could not identify him until he noticed the ornament the man wore on a chain around his neck. It was a bronze pendant of great antiquity and vaguely Gaulish style; a triskele, emblem of druidry.

"What are you doing here!" the abbot challenged, extending his blackthorn walking stick to bar their way.

"Our father sent us to help repair Kincora," Padraic's eldest son replied. "He is of the Dal Cais; it is our responsibility."

"We don't need your help. We have plenty of Christians to do the work, God-fearing men who will not leave pagan charms hidden under lintels."

Torccan's eyes flashed but he said evenly, "We merely seek to be useful. My brothers and I are able carpenters, and our sister can mix limewash and trim thatch. We do all the work on our father's holding; we can turn our hands to anything."

"Be that as it may, we have no need of you! Go back where you came from or . . . or . . ." Cathal choked on outrage. To regain his composure he lowered the walking stick and reached for the cross he always wore.

The moment his fingers closed on the holy symbol, words seemed to flow into his mouth. ". . . Unless you are willing to renounce your idolatry of sun and tree and embrace the true faith?"

No sooner did he utter the words than the abbot was suffused with a warm glow. His imagination leaped ahead to the spiritual rapture of conversion: impassioned prayer, patriarchal instruction, the opportunity to emulate sainted Patrick and bring the light of Christ's message to the benighted. God worked in mysterious ways. Perhaps the destruction wrought upon Kill Dalua and Kincora had been for the express purpose of drawing Thomond's remaining pagans out of the hills and delivering them to Cathal's ministry.

But Torccan was shaking his head. "We are not interested. You have your beliefs; we have ours. They have nothing to do with rebuilding Kincora."

I must keep my patience with these people, Cathal warned himself. An injudicious remark now might destroy a God-sent opportunity. "I remember your father as a Christian. Surely he would not deny his children the benefits of faith?"

Onchu, who had fierce blue eyes and a wedge-shaped jaw, spoke up. "We have faith, the Old Faith," he informed the abbot. "And we have knowledge, the true knowledge that comes from earth and sky and not from the minds of men no better than ourselves."

Druid rantings! thought Cathal, refusing to be insulted. He kept a firm hold on his cross. But at that moment he heard the wind moan on the slope of Crag Liath, and in spite of himself cast a superstitious glance in the direction of the mountain.

Following his glance, the youngest brother spoke. "You hear the voice of the gods," said Daman. "The old gods speak to us through the elements in language we understand; we need no Church to translate for us."

Daman was shorter than his brothers, thickset and stolid in appearance, but his face was stamped with an indestructible innocence. Be gentle with this one, Cathal cautioned himself. Be persuasive. Find common ground upon which to build, as the saints did in their first contacts with the pagans of Ireland.

"In the words of the blessed Patrick for whom your own father was named," Cathal said in his kindest tones, "our God is the God of all the people and also of the sun and the moon and the stars, of the high mountains and the deep valleys."

Daman blinked like a sleepy ox. "Then you and I worship the same gods already."

Cathal inhaled sharply. "Not gods. God. One God! He has one Son who is coeternal with Him, and together with the Holy Spirit they . . ."

"I thought you said one god," remarked Torccan, shifting weight from one hip to the other and folding his arms. "Now you're talking about three."

"Three in One, the Trinity. It is a great mystery that will be clarified when . . ."

"Mysteries are not meant to be clarified," a smiling Torccan said as if he was instructing a child. "Mysteries are necessary to remind us that there are things beyond our understanding and to keep us from being arrogant; they encourage the ecstasy of worship. We worship life. We enjoy everything it brings us, from the warmth of the sun to the refreshment of the rain. We do not know the source of either, but we hold them both holy and are enraptured by them.

"You Christ-men gain power by channeling man's inborn need to worship through yourselves as sole inter-preters of the spirits. You erect buildings and claim they house your god—as if a god could be contained in a building. But are you not discouraging people from learning to hear the voices of the Otherworld for themselves? And I wonder—do they find as much joy in your roofed rituals as we do in the singing of the grass?"

Cathal started to voice a protest, but Torccan went on relentlessly. "I must tell you, we find your custom of cele-brating the torture of your god and then eating him repel-lent. But if such practices make you feel better, that is your business—provided you do not try to force them on others. As for us, we neither need nor want your services. We only want to offer assistance to Prince Teigue."

The words of the despised pagan demonstrated such mis-guided intelligence and reasoning ability that Cathal was severely tempted to abandon his Christian forbearance and hit Torccan in the mouth.

But at that moment the woman in the cloak stepped forward. Pushing back her hood to reveal her face, Cera inquired sweetly, "Please, can you tell me if Prince Donough postponed his trip to Alba to help rebuild Kincora?"

Cathal was disconcerted. "What business is that of yours? What possible . . . ah . . . did I not see you at his wedding?"

When Cera lowered her eyes her thick lashes swept her cheeks. "We were outside. We were not allowed in."

A horrified Cathal was hastily fitting pieces together in his mind. "And his young wife died not long thereafter. You were angry at being excluded, so you put a curse on her. A pagan curse!" His face suffused with blood. "I demand you leave this place now and never return!"

Onchu said in a good-natured drawl, "I thought you wanted us to convert to Christianity."

Suddenly Cathal understood everything. These were demons sent to torment him. There had never been any hope of conversion; indeed, they were probably responsible for the wind that kept tearing the new roof off the chapel. They outnumbered him but he was not afraid. He would not let himself be afraid. He was Dal Cais, born to be a warrior. And God was with him.

They might tear and rend his body but they could not harm his Christian soul!

Shouting, "Begone, demons!" the Abbot of Kill Dalua brandished his walking stick like a spear and crouched in anticipation of their attack.

The four stared at him but made no move.

When the tension became unbearable, Cathal dropped to his knees and bent his head in prayer, beseeching God to be with him.

Torccan exchanged glances with the others, then with no word passing between them, the four edged away from the man who knelt like Saul on the road to Damascus.

Cathal did not hear them go, for his heart was pounding

too loudly in his breast. To the best of his knowledge no Christian had yet died at druid hands in Ireland; perhaps this was a special honor God had reserved for him. He waited, alternately cold with terror and hot with exultation. Time passed. A great wind soughed along the roadway, ruffling the trees on either side and lifting the hair at the edge of Cathal's tonsure.

He opened his eyes.

He was alone.

They followed the winding pathway up the shoulder of Crag Liath. Torccan led the way. As he shouldered through holly and hazel and hawthorn he could feel the summer-life draining from them, flowing back into the earth which would keep it safe until the next leaf-spring. There was peace on the mountain, the peace of time measured in seasons.

Over his shoulder he said, "It would be a mistake for us to go to Kincora now; it would only cause trouble."

"It would," Onchu agreed. "The abbot hates us."

Daman chuckled. "We did nothing to encourage him to like us." In a more sober voice he added, "We don't try to convert Christians, so why does the abbot want to convert us?"

"It is a tenet of the Christ-faith," replied his oldest brother, "that they must extend it to everyone."

"Why?"

"They think only they know the truth."

Onchu barked a laugh. "But there are as many truths as there are people! As soon insist we all have the same shape of teeth."

A mist descended, damp and clinging. Cera licked her lips to taste the moisture clinging to them. Sweet; so sweet.

Water in all its forms was holy.

The quartet emerged from a clump of trees to find themselves facing the bare gray rock for which the crag was named. As if at a signal, the mist lifted. When they turned around Thomond lay spread out below them. "I can see Kincora!" Cera cried with delight. "Och, Torccan; are you sure we cannot go there?"

"Father told us to stay out of trouble, especially since you are with us. It would have been better, little sister, if you had stayed at home with him."

"Failenn's at home with him," Cera replied with a toss of her head. "Besides, I insisted."

Daman chuckled again. "And we all know how stubborn you are."

"What if I am? Life is stubborn." She took a few steps down the slope and gazed toward the sprawling fortress below. Was he there? Would he feel her on the height above him?

But when she searched with her mind and spirit, she could feel no trace of Donough Mac Brian.

Her shoulders drooped.

Torccan said briskly, "Come now, Cera, we have things to do."

With a sigh, she turned and made her way back up to her brothers. From a pack on Torccan's back Onchu took a parcel neatly wrapped in deerskin. The others crowded close, each placing a hand on the parcel so that together they laid their offering before the stone.

Then they stood for a time in silence; Being With.

At last Daman said, "If we can't go to Kincora, how can we take part in the rebuilding as Father wanted?"

Cera smiled. "I know the answer to that question. We shall send strength to the builders."

Torccan nodded his approval.

"Will we do a pattern?" Onchu asked his sister.

"A wheel of strength," she affirmed. "Sunwise round." She reached for Daman's hand and took a step forward, bare foot against bare earth. Torccan and Onchu fell in behind them. With unselfconscious grace, Padraic's children began a druid dance. The rhythm they would follow was as old as time, and deep in their bones.

They sprang lightly off the ground, landing on the toes of their feet. The earth cushioned them. In perfect harmony they raised their right feet and placed them to the second beat of the silent music within them, then followed this step with a lightning-swift placement of the left foot. Right and left again for seven beats, ending with the left foot as they were turning to the right; sunwise.

Then one, two, three, backward and forward, flying feet, bodies as light as air, leaping, sidestepping, weaving through an ancient pattern.

When one full wheel was completed and before they began the next, Cera lifted her voice in song.

Below in Kincora, the men laboring to rebuild the damaged fort heard the larks of summer singing, though the day was chill with autumn. They redoubled their efforts, feeling more energetic, as if new life flowed through their veins.

The leader of the construction crew had just received a tongue lashing from the Abbot of Kill Dalua and was in no good mood, but even he relaxed and began to hum under his breath as he worked, forgetting the recent unpleasantness.

On his way back to the monastery, Cathal heard a sound which seemed to emanate from the dome of the sky. He paused, turned around, looked up. Saw nothing. But a chill ran up his spine and he began to trot, pounding the end of his walking stick into the ground with every step he took.

The sound followed him. He thought it a shriek, a moan, a demon's voice. By the time he reached the sanctuary of Kill Dalua he was red-faced and sweating.

"The ban shee!" he cried to an alarmed Brother Declan. "I heard the ban shee, and I am Dal Cais!"

Chapter Thirty-eight

In the autumn of 1017, Donough's hired longship had followed the Irish coast as far north as Rathlin Island, where they took aboard additional supplies, then struck out across open water. Upon reaching Islay, they had turned north again, hugging the deeply indented coastline and putting ashore at night to make camp.

In spite of Ragnald's frequent exhortations to Odin, the wind had been against them. Most of the time the ship relied on oar power rather than its one square sail. Beneath darkly overcast skies, daylight hours were defined by the relentless rhythm of the oars.

Donough's plan had been to circle northern Alba and come down the eastern shore almost to the Firth of Tay, which would put them near Glamis. A sea voyage had seemed preferable to a long and dangerous overland trek in unknown territory.

In actuality sea travel could be more hazardous than traversing the land, as the ship's owner reminded his passengers once their fare was paid and they were underway. "Raiders abound in these waters," said Ragnald, an axe-faced Dane with dark gold hair and a thrusting, predatory nose. "Not me, you understand," he added quickly. "I don't go Viking, I'm just a hard-working trader." His weatherbeaten face shone with unconvincing sincerity. "But as we round the northern coast of Alba we'll pass very close to the Orkneys, and no matter what the season, the Orkneymen take to the sea like sharks in search of prey."

"My son is well able for them," Gormlaith assured him.

But Donough spent considerable time clutching the gun-wale, scanning the horizon and speculating on just how one fought off Vikings at sea.

As the weather worsened he, like the rest of his party, had another reason for clinging to the gunwales. Their stomachs rolled and lurched like the waves beneath the boat. Even Ronan turned a peculiar shade of green.

Only Gormlaith did not surrender to her stomach. With a mighty effort of will, she stood erect in the dragon-headed prow with her face to the gale as if she was enjoying every moment. Her unbound hair whipped behind her like a banner. When nausea overcame her she simply leaned for-ward and pretended to be examining some object of intense interest in the waves.

"I love storms!" she proclaimed.

"That woman *is* a storm," Fergal muttered as he sat slouched in the bottom of the boat, hugging his stomach and tasting bile.

At the helm, Ragnald silently concurred. They had been underway less than a day when he realized his female pas-senger was none other than the infamous Kormlada. Old she might be, but it was said no female in Ireland was more skillful in pleasuring a man's private parts.

The very first night they camped ashore he had sidled up to Gormlaith as she sat amid a small collection of bags and boxes she insisted on unloading and keeping with her at all times. Her eyes had been fixed on the campfire, but she cut them in his direction.

"My women call me Ragnald Long-Knife. Can you guess why?" he inquired.

Recognizing the smug innuendo she had heard in a thou-sand other male voices, Gormlaith yawned with boredom. "No," she said tersely. She turned away from him and resumed gazing at the fire.

Ragnald had not expected a rebuff. Surely such an old

woman should be grateful for the attentions of a virile and vigorous Dane to heat the blood in her veins. He tried again. "We have a long journey ahead of us and the farther north we go, the colder the nights will be."

"Good. I like the cold."

"I have warm furs for my bed."

"Enjoy them. Fur makes me sneeze," she lied.

"Then perhaps we would be more comfortable in your bed?"

Gormlaith swung around and this time looked squarely at the man. Her eyes glowed like coals in their deep hollows. "You aren't going to be in my bed."

Something flashed in the firelight. To Ragnald's astonishment Gormlaith produced a knife out of nowhere; not the little household knife Viking women wore along with their shears and keys, but a serious dagger, honed sharp. In one lithe motion she was on her feet, holding its point to his groin.

"This is *my* long knife," she said in a conversational tone which was all the more deadly for its lack of emotion. "I am quite capable of using it to amputate yours."

Ragnald did not doubt she meant every word.

Nonplussed, he returned to his men and spent that night, and every night after, safely embedded among the Danish crew.

The Irish chuckled about the incident but kept their mirth to themselves. It would be unwise to offend men on whom their lives depended.

Gormlaith had no such inhibitions. Whenever Ragnald came too close to her, she openly sneered at him.

"The man's a sea raider for all he claims otherwise," Ronan advised Donough. "Can't you get your mother to be nice to him? He could slit our throats and toss us overboard any time he likes."

Donough gave Ronan a sardonic glance. "What makes you think I can get my mother to do anything?"

Gormlaith had nothing but contempt for Ragnald and his
kind. She was weary to the soul of the mindless lust of men
who neither knew nor cared about the person inside her
head. Furthermore the Danes stank, having rubbed themselves copiously with rancid grease to keep out the cold.
They could neither read nor write; she could not carry on
an intelligent conversation with any of them about subjects
that interested her. And as she told Donough, "I've seen
much bigger ships than this in the harbor at Dublin. Your
Ragnald is no wealthy merchant; he's a common pirate and
not a very successful one at that, to judge by his ship and
crew. You could have hired him for a great deal less."

"They cost so much," Donough informed his mother,
"because I had to bribe them to transport a red-haired
woman. Without you I could have saved half the fare."

Gormlaith shrugged one shoulder. "I'm worth it," was all
she said.

From the first day it loomed out of the mist, she thought
the west coast of Alba very beautiful. Deeply cut inlets and
innumerable small islands provided excellent hiding places
for sea raiders, but the overall effect was one of rugged
grandeur.

Past Cape Wrath, bouldered headlands soared up from
the sea like mythical beasts with gleaming shoulders. They
lacked the softening luxuriance of verdure, but Gormlaith
liked them the better for it. Taking an engraved mirror from
her chest of belongings, she gazed into its polished surface.

The softness is gone from my face too, she thought. Worn
away by the storms of my life. Now the bones show, and
they also have a rugged grandeur.

Putting the mirror away, she returned to her favorite
position in the prow of the longship. This time she did not
look ahead, however, but back; back toward the oarsmen
laboring on their benches.

I am old, thought Gormlaith, as men reckon old. I should
be wrapped in blankets and crouching by a smoky fire,

gumming my food. Instead I ride behind the dragon and Vikings—Vikings!—are taking me to Alba, a land even Brian Boru never saw.

She threw wide her arms and laughed.

Although the northern coastline appeared desolate at a casual glance, numerous small settlements were snugged behind the headlands. Coast-dwellers always anticipated trouble, and did not wait to learn if strangers were travelers or raiders. Whenever the longship drew close to shore, it met a rain of spears and shouted imprecations.

"Can they not tell us from Orkneymen?" Fergal asked Ragnald.

"They don't care. Anyone in a longship is a menace as far as these people are concerned."

Fortunately the Dane knew the area well enough to locate safe sites ashore for night camps, but nevertheless both he and Donough posted sentries.

Near Arbroath, they dragged their ship ashore and made a final night camp. Beyond a meadow of bracken, stands of pine and larch cut off their view inland. No sooner had they built a fire than a herd of excessively shaggy cattle with impossibly long horns materialized like ghosts at the edge of the meadow and stared curiously at the strangers. "I've not seen their like in the five provinces," Ronan murmured in wonder. But when he tried to get close for a better view they stampeded.

The others laughed. "I hope you have better luck with Alban women," jeered Fergal.

When Donough announced they would set out for Glamis at sunrise, his mother scowled. "Nonsense. You are a prince of Ireland, you cannot appear like a beggar at Malcolm's gates. It's a good thing I came with you to instruct you in proper behavior.

"We wait right here and send a messenger to Glamis with a formal announcement of your arrival, and request for a royal escort. We don't put one foot in front of the other until they come for us."

"But we're perfectly able to . . ."

Gormlaith's scowl deepened. "You are perfectly able to look like a total fool who knows nothing. Listen to me."

Fergal sided with Gormlaith. "The woman knows more about royal courts than any of us, yourself included," he said. "I would listen to her if I were you. You don't want to be left-footed here."

At Donough's request, Ragnald dispatched four of his men to Glamis to inform Malcolm of his guests' arrival.

Then they waited.

"We should have gone, Donough," fumed Ronan. "Myself and Fergal."

"Do you know the way to Glamis?"

"I do not, but I doubt if those Danes do either."

Donough smiled. "I'm sure they do. Ragnald knows Alba far too well; I would say his ship has sailed these waters many times before, and not on innocent trading ventures."

"If that is so, will the Scots let his men get anywhere near Glamis?"

"They carry a formal message from a prince of Ireland, written in his own hand," Gormlaith interjected. "No matter what the circumstances, only a sentry who did not value his head would refuse to take them to his king. A messenger must be as sacrosanct as a bard or nothing could be accomplished."

While they waited for word from Malcolm, Donough tried to keep his mind occupied by envisioning the future. *If Malcolm likes me, if I can form some sort of alliance with him—then how do I use it? To challenge Teigue for Munster?*

Or to challenge Malachi Mor?

Donough ambled down to the edge of the dark water that had carried him this far, and stood gazing not outward, but inward, troubled by the amorphous quality of his ambition.

I should have a more exact idea of what I mean to do. Life is short, any warrior knows that much.

I want . . . but what do I want?

What did my father want when he was young?

Peace, surely. Ireland in his youth was ravaged by warfare, Gael and Viking at each other's throats. Brian won his battles and lived long enough to know he'd won them. But things are more complicated now. Clontarf forced the Northmen to abandon their dream of ruling Ireland, yet peace has slipped away from us again. We are plagued by struggles for power among the princes of the various provinces, while tribes and even clans fight among themselves. Then there are the outlaws . . .

The Ard Ri is supposed to solve all these problems; to settle quarrels and make judgments and rule the island in the pattern my father established. If Malachi Mor fails to do so, the next High King must. The Irish grew accustomed to stability under Brian Boru, that's why there is so much upheaval now. They want the old days back.

As Ard Ri, I will be expected to restore them.

To devote my life . . .

Donough gazed unseeing at the dark water.

It was not too late. He might still say to his mother, "This is a mistake, I want to go back to Ireland and . . . and . . ."

He could not think of what else he might do. Princes followed the path their fathers trod; it was ever so. How could it be otherwise?

Unwilling to be alone with his thoughts any longer, Donough returned to camp. His men were sitting around the fire, telling tales of war. Gormlaith occasionally joined in, taking evident relish in describing battles fought and men killed for her sake.

Donough stood outside the ring of firelight, listening. His brooding gaze wandered over the familiar faces in the gilding light. How simple things were—for them.

War and war and war, a voice said clearly. Startled, he whirled around. But there was no one there.

Yet the voice went on. *Kill or be killed, and where's the glory in it? When a sword runs through you, your bowels open and you die in your own stink.*

"Is that you?" Donough whispered, shocked. *"Father?"*

No one answered.

In due course an escort from Glamis arrived: a company of men in heavy woolen tunics, with gaudy plaids slung over their shoulders. Their features were similar to the Irish and they spoke, roughly, the same tongue, but their accents were so thick Donough could scarcely understand them.

They brought sturdy Pictish ponies onto which they loaded the travelers' baggage. There was no cart for Gormlaith, but their leader explained that no one had mentioned a female being with the party. "Besides," he added, "what kind of woman are ye that your legs don't work?"

Crimson flamed in Gormlaith's cheeks. Without a word, she strode out ahead of them, determined to walk them all into the ground before they reached Glamis.

Ragnald and his men were busily preparing the longship for the return voyage to Ireland. "Real winter is a snowflake away," the Dane told Donough. "No one sails these seas then. You are here until spring; I trust you know that?"

"We know."

"You are here no matter what happens. Do you understand me?"

"Are you giving me a warning?"

"I'm just saying that you cannot leave Alba until the seaways open again. And take it from one who knows—these people, for all they look like you, are not Irish. They have been here too long, they sing different songs now. Don't trust them."

Donough laughed. "This, coming from a Viking!"

Ragnald shrugged. Having delivered his passengers, he had no further interest in their fate.

But as Donough and his party entered the first stand of

trees between themselves and Glamis, the Dane impulsively cupped his mouth with his hands and bellowed, "Remember what I said!"

Chapter Thirty-nine

The composure for which Blanaid was famous deserted her entirely.

She had been delighted to learn that her brother was actually in Alba. With Malcolm—as so often—away from Glamis, holding court at Scone, it fell to his wife to organize an escort to bring the guests to the castle. While she waited she busied herself with ordering a feast and overseeing the airing of a chamber suitable for a prince.

When Donough's party arrived, Blanaid was waiting for them at the entrance to the great hall. Her face was wreathed in smiles as she held out both her hands to her brother, recognizing him at once by his likeness to Brian Boru. He towered a head taller than the men around him.

"I apologize for not having an attendant waiting for you," Blanaid said to the person who pushed forward to stand beside him. "I did not know my brother was bringing a woman with him."

"Not just a woman," came the swift reply. "I am his mother."

Blanaid was taken aback. "Gormlaith of Leinster?"

"Of course," snapped the other woman. "How many mothers has he?" She strode imperiously past Blanaid and surveyed the hall through narrowed eyes. "So this is Glamis. Well, I must say, it looks no better from inside than from out. What a dark, dismal place. You have no windows!"

Blanaid made a swift recovery. "Glamis," she said coldly, "has been a noble stronghold for generations and is now the primary residence of the King of the Scots and the Picts. May I remind you that you are a guest here, and as such you have no right to insult . . ."

Gormlaith chuckled. "Och, may I remind you I'm no guest here. You never invited me. I just came."

Blanaid turned toward Donough. In the moment before her eyes met his she could have sworn he was grinning, but when she looked at him full face he was suitably sober. "The Princess Gormlaith is a law unto herself," he told his sister.

Blanaid was trembling. Her face felt bloodless. "My . . . our father is dead because of her. How dare you bring her here!"

This time Gormlaith laughed outright, a rich, throaty sound as disconcerting as it was unexpected. "He couldn't have stopped me. And your father is not dead because of me. He's dead because your daughter's husband Sigurd, among others, tried to wrest control of Ireland from him."

"The 'others' you mention include your own son Sitric and your brother Maelmordha!" Blanaid retorted furiously.

"They're all dead now," the other replied, unruffled, "except my son Sitric, and he doesn't amount to much if the truth be known. This one here is twice the man, that's why I thought it was time you two should meet."

"*You* thought . . ."

"Of course. Donough was not going to come, but I insisted. And a long journey it has been, I must say. Days at sea in an open boat, nights sleeping on cold ground—and I hate the cold! Surely you intend to offer us some heated water for bathing our faces and feet, and then a hot meal?" Gormlaith fixed Blanaid with a wide-eyed, ingenuous gaze. "I have it on good authority that no one will cross the sea in winter, so we shall be with you for months and months."

No member of Malcolm's court had ever seen his Irish

wife nonplussed—until she faced the Princess of Leinster. While she recovered, Blanaid fell back on the immutable tradition of Gaelic hospitality which was the same in Alba as in Ireland. Guests, even if they were mortal enemies, were entitled to the best a household had to offer.

Malcolm would not forgive her if she did less.

But the emotions surging through her were hard to control.

Seeing Donough was almost like seeing a youthful version of her father. She wanted to throw her arms around him, draw him down beside her and talk about Ireland and Kincora, invoke the song of the cuckoo and the screech of the corncrake, the taste of buttermilk, the baying of a red-eared hound. She wanted him to take her home again with his words and memories.

Instead he had brought Gormlaith.

In the king's absence, Blanaid presided over the banquet in the hall. "Make certain only the best of everything is served," she instructed Malcolm's steward, "and seat my brother's mother with us, as you would any visiting noble. Just put her as far from me as possible. You understand?"

She spoke coldly, precisely, her spine rigid with indignation. Malcolm when he returned would find no fault with her hospitality in his name. Pride would carry her through.

The banquet was served in the hall, with the guests seated on benches drawn up to a massive single slab of oak, and the rest of Malcolm's court eating from small trestle tables. As at Kincora, great hounds roamed through the room, devouring the gnawed bones that were tossed onto the straw-strewn floor. But Glamis was darker than Kincora. It was built entirely of stone, and interior illumination was provided exclusively by torches soaked in pine pitch then mounted in iron holders on the walls. They cast a flickering, baleful glow. The air smelled resinous.

Gormlaith remarked irritably, "There's no grianan in this

wretched place. How do women survive here without a sunny-room?"

Fergal Mac Anluan took note of the fact that the shields hung on the walls, painted in unfamiliar designs and color combinations, were badly dented. "I think survival does not come easy here for anyone," he said.

The meal was a nightmare for Blanaid. She could not eat, could only jab at her food with the point of her scian dubh. But Gormlaith ate enough for two, devouring roast venison and eel boiled in milk with an enthusiasm that belied her years.

"I thought old people lost their appetites," Blanaid murmured under her breath.

Seated at her right hand, Donough overheard. "As far as I know, my mother has lost none of her appetites," he told his sister. "I'm sorry about this. I can see it is hard for you. But she is my responsibility; I could not just go away and leave her."

"Could Sitric Silkbeard not have taken her in?" Blanaid inquired, the name bitter in her mouth.

Donough lowered his eyes. "Sitric doesn't want her. Or rather, his wife Emer doesn't want her. Gormlaith does live part of each year with them, but it invariably degenerates into war. And with Maelmordha dead she has no other close living kin except myself."

"Tell me of Emer," Blanaid said brightly, to change the subject.

But Donough could tell her little about their mutual half-sister. Emer, like Blanaid, lived a life apart from his, a life shaped by her marriage.

"She is as much a Viking now, I suppose, as I am Scots," Blanaid remarked, fingers plucking absentmindedly at the plaid shawl around her shoulders.

Brian's blood flows in surprising directions, mused Donough. By the light of smoking torches in iron sconces affixed to the walls, he covertly studied Blanaid's features, trying to find something familiar in her face. But she was a stranger to him. *I would not know her if I met her on the road. How odd.*

Then Gormlaith's laugh rang out in response to something one of the men said. Blanaid lifted her chin and squared her shoulders as if for battle, and in that proud, defiant gesture Donough found his sister.

"Why are you smiling?" she asked him.

"Because I remember our father carrying himself just so, the last time I saw him."

Catching Donough's hand, Blanaid gave it an impulsive squeeze.

That night a Scottish piper played in the hall at Glamis, and a troupe of jugglers put on a performance marred by missed catches. "They are tenants of my husband," Blanaid explained to Donough. "In Alba the king has the right to food-rent, and also to 'conveth,' to demand a night's entertainment from those who occupy his land."

"Is entertaining the king not an honor to be sought?" Donough wondered. His thoughts strayed to the harp in its leather bag with his other belongings.

"By some. We have our bards. But others"— Blanaid nodded toward the forlorn jugglers—"perform because they must. Otherwise they would be dispossessed."

"Does the land not belong to the tribe itself then, as in Ireland?"

"Alba is different, my brother. Here, a man claims as his own all the land he can conquer. The Brehon Law that still pertains in Ireland has been subsumed into other laws, other customs, in Alba. But the king is not a despot. Malcolm rules justly; he has a council of priests and mormaers to whom he must answer."

"Mormaers?"

"Somewhat like tribal tanists, men of royal blood who might conceivably have a claim on the throne. One such was Donall, the Great Steward of Mar, whom Malcolm sent to fight on the side of Brian Boru at Clontarf."

A movement at the end of the table alerted Donough to the fact that his mother had leaned forward and was listening avidly to this conversation. "How clever of Malcolm!" Gormlaith cried. "Imagine being represented by both Sigurd of Orkney and the Steward of Mar. I admire a man who fights on both sides at the same time. He cannot lose."

Donough shot his mother a warning glare, but she ignored him.

As the torches began to burn out and courtiers were nodding over their cups of ale, the blast of a horn reverberated outside like a shriek of doom. There were immediate sounds of uproar in the courtyard, and through the open doors of the hall Donough heard a hoarse male voice shouting invective.

"My husband," Blanaid remarked calmly, "seems to have returned early."

Soon Malcolm strode into the hall, bringing with him the smell of sweat and horse dung and fresh night air. "Where's Brian Boru's son?" he demanded to know.

Before Blanaid could answer, Donough was on his feet. He lifted his chin and squared his shoulders as if for battle.

Then he deliberately kicked over the bench on which he had been sitting.

"I am Donough of Thomond," he said.

They talked late into the night. Or rather, Donough talked and Malcolm listened. The King of Alba wanted to hear all his guest could tell him of the battle of Clontarf and the ensuing political situation in Ireland. Donough gave him as many facts as he could, aware that from time to time Malcolm nodded as if comparing his words with those of other informants.

This would be a dangerous man to lie to, warned the voice in his head.

At last Malcolm sat back and thoughtfully fingered the massive silver cup from which he drank his ale. "Now tell me about yourself," he commanded. "You come from a race of warriors; what sort of fighter are you?"

Donough had never heard the question put quite so bluntly. "I am adept with sword or axe, and I can hurl a spear for at least a . . . "

"That isn't what I mean. Do you fight because you must, or do you enjoy it?"

Donough paused to consider. "I enjoy winning."

"Ah." Malcolm's dark eyes glowed. "Which do you feel more strongly? The desire to win—or the fear of losing?"

Again Donough paused. Then he chose the heroic answer, thinking it was expected. "The desire to win, of course. I have no fears."

Malcolm laughed. "By the holy rood, lad, you have a lot to learn! When the day arrives—and it will—that you feel a healthy jolt of pure terror, come to me and I may have some use for you in my army. A fighting man needs to know fear and how to get beyond it, or he's no use."

"I have no interest in fighting in Alba. There are wars enough in Ireland to keep me occupied."

"And what do you hope to get out of them, those Irish wars? From what I understand, you have no kingship and no power. Do you not covet your brother's Munster?"

Do not answer. That is not a question to be answered publicly or to this man.

"I want only what I deserve," Donough said carefully.

Malcolm leaned forward. "And your inheritance, did you not deserve that? Ah, don't look so surprised. We know many things here. For example, I know that you were hard-done-by, Donough, and you have every reason to be resentful."

"I'm not resentful."

"Nor afraid. You are a wonder, a creature with no human feelings at all," Malcolm said sarcastically. Then his tone changed. "But we might make a man of you yet. You will stop with us for the winter and perhaps we may be of benefit to one another.

"Your father was an ally of mine, though we never met in person. I admired him, and he entrusted me with his daughter. For that I owed him."

Donough suddenly felt uncomfortable. "Do you resent my bringing Gormlaith with me? Blanaid does, she already made that plain. Like many people, she holds my mother guilty, at least in part, for my father's death."

Malcolm gave a negligible wave of his hand. "No woman is capable of bringing down a giant. The Princess of Leinster was part of the bait, but the battle would have been fought with or without her. Ireland is a rich prize and your father had made too many enemies.

"It was just unfortunate that one of them was your mother." Malcolm added, light rekindling in his eyes. "Perhaps a different man would have been more able for her."

A thin gray light was seeping into the hall when at last Donough was able to leave Malcolm and seek his bed. Blanaid had given him a chamber little bigger than a closet, but the best guest accommodation the castle had to offer. He must share it with his noble cousin Fergal, however. Ronan and the other men were already asleep on the floor of the hall, and Gormlaith had been ushered to some closet of her own, arranged at the last minute at her vehement insistence.

Weary beyond weariness, Donough tumbled onto the feather-filled pallet where Fergal already lay snoring. But when he closed his eyes they would not stay closed.

He nudged Fergal. "Do you want to hear something surprising?"

"Yes," muttered the other. "I want to hear that you'll let me sleep."

"The King of Alba is interested in Gormlaith."

With a strangled snort, Fergel came fully awake. "What do you mean?"

"I mean he asked me all sorts of questions about her, personal questions. And the look on his face . . . "

"But she's an old woman." Fergal would have been shocked—had it been anyone other than Gormlaith.

"Malcolm's older than she is. Besides, did you notice her after he joined us in the hall? It might have been a trick of the torchlight, but I could have sworn she seemed prettier somehow."

"There are certain men, apparently," Fergal observed, "to whom your mother responds no matter what her age."

"And I'm telling you, Malcolm responds to her."

Fergal considered this in silence for a time, then said, "Well, I shouldn't think he would do anything about it. Don't take offense, but everyone knows what Gormlaith is—even if she is your mother."

Donough took no offense. Yet he could not help wondering before he finally fell asleep how many more surprises Alba would have in store for him.

From the moment Malcolm had learned her identity, Gormlaith had been aware of his eyes on her. Aside from a perfunctory greeting he did not speak to her while they were in the hall, but when an attendant led her from the room on her way to her chamber, he had nodded to her.

Gormlaith needed no one to interpret the nod.

Before collapsing on her pallet she opened some of the baggage she had brought and took out a carved wooden casket, heavily ornamented with silver and gems like a gospel shrine. By the light of a Norse seal-oil lamp she raised the lid, peered in, and smiled.

Malcolm spent the following day in consultation with his

council. When the sun began to set he was just heading for the hall when he encountered Gormlaith in a passageway.

She had slept most of the day. Upon arising, she sent for heated water into which she poured perfumed oil, then bathed her face, her body, her hair, refusing the help of an attendant. She had passed the stage where she was willing for any other woman to see her naked.

From an assortment of pots and jars she scooped various unguents which she applied assiduously. She stared critically into her mirror, wiped off some and reapplied others. Crushed ruam in beeswax was used to trace the rim of her ears, giving them a youthful flush; then she, with a bemused expression, cleaned her stained fingertips on the aureole of her nipples, rouging them too. Finally she poured a little more of the perfumed oil into the palm of her hand and rubbed it between her legs, at the tops of her thighs, where the curls were still red and springy.

She recalled with a stab of pain the very last time she had so decorated herself. For *him* . . .

But that was long ago. And very far away.

Gormlaith tried on half a dozen gowns before selecting one of sheerest linen, through which the shape of her breasts and belly was clearly visible. Satisfied with the effect, she combed her hair with a willow-wood comb and arranged its faded silk into elaborate swirls around her head and shoulders. Then she stood in the center of the small chamber, closed her eyes, and ran her hands slowly down over her body.

When Malcolm met her in the passageway, for a moment he did not recognize her. Last night it had been her notoriety that engaged his interest; her physical self, gaunt and aged and travel-worn, held no appeal.

But the Gormlaith he found himself facing now was transformed. Tall, glowing, she sauntered confidently toward him with a youthful sway of hips that distracted his eye from the lines on her face. In truth those lines seemed much less deep than he had first thought. She looked no older than his wife.

"Has my son given you the presents he brought? The cloaks?" she inquired.

"He did, last night in the hall after you had retired. A princely gift; I was grateful."

"I also have a gift for you," said Gormlaith. Her voice dropped into a lower register; husky, intimate. "But I would rather not present it in public, in the hall. When you see what it is, you will understand."

Malcolm drew a deep breath.

He knew exactly what this woman was—or thought he did. She radiated danger as a bar of copper left long in the sunshine radiated heat. But for a mature man like himself, who had seen and done much and knew how to handle himself in any situation, surely there was nothing to fear. He loved his wife as much as he was capable of loving anyone; he was not emotionally vulnerable to Gormlaith.

She would be merely a diversion; a form of exotica in a life which had offered nothing exotic before.

"I have a private chamber," he said.

Chapter Forty

The King of the Scots and the Picts was no skilled voluptuary, but had what he considered an adequate experience of women. From the first lass he had tumbled in a cow-byre when he was little more than a child, he had enjoyed the female sex as he enjoyed meat and drink and a good scratch. He was well acquainted with the landscape of the female body, and he knew enough about female moods to ignore them. In fact, apart from the occasional sexual conquests he still undertook when away from Glamis, he tended to ignore women. The fires of youth were far behind him and he had more important matters on his mind.

Yet from the moment Gormlaith swept into his private chamber carrying an ornamented casket, he felt as if he had been catapulted into unfamiliar territory.

"Sit there," she said peremptorily, indicating with a nod the bench next to the brazier where a fresh fire crackled. He started to protest, thought better of it, and, bemused, sat as she requested.

Pushing a small table in front of the bench, she placed the unopened casket upon it. Polished silver gleamed in the firelight. "No looking yet," she warned. "Have you mead, or is Alba too cold for bees and apples? That Danish ale you served last night is good enough for woodcutters and leather tanners, but I have a finer palate."

"We have good mead," Malcolm assured her, feeling uncharacteristically defensive. Raising his voice, he bellowed "Mead! To the king now!" The cry rang through stone passageways and a servant arrived at the run with a pitcher in hand.

Gormlaith stood waiting until two silver cups were brimming with the fragrant golden liquid, then she downed hers in a long, appreciative gulp, as straightforward as a man. She set the cup back on the table and glared at the servant. "Go!" she commanded.

The man went.

Gormlaith turned back to Malcolm. There was a smile in her eyes but not yet on her lips; a slow warmth full of possibilities. "Do you want to see what I brought you now?" she asked in that husky voice he remembered.

His mouth being unaccountably dry in spite of the mead, he merely nodded.

Gormlaith opened the casket. "A king should have a

king's gift," she murmured, bending forward to remove the contents.

Malcolm found himself staring into the neckline of her gown.

From the ornamented box, Gormlaith began removing chess pieces, intricately carved figures in ivory and polished basalt. Each piece was decorated with gold or silver, and the larger ones were set with gems. The white, Malcolm saw, were in Gaelic costume; the black pieces represented Vikings.

Pressing a panel on the bottom of the casket, Gormlaith revealed a folded chessboard that swung open to full size. Its squares were inlaid with the same ivory and black, and each square was outlined with a minute Celtic knotwork of gold wire.

It was the most beautiful object Malcolm had ever seen.

Gormlaith read the appreciation in his eyes. The smile in hers extended to her lips. "This was the chess set of . . . the former Ard Ri," she said.

He dragged his gaze away from the chess set and looked up at her. "How did you come by it?"

"I stole it."

"You what?"

She shrugged. "I stole it from Kincora. When I, ah, left there after our marriage was set aside, all I took was the clothes on my back, but later . . ."

"I heard that Brian threw you out."

Her eyes flashed. "We mutually tired of one another. But the point is, he did not return my full dowry to me; I was entitled to more. The last time I was at Kincora I took his chess set as part compensation, and now I give it to you."

Malcolm gaped at her, dumbfounded.

She arched an eyebrow. "Can it be you don't know how to play? Perhaps you might know one of the simpler Irish games, then; fidchell, or bran dubh? I'm sure my son has . . ."

"Of course I can play chess," he snapped, on the defensive again. "I learned on the Isle of Lewis."

"Then you will grant me a match?" Before he could answer she had drawn up a stool and seated herself facing him. She took a black pawn in one fist and a white in the other. "Choose one."

When he tapped her left fist with his forefinger, he felt a spark jump between them.

Never in his life had Malcolm played chess with a woman. Such games were an extension of warfare, requiring a masculine mind. But from the first moves, it was obvious Gormlaith was a skilled player. Soon he was fighting for survival as surely as he had ever fought on a battlefield.

He could feel sweat rolling down his back.

To his consternation, Gormlaith was able to play while carrying on a conversation. No sooner were they into the game than she began questioning him about his recent campaigns.

"I understand you recently defeated a large army of Northumbrians at Carham and now claim everything to the Cheviot Hills," she remarked as she moved a pawn deep into his territory.

Malcolm frowned at the chessboard. "You give me credit for my ambitions but not necessarily my achievements. There are regions not yet secure. Perhaps with the help of foreign allies . . . ?"

She glanced up with a demure smile. "I'm sure you will triumph," she told him.

When he looked down again he discovered she had captured his queen's bishop.

The pace of the game slowed. Gormlaith kept asking Malcolm questions he felt impelled to answer, which spoiled his concentration, and he was increasingly aware of her sensually, an awareness that grew into a thundering tension that was giving him a headache.

"What do you think of my son?" she inquired as she put one of Malcolm's rooks in jeopardy.

"When we met he kicked his bench aside. A bold gesture that attracted me immediately, I must admit. I tend to judge a man by small things." As he spoke Malcolm made a countermove he immediately regretted, certain it was a mistake.

"Och, he's bold enough. He just needs a little push, so to speak, to come into his own. I do what I can to counsel him and guide his moves . . . "—she moved her queen unexpectedly, devouring Malcolm's bishop—" . . . so that he can rise to the eminence he deserves."

The Scot gave her an appraising look from beneath his heavy eyebrows. "And you? A rise in status for Donough would elevate you as well, I presume."

She bit her lower lip and studied the chessboard.

"You like being allied to power, don't you?" guessed Malcolm.

Her green eyes met his with jolting force. "I like *having* power," Gormlaith replied.

The game continued.

The flickering firelight from the brazier cast grotesque shadows on the chamber walls. Malcolm was seated at an angle that left his face in darkness, though his hands were clearly visible on the chessboard. Gormlaith found herself studying them while she and the king discussed power and politics, schemes and strategy.

How pleasant it is, she thought, to converse once more with an equal. She was reminded of years ago, when *he* taught her to play chess and they used to talk for hours, long after everyone else had gone to bed, while the pieces swooped around the board and wars were won and lost.

Flattered by Gormlaith's interest, Malcolm began describing his successful campaign against an invading force of Orkneymen in Moray in 1010. "The Orkneys are a major base for the sea empire of the Norsemen," he explained. "In order to safeguard Alba from their depredations I had to prove I could defeat them in battle, but I also took the pre-caution of arranging an alliance with their most powerful family through marriage to one of my daughters. Since Sigurd's death, the son of that marriage is here with us at Glamis. A hard little boy called Thorfinn; I like to think I see something of myself in him."

"Perhaps we can profit from your example," Gormlaith commented.

"What do you mean?"

"If my son Donough is to attain the power he deserves, he needs an advantageous marriage. Left to his own devices he'll accept someone as unsuitable as his first wife. The poor thing was nothing more than a cattle lord's daughter; he could have done much better. Perhaps you and I can think of someone who would enhance his opportunities?" Her hands hovered over the chessboard.

"There are advantages to be gained from a clever politi-cal marriage," Malcolm agreed. "Unfortunately all my daughters are wed now or I would . . . " He fell silent, frowning over strategy.

Gormlaith heard what he did not say. "Your relations with Orkney may be amicable enough these days—but a king is always under siege of one sort or another. Perhaps we could marry my son to a woman whose connections would be of benefit to you. Since there are already alliances established between us," she added, smiling meaningfully.

The woman astonished him. Her mind went straight to the point like a well-thrown spear. Even as she was speaking he was thinking of Canute, of Dane and of Saxon to the south, of the great power struggle he sensed coming.

As the game progressed, Gormlaith became more and more aware of Malcolm's hands. Huge hands, with strong, well-shaped fingers. In the dim room it was impossible to tell if the hair on their backs was dark or bright.

It might have been red-gold.

She did not look up at his face. As long as she watched only his hands, she could almost imagine that someone else sat across the chessboard from her. Another king . . . another powerful man . . .

She drank a fourth cup of mead, a fifth, the fumes dancing in her brain. She laughed, she flirted, she dazzled him with the extent of her intellect. Sparkling like a polished gemstone, she displayed a dozen facets of Gormlaith.

The man whose face was in shadow became not one specific person, but the male audience for whom she had always performed. Moment by moment she felt the flesh growing firmer on her bones, the age melting out of her muscles. Like a river reversed, the years flowed backward until she was in Glamis no longer, but somewhere else . . .

. . . facing someone else across the chessboard . . .

The hair on the backs of his hands was a burnished red-gold.

Emotion she had thought long dead welled up in Gormlaith. Her eyes stung with long-forgotten tears.

A great, aching tenderness swept through her. She fought it back; to be tender was to be vulnerable, to be feminine and weak. Men took advantage of female vulnerability; she had learned that lesson with the first flush of her beauty.

There had been a time when she wanted desperately to explore the soft side of her nature. There had been one man to whom she longed to present the varied facets of Gormlaith; for him she would have been child and woman, devil and angel, seductress and playmate and friend. But fate had made them adversaries, even in the marriage bed. And he had died at Clontarf . . .

He had not died. He sat across from her now. She knew those hands, knew the skill with which they suddenly began to maneuver the chess pieces. She had never succeeded in defeating Brian Boru.

Gormlaith gave a little sob.

Startled, Malcolm glanced at her face.

Her eyes were immense and full of light. By some trick of the firelight she looked like a young woman, a spectacularly beautiful woman whose face glowed with passion.

Malcolm held power by never failing to recognize and take advantage of an opportunity.

With a sweep of his arm he knocked the priceless chess pieces off the board and onto the floor. He leaned across the emptied table and caught Gormlaith by the shoulders, drawing her face toward his.

Before the light could reveal his features, she closed her eyes.

The lips that crushed hers were hard and bruising, but she did not respond in kind. *Not this time. I have learned my lesson*, she thought. *He has come back to me and I have learned my lesson.*

She let her mouth go soft; let her body go soft in his arms as he stood and pulled her against him. All of her was a yielding and a giving, so opposite from what Malcolm had expected that he almost dropped her. He had thought to embrace a tiger; instead he held a virginal girl.

The change confounded him. He sought to soften his kiss and meet her gentleness with gentleness, but he did not know how. His mouth could only seize and devour. Angered by failure, he became more fierce than ever, running his hands down her body and ripping away her robe. The fabric bruised her flesh as it pulled and tore and she winced, but he paid no attention.

He thought she murmured, "Please, not this time," into his mouth, but he would not accept guidance from a mere female. He forced her backward and threw her down onto the floor, then hurled himself atop her.

"Lie still, woman; you're going to bed another king."

When she began to struggle he laughed. He forced a knee between her legs and fumbled with his clothes, aware that he had a massive erection.

Gormlaith! The ultimate prize, in his chamber, beneath him!

Chapter Forty-one

Contrary to his expectations, Cathal Mac Maine did not die. He was convinced he had heard the ban shee wail for him, but days, weeks, months passed, and the worst fate that befell him was increasingly severe rheumatism during a long, wet winter.

His dreams were haunted by echoes. Usually they took the form of a ban shee's keening, but occasionally they contained an underlying, mocking laughter.

"Those pagans have cursed me!" he complained bitterly to Brother Declan. "They put the ague in my bones."

Though the scribe had heard Cathal complain of joint pain for years, he dare not contradict his abbot. Keeping his thoughts to himself, he dutifully updated the annals and transcribed Cathal's letters. Early in 1018 sympathy was expressed to the Abbot of Kildare, whose monastery had been struck by lightning, and to the Abbot of Kells, whose abbey was plundered by Sitric Silkbeard and the Danes of Dublin. Cathal viewed both disasters in the same light.

For a letter to Malachi Mor, Cathal dictated, "We share your grief in this time of your trouble. The death of two of your sons, Ardgal and Ardchu, is a great loss. Sad it is for them that they were slain by the treacherous tribe of the Cenel Eoghain, rising against your authority. They shall be remembered in our prayers at Kill Dalua for a seven-night."

Privately, Declan thought a seven-night was a bit mean; the sons of the Ard Ri surely deserved a longer period of mourning. But everyone knew that during the reign of a good Ard Ri grain overflowed the storehouses and every cow had twins, while a bad Ard Ri inevitably brought on an era of calamities.

Disasters were indeed occurring, but Cathal was increasingly attributing them to the lingering paganism in Ireland, and more specifically to the druids themselves.

In this he was in the minority, even among his fellow clerics, as Declan well knew. Since the coming of Christianity to Ireland in the fifth century, a degree of tacit coexistence had marked the relationship of the Church with druidry. Christian missionaries almost from the beginning had realized that the druids had smoothed their path for them by teaching that the soul was immortal. Having this central belief in common helped make the conversion of Ireland bloodless. The New Faith was not so radically different as to be unacceptable to druids; in many instances, it was just a matter of changing the names of festival days, or grafting one superstition onto another.

Druids were members of the *filidh*, the intellectual class of Irish society which included teachers, sacrificers, healers, brehons, historians, philosophers, and poets. Some of these functions the Church appropriated unto itself, but others were still very much the realm of the druid. Christianity had as yet made no concerted effort to supplant them.

Over the centuries the balance of power had shifted as members of the *filidh* accepted the New Faith. They did not abandon their sacral reverence for the land, however; they merely enlarged their view of godhood, recognizing the god of the Christians as immanent in his creations. Such innocent pantheism added a new dimension to the Church, giving it a uniquely Celtic flavor. In lonely ascetic cells, Irish monks composed poems celebrating the beauties of nature and thus affirming spiritual kinship with the pagans.

But there were still those in the vast dark forests who practiced the Old Faith undiluted by Christianity.

Irish druids did not engage in human sacrifice as their continental counterparts had done, but they manipulated the environment through techniques the Church called sorcery. They healed the sick, cursed the wrongdoer, instructed the young—aside from the sons of princes who were educated in the great monastic schools—and continued to devote themselves to the natural sciences as they had done for a thousand years.

Such practices were tolerated if not condoned. In the soft mists of Ireland old gods and new had intermingled, and the bitter plant of intolerance had yet to take root.

Christian chapels were sometimes ornamented with the carved, stylized heads of men and animals, a purely pagan embellishment not intended to represent saints. Brehon Law still governed such customs as marriage, allowing polygamy and divorce and denying the concept of illegitimacy, because every union that could result in a child was considered a form of marriage.

This enduring pagan influence was increasingly resented as the Church sought to expand its power, however, and Cathal Mac Maine was more resentful than most. He saw the druids as being in direct competition with the Church, and their intention as the destruction of Christianity.

"My confrontation with Torccan Mac Padraic was all the proof I need," he confided to Brother Declan. "The man demonstrated a reasoning ability no enlightened pagan could possess. It is the work of Lucifer."

Torccan's intelligence was not all that upset the abbot, however. Padraic's children radiated an inner serenity that scandalized Cathal. Such a gift should belong only to Christ's annointed. To make matters worse, they took a heathenish pleasure in being alive.

"This temporal existence is a burden and a punishment, an ordeal to be endured so we may earn an eternity in the company of Christ," the abbot frequently lectured his monks. The druidic joy in life was a refutation of his personal philosophy.

"We are taught that unquestioning obedience to the Church," Cathal sternly reminded Declan, "is the only path to true happiness. How then can we tolerate the dangerous example the druids set?"

He began to write letters to the hierarchy expressing his fear and loathing and urging that something be done, once and for all, to destroy druidry. But the bishops he addressed were, like himself, Irish. Their Christianity, no matter how ardent, overlaid a respect for ancient wisdom bred deep in their bones. They were not prepared to attack the druids overtly.

"Pray for their souls," Cathal was advised, "that they may find the path of redemption."

Sworn to obedience, he tried. He prayed long and hard on the cold stone flags of the chapel and arose with painfully stiffened knees. These he offered as a sacrifice to God, but his heart was not softened. Having recognized the menace, he saw it everywhere. Ireland abounded in druidic seductions.

Cathal loved the Church with all the passion of a man who has felt only one passion in his life. His was a fierce, proprietary devotion. Were it possible for him to convert Padraic's children he would have done so, but instead, as in a vision, he saw himself singlehandedly defending Christianity against them.

The warrior in him thrilled. The Church Triumphant.

Chapter Forty-two

Gormlaith awoke; a layered process beginning with a foggy awareness of self, then of a hard surface beneath her, lastly of a throbbing head. She was lying on the floor. Someone had wrapped a woolen robe around her and jammed the ends under her body. When she moved she felt another sort of throbbing lower down, a sweet, familiar soreness in her female parts.

Her eyes opened the merest slit. An arm's length from her face lay a tumble of chess pieces.

Brian's chess pieces.

She stared at them blankly for a moment—then saw, in clear and perfect memory, a large hand hover over the pawns. A hand with red-gold hair on the back.

Her body turned to ice; to fire.

He was alive!

Of course he was alive. How could she have been so foolish as to think otherwise? The man had not been born who could kill Brian Boru!

He was alive and the terrible past was relegated to nightmare.

All my sins are forgiven me, Gormlaith thought gratefully. She dragged herself to her knees and signed the Cross on her breast.

Soon he will come through the door, she told herself, and we will be together again as we were in the beginning, or as we should have been, if I had been content to love him as a woman loves a man, and not compete with him. This time things will be different.

She glanced down at her hands. In the dim light they looked young and smooth. When she raised her fingers to her throat and stroked the skin, it felt firm to her touch.

The years have been rolled back, she thought in amazement. I am a girl again, and he will be the only man I ever know. I shall make him happy, oh, I shall make him so very happy!

Gormlaith gazed around the chamber, looking for a basin in which to wash her face, or a comb for her tangled hair. He must never see her so rumpled. She must be beautiful for him; beautiful and young. As he would be beautiful and young, so tall, so strong, blazing, and crackling with that ferocious, irresistible energy that had won Ireland . . .

No. If he was young, his great victories were still ahead of him. Kincora was not yet built . . .

"So where am I?" Gormlaith asked of the stone walls.

They kept silent.

She got slowly to her feet. Sleeping on the stone floor had left her very stiff, but she ignored the pain. It was nothing to someone so young. A torn gown she did not recognize lay on the floor, but she did not pick it up. Let him return and find her naked, and they would . . .

There were footsteps in the passage. Her heart was pounding so hard she could barely breathe. As the door opened a cold draught blew across the floor and she shivered, but the smile she put on for him was radiant.

"Brian." Her lips shaped his name silently. Like a prayer.

He stood in the doorway, a big man, filling the space. Suddenly she was as shy as a virgin. She stood waiting for him to take her in his arms, and as he came toward her, she saw with perfect clarity the noble forehead, the long, straight nose, the stark cheekbones. The luminous gray eyes in their deeply carved sockets.

He was alive.

Gormlaith could not wait any longer, but hurled herself into his arms.

A moment later her scream rang wildly through the corridors of Glamis.

In the days that followed, Gormlaith's use of paints and dyes grew more lavish, accentuating her age, yet she took to wearing the simple gowns of an unmarried girl. She was by turns giddy, querulous, diffident, and demanding.

But the king continued to welcome her to his bed.

She had given him a fright on that first occasion, screaming like a madwoman when he returned to his chamber. Malcolm had hastily clamped his arms around her and put one hand over her mouth to muffle her screams. Then, when she was quiet, he let his hand slide down her body, enjoying her heaving breasts.

"I thought you were Brian," she murmured.

"You were groggy and half-awake, it was just a dream," he insisted.

She almost believed him.

But not quite.

She closed her eyes and let him fondle her, however, and in the dark behind her eyelids the alchemy of desire changed one king into another.

"Brian," Gormlaith whispered, parting her thighs for him.

Malcolm had smiled grimly to himself. So that was the game she preferred to play, was it? Well, he was able for her—particularly since he was the beneficiary of her passion.

The next night he again invited her to his chamber and kept the room in darkness, and when she called him Brian he did not contradict her.

If she had been good before, she then became extraordinary.

Thereafter Malcolm slept with her as often as the desire took him, which was often indeed. The fires of his youth flamed again, an unexpected spring interrupting the onset of winter.

And in the dark, afterward, he found himself talking with her as he had never talked with any of his other women.

Not a passive confidante like Blanaid, Gormlaith demonstrated an uncanny understanding of the male world of politics and power. She was a font of stratagems. Privately, his courtiers grumbled that the king's bedchamber became his council chamber when the Princess of Leinster arrived.

The winter Donough spent at the court of Malcolm the Second was the coldest of his life. But as fire tempers a sword blade, harsh Alba tempered him. A young man had arrived at Glamis; a man full-grown would leave it.

During the gray months, Malcolm kept the Irish prince close by his side. Donough answered the questions he asked, but more frequently was content to listen. The older man was wily and experienced and did not seem to mind passing on his wisdom.

But on an evening when he had drunk too much Danish ale at a banquet to entertain a chieftain from Strathclyde, Donough remarked to Cumara, "Malcolm is not easy company. My mother gets along with him, but I always feel as if he's watching me over the edge of a shield."

"Does it bother you, knowing they sleep together?" the poet's son asked bluntly. He too had drunk an excess of ale.

Donough hesitated before answering. "At first it did. It seemed a betrayal of my father. Then I reminded myself that he had ended their marriage, and if she married one man or slept with a thousand it no longer had anything to do with him. Now I am glad that she has found some pleasure in life again."

"Do you really mean that?"

Donough stiffened. "I do of course."

"You answered just a bit too quickly."

"Nonsense, Cumara, you're imagining things."

Yet at night, when he lay in his bed knowing full well Gormlaith had gone to Malcolm's chamber, Donough tossed and turned. His fevered imagination presented him with a hundred different images of his mother in the arms of the swarthy Scot.

Late one night he could bear it no longer. He rose, threw on a fur-lined brat, and went out into the passageway. He had no destination in mind other than escape from his thoughts, but he had gone only a short distance when he met his sister.

In the light from a torch still burning on the passage wall Donough could see that his sister's face was drawn, her eyes red-rimmed.

"Is anything wrong?" he asked. He felt a sudden urge to take her in his arms and comfort her, but she had done nothing so far to encourage such an intimacy.

Blanaid lifted her chin. "Of course not, I merely wanted a breath of air."

"I do myself. Shall I go with you?"

When she nodded assent they continued along the passage together, then made their way single-file down a narrow stone staircase and out into the great hall. Humans and hounds slept together on the rush-strewn floor, keeping one another warm. The fire on the hearth had gone out. The stale air smelled of dead ash and sleep.

Donough and Blanaid passed through the hall without waking anyone. A yawning guard unbolted a massive oak door for them with a curious glance but no question, and they went outside.

The night was bitterly cold. There was no moon; the stars were so bright they stabbed at the eyes. Blanaid drew her cloak more tightly around her and gazed upward. "Winter nights here have their own sort of beauty," she said conversationally.

"They do."

A pause ensued. "Is Alba what you expected?" she asked at last.

"I don't know what I expected."

"Why then did you come?"

"I'm not sure of that either," he replied honestly. "My mother . . ."

"Ah yes. Your mother." Blanaid's voice was carefully neutral. "She was something I did not expect."

Donough laughed. "No one is ever prepared for Gormlaith."

In spite of herself, Blanaid laughed too. "No, I suppose not."

Donough tried to read her face in the starlight. "Is she the reason you were crying?"

"I wasn't crying. My husband has always had women; he's a king. It means nothing to me."

"No," he agreed amiably. He slouched against the wall beside her, and together they watched the sky as if messages were concealed among the stars.

"How strange it must be," Blanaid remarked after a while, "to have that woman as a mother."

"She's the only mother I've ever had, so I've no comparison. But most of the time I don't think of her as my mother."

"You don't? How do you think of her?"

"Just as Gormlaith."

"And our father?"

Donough drew a deep breath. When he spoke his voice was so deep and so familiar it startled Blanaid. *"Ard Ri."*

She whirled to stare at him. "You sound just like him."

"Do I?"

Blanaid's throat closed. Her eyes began to sting again. *Not fair!* she thought. *I have not wept in years, and now twice in the same night . . .*

Donough exclaimed, "Look! Look there!"

She blinked hard and followed his pointing finger in time to see a shooting star. "The druids used to say a shooting star meant the death of a king," she said around the lump in her throat.

At the mention of druids, Cera leaped into Donough's

mind. Overcome by an echo of sweet laughter and a smell of the wild woods, he stared unseeing into the night, his thoughts very far away.

Suddenly, unexpectedly, Blanaid broke. A storm of sobs shook her. She did not know if she was crying because Brian Boru was dead, because Malcolm was with Gormlaith, or simply because the sight of her brother had brought back Ireland with painful intensity.

In the next moment her brother's arms were around her and his hand at the back of her head was gently pressing her face into the hollow of his shoulder.

"Sssh," he whispered. "It's all right. Sssh now."

Never in his life had Donough held sister or mother as he held Blanaid now. The emotions engendered were a revelation to him.

Surely what he had felt for Cera was love; a love that time and distance were gradually investing with a nostalgic melancholy. His feelings for Blanaid lacked the sexual excitement, but they were equally tender, and to his surprise they gave him a sense of family which he had never experienced with Gormlaith.

As he held his sister he was very aware that they shared the same father, a connection that was almost tangible. *Links in a chain*, Donough thought musingly. It was impossible to imagine putting his arms around Brian Boru, yet through his sister he was somehow embracing the man.

Love had a life of its own, then, an immortality that had nothing to do with death or distance. With Blanaid in his arms, Donough had a sense of forces much larger than himself.

Cera, he thought again.

Brother and sister stood together under the stars.

They never spoke of that night afterward. Blanaid's acquired Scottish reticence kept her silent, and Donough would not bring up the subject on his own, but he knew the same thing had happened to both of them. They had found family. When their eyes met in the hall or the courtyard or as they passed one another in some corridor, a warmth leaped between them that did not depend on words.

Across the Irish Sea, another member of Donough's family was thinking of him, though not tenderly. Carroll the historian made it his business to follow the fortunes of Brian's children, and had innocently mentioned Donough's trip during a conversation with Teigue.

They were in the great hall at Cashel, where Teigue now spent most of his time. Because the restoration of Kincora was taking longer than anticipated, he was keeping his family in the traditional fortress of the Munster kings. Cashel was magnificent in a forbidding way, comprised of a cluster of stone buildings perched atop a huge limestone outcropping with a view spanning much of Munster.

Teigue had begun taking several walks a day around the perimeter of the height. He would pause at various points and stand motionless, gazing out across the rolling, fertile land with a self-satisfied expression.

But Carroll would always prefer Kincora. He said as much, then added offhandedly, "I daresay Donough would agree with me. He must be finding Alba inhospitable by comparison."

Teigue stiffened. "What's he doing in Alba? Why did someone not tell me sooner?"

"I thought you knew already," replied Carroll.

"I did not know. Is he on a pilgrimage? To Iona, perhaps?"

"It seems to be a family visit. Your sister Blanaid invited him to Malcolm's stronghold at Glamis, so he and Gormlaith . . ."

"Donough took that woman? To Alba?!"

"He did."

"Then it's no family visit," Teigue snapped. "If Gormlaith is involved it can only be a conspiracy. What's she scheming to do now, have him take Munster from me?"

Carroll said soothingly, "Och, I'm sure neither of them has designs on your kingship."

"You're almost right," Teigue shot back. "Munster is not their final objective, one province would never satisfy Gormlaith. She intends her son to be Ard Ri, and this visit to Malcolm's court is her way of promoting that ambition. It should be perfectly obvious to anyone who knows the woman!

"The very fact that Donough is her son condemns him. He must never be allowed power; a door that opens the slightest for him lets Gormlaith enter.

"I did not seek to be King of Munster, but now that I am, Donough will not make Cashel his steppingstone to Tara. I won't let him. With Brian Boru's own sword I will bar his way."

Carroll's jaw dropped. "Brian's sword? You have Brian's sword?"

A sly light, which once would have been uncharacteristic of Teigue, crept into his eyes. "I might know where it is."

He would say no more, but Carroll was like a hound with a bone. The historian began quietly questioning the sentries, the spear carriers, the lower echelon who always knew more than the nobility.

He never mentioned the sword directly, but in time he had the answer he sought. It was not the answer he expected.

Chapter Forty-three

In addition to being King of the Scots and the Picts, Malcolm had been, since the death of a cousin in 991, Prince of

Cumbria, the northwestern region along the Irish Sea. With his defeat of the Northumbrian army at Carham in 1016, he had extended his reign south to the Cheviot Hills. The control of so much territory required not only constant military vigilance, but considerable monarchical administration.

For this purpose he held court at Scone, to which he invited Donough and his men to accompany him. The distance was not great, a long day's ride along a well-beaten road through valleys carpeted with dead bracken. Gray crows wheeled above in gray sky, calling harshly to one another.

Scone was an ancient assembly site predating Christianity. The buildings that now stood there were constructed of stone-kerbed timbers, with sod roofs upon which rank grasses grew. Built in the manner of an ancient broch, they comprised a cluster of round chambers, low-ceilinged, smelling of the earth.

"The Picts prefer this to Glamis," Malcolm explained to Donough on their first visit. "They are, or were, cave-dwellers, short-statured folk who feel comfortable in these surroundings. Skilled artisans, though. The silver ornamentation you see all around you is their work."

Scone felt old, Donough thought. And not Celtic. There was something else here, a different flavor in the air. The scent of metal and stone-dust.

Malcolm personally escorted his Irish guests to the tree-girded Moot Hill, or Assembly Site. "This mound was formed centuries ago of earth collected from throughout Pictland," he said proudly. "And there you see the Stone of Scone, believed to be part of the original stone pillow upon which the biblical patriarch Jacob rested while seeing his vision of angels."

With a proprietary sweep of his arm, he indicated a rectangular block of pale yellow sandstone at the top of the mound. "Jacob's Pillow eventually made its way to Ireland—some say with the Tuatha De Danann—where it was placed on the Hill of Tara. There it was called the Lia Fail, the Stone of Destiny, and became the inauguration stone of the Irish high kings. My predecessor, Kenneth Mac Alpin, acquired a piece of the Lia Fail for his own inauguration as the first King of the Scots and the Picts—his mother was a Pictish princess—and named it the Stone of Scone. Each King of Alba since then has seated himself upon it. Rather than being crowned, we are 'set upon the Stone.'

"Go on, look at it. You may touch it if you like, Donough," Malcolm added magnanimously. "You are of kingly blood."

Donough and his companions gathered around the revered stone, embedded like a jewel in the grass. After one good look, Ronan snorted and nudged Donough with his elbow.

When Malcolm was out of earshot, he said, "That's no more part of the Lia Fail than I am. I was on Tara, a mere lad in my first company of warriors, when your father stood upon the Lia Fail and it shrieked aloud, proclaiming him the true Ard Ri. I'll never forget that day nor anything about it—including the fact that the Lia Fail is gray, not yellow like Malcolm's rock. A different stone entirely."

"Is that true?" Fergal asked Donough.

"I don't know, I've never seen the Lia Fail. When my father went to Tara to be inaugurated, he left my mother and me at Kincora."

"Good job too," commented Cumara. "Gormlaith had been married to Malachi Mor, and Brian was taking Malachi's high kingship away from him. It would have been too grave an insult to flaunt the fact that he had also married Malachi's former wife."

Donough knew, but did not say, that Gormlaith had never forgiven Brian for denying her her moment of glory at Tara, her chance to be honored as the new Ard Ri's wife in front of Malachi Mor. Their subsequent arguments about it were his earliest memories of his father.

* * *

Chieftains traveled to Scone from the far corners of Alba to do homage to Malcolm. Donough listened attentively as the wily Scot played off one against another, always to his own advantage.

From time to time he would look up and catch Donough's eye and give the slow, solemn wink of shared conspiracy.

"The king is trying to impress me," Donough remarked to Fergal on a rare winter afternoon of radiant sunshine, when they were enjoying a stag hunt Malcolm had arranged for the new Mormaer of Ce. "He must believe I'm more powerful than I am."

Before Fergal could reply, Donough felt an unseen presence at his shoulder and in his head sounded the deep, slow voice he knew so well. *Perceptions are important*, it counseled. *If Malcolm thinks you have hundreds of warriors at your command in Ireland, do not disillusion him.*

Donough began dropping offhand references to "my armies at home" into casual conversation.

At Scone he met a variety of powerful men come to negotiate with Malcolm for various reasons; the King of Man, the Lord of the Western Isles, the Mormaers of Caithness and Argyll, abbots and bishops and silver-haired Norse jarls and dark Pictish chieftains. To all of these Malcolm unabashedly presented Donough as, "The son of the Emperor of the Irish," and Donough watched their eyes kindle with respect.

In Alba he was accorded a stature he did not possess at home.

He ordered Fergal and Ronan to flank his seat in the hall, holding spears at a ceremonial angle. Ronan obeyed without question, but Fergal took offense. "I'm entitled to have spear carriers of my own; I'm a prince of the Dal Cais!"

"I'm Brian Boru's son," Donough replied inarguably.

* * *

While Malcolm held court at Scone, Gormlaith was left at Glamis with the other women. Her son was relieved. He was finding her behavior increasingly disturbing. She howled with laughter at inappropriate times, which was bad enough, but her tendency to stare at Malcolm and then burst into tears unnerved him.

Donough had never before seen his mother cry.

Blanaid also remained in residence at Glamis, with Sigurd's widow, Thora, and the boy Thorfinn. She avoided Gormlaith whenever she could, which was not easy, as the big Irish woman dominated whatever space she occupied. Blanaid held her temper and her dignity until the arrival of her oldest daughter, Bethoc, with her husband Crinan, Abbot of Dunkeld, and their son, young Duncan.

Being of an age and like disposition, Duncan and Thorfinn immediately became companions-in-mischief. Bethoc was reunited with her sister Thora, whom she had not seen in some years.

And Gormlaith flirted outrageously with the Abbot of Dunkeld.

Bethoc complained to her mother. When Malcolm next returned to Glamis he was unpleasantly surprised by a confrontation with his wife. Blanaid would not fight him on her own behalf, but she was a tigress where her cubs were concerned. "Do something about that woman!" she demanded.

"Short of locking her in her chamber," Malcolm replied, "I cannot keep Gormlaith out of the hall. I don't want to alienate Donough Mac Brian by abusing his mother."

"You abuse her often enough in your bedchamber."

His black brows swooped together. "That's my business. And it isn't abuse."

"No? Taking advantage of a demented . . ."

"She is not demented."

"I thought you more observant than that," said Blanaid coldly. "I warn you, husband. Keep Gormlaith out of sight henceforth, or I myself will see that Donough is never an ally of yours."

She held her shoulders square and her head high, and in the proud set of her jaw, Malcolm read implacability.

That night he told Gormlaith, "When I return to Scone, you will go with me."

"He wants me at his side," Gormlaith smugly reported to her son.

Of course she found Scone even less appealing than Glamis, and did not hesitate to say so. In an effort to win her interest, Malcolm took her to see the famous Stone.

Donough accompanied them out of politeness and a secret amusement. *Perceptions*, he thought. *The Albans perceive this to be a legitimate king-stone, so for them it is. Old Kenneth Mac Alpin must have been very clever.*

Lost in his own thoughts, he walked beside his mother and Malcolm toward the Stone of Scone.

Neither man was prepared for Gormlaith's reaction.

No sooner had Malcolm delivered his speech about the stone's provenance than she swept past him, up the gentle breast of the manmade hill, and threw herself down beside the stone. As the two men watched in consternation she pressed her cheek against its cold surface.

"Just so," Gormlaith whispered throatily. "Just so. You stood on this stone in the sun; I remember. You stood, and I at your side, and it screamed aloud for us."

"What is she talking about?" Malcolm asked Donough. "We don't stand on this, it's the throne, the king-seat."

The younger man shook his head, unable to speak.

Gormlaith was running her hands over the stone as a woman would caress a man's body, with infinite love. "Ard Ri," she murmured.

She was crying.

Donough felt a terrible pain flare through his chest as if someone had opened him with a sword. *She loved him. She actually loved him, and none of us ever knew.*

He ran up the hill and put his hands on his mother's shoulders to try to lift her, but she fought him off. "Leave me! Leave me with him! I belong with him, don't you know that? Don't any of you know that?"

In a moment Malcolm was beside Donough. Together they wrestled Gormlaith to her feet but she fought them like a wildcat, screaming. They had to drag her down the hill, and she was constantly twisting backward to shout at the stone, "Don't let them take me!"

That night Malcolm's personal physician spent a long time closeted with Gormlaith in a small chamber with a guard at the door, then emerged shaking his head. "Her reason is addled," he reported. "A pity. Such a big, strong woman. But she keeps talking to someone else in the chamber, someone who is not there."

I talk to him too, thought Donough, inwardly flinching. *Does that mean my wits are addled? Or is he really with us?*

There was no answer. Try as he might he could not sense the towering presence behind him, but felt suddenly, terribly, alone, as if his back were unshielded at the height of battle.

His feelings about his mother, always ambivalent, underwent a sea-change. The last emotion Gormlaith would want to inspire was pity, yet it was pity he felt for her.

Malcolm's attitude toward Gormlaith also changed. When she was rational, which was most of the time, her intelligence was as keen as ever and he continued to enjoy talking with her. But whatever ardor he had felt was gone. He could not bring himself to take her into his bedchamber again.

Gormlaith was plainly hurt by the king's rejection. She put a brave face on it, however. "I've grown tired of him," she announced to Donough. "He's thick in the belly and too old for me, and his spear is blunted."

This open reference to her sexual life made Donough uncomfortable, and struck him as further proof of her failing

sanity. He began to be anxious to take her home to Ireland.
Exposing his mother, in her weakness, to the eyes of
strangers seemed a betrayal.

But he was torn. The visit to Alba was providing him with
knowledge, experience, and a circle of powerful acquain-
tances. To leave now would be to lose opportunities that
might not come again. In Alba he was looked upon as the
next Ard Ri of the Irish. At home he was not even a provincial king.

On the first day that carried a hint of spring in the air,
Donough was with Malcolm in the low-ceilinged audience
chamber, conferring with clan chiefs of Angus and of Fife,
when their conversation was interrupted by the blast of a
horn. Within moments a foreign delegation was ushered
into the chamber.

The leader of the group was thickset, with a tawny beard
and snapping blue eyes in a square Saxon face. Beneath a
mantle of woven wool he was garbed in the sleeved, short-
skirted coat and loose trousers worn by men of Albion, now
called by its inhabitants the land of the Anglo-Saxons, or
England.

"My lord Godwine, Earl of Wessex and Kent," announced the small boy who trotted beside him, panting.

Malcolm sat bolt upright on his bench, his face impassive. But the hands that clasped his knees were suddenly
white-knuckled.

Power meets power, whispered a voice in Donough's head.
Watch for your own opportunity here.

Chapter Forty-four

On that day at Scone Donough's horizon expanded in a way he had never anticipated. The trip to Alba was a mighty adventure, but with the arrival of Earl Godwine it became obvious that Alba was only a threshold; a much larger world lay beyond.

He listened, fascinated, as the Earl and Malcolm spoke of London and Normandy and Rome, of shifts in power both temporal and spiritual, of warfare and politics and the reshaping of the Anglo-Saxon kingdom.

"Canute is nothing short of brilliant," stated Earl Godwine unequivocally. "When he arrived off our coast in the summer of 1015 with a fleet of Danish ships, many thought him little more than an untried youth. There were even jokes about the boy King of Denmark; some claimed he brought a wet nurse with him.

"But within four months no one was joking. Canute had complete military control of Wessex and was not only extending Swein's conquests but making new ones. I thought it expedient then to ally with him—a decision I have never regretted. I owe my recent earldom to him. My wife is a full-blooded Dane and her brother Ulf is married to one of Canute's sisters. Our children will ascend with Canute's star.

"At the time Canute began his military campaign there was already great dissatisfaction, even rebellion, against the Saxon King Aethelred. Eadric of Mercia, one of his foremost critics, openly allied himself with the Danes. He did return to the king's side, however—for a while.

"Much too late, Aethelred raised an army. When the London militia refused to join them, it disintegrated. Meanwhile, Canute played on the fears of the people by harrying the unprotected shires. One after another, they fell to him.

"When Aethelred conveniently died his son succeeded him, but Edmund Ironside had little more success against Canute than his father before him. A great battle was fought for London, and Eadric of Mercia fled the field, taking many warriors with him."

"I heard that he deliberately betrayed the king," Malcolm commented.

"I was told you had long ears," replied Godwine with respect. "Your informants are correct. In the event, the Anglo-Saxon defense collapsed.

"But I must admit Edmund Ironside proved so formidable in the face of disaster that he won the hearts of many who had not previously supported him. Canute was shrewd enough to recognize this. He met Edmund on an island in the Severn and the two made a pact by which the land was divided, with Wessex going to Edmund and the country beyond the Thames to Canute. Even Canute's enemies were impressed by this example of generosity to a gallant foe.

"Such a division could not last, of course. When Edmund died not long after, Canute became King of England almost by acclamation. The people were hungry for a strong man."

Ireland, said the voice in Donough's head. *The people are hungry for a strong man.*

He leaned forward on his bench, absorbing every word as Earl Godwine described the means by which Canute had consolidated his hold on England. Although Swein had been a pagan, his son Canute undertook to promote the Christian religion and protect and enrich its clerics. He became the first Viking leader to join the exclusive ranks of Christian kings. Thus he was brought into contact with

Rome and acquired political connections none of his race had enjoyed before.

He had also married Emma, the widow of the dead King Aethelred.

Malcolm looked surprised. Clearly this, at least, was news to him. "But did Canute not already have a wife?"

Godwine's blue eyes twinkled. "He did. He had married the daughter of a wealthy Northumbrian landowner not long after arriving in England, and she bore him two sons in very short order. But once he became king, he faced a threat in the form of the late Aethelred's sons. Their mother, Emma, was a sister of the Duke of Normandy, and it was feared Normandy would use them to lay a claim to the English crown.

"He may be a professed Christian, but our good Canute still has a strong streak of the barbarian in him; he does not accept the conventions that limit lesser men," Godwine continued. "He promptly announced that his arrangement with the Northumbrian woman had never been formalized by the Church, and therefore as a Christian king he could not consider himself lawfully bound to her.

"Then he married Emma.

"He now has control of Aethelred's sons plus the Duke of Normandy for a brother-in-law. Under the circumstances I seriously doubt if Normandy will dispute Canute's right to be King of England."

When Donough at last retired, grainy-eyed and weary yet exhilarated, he found Gormlaith waiting for him. She wanted to hear every detail concerning the Saxon visitors.

Once he would have tried to avoid her. Now, in pity, he spent as much time with her as he could.

"Why has this Godwine come to Malcolm's court?" she wanted to know after Donough recounted all he could recall of the conversation in the audience chamber.

"For the same reason everyone else comes—to gain

something for himself. Nothing was said in my hearing, but I have the profound conviction that Malcolm summoned him, or at least invited him, for a very specific reason."

"What?"

"As Godwine made clear in the audience chamber today, he has the ear and the trust of King Canute. I think Malcolm will make him a generous offer in return for Godwine's using his influence to dissuade Canute from attempting the conquest of Alba."

"What has Malcolm to offer that Godwine would want?"

Donough's eyes narrowed to slits in the torchlight. But Gormlaith was not looking at his eyes. She found herself staring at his hand, upon which gleamed the ring of Brian Boru.

"A powerful ally in Ireland," said the deep voice she knew so well.

Gormlaith smiled.

"Godwine has his own ambitions," Donough went on. "He said quite candidly that he would not mind seeing a son of his on the English king-seat one day. An alliance with the Irish Ard Ri would be very beneficial in such a circumstance, and that, I suspect, is what Malcolm means to offer him."

"Games," murmured Gormlaith. "The old games; ah, how well I know them. And how perfectly this comes together for you! An alliance with the King of England . . ." Reaching out, she stroked the massive gold ring on her son's finger.

"That potential alliance is based on my being Ard Ri, which I am not," Donough reminded his mother.

When Gormlaith's eyes met him they were glazed; they looked almost blind. He wondered if she saw him at all.

Yet she seemed to know who he was. She said, "With such forces behind you as you are now gathering, who could stand against you? Not that flabby old man Malachi, surely."

"I cannot be Ard Ri without first being King of Munster.

That, need I remind you, is a title my brother holds with all the determination of a hound clinging to the throat of a stag."

Gormlaith gave a negligible wave of her hand. "A temporary inconvenience."

"What do you mean?"

"Ask Malcolm—he will tell you. Ask him just how he arranged to become King of Alba."

But when Donough questioned Malcolm on the subject, he was met with such evasions he began to suspect a valuable secret was being withheld from him.

"When Godwine has gone and we return to Glamis," Malcolm said, "we can discuss these things. There are some matters one should not mention when foreigners are about."

I am a foreigner, thought Donough. *How much is being kept from me?*

The fact that he was not privy to all of Malcolm's conversations with Godwine heightened his suspicions.

After a fortnight Godwine departed with the air of a man who has got all he came for, and the King of Alba and his retinue set out for Glamis.

The pile of dark stone looked more forbidding than ever as they approached it through a driving rain. Gormlaith, wrapped in leather cloaks and seated upon a sure-footed pony, stared at the Alban stronghold as if she had never seen it before, then gazed wildly around and called out, "Where is this? Where are we?"

Donough left Malcolm and went to ride beside her, talking gently to her in a voice she did not seem to hear. But by the time they were inside she seemed herself again.

Within the stern walls there were fires blazing cheerfully, and the air rang with the squeals of children. The two little boys, Thorfinn and Duncan, were racing through the castle, playing at war. The King of Alba had no sooner entered his hall than they caromed into him, glanced off, laughed, and ran on without so much as a backward glance.

Malcolm smiled indulgently. "Have you sons?" he asked Donough as Blanaid came forward to greet them.

"Not yet. My wife died before any children were born to us."

Malcolm turned and met Gormlaith's eyes. Intercepting the look that passed between them, Donough recognized conspiracy.

That same night Donough repeated the question Gormlaith had bade him ask Malcolm. He even used the same wording she had used, a fact not lost on the king.

"Arranged?" Malcolm repeated. "Who said I 'arranged' to become king?"

"My mother."

"Ah." For a moment the Scot's face looked more somber than usual. "She was referring to . . . to pillow talk, I believe. One should be careful what one says in the dark to a woman."

"I suspect my mother has a gift for working secrets out of men."

"Your mother has many gifts. In a way I shall be sorry to see her leave; some of her ideas have been . . . very valuable. I shall answer your question as a favor to her." With his eyes, Malcolm summoned a servant, who hastily refilled his and Donough's cups. Then the king led the way to his private chamber.

It was Donough's first visit to the chamber. He was careful not to let his eyes linger on the bed.

Seating himself on a bench beside a low table that held a richly ornamented silver casket, Malcolm took a deep drink from his cup, then began. "Before me, Kenneth the Second considered himself King of the Scots and the Picts. Like myself, he was descended from Kenneth Mac Alpin. As is sometimes the case in Ireland, I believe, kings in Alba are chosen from alternate branches of the royal house, but my predecessor came from a secondary branch and was not entitled to the kingship. Not by my reckoning.

"Besides, he was a bad king, weak in battle and vacillating in judgment."

Malcolm paused and drew a deep breath, flaring his nostrils. "So I killed him."

"You . . ."

"Killed him. An ancient and honorable way of proving oneself the better man."

"Is it? Ancient, indeed, but honorable? My father did not kill Malachi Mor; he proved himself the better man without bloodshed."

"And overthrew the concept of alternate succession for the high kingship; yes, I know. It is dangerous, young Donough, this breaking with tradition. Listen to a man who has had considerable experience. The old ways are best; simple and straightforward.

"Your father changed things too much too fast in Ireland. Now he is gone, the old verities are swept away, and there has not been time for a new tradition to grow strong roots. Malachi Mor can neither replace Brian Boru, nor restore the system that was destroyed.

"So I do not advocate your father's methods. If he had killed Malachi, you would not have him standing between you and the high kingship."

"You are a Christian king . . ."

"I am, I endow churches and monasteries."

". . . yet you advocate murdering your rivals?" Donough finished.

"Murder is the wrong term. I advocate political assassination when necessary, for the, ah, greater good."

"And does it not weigh heavily on your conscience?"

Malcolm did not blink. "No. A king cannot afford a conscience. There are other things he requires, however. Your mother and I have discussed this and she made an excellent suggestion."

"Any suggestion of hers would be suspect. My mother is no longer sane." Saying the words hurt, but honesty impelled Donough to say them.

Malcolm's mouth twisted. "Who is sane? She is still clever. She put forward a proposal on your behalf which will be advantageous to all of us."

"My mother has no authority to make proposals on my behalf," said Donough heatedly.

"Don't get prickly with me, lad. Just listen. This may be the last thing your poor mother ever asks of you."

Chapter Forty-five

We returned to Ireland in an Orkney longship arranged by Malcolm. With us we carried numerous gifts he had given me, the plans and dreams the visit had instilled in me, and a strong, silent Scot whose sole function was to take care of my mother.

By the time we left Alba it was obvious to everyone that the Princess of Leinster was mad.

She who had not spoken the name of Brian Boru for years had begun talking to him constantly. Sometimes she was looking at Malcolm as she spoke; sometimes at me. But she was talking only to Brian. She would no longer respond to anyone else.

The spring winds were kind to us; the Viking ship with its shallow draught flew like a bird over the waves.

Sitting in its waist, I passed the time by endeavoring

to play my father's harp. Cumara taught me what he had learned from Mac Liag. I could see why Cumara had never followed his father as a bard, however. He did not have an instinctive understanding of the music inherent in words or in an instrument. He knew which strings to pluck in what order, but he could not make the harp sing.

After a bit of instruction, my fingers sought the strings with a will of their own, and the sounds I summoned, if not always accurate, were at least musical.

The damp sea air was bad for the harp, and her voice was soon tarnished. Yet she answered my touch as if she knew me, and I rejoiced in her company.

One evening the dark caught us before we had found a suitable harborage, and the ship glided on for a time, propelled by her sail. A silence descended; the hard-bitten men of Orkney rested on their oars and listened to me play. The air was unseasonably warm, and soft. A rising moon shone silver.

In memory I can still see that pale face, wreathed in shreds of cloud.

In memory I can still see my mother come swaying toward me, with her keeper following to see she did not hurt herself. She made her way the length of the ship to kneel at my feet and rest her head against my knee.

"Play," she said softly. "Play the music you composed for me, my Brian."

Chapter Forty-six

Never before had Cera celebrated the rites of spring with such happy abandon. She danced, she hummed, she glowed.

"Donough will return to us with the leaves," she explained to her father.

"To us? You mean, to you."

"Perhaps I do."

The blind man put his hand on his daughter's arm. "Don't start living in the future until it arrives, pet. Prince Donough may indeed return to Ireland soon—or he may not, there is no predicting the movements of princes. But either way, he will have things on his mind that have nothing to do with you. Do not expect him to come running to you the day he sets foot on the shore."

Living with druids had amplified Padraic's senses. He could not see Cera, but he could feel waves of heat radiating from her spirit. "Listen to me," he said emphatically. "Be patient, bide your time. What is for you will . . ."

". . . not pass by me, I know, you've told me that for as long as I can remember. But how can I sit with my hands folded and do nothing? Life is to be lived; you've told me that, too!"

She pulled away from her father and ran from the cabin.

Beyond the oak woods that embraced their home, the land rose into a succession of rocky hills. A swift-flowing stream ran through these hills on its way to the Fergus, watering the roots of numerous rowan trees. On summer nights white moths collected amid the rowan. In the autumn, Cera's sister brewed a refreshing beverage from fermented rowan berries. But in early spring the power of the rowan was most potent, shimmering almost visibly through the silver-gray bark.

This was the tree Cera now sought, the fabled tree of speed and protection, the tree of summoning and welcoming. When she found a specimen whose branches extended eastward like outreaching arms, she knelt at its base and made a small offering. Then she set to work.

Aboard the Orkney longship, Donough put aside his harp to gaze out across the greenish-blue water. He avoided looking at Gormlaith. To calm her last night the captain of the longship had donated his own measure of ale, and the big Scot held her down while Donough forced her to drink all of it. Today she was bleary-eyed and nauseated, but at least she was quïet. Huddled in a blanket, she sat inert and unaware.

"I shall have to take her to Dublin, to Sitric," Donough told Fergal. "Advise our captain accordingly. I cannot keep her with me under the circumstances, her presence would be crippling."

Once he made this decision, all his plans became more substantial. Making arrangements for Gormlaith was now the first step in a careful campaign. Donough expected Sitric to complain mightily, but at the end of the day he would not throw Gormlaith out into the road.

As he watched the sea slipping past the prow, in his mind Donough was already taking the next step. Upon returning to Thomond he would rally as many followers as he could, then request a convening of the brehons at Cashel. He would . . .

A shiver ran across his shoulders. It was cold on the sea but he wore a heavy fur mantle, the gift of Malcolm. He should not have felt the . . .

There it was again. With the shiver came a longing so

painful it was like a fist to the belly. "Cera!" Donough heard himself call out.

"What?" Fergal glanced toward him. "Did you say something to me?"

"I . . . ah, I did not. I was just thinking aloud, I suppose."

His cousin squinted at him. "Are you all right, Donough? You've gone very pale."

"I'm fine. Just eager to be home again, to make things happen."

Fergal grinned. "You will make things happen; there's no doubt of it. Just don't forget your old friends."

A shadow crossed Donough's face. For just one moment he smelled green grass, flowers blooming, felt Cera in his arms. "I never forget," he said.

The pain in his voice puzzled his cousin.

Donough sat very still, waiting.

The feeling, when it came again, was almost overpowering. It was all he could do to keep from leaping from the ship and swimming frantically toward Ireland.

"Hurry!" he shouted to the captain. "Can you not go any faster?"

The Orkneyman was losing patience with his passengers. That business with the woman last night was bad enough; he resented having a landman criticize the way he sailed. "You'll get there when you get there," he responded in a surly tone, "and not a moment sooner."

When they caught their first glimpse of the Irish coastline, Donough thought his heart would leap from his breast. But there were practical considerations to distract him. The decision to put ashore at Dublin added to their sailing time, and also meant they would receive an uncertain welcome.

"I have done some trading with the Dublin Danes," the Orkney captain said, "but if the Irish hold the city now, they might meet my crew with spears."

"If the Irish hold Dublin you'll be safe, because you're in the employ of an Irish prince," Donough assured him. Privately he wondered, however, just what the situation might be in Dublin. Was it possible Malachi could have seized the city?

They beached the longship at the mouth of the Liffey, where the Vikings had built wooden wharves to facilitate the loading and unloading of cargo. Even before they went ashore it was obvious that the city was still under Viking control, although an occasional, unmistakably Gaelic face appeared in the crowds thronging the quayside.

As the stench of the city enfolded him, Donough felt his sense of Cera receding. She was a creature of meadow and mountain; her voice was lost in the clamor of Dublin.

"Keep a firm hold on my mother," he advised the big Scot as, surrounded by his men, he set out for Sitric's stronghold.

Sitric was far from pleased to see his half-brother—or their mother. When the sentries announced Donough's arrival, the Dane left them waiting at the gates for a long time before they were finally ushered into the hall.

"What do you want here?" was Sitric Silkbeard's greeting.

Armed warriors ringed the room. Although they were indoors, at Sitric's command they had donned their Viking helmets, conical metal caps with nose protectors and eye-slits that gave them a uniquely sinister appearance.

Donough was not intimidated; he understood the game. "Put down your weapons at the door," he said loudly to his men. "We won't need them here."

Then he met Sitric's eyes. "Will we." It was not a question.

The Viking hesitated. "No," he said at last. "Put down your spears," he ordered his guards. "Now, Donough. What's this about?"

"I have to leave Gormlaith with you, as I cannot keep her any longer."

Sitric scowled. "Not even for half the year?"

"Not even for a day, not now. I shall be traveling light and fast, as I have much to do. She will be better off here."

Sitric looked past Donough to the silent woman who stood wrapped in a mantle, her head hanging apathetically. He noted the Scot who kept a firm grip on her shoulder. "Is this what you want, Mother?" he inquired.

Gormlaith did not respond. She did not even lift her head.

Sitric strode toward her and bent slightly to get a good look at her downturned face. What he saw horrified him. Her eyes were perfectly blank and a thin drool of spittle ran down her chin.

"What have you done to her?" he demanded of Donough.

"Nothing. I took her to Alba with me because she insisted on going, and while we were there she began to see things. Hear things. Talk to thin air. She was not injured in any way, she just . . ." He lifted his hands palm upward in a gesture of helplessness.

"Just went mad," Sitric finished for him.

"Indeed. I regret it bitterly, but it was nothing anyone did to her. She was still sane, at least part of the time, until we left Alba. Sane enough to extract promises from me," he added under his breath. "But once we were on the open sea she became as she is now. I don't think there's any way back for her."

When Sitric put a tentative hand on Gormlaith's shoulder she gave no sign of recognition. Only the big Scot responded, watching the Viking warily.

Sitric turned back to Donough. "I think we had better talk," he said.

A chamber was found for Gormlaith. Emer refused to have anything to do with her, so her Scottish attendant bathed her, fed her, put her into bed. Meanwhile Donough's men circulated uneasily among the Vikings in the stronghold, and Donough and Sitric talked.

Food and drink were provided: roast meat, dried fruit, horns of Danish ale. But neither man had much appetite—except for the ale.

They were natural enemies with nothing in common but the womb that bore them. Yet the tragedy of Gormlaith was enough to allow them to speak to one another with tense civility.

"Under Brehon Law," Donough told Sitric, "her kindred must care for her. But in truth she has few kindred left alive, only yourself and myself. And I don't suppose you recognize Brehon Law anyway."

"I do not. The same custom pertains among the Vikings, however. We would not put a madwoman out in the snow—at least, not so long as we had enough food for her without starving ourselves."

"And do you?"

"Things have not gone well since Clontarf," admitted Sitric, "but I can fill another mouth. I'm still king of the Dublin Danes, and as you no doubt saw down at the quay, trade continues. Trade always continues, no matter who's in power," he added.

Donough cocked his head for a moment, then smiled and said, "It's a trade I have to offer you."

"You brought me riches from Alba?"

"In a manner of speaking. In Alba I acquired some powerful allies, not the least of them being King Malcolm. I now have more supporters across the sea than Malachi Mor could ever call upon. What does that suggest to you, Sitric?"

The Dane folded his arms across his chest. "Go on, I'm listening."

"I can make life very hard for you, or not, as I see fit."

"Malachi's been making life hard enough for me. He and his followers attack my people on any pretext. He's worse than a rash of nettles. That old man's trying to bash his way back into a kingly reputation."

"There are better ways to win a kingly reputation, Sitric."

"Are you suggesting a truce between us if I'm willing to take Gormlaith off your hands permanently?"

Donough cocked his head again. "Is a truce possible between us, after Clontarf?"

"Malachi would say no."

"I'm not asking Malachi. I'm asking my brother."

Sitric took a long pull of ale from his drinking horn. "Half-brother," he corrected. "That makes a difference. Your father was a Gael, mine a Dane. Born enemies, some might say."

"That doesn't mean we can't come to an accommodation now. The world has moved on. Ireland has moved on."

"You may think so, but some things don't change," Sitric replied. "My wife hates Gormlaith as water hates fire."

"Emer and I are blood kin too. If I could persuade her to accept the arrangement, what then?"

Sitric dug into his beard, scratching with blackened fingernails. "Old enmities go deep. You don't like me, I don't like you. And Clontarf is an open wound."

"It is," Donough agreed somberly. "But it's over. No one can bring back the dead, on your side or mine. Here's what I propose, Sitric: Give Gormlaith a home for the rest of her life, and in return, I shall never take up arms against you or your people without first meeting you and making every effort to resolve our differences."

"You're as mad as she is. That isn't the way things are done."

"That's how my father did them."

A muscle jumped in Sitric's jaw. "Your father. Yes. But he was . . ."

"Whatever he was, I mean to be. Have we an agreement or not?"

Sitric eyed Donough with a grudging respect. "You really think you're going to be Ard Ri?"

"Answer my question."

"You don't know what you're asking of me. Any time

spent under the same roof with Emer and Gormlaith together is enough to make a man tear out his hair with both hands. You are requiring a great sacrifice on my part—in return for what?"

"In return for my solemn pledge that, when I am Ard Ri, you shall be undisputed king of the Dublin Danes, and the penalties exacted against you since Clontarf shall be rescinded."

"What about Malachi Mor?"

"I cannot speak for Malachi Mor. As long as he is Ard Ri . . ." Donough deliberately left the sentence unfinished.

Sitric took another drink of ale. Then, unexpectedly, he laughed. "You're good! I give you that, you're very good. I might almost hear your father talking. I suppose this means you will expect my support when you undertake to claim the high kingship?"

"It would be to your advantage," Donough told him. "But it won't make any substantial difference. I told you, I have Malcolm of Alba. And for that matter," he added casually, "an alliance with the King of England."

Sitric's jaw dropped. "You *what*?"

At Kill Dalua, Brother Declan was continuing to record the litany of carnage and pillage sweeping the country. No longer was he concentrating on Viking depredations; he wrote of Irish princes renewing old battles for supremacy.

"Malachi Mor endeavors to control the violence with greater violence," he entered in the annals, "but he is not successful. Flaherty, grandson of Eochaid, King of Ulster, has been blinded by Niall, son of Eochaid. The men of Brega have slain a chieftain of Mugorn. The Tanist of Delbhna was brutally murdered in his own home. Ruadri of the Nechach has been killed by a rival from Fernmai."

"No one is safe in Ireland these days," complained Cathal Mac Maine grimly. "The land is cursed."

He knew the source of the curse. He reviewed his epistolary

bombardment of his superiors, demanding extirpation of the druids.

Once Donough had come to an agreement with Sitric, he had a long and unpleasant conversation with Emer. He could not offer his half-sister the same inducements. Nothing would make her accept Gormlaith gladly. "And if my husband does, or says he does, you should not trust him," she warned Donough.

"Och, I don't trust him. But I understand him; he only respects strength. As long as I have sufficient strength, he will keep his word to me."

"He didn't keep the truce he made with our father," Emer reminded her half-brother.

"He had Gormlaith at his shoulder, urging him on. It would take a stronger man than Sitric Silkbeard to resist Gormlaith at the height of her powers. But those powers are gone now, and it is my duty to do what I can to care for her. I ask you to do the same, in the name of our kinship. Father would want that," he added.

Tears shimmered in Emer's eyes. "You cannot speak for him, and you have no right to invoke his name that way. It isn't fair."

"I can speak for him," said Donough Mac Brian.

He paid his mother one last visit before leaving her in Dublin. He did not think she would recognize him, but when he entered her chamber her Scottish attendant said, "She's having a good day."

Donough looked at the empty-faced woman slumped on a bench. "How can you tell?"

"I'm used to her ways now."

"That's why I want you to stay with her. Sitric will give her shelter and food, but the only way I can guarantee she will be properly cared for is if her attendant is answerable to me. I shall reward you handsomely, and when . . . when you are no longer needed, you may either return to Alba or I shall give you land here; good land, fertile soil."

The Scot did not hesitate. "I'm your man," he said. "I won't go back. It's cold in Alba."

Donough sat down beside his mother. He wanted to take her hand, but such gestures had never been employed between them and would seem unnatural now. Not knowing what else to do, he spoke of his plans to her for a while, then, when she was unresponsive, he stood up with a sigh. "I'd best be going," he told the Scot. "Be good to her."

He was almost out the door when he heard her voice, as thin and insubstantial as that of a ghost.

"Remember your promise to me," said Gormlaith.

Donough whirled around.

Her faded eyes met his. "You made me a promise. The last thing I shall ever ask of you."

"I won't forget," he said hoarsely. "I will keep my vow to you . . . Mother."

After he had gone, Gormlaith stared at the empty doorway for a long time. Then her dry, cracked lips shaped a name.

Chapter Forty-seven

Malachi Mor felt stretched very thin. He had never fully recovered from the deaths of his sons, but as long as he kept busy he could avoid thinking about them. His years were against him, however. Each day he felt wearier, more despondent; each day he fought back with all the fury he could muster.

But he had to admit to himself it was not enough.

Learning that Donough Mac Brian had returned to Ireland and gone straight to Sitric Silkbeard did not improve his humor. "He's a schemer like his father," Malachi told his courtiers. "No doubt he's plotting some evil with the Dublin Danes."

So he was astonished when Donough arrived at Dun na Sciath and offered to put himself and his followers at Malachi's service.

It was the first time the two had met face to face. The Ard Ri expected an impudent youth; he found himself facing a disturbingly familiar man.

"Why would you want to help me?" Malachi asked suspiciously. "What benefit do you seek?"

Donough replied with a disarming smile, "You have lost sons who should be fighting beside you. I have lost a father."

"I can't replace your father."

"Nor can I replace your sons," Donough replied, aware of the irony in the Ard Ri's words even if Malachi was not. "But I have a number of supporters in Thomond, good fighting men all of them. I think an alliance would be to the advantage of both of us."

At Cashel, Carroll could hardly contain himself. Messengers from the northeast had begun reporting a succession of victories on the part of the Ard Ri, and the name of Donough Mac Brian was always prominently mentioned.

"He is acquitting himself in a way that would make his father proud," the historian said. "Prince Donough is helping the Ard Ri to restore, at last, a modicum of order."

"Why is my brother fighting for the High King?" Teigue asked peevishly. "Is not his place here in Munster?"

Maeve felt compelled to be fair. "You denied him a place in Munster," she reminded her husband.

"I did no such thing. I just refused to allow him to take over Kincora."

"Yet you no longer live there yourself."

"I shall when it is fully rebuilt."

"All the work is done, they say."

"Are you so anxious to go back there?"

Maeve sighed. "I would really like to go back to our home in the valley west of Kincora," she said wistfully. "But I suppose . . ."

"No," Teigue said. "I am King of Munster now."

In the cabin among the oaks, Cera waited. She knew Donough was in Ireland; she could feel him. But he was a great distance from her and she could not draw him closer.

Sometimes she felt that he was in great danger. Then she employed all she knew of druidry to keep him safe.

The Ui Caisin had long been an exceptionally contentious tribe. Their neighbors feared and hated them, and their incessant cattle raiding had sparked a hundred bitter feuds. So many had complained to the Ard Ri that at last Malachi, with Donough beside him, led a small army south and west from Kildare to the territory of the Ui Caisin.

The season was high summer. Hedgerows hummed with insect life, and as he sat at ease on his lightly sweating horse, Donough could smell the fragrance of sun-warmed earth. He rode at the head of the warrior band, allowing only Malachi to precede him. Having learned a lesson from the head wound at Annacotty, he now never went on such expeditions without wearing a padded iron helmet and a shirt of iron links in the Viking style. He did not include a Viking axe among his weaponry, however.

Donough preferred the sword.

In the bright sunshine, his helmet was too hot. He debated with himself about removing it, then decided to keep it on. He would not let the men see him giving in to discomfort. He was stronger than the Ard Ri.

Malachi was finding such campaigns increasingly difficult. In recent years he had been plagued with hemorrhoids, which made riding an agony, but he was too old to walk. Face white with pain, he rode on a saddle thickly padded with fur cushions, and insisted that his mounts either walk or canter, but never trot.

Donough was contemptuous. "That pathetic old man," he said privately to Fergal and Ronan. He did not say it in Cumara's presence, however. Cumara had spent years taking care of an old man, and his sympathies were with Malachi.

As they neared the land of the Ui Caisin, the Ard Ri seemed to shrink in upon himself. He was gathering his energies as best he could for another of those battles he had come to dread.

But he was not prepared for the Ui Caisin when they came exploding out of the undergrowth.

Even Donough was caught by surprise. Almost before he knew what was happening, a warrior had grabbed the bridle of his horse and was wrenching the animal's head around, trying to make it fall and pin its rider.

"Maggot!" screamed Donough. He tore his sword from its sheath and hacked furiously at the man on the ground, driving him back. Meanwhile another of the enemy vaulted onto his horse from behind and tried to strangle him, but Donough twisted around and knocked his attacker off the horse, then slid to the ground himself, ready to fight.

By now Donough was very familiar with battle. It had a rhythm: lunge forward, slash and thrust, fall back, adjust your balance, attack again. A good sword could weave a shield of metal in the air around you. And there was always a man guarding his back; usually Fergal.

He was young and it was summer, and he thought himself invulnerable.

Catharnach, son of Aedh, chieftain of the Ui Caisin, did not know the identities of any of the warriors who had invaded his homeland under the banner of the Ard Ri. As far as he was concerned they were all The Enemy. But he did want credit for bringing down the most able of them, the champion. And from the way he was fighting, dancing on the balls of his feet, the champion appeared to be the very tall man with the flowing auburn moustache.

Brandishing an axe, Catharnach ran toward Donough.

Cera was kneeling beside a stream, washing her hair, when a cold white lightning burst over her. She sat up abruptly, slinging back her hair. Water cascaded from her head and ran down inside her clothes, but she did not notice.

The lightning vanished, and the light with it. Yet the sun was still visible. A strange murky grayness had descended, however, and a chilling cold.

She could taste blood in her mouth.

She leaped to her feet and ran toward the rowan trees.

Donough was jarred by the impact as his sword grated against bone. The man whose ribs he had just laid bare shrieked in pain and spun away from him, staggered, fell. Donough temporarily switched the sword to his left hand and gave his right arm a vigorous shake to relieve the shock. At that moment a florid young man with a button nose and sweat-drenched yellow curls flung himself forward, screaming a battle cry. He swung a mighty sideways axe blow at Donough's neck, meaning to decapitate him.

The attack caught Donough off-balance. He flung up his right hand instinctively, deflecting the blow, and heard the axe boom against his iron helmet.

For a measureless moment there was no pain, only a blinding white light. Donough rocked on his feet. In his left hand his sword seemed incredibly heavy; he could hardly lift it. When he tried to launch a counterblow dizziness washed over him and his effort was weak, badly aimed. The man leaped nimbly out of range then came toward him again, grinning in anticipation of an easy kill.

Fergal cut him down from behind. Catharnach fell without ever knowing what hit him.

Fergal caught Donough before he collapsed. "Over here . . . this way . . ." He half-carried his cousin away from the fighting toward the shelter of a copse of trees.

Donough still had not realized that he was injured. He could not understand why the countryside seemed to be spinning around him. In his ears a roaring rose and fell like the voice of the sea; he was very nauseated.

Looking up, he tried to focus on his rescuer's face. "I'm not seasick," he mumbled. "I don't get seasick anymore, Fergal."

The other laughed without humor. "We're a long way from the sea. You're axe-sick, you are. And it looks like you've lost a hand."

Chapter Forty-eight

Cera was frantic with anxiety. He was badly hurt and she did not know where he was, nor was there time to find him.

She had tasted his blood in her mouth.

Until long after moonrise she was scouring the fields and forests for every form of medicament that might be of use. Gathering them with the appropriate signs and spells, she carried them to the bank of the stream. There she built a large fire. When the heat was enough to warm the sap in the nearest trees and thick smoke was billowing out over the swift-flowing water, she consigned her collection to the flames.

* * *

For the second time in his life Donough had lost consciousness as the result of a battle injury, but this time he did not wake up with his head in someone's lap. Nor was his awakening painless.

"Sweet Jesus," he groaned as he became aware of an agonizing throbbing all along the right side of his body. His arm felt as if it were being crushed between giant jaws.

With an effort of concentration, he recalled the battle. He had a dim memory of an axe flashing in the sun; then nothing. He groaned again. Footsteps approached and he heard Fergal's voice as if from a great distance. "You're awake then? God be praised; we thought we'd lost you."

"Fergal?" Donough's tongue seemed to fill his mouth, making it hard to speak clearly.

His cousin squatted beside him, saying, "Don't try to talk, save your strength. If you really are going to live, we'll make a litter for carrying you."

"Malachi . . ."

"Celebrating victory. He'll start for Dun na Sciath tomorrow."

"I can't . . ."

"Of course you can't, it's too far. We'll take you on to Thomond, it's much nearer and you'll be safe there. Drink this, then rest."

Fergal held a cup of water to his lips and Donough sipped obediently, though even that effort made his arm throb.

He slid away into a buzzing darkness.

By dawnlight he learned the extent of his injury. When he awoke, in spite of the pain he made himself unwrap the bloodstained cloth someone had bound around his right arm. The fingers of his left hand were stiff and clumsy as if shrinking from their task. Before he had finished a clammy sweat formed on his forehead.

Then the arm lay revealed.

It was so purple and swollen at first he could not tell its true condition, only that the contours were wrong.

He peered closer. Nausea swept over him again.

Most of his hand was missing.

The axe had sheared off his fingers at an angle from between thumb and forefinger to just above the knob of wristbone. Only the thumb itself remained. Stubs of splintered bone and severed tendon fibers protruded from a crust of dried blood.

Donough could only stare.

Fergal bent over him. "Nasty," he commented. "Ronan said you would probably die."

Donough gritted his teeth. "Tell him I appreciate his faith in me."

With a laugh, Fergal straightened. "Och, you're better. You shouldn't be, but you are. Cumara!" he shouted. "Come here and take a look at this."

Cumara joined them, looking, as always, worried. He examined the exposed injury, then shook his head. "Ronan told us the hand would fester and we would have to cut off the whole arm."

Donough's toes curled in anguished anticipation. "Not my arm, you don't! It isn't festering, see?"

"It doesn't appear to be," Cumara reluctantly agreed. "But it should. We had nothing with which to treat the wound, all we did was wash away the worst of the blood with water from a stream. I cannot understand why . . ."

"I am healing to spite Ronan," Donough interrupted. "Where is he?"

Fergal's scowl of disapproval told the story. "He's gone with Malachi. Said he was a warrior and you would not be fighting any more battles, so . . ."

"So." The pain in Donough's arm was excruciating, but no less than his sense of betrayal. He was determined to let neither show. Keeping his face stony, he said, "The next time we go to war we will be better off without him."

"The next time?" Fergal looked quizzical.

"There will be a next time," Donough promised. "I've only lost part of a hand. I'm a long way from dead, no matter what Ronan thinks." He looked at Cumara. "I shall need some place to rest and heal. Can we go to your house on Lough Derg?"

"I gave it up to someone else when I joined you," Mac Liag's son replied. "There's Kincora, of course."

"Not yet. Not until I walk through those gates with the full approval of the law."

"What about Kill Dalua?" suggested Fergal. "The physician of the Dal Cais can take a look at that arm, though in truth there seems little for him to do. And the good brothers can care for you until you recover."

Donough started trying to rewrap the arm, but he was too clumsy. A solicitous Cumara took over the task.

Looking the other way, Donough said, "Kill Dalua would not be my first choice, but I suppose it's the best under the circumstances. And I won't need a litter. If you will lead my horse, Fergal, I can ride."

The rebuilt monastery at Kill Dalua was Cathal Mac Maine's pride and joy. The abbot went on a tour of inspection almost daily, feasting his eyes on sturdy oak gates and freshly quarried stone walls. If the new structure looked more like a fortress than a monastery, the resemblance was intentional.

Cathal now thought of Kill Dalua as a Christian stronghold against the pagan forces arrayed against him.

When the injured Dalcassian prince was brought to him to recover from his injury, Cathal welcomed him effusively. The abbot's disenchantment with Teigue continued, and having Donough under his influence for a time was a heaven-sent opportunity.

"You will be the first guest in our new guesting house," a beaming Cathal informed Donough. "Anything you require, you have only to ask for. We are now brewing some very fine mead from our own honey and apples, and I shall see that a jug is kept by your bedside to ease your pain."

Cathal was too friendly, instinct warned Donough. But he was wounded and weary and it was enough to lie beneath a linen sheet, listening dreamily to the angelic voices of the brothers as they changed their offices.

The abbot assigned several monks to tend to his needs. Foremost among them was a young local man called Brother Senan, who had a round Thomond face and a great gap between his front teeth, about which he was inclined to make jokes.

Under Brother Senan's watchful eye Donough slept, ate, slept again. The arm healed with astonishing rapidity. Sometimes, as he lay on his bed gazing out the window at the sky beyond, he thought of Cera.

She could feel him; much closer now. At least he was still alive. But she could feel a darkness, too, like a bruise in fruit. An injury. In spite of all her efforts he was damaged, and the knowledge tormented her.

She spent more and more time away from the cabin among the oaks. She could not bear to be under a roof or within the embrace of four walls.

She did not confide in Padraic. A change had taken place within her; she wanted to confide her inmost thoughts only to Donough. Everything of value in herself was his now.

Her longing reached out to him.

As his health improved Donough began to read voraciously, demanding books be brought to him from the abbot's library. His mind was as restless as his body was lacking in vigor. He resented the periodic exhaustion that still incapacitated him, although Ferchar, chief physician of the Dal Cais, assured him it was normal for someone who had suffered such an injury. "Just rest and give yourself time," he counseled.

But it was hard to rest, hard to feel life going on without him.

Donough spoke to Brother Senan. "The abbot said I could have anything I wanted, so I need you to do something for me."

"Of course," the monk agreed as he put a fresh sheet of linen on Donough's mattress. Smoothing the fabric over the bag of feathers he felt a momentary envy, but he quickly extinguished it and thanked God instead that he was allowed to sleep on a plank.

Donough was saying, "I want to send word to Cera Ni Padraic that I am injured and would like to see her. She's the daughter of my father's spear carrier; she lives near Ennis."

Brother Senan flashed a pleasant, gap-toothed grin. "If she sees my smile first, she may forget all about you," he warned.

"I'm willing to take that chance," replied Donough, grinning back at him.

When Senan dutifully reported the request to the abbot, he was startled by Cathal's response. "Forget we ever had this conversation."

"Forget? But Prince Donough wants . . ."

"He doesn't know what's good for him. A woman like that has no business coming within a day's journey of Prince Donough, and I mean to protect him from her."

"But what shall I tell him?"

"Don't tell him anything. Let him assume the message has been sent—and ignored."

Senan was a scrupulously honest man and any deception troubled him, but he was obedient.

While Donough waited for Cera to come to him, he began working to restore his strength. Every day he pushed himself harder, ignoring the order to rest. It was bad enough

that Cera would find him maimed; he did not want her to
see him weak as well.

He was a warrior. He could not think of himself as anything other than a warrior. And a warrior must fight, so he
had to relearn the use of weapons. Cumara had gone with
Fergal to the latter's home during Donough's recuperation,
so Brother Senan was pressed into service. The bemused
monk became a training partner, helping Donough adjust
to using his sword left-handed.

The weapon was made for a right-handed man, however.
The hilt was awkward in his left hand, the balance of the
blade was wrong. "I'll need a new sword," Donough told
Senan. "Send word to Odar the smith, at Kincora. Have
him come to me and we shall discuss its forging."

Odar soon arrived and a long afternoon was spent in
discussion of hilt shape and blade balance. The forge at
Kincora was heated white-hot; a new weapon was manu-
factured. The final result, when Odar delivered it to Kill
Dalua, was handsome and well balanced, but Donough
could not help thinking how little it resembled the sword of
Brian Boru.

"With the sword in my left hand I have to carry the shield
on my right arm," he said to Senan, "which may be of
advantage. When my hand is hidden behind the shield, no
opponent can tell I'm injured. And listen here to me, Senan:
Why not bind a knife to my right wrist, with the blade like
an extension of my thumb? That way if I lose the shield I'll
still have a weapon in either hand."

"Except you don't have two hands."

"I shall make a hand and a half enough," Donough
replied.

As he gained in strength, he undertook daily practice ses-
sions in the orchard beyond the refectory. Brother Bressal
complained that it disturbed his bees and would lower
honey production, but the other monks made a point of visiting the orchard as often as they could, for the pleasure of

watching. They were sworn to God, but they were born of a warrior race.

To a man, they admired Donough. He never spoke of his mutilation and made no excuses for it. Nor did he try to conceal it, except when carrying the shield. The rest of the time he displayed his damaged arm as freely as the other, and soon no one took any notice of it.

When the sunlight took on the golden slant of autumn and harvested apples piled high in baskets, Donough began to wonder when Cera would arrive.

She had waited as long as she could, but at last she wrapped a shawl around her shoulders, kissed her father good-bye, and set off eastward, feet white and bare beneath the hem of her red skirt. Cera trusted her intuition to lead her to Donough as surely as instinct brought mated birds back to last summer's nest.

She could feel him. Three days' determined walking should take her to him.

When she appeared outside the gates of Kill Dalua she found them closed. But a bronze bell had been set up in a niche, and she rang this energetically.

A small panel set flush in the left-hand gate slid open with a squeal of wood, and a tonsured head peered out.

"I want to see Prince Donough Mac Brian," Cera announced.

The monk regarded her owlishly. "Your name?"

When she told him, he slid the panel shut.

Cera waited with the taste of anticipation tingling like mint on her tongue. At last she rang the bell again.

A different monk looked out at her and she repeated her request. This time she was told, "The abbot has been informed."

"I am not here to see the abbot, but Prince Donough. I am . . . a friend of his, and I want to know if he's all right."

"Please wait." Once more the panel closed.

The third time the panel opened, it was Cathal Mac Maine himself who gazed out at her. She recognized him immediately and braced herself for another unpleasant confrontation, but instead he arranged his features in an expression of polite regret.

"You have come to visit Prince Donough, I believe?"

"I have."

"Then I am sorry to have to tell you he will not see you."

Cera stared at the abbot. "But I've come a long way . . ."

"Then I am doubly sorry."

Her small chin lifted stubbornly. "Let him tell me himself that he does not want to see me."

Cathal smiled. "He cannot do that without seeing you, and he refuses. There is nothing I can do. He is our guest; we cannot ignore his wishes in the matter."

"But he's been hurt!"

The abbot looked surprised, but quickly recovered. "How did you . . . indeed, he was injured in a battle, but he is almost well now. You need not concern yourself about him."

She was sure he was lying. Faced with his unyielding determination, the closed gates, the high stone wall, she was effectively blocked, however. She could not simply push her way in.

But when Cathal said, "I am sorry," a third time, he sounded so sincere her conviction was shaken. She was not born to noble rank, her woman's heart reminded her. Perhaps she was only a pleasant interlude in the life of a prince, and Donough really did not want to see her again. Perhaps when he sailed away to Alba he had forgotten all about her. She had no proof otherwise.

Reading self-doubt in her eyes, Cathal saw his victory.

He could afford to be generous now, if only for the sake of keeping the enemy off-guard. It was not hypocrisy, merely clever strategy. Anything was permissable for the greater good of the Church.

"Wait there and I will have one of the brothers bring you a small cask of mead to take home with you," he said.

Chapter Forty-nine

As the days passed with no word of Cera, I began to feel anxious. It had been necessary to establish an alliance with Malachi as soon as I returned to Ireland, but I had meant to go to her straight from Ui Caisin territory. There were things I needed to say to her, and explanations to be made in a way she would understand.

Instead I had been injured.

It was Cathal himself who informed me she was not coming to me. "We sent a request as you asked, but she has refused. There is nothing more we can do, Prince Donough."

"Why did she refuse?"

Cathal gave a noncommittal shrug. "I cannot explain the ways of women. I can only assume, in the light of your mutilation . . ." He paused meaningfully.

I stared down at my hand. "She was told of this?"

"Of your injury, of course."

When he had gone, I sat for a long time just looking at my hand—or what was left of my hand. The pain I felt was much greater than it had been on the day the axe cut through me.

Chapter Fifty

In him was an anger that simmered and seethed. At times it lay almost quiescent, no more than a dull heat beneath the surface of his soul. Then it would erupt for no reason he could consciously identify, lashing out with a white-hot fury that scorched himself as much as those around him.

When Ferchar told him the hand had healed as much as it ever would, Donough left Kill Dalua. He summoned Fergal and Cumara to accompany him and crossed the Shannon into Ely territory. Like the Dal Cais and the Owen-nachts, the Ely had extensive tribal landholdings in Munster. Their territory ran from the east bank of the Shannon north to Meath and south as far as Cashel. Eight powerful clans comprised the tribe, whose tribal king was tributary to the King of Munster.

Donough and his companions set up camp near the fort of a cattle lord called Lethgen, who promptly came out with a pair of spear carriers to question their intentions.

When Donough identified himself Lethgen was visibly impressed. "A kinsman of mine was historian to your father," he boasted. "Maelsuthainn O Carroll of the line of King Cearbhaill, the greatest of the chieftains of Ely."

"He is a very good friend of mine," Donough asserted. "As a child at Kincora I sat on his knee while he taught me my letters. We Dalcassians have always referred to him simply as Carroll, however; he prefers it."

Satisfied that Donough did indeed know his kinsman, Lethgen beamed. "I am certain he would expect me to give you the utmost hospitality," said the cattle lord, a bandy-legged, barrel-chested man with ruddy cheeks and the roseate nose of a confirmed ale-lover. "What may I offer you?"

"Land."

Lethgen was taken aback. His smile slipped. "What?"

"I need a holding, some land."

"As a prince of the Dal Cais, surely you have holdings in Thomond."

"I want to build a stronghold somewhere else," Donough replied, "and gather an army."

Lethgen was thinking fast. Here was another of the line O Brian, obviously extending his grasp. It would be wise to accommodate him. "This army of yours—it would protect your holding? And support your allies?"

"Indeed."

"Now that I think of it, Prince Donough, there is a hilltop not far from here with a grand view of the countryside; no one could sneak up on you at all. I have plenty of grassland, I could certainly grant you a holding as a kindness to my kinsman."

Donough smiled. "You are the soul of generosity," he assured the lord of Ely.

Learning his whereabouts, Dalcassians came to him: the loyal, the disaffected, the bored. From them he assembled a personal army, and from Ely timber he built a new fort with no old memories to taint the walls.

And no women, not even bondservants. In the beginning Donough's fort was an exclusively male stronghold where he sought to reproduce the masculine atmosphere of the Kincora he remembered.

Countless warriors had postured and swaggered through his father's hall, boasting of everything from their battle skills to the size of their genitals. As a child, Donough had hung on their every word. He had regarded them as demi-gods in a pantheon whose chief deity was Brian Boru.

Now similar men gathered under his banner in Ely and pledged their allegiance to him.

On the day each new man joined him, Donough held out his right arm in a way that forced them to observe the damage. "This is a battle wound," he said, "gained in honorable combat. I am not ashamed of it. Look your fill now. Then we can talk of things that matter."

Wounds more disfiguring than his were common in a warrior society, but never exhibited so blatantly. By calling attention to the mutilation, in a curious way he diminished its power. His men soon ignored it, which was his purpose.

He demanded to be treated as a whole man.

"I have lost enough," he told Cumara one night as they sat late beside the fire, "and I don't intend to lose any more." As he spoke he withdrew the harp from its bag beside his bench. He did not ask Cumara to help him. "The time has come to teach myself to play this with my left hand," he said.

Cumara looked dubious. "We can find a harper for you if you want music, it would be easier."

"I don't need anything to be made easier."

Donough rested the ruin of his right hand on the forepillar of the harp, holding the beautiful instrument in place with a purple-scarred stump ending in a single thumb like a hook. A webwork of exceptional musculature developed by wielding the sword remained at the base of the thumb. As the wound healed it had tried to contract and stiffen, but he fought back, manipulating the thumb, forcing the joints to flex and stay functional.

With grim determination he had taught himself to do many things using his maimed right hand, things that Cumara would have thought impossible. He would undoubtedly teach himself to play the harp with his left.

Donough's hall was silent except for the crackling of the fire. The first notes he evoked from the harp strings sounded tortured.

But he persevered.

Several warriors passing the hall overheard the attempt at music but did not realize who was responsible. There was a bark of derisive laughter.

Donough carefully laid the harp aside, then rose to his full height and hurled himself through the open doorway. In two strides he reached the surprised warriors. Seizing the nearest man by the shoulder in a punishing grip, he doubled his right arm and slammed it into his hapless victim's windpipe.

The warrior sagged in Donough's grasp. He gasped and made gurgling noises. His companions tried to intercede, but Donough gave them such a ferocious glare they fell back. With an oath he flung the laugher away from him, then ran after him and punched him in the face two or three times with his left fist.

When the man was lying inert and unconscious Donough turned without a word and stalked back into the hall. He picked up the harp and resumed practice as if nothing had happened.

After that no one laughed at his playing.

Learning that Donough had built himself a fort in Ely territory, Carroll decided to visit that branch of his clan which dwelt east of the Shannon.

He had grown too old and too stout for traveling by foot, so he made his journey in a wicker cart driven by a pungent bondservant. The man was disinclined to bathe but loved to talk, and his only topic was himself. He had an endless supply of pointless personal anecdotes. Occasionally Carroll interjected polite murmurs, but as they jolted along the rutted trackways the historian's thoughts wandered.

During a rare silence on the part of his driver he remarked, "As a scholar I have been singularly blessed. I was thinking about that just now, counting my blessings if you will. I have witnessed momentous events and been the confidante of kings. Words I have written will be carried to lands I shall never see, and speak, long after I am dead, to people as yet unborn."

"Annh," grunted the driver. "I don't read, myself. Bond-servants aren't entitled to an education like you lot. You nobles. But I have other skills. Did I ever tell you about the time I beat my cousin at arm wrestling? Four times running?"

Carroll sighed. "Please do," he murmured patiently.

But before the driver could launch into this new tale, a column of dark smoke on the horizon drew his attention.

"Outlaws burning some homestead," he said, pointing. "It's a disgrace. I am an honest man, and while there are days I feel hard done by, I would never . . ."

I have seen Ireland at her zenith, Carroll thought sadly. Now I am witness to her decline.

But at least there is Donough.

Like a traveler at sea, Carroll found himself pinning his hopes on a star.

When he found Donough he was shocked, though he tried to hide his reaction. Instead of the merry, arrogant youth he remembered, Carroll saw a man who wore his tragedies in his eyes.

The hand was the least of it. "Have a look," Donough offered casually. "It's healed remarkably well, they tell me."

Carroll glanced, then quickly looked away. He had seen too many battle injuries; he did not want to see any more. "I had no idea you'd lost an arm."

"I haven't lost my arm. Look again. Only part of my hand is gone. I can do everything I used to do, I'm not crippled," Donough said as if daring the historian to con-tradict him.

Carroll turned to see his baggage being carried into the

hall by his bondservant. "Be careful!" he called sharply. "My writing desk is in there, and my quills."

Donough raised an eyebrow. "All that baggage for a portable desk and some quills?"

"I have a few other things. You know. Clothes. Books. Mementos. One accumulates a certain amount of property over the years."

"From the looks of it you've brought most of your property with you."

Carroll lowered his eyes. "I have, actually."

"You intend a long stay?"

"If you have no objections. I would prefer to spend my remaining days with you than with . . ."

"With my brother? But surely Teigue can make you more comfortable than I can." As he spoke, Donough was gesturing to his men to bring a basin of heated water.

Carroll replied, "At Kincora, perhaps. But he does not live at Kincora these days. Cashel seems to please him better, being less Brian Boru's place and more his own. Our Teigue has become quite fond of the perquisites of being King of Munster. Ah, that's nice," the historian added as a steaming basin was offered for bathing his hands and feet.

While these ablutions took place, Donough steeled himself to ask, "Who occupies Kincora now?"

"The king keeps a garrison there so it does not stand empty."

The tall young man with eyes like winter lakes said softly, bitterly, "Teigue could have offered it to me."

Carroll did not reply. He devoted himself to removing the dust of the road.

Donough made the historian welcome and ordered a separate chamber built for him on the east side of the stronghold, where the morning sun would awaken him. "You and I seem destined to take care of old men," he remarked to Cumara.

"At least we don't have Gormlaith."

One of Donough's increasingly rare smiles flickered across his face. "Strangely enough, I almost miss her."

"And your father?"

Donough looked at some point over Cumara's shoulder. "I used to think he was with me . . . most of the time. Though not the way my mother seems to."

"It's not uncommon. After Mac Liag died I had a sense of his presence for months. I take it you no longer sense Brian Boru beside you, though?"

The skin around Donough's eyes tightened with pain. "No," he said.

A messenger arrived from Malachi, who was currently holding court at Tara. Was Prince Donough prepared to send some of his warriors to the Ard Ri's service?

Donough gave a cynical laugh. "The tide of battle must have turned against him again. But I'll go myself. It will amuse me to show him I'm not the cripple he no doubt imagines."

"Can you wield a sword?" Carroll wanted to know.

"Come out on the grass and I'll show you."

The historian was impressed. Donough brandished the weapon as if he were naturally left-handed.

"It is a pity," said Carroll, "that you don't have your father's sword, since you wear his ring and play his harp."

"I thought he was supposed to have been entombed with his sword," Donough replied. Suddenly he was tense. Something he heard in Carroll's voice alerted him.

"Supposed to have been. Yes. You put it very well. I myself saw it laid upon his body. But the vault was not sealed for several days, and during that time . . ."

"Someone took the sword," Donough concluded. He did not sound particularly surprised.

"Indeed. Once no man in Ireland would have desecrated a grave, but times are changing. Changing very fast."

"What happened to the sword?"

"The warrior who took it—and I shan't tell you his name, it is of no importance—was a Dalcassian. He took the sword because he loved Brian, I think. It went back to Thomond with him, but in time his conscience got the better of him and he presented it to the King of Munster."

Donough's features hardened into a rigid mask. "Teigue has my father's sword?"

"Yes and no. He thought it would be, ah, presumptuous of him to display the sword of the Ard Ri, and quite honestly I think he's afraid the Owenachts might try to steal it. So he had his servants secretly bury Brian's sword.

"At Cashel."

Chapter Fifty-one

Life was increasingly hectic for Malcolm of Alba. He had begun delegating some authority to the mormaers to collect tributes and be responsible for the execution of the king's law. But it was not easy for him to relinquish power, even to those he trusted. He spent much of his time traveling from one region to another to assure himself the king's word remained absolute in Alba.

Another of Malcolm's worries was the lack of a son. As the years passed, he had become obsessed with securing for his grandson, Duncan, the throne he must someday vacate. Mindful of the disaster whereby the Battle of Clontarf had destroyed Brian Boru's plans for an inherited and stable monarchy, he had even discussed the situation with Gormlaith during her visit. Talking together long into the night, they had agreed on the most pragmatic course of action.

In 1020, Malcolm put their plan into effect. Having slain
Kenneth the Second to gain the kingship, he now had the
grandson of his predecessor killed. By this deed he satisfied
himself there were no stronger claimants for the throne than
young Duncan. He was unfortunately unaware that the
murder victim left a daughter, Gruoch, who was betrothed
to a young Scot called Mac Beth, Mormaer of Moray, a
man also of royal descent.

With the murder of Kenneth's grandson, Malcolm's
hands felt no more bloody than they had before. "Kingship," as he had remarked to Gormlaith, "is only for the
able."

Although he doubted she any longer had the mental
capacity to understand, early in the year 1020 he sent
Gormlaith a letter. In it he wrote, "Our mutual plan for
Duncan's benefit is accomplished. Now I am prepared to
turn my energies toward your son, as we agreed."

Malcolm had been following Donough's career with
interest, welcoming every bit of news from Ireland.
"Duncan will not have an easy time when he is king," he
told Blanaid. "I mean for him to have all the allies I can
arrange, as I foresee the day he might need to call upon an
army of the Irish Gael to keep his place on the king-seat.
Therefore I want to be sure your brother is indebted to me."

Blanaid had had her fill of kingly manipulations. Gormlaith had inserted a wedge between herself and Malcolm
and she was no longer sympathetic to his political machina-
tions. Nor did she like the idea of having her brother used.
She told Malcolm so in no uncertain terms, surprising him.

"What has become of my compliant wife?" he asked,
meaning to tease her.

Blanaid's expression hardened. "She's Irish," was the
reply, "and not as compliant as you think!"

Thereafter Malcolm did not confide in her listening ear.
When he sent two more letters, first one to Earl Godwine

and, sometime later, one to Donough Mac Brian, he neglected to tell his wife.

Malcolm's letter reached Donough at Tara, where he had gone to join Malachi.

Once known as Tara of the Kings, the ancient royal seat had begun to show signs of dilapidation. The palisaded complex of timber forts and chambers sprawling along the green ridge was badly in need of limewash and rethatching. Preferring Kincora, Brian Boru had never made Tara his principal residence. Malachi Mor now followed his example.

This was Donough's first visit to the fabled hill, and he was disappointed.

He had brought his personal army with him, regaling them along the way with tales from his father's time. "When Brian stood upon the Stone of Fal it cried aloud for him as the true Ard Ri!" he repeated in ringing tones.

But when he saw the Stone of Fal, supposed parent to the Stone of Scone, he found it hard to imagine the scene that had taken place there only eighteen years earlier. Weeds were growing up around the roughly formed gray pillar-stone that lay on its side atop the Mound of the Hostages. Bird droppings like white lichens disfigured its surface.

Even the great banqueting hall and the House of the King looked shabby. A few sodden banners hung beside the fourteen doorways of the hall, and there was a fire on the hearth in the royal residence, but all Tara bore an air of dejection.

Malachi seemed cheerful, however, though it was a forced jollity born of growing desperation. "You are a hundred times welcome," cried the old High King as he hurried forward to greet Donough with outstretched hands. Then Malachi's eyes dropped. "I . . . ah . . . I heard you were injured, but . . ."

"But nothing. I'll fight any champion you care to name."

"Of course, of course." Smiling broadly, Malachi looked past Donough to the large company of able-bodied men he had brought. "We are glad to have all of you," he said. "There is rebellion in the west and the Connachtmen have plundered Clonmacnois. I have summoned additional warriors from both Leinster and Ulster but they have not yet arrived." The smile faded from his face as he spoke, revealing a troubled man approaching the end of his reign.

When *I* step upon the Stone of Fal it will cry aloud for me, Donough told himself. And there will be no weeds around it, either.

While the Ard Ri waited for more warriors to arrive, Malcolm's letter was brought to Donough by a messenger from Dublin. "The arrangements have been undertaken and completed," the king had written. "This day I have heard from the Earl Godwine that he accepts your proposal for his daughter Driella. She will be sent to you in Ireland as soon as she is of an age to consummate the marriage, and you will thus be related to the most powerful families in England.

"Remember who made this possible.

"Malcolm the Second, King of the Scots and the Picts."

Donough put the letter down and stared thoughtfully into space. For a man who had just learned he was betrothed, his expression was bleak.

He did not mention the contents of the letter to Fergal and Cumara until Malachi's combined army was marching toward Connacht. Then he remarked offhandedly, "In a year or two I shall have a new wife."

His two friends turned on their horses to stare at him. "A wife?" Fergal asked in surprise. "You're a deep one; you never mentioned this before. What cattle lord is being enriched with your bride-gifts this time?"

Donough's eyes twinkled. "No cattle lord, but Godwine, Earl of Wessex and Kent."

Their gape-mouthed astonishment provoked the first laughter he had enjoyed in a long time.

Fergal was the first to recover. "Why in God's name would you marry a square-headed Saxon?"

"Her mother is a Dane, actually. And her uncle is married to a sister of Canute, King of England."

For once even Fergal was speechless. It remained for Cumara to ask, "How did all this come about?"

"Through Malcolm. And my mother. It is something she wanted very much, and I . . . I saw no reason why not. While I was still at Kill Dalua I sent a letter to Malcolm to make the arrangements."

Edging his horse closer to Donough's, Cumara studied his face. "You don't seem very happy about this."

"Happiness is a tale told to children. I am making a most advantageous marriage. No other prince in Ireland will have such a connection. My sister is married to the King of Alba, and I shall be . . ."

"Ard Ri," concluded Fergal.

Cumara shook his head. "Even with the support of the King of England, that won't be easy. The brehons will argue you're blemished, and a blemished man cannot be king."

Donough replied scornfully, "That grass won't feed cattle any more. While I was recovering at Kill Dalua I read some of the *Senchus Mor*, the books containing Brehon Law. Kings had to be whole so they could be warriors, but I'm as good a warrior as any man in this company and I mean to prove it to the satisfaction of the brehons and anyone else. My father overthrew outdated traditions and so shall I."

They rode on into the west, following the banner of Malachi Mor. In his mind's eye, however, Donough was seeing his own banner at the head of the army.

Later the annalists would write: "An army was led by Malachi Mor and Donough Mac Brian to the Shannon, and there a great battle was fought. The forces of the Ard

Ri were triumphant, and he was given the hostages of Connacht."

The warriors who actually took part in the battle would remember it in much more colorful terms. Even with one hand, Donough fought like a man possessed. His left arm rose and fell, rose and fell, until the sword that had gleamed in the autumn sunshine was coated with blood. When a concerted rush by several Connachtmen succeeded in tearing his shield away from his right arm, the knife strapped to his wrist fatally skewered his nearest opponent. The others were so surprised they lost the all-important rhythm of the battle and Donough's men quickly overpowered them.

Below his helmet, Donough's face was radiant with victory. "Boru!" he screamed. "Boru!"

The sound of that cry froze the remaining Connachtmen in their tracks. The High King's army poured over them like a wave.

That night in the leather tent his men had erected for him beside Malachi's command tent, Donough tried to imagine his father beside him. "I fought well today," he whispered. "You would have been proud of me."

The night was very still. No voice answered him.

The Connacht campaign was a great success, but that same autumn Kildare was burnt and pillaged, the monasteries at Glendalough and at Swords were plundered, the bell of Saint Patrick was stolen and Armagh itself was burnt, with only the library being saved.

Malachi hurried north and east, south and west, putting out small fires while larger ones flamed up behind him. Only the onset of winter saved the old High King from a total collapse due to exhaustion. "Malachi is a spent force," Donough said privately to Fergal. "It's just a matter of time now, and while we wait for the inevitable I can be strengthening my base of support."

The combined army disbanded. Its members went home

to their various tribelands for the winter, aware that a new battle season surely awaited them the following year.

But something more awaited Donough. He had no sooner returned to his stronghold in Ely territory than another message reached him. Driella, daughter of the Earl of Wessex and Kent, would arrive in the spring.

A tall man with troubled gray eyes stood in the doorway of a timber hall, gazing out at a somber sky.

A wife. Another wife, a woman I've never seen. A woman who probably doesn't even speak Irish. How am I to talk with her? Will she know any Latin? What sort of education do Saxon women have?

But Driella was of noble blood, surely she would be educated as such women were in Ireland.

What will we talk about? Have we anything in common? She will be barely grown, her experiences surely limited. Perhaps all we will have in common are our bodies.

Bodies. A strange woman in his bed.

Heat throbbed in him, but it was a heat oddly disassociated from his mind.

Since his injury he had bedded no woman. Believing that Cera shunned him because of his mutilation made him wary. He did not want to subject himself to female pity.

Driella might pity him, but he resolved not to let it bother him if she did. She would be his connection to that great world that glimmered beyond the Irish horizon.

As he thought of marriage a figure took shape in his mind. But it was not the figure of a Saxon woman.

Staring down from his hilltop and across the plains of Tipperary, named after a holy well, Donough spent an imagined lifetime in the company of a slender Irish woman with huge, dark eyes.

They laughed a lot and he played the harp for her.

Blackbirds circled in the wintry sky, cawing derisively. Summoning him back to reality.

He went back into his hall and slammed the door.

Chapter Fifty-two

Dublin in the late spring teemed with activity. Seagoing vessels of every description sailed into the mouth of the Liffey to jostle one another for space at quayside. Traders from throughout western Europe unloaded merchandise, haggled, gesticulated, argued, and finally reloaded their ships with the wealth of Ireland. No one cared about the origins of the man he did business with, so long as a profit was made.

When Donough arrived to await Driella's ship, he went straight to the king of the Dublin Danes.

"You don't want to see her," Sitric assured him. "She won't recognize you; she doesn't know anyone any more."

"I've come to tell her I've kept my promise. She'll understand."

"She won't. But go ahead if you insist. I'll have someone show you where she is."

Gormlaith was being kept in a stone chamber at some distance from Sitric's hall. There was one heavy oak door with a bar on the outside, and a pair of opposed windows too small for anyone to squeeze through. Relieved to find her Scottish attendant still with her, Donough gave the man a leather pouch full of coins stamped with the image of Sitric Silkbeard—valuable in Dublin if not in the rest of Ireland, where cattle or bondwomen still comprised the medium of exchange.

Then he turned his attention to Gormlaith.

Seeing her, he wished he had followed Sitric's advice. He did not want to remember her as she was now, shrunken and wizened and gray. She was wrapped in warm robes and the Scot kept her clean and fed, but she seemed no more than an empty husk. When he addressed her as Mother, Gormlaith did not respond at all.

Donough sat down beside her and took her right hand in his left while he told her of his betrothal. She gave no indication of awareness. "Are you not pleased?" he asked earnestly. "Is this not what you wanted for me?"

With her head sunk on her breast, she picked idly at a thread on her sleeve.

In frustration he burst out, "Does she even know I'm here?"

"I cannot say," the Scot answered. "But if I ask her to stand up or sit down she does, so there is something left in her poor old head."

Eventually Donough joined Sitric in the Viking hall, where he drank four horns of ale in swift succession.

"Well?" said the Viking. "Did she recognize you?"

"No."

"Did you say what you came to say to her?"

"I did."

"Any reaction?"

"No. I'll be going now, Sitric. Thank you for your goodness to her."

His half-brother hesitated. "You can . . . you can stay here if you're going to be in Dublin for a while."

Donough gave him a measured smile, warm enough to be polite, cool enough to discourage intimacy. "I think not. It would not look good for either of us. You're still pillaging my people whenever you can get away with it."

"*Your* people?" Sitric stroked his beard. "So that's the way the wind is blowing?"

"You will have to meet me someday as we agreed, to negotiate," replied Donough. "Until that time, it is best if we develop no personal friendship."

Sitric threw back his head and laughed. "Friendship! With you? There was never any danger of that!"

In her chamber, Gormlaith repeatedly ran the tip of her tongue over her lips. The Scot left her to fetch a pitcher of fresh water. When he had gone she lifted her head and regarded the closed door.

"A marriage," she muttered, frowning, trying to think clearly. But her head was full of shapes and memories that flowed into one another uncontrollably. "Marrying . . ." She could not hold the thought. It slipped through her mental fingers like drops of water and was gone. Overwhelmed by the tides of time, Gormlaith was swept back to a wedding day of her own and saw herself at Kincora beside a copper-haired giant. They might have been of another race, ageless and more beautiful than mere mortals.

Donough and his men pitched tents outside the walls of Dublin, not far from his first sight of the city almost a decade earlier. Leaving the others behind, he went alone to Kilmainham and stood a long time before a rough gray standing stone carved with a Celtic sword.

"Murrough," he called in a low voice to the brother who lay beneath the stone.

"I am living the life that was meant for you. You were to follow our father as Ard Ri. How unexpected are the events that actually shape our lives! It is never the thing we plan for; always something else. Fate . . . or God? Or random chance? How much of it is in our own hands? Anything?"

Donough realized he was afraid of the answer.

A runner brought news of a Saxon ship in the bay. Dressed in princely style with his gold torc prominently displayed, Donough went into Dublin to meet his bride.

Accompanied by Fergal and Cumara, he waited impatiently at quayside while the wide-bellied, square-sailed

Saxon vessel was maneuvered into position. As he scanned
the faces waiting at the rail he saw no one who might be the
daughter of Earl Godwine.

"Perhaps," said Fergal jocularly, "she changed her mind
and didn't come."

Donough replied through gritted teeth. "She couldn't
change her mind. Their laws are different from ours; Saxon
women are property. Her father would make her come."

"There she is!" Cumara cried, pointing.

A chubby girl with corn-colored braids looped around
her ears had appeared at the railing. Her face was broad,
bland, and wind-chapped, and she was chewing on her
thumb. She could not have been older than fourteen.

Donough strode forward as she disembarked with a small
escort. Earl Godwine had sent four Saxon housecarles with
his daughter, sturdy men-at-arms who cast suspicious eyes
on everything they saw. There was also, to Donough's surprise, a Saxon priest.

Language was a problem. Driella spoke no Irish, and
when her intended husband tried to welcome her in Latin
she stared at him blankly. Then her eyes dropped to the
mutilated hand he made no effort to hide. She turned to the
dark-visaged young man in clerical garb beside her and jab-
bered away in her own tongue.

The priest suppressed a smile. To Donough he said, in
polished Latin, "I am called Geoffrey of the Fens. I am sent
by the Earl Godwine to guard his daughter's virtue and see
that she is married properly."

"What did she just say to you?" Donough demanded
to know.

"She remarked that you are a comely man," Geoffrey
replied smoothly.

Donough did not believe him.

Deep down, he was angry. Did the Saxons think the Irish
were such heathen they had to send one of their own
priests?

They shepherded the Saxons through Dublin, down narrow alleys where the local Vikings stared at them and stray dogs barked at them. The brightly painted wicker cart Donough had provided for Driella was waiting just outside the eastern gateway. A company of his men were guarding the cart and holding horses for himself, Fergal, and Cumara, but there were none for the Saxon soldiers or the priest.

Geoffrey of the Fens promptly climbed into the car beside his young charge.

All communications with Driella subsequently took place through Geoffrey, a fact that amused Donough's men not a little.

"I wonder if he'll stand beside the marriage bed and give her instructions," Fergal muttered to Cumara.

The other guffawed.

During the long journey to Tipperary, Donough had ample opportunity to study his intended bride. "She could be worse," he finally said to Fergal.

"She could be," his cousin assured him. "She has two expressions: stupid, and scared. It would be worse if she had only one. And at least she possesses good wide hips, she'll give you sons."

Wide hips and a noble family constituted most of Driella's assets. She had brought the requisite dowry, Saxon coin and Flemish cloth, but she seemed woefully deficient in personality. Nor was she interested in much beside the priest, to whom she clung like a child afraid of strangers. For much of the journey he kept one arm around her to cushion her from the jolting of the cart.

When at last they reached Donough's fort she clapped her hands together and made some remark to Geoffrey.

"She says you have a magnificent palace," the priest translated to Donough.

Fergal sniggered. "If she thinks this fort is a palace, what sort of place do you suppose a Saxon earl inhabits?"

Donough's plan was to marry Driella in Saint Flannan's Chapel, with Cathal Mac Maine officiating as before. He took great pleasure in sending a message to Teigue, formally requesting the use of Kincora for the wedding. "My marriage to a niece of the King of England," was the way he put it.

"That is not strictly true," Carroll pointed out. "Her uncle is married to the king's sister, which makes your Driella . . ."

"Whatever I say she is," Donough snapped.

Whatever the niceties of the connection, Teigue was thunderstruck by the news, as Donough had intended he should be. He saw the ramifications at once.

"I suppose I must let him use Kincora—temporarily. But we will not go to that wedding," he told his wife.

Maeve put a gentle hand on his arm. "But we must, and not just because he's your brother. How would such an open split among the Dalcassians look to outsiders?"

"There is already a split; everyone knows it."

"But why make it wider? Let's go to Donough's wedding and perhaps use the opportunity to mend things between you."

The wedding was ruffling other feathers, however.

Cathal Mac Maine was irritated by the proposed presence of Geoffrey of the Fens, and when he learned Geoffrey intended to say "some sort of Saxon rite" over the couple, his temper exploded.

Donough sent Carroll to placate him. "The occasion will mark a most signal honor for the Dal Cais," the historian pointed out, "and for Saint Flannan's. Prince Donough is not marrying just anyone, but a niece of the King of England." The phrase did not stick in his throat. "Your joint participation with the Saxon priest will set a new tradition. No doubt there will be pleasure in Rome when the Church learns of this."

As ever, Carroll was persuasive. Cathal agreed and the date for the wedding was set.

Donough invited almost every free person in Thomond. He went to his father's fortress in order to supervise all the arrangements himself. For weeks in advance, supplies were carted into Kincora to feed the expected horde.

When Teigue and Maeve arrived they were astonished at the lavishness of the hospitality being provided. "My brother cannot pay for all this himself," Teigue told his wife. "And I will not!"

But Donough asked nothing of Teigue. Every action of his emphasized his independence from his brother.

When a group of young people gathered at the river, the bellows-boy who worked in the forge of Odar the smith remarked to a comely bondwoman who worked in the kitchens, "If Prince Donough is marrying the King of England's daughter, does that mean an army from England will be coming here?"

The girl scratched her head. It was a bad year for lice. "I hope not. We have all we can do now, preparing food for the marriage feast. If another army is coming I don't know how they will be fed. I don't even know where all this food is coming from."

A porter who brought supplies to the kitchens joined the conversation. "The O Carrolls of Ely are furnishing most of it themselves. This morning six carts piled high with slaughtered boars forded the Shannon, followed by twelve carts loaded with casks of ale and wine. Brian Boru's old wine cellar is so full we're having to open a new one."

"Why are the Ely being so generous?" wondered the girl. But her companions could not explain the abstractions of politics.

Teigue, however, thought he understood very well. "Donough has made allies of the Ely in order to outnumber the Dalcassians who are loyal to me," he told Maeve. "He intends to use this wedding to show everyone he has more supporters than I have. I don't have to stay here and suffer this, I'm going back to Cashel and taking my men with me, so no one can count them and make comparisons."

"But the wedding . . ."

"You stay if you want. Women love weddings."

The departure of the King of Munster was observed by everyone and commented upon by most, but Donough was not displeased. "In addition to his other failings, now my brother reveals himself as petty and mean-spirited," he remarked.

The wedding proved to be the spectacular event he had planned, with the four ranks of Irish kingship represented. The Ard Ri did not attend personally but he sent gifts. The eldest sons of two of the provincial kings, those of Leinster and of Connacht, did arrive, duly impressed to find Donough in apparent possession of Kincora. Several tribal kings such as the king of the Ely were among the guests, and a number of clan chieftains.

Padraic of Ennis and his family did not attend.

When Donough and Driella emerged from the chapel he found himself half-hoping, half-fearing to see Cera there. For one wild moment he imagined leaving the dumpy girl by his side and running to the druid. Sweeping her up in his arms, carrying her out of Kincora forever, taking her into the wild hills of Thomond and . . .

"Hoos-band," said Driella, giving his left arm a proprietary squeeze.

Then she laughed. It was the first time Donough had heard her laugh; the sound was like the breaking of eggs.

Chapter Fifty-three

✠

Deep in his bones, Malachi Mor sensed the approach of death. The rats of mortality gnawed with sharp teeth. He awoke in the night gasping for breath, listening to the increasingly irregular thudding of his heart.

As he told his confessor, "I am not afraid to die; every warrior has faced death so many times the fear is replaced with familiarity."

He had another reason for lack of fear, however; an over-riding emotion. In death Malachi meant to triumph at last over his greatest rival. He would thwart forever the dreams of Brian Boru.

Malachi's sons had died in battle and fallen to disease, even the youngest of them, but he was expected to name a tanist. Under the very rule of succession that Brian had established to benefit his own son Murrough, Malachi's tanist would succeed him as High King.

"Donough Mac Brian has worked very hard to win my trust and support," he told the clan chieftains of Meath when he entertained them in the hall of Dun na Sciath. "He hopes I will go outside my tribe and name him to succeed me. It is the sort of break with tradition his father espoused."

"No!" the chieftains thundered, pounding their fists on the table.

Smiling serenely, Malachi continued. "Donough has built himself a formidable power base in Munster. I know why; he means to wrest Cashel from his brother. As King of Munster he would be following in his father's footsteps on his way to Tara.

"Do not scowl at me, good friends. The high kingship is not to be taken away from our tribe and our blood, I swear this to you on the sacred wounds of Christ. There are several moves by which I shall forestall the ambitions of the clan O Brian. The first concerns Tara, and for this I need your support."

Tara was the ultimate symbol of high kingship. Malachi now proposed to abandon the ancient royal site altogether. By this official act he meant to deny its possession to whoever succeeded him.

He vowed that no son of Brian Boru would ever hold court in the banqueting hall with the fourteen doorways.

With some reluctance, the chieftains agreed to his plan. Ending the supremacy of Tara would be a blow to Meath prestige, but they would rather see it fall into final decay than revert into the hands of Munstermen.

With a weariness he would admit to no one, Malachi visited Tara one last time. He rode in an old-fashioned chariot bedecked with plumes and gaudy with colors, and he took as escort the battle-champions of Meath.

In the end, however, he paid his final visit alone.

"Wait for me," he instructed his driver. Stepping down from the chariot, he entered through the great northern gateway and proceeded up the ceremonial avenue on foot.

A cold wind was blowing. The rats chewing Malachi's old bones bit deeper.

For eight hundred years this had been Tara of the Kings, and before that the stronghold of the Tuatha De Danann. But whatever sorcery might still linger could not prevail against the power of time. Earthwork embankments that once stood taller than six men were gradually sinking, victims of centuries of human wear and elemental erosion. The timber palisades that encircled the site, mile upon mile of them, were rotting. An attacking force could breach them with little effort.

But no one would attempt Tara now; its symbolic value was ended. The Ard Ri had so decreed.

Malachi shivered. Suddenly he wanted very much to be gone from here. Tara had never been his, not since Brian Boru stood on the Stone of Fal and it screamed aloud for him.

The Stone had never screamed for Malachi.

When he realized the sun was beginning to set he trudged back down the ceremonial avenue. The farewell tour was over, the silent good-byes said. His chariot was waiting just beyond the gateway; a brisk drive would take him back to Dun na Sciath, to hearth fires and ale and the forgetfulness of old men.

At the gate he paused without meaning to and looked back. The westering sun gilded Tara. Decaying thatch blazed gold.

Atop the Mound of the Hostages, the recumbent Stone of Fal was struck by a slanting sunbeam.

Malachi gasped.

For just one moment he thought a man stood there, his coppery hair aflame in the setting sun.

A giant.

Chapter Fifty-four

Cumara was worried. Anxiety came naturally to him; the permanent frown on his forehead had been stitched there when he was still a young boy. It was his lifelong habit to awaken each morning asking himself what might go wrong in the day ahead.

But now he did not have to ask. He knew.

The stronghold was no longer a comfortable place for a man to be. Since his marriage to Driella, Donough was more short-tempered than ever. Even Fergal had begun guarding his tongue; his sarcasm no longer amused Donough but made him angry.

Almost anything could make Donough angry.

No one knew when they might receive the sharp edge of his tongue. He took the most casual comment the wrong way, seeing insult where none was intended. For the first time, he began wearing sleeves so long they concealed his mutilated arm. If he thought anyone was looking at it he glared at them savagely.

Cumara told Fergal, "I'm going to leave here and go back to Thomond. The atmosphere in this place makes me nervous; it's as if the fire on the hearth is about to explode."

Fergal said quickly, "Don't go! You're a good influence on him. At least he plays the harp occasionally for you, the only time he seems to be in relative good humor."

"I'm a poet's son," Cumara pointed out, "and I have my father's temperament if not his talent. Discord upsets me. It's all very well for you; warriors thrive on conflict. But some nights I can't even eat my meal, my stomach is so roiled. A couple of times recently I've vomited blood. I'm going back to Thomond."

"I thought you gave your house away."

"I did, but I have friends who will take me in. Friends of my father's will welcome me in his name."

"What will Donough do if you go?"

"I worry about that," Cumara replied.

But he left; an act of self-preservation after a life dedicated to others.

Donough was too proud to ask him the reasons for his leaving, although deep in his heart, he knew.

As Cumara was taking his leave of Carroll, he warned the old man, "Keep an eye on that Saxon priest, will you?"

"What can I do? I'm a guest here, I have no right to interfere."

Cumara's naturally lugubrious face lightened briefly. "When did you not interfere, Carroll?"

Donough needed no warning about Geoffrey of the Fens. The man's presence was a constant irritant, yet he could not send him away. Only Geoffrey could translate what he said to Driella, or she to him, and the young woman seemed unable to learn any language other than Saxon.

At first Donough agreed with Fergal; she was simply stupid. But as time passed he began to suspect she was deliberately refusing to learn so she would have to keep Geoffrey with her.

Yet he never caught them together in any compromising position.

When Carroll remarked on their constant companionship, and Driella's total dependence on Geoffrey, Donough's pride made him say in her defense, "I cannot imagine my wife betraying me with a priest or anyone else. She's nothing like my . . ."

"Like your mother? No, she is nothing like Gormlaith," Carroll agreed.

But Driella had other faults, he observed.

A lifetime spent absorbing every tenet of the Church with no sense of discrimination had rubbed away her own personality, leaving her as featureless as an ocean-scoured pebble. She was submissive and self-effacing to an infuriating degree.

Old as he was, Carroll began speculating about what it was like to bed such a woman.

The first night had been awkward, but no more than Donough expected. Driella was a virgin and there were tears and blood and moans of pain.

Cera had been a virgin, he recalled against his will. And

there had been blood, but no tears, only radiant smiles and . . .

Driella had submitted totally to him in spite of her pain, spreading herself beneath him like a sacrifice. She lay with eyes screwed tight shut and endured him. Had there not been so much pent-up lust in his body, Donough would have got off her and walked away. He felt as if he were pounding himself into a piece of meat.

The next morning he had barely left their bed when Geoffrey came bustling in, all unctuous sympathy, and knelt to pray with the deflowered bride.

"No one sent for you," Donough had said coldly, but the priest replied, "I'm only here to help. This child needs me now; due to the rigors of the voyage she brought no womenfolk of her own. Surely you have enough delicacy to understand?"

That same day Donough arranged for female bond-servants but they proved of little use except for menial tasks. They spoke no Saxon.

Geoffrey seemed to be constantly counseling Driella. When Donough bit back his pride long enough to ask what they were discussing, the priest replied, "I am giving her advice as to her conjugal duties."

Yet Driella's response in the marriage bed did not improve. She accepted. She endured. The only emotion she ever displayed was when she shrank from the most inadvertent touch of her husband's maimed arm.

After each night spent with Donough, in the morning her first act was to pray with Geoffrey.

"We are praying that she will conceive," Geoffrey said.

Donough discovered a curious thing about himself. Passion was a powerful, compelling force in him, but he could direct it into other channels such as fighting—so long as there was not a woman to focus his desire.

With the plump young Saxon in his bed, however, he thought constantly of sex. If he did not have intercourse with Driella he lay awake, smelling her skin and hair, intensely aware of her slightest movement, suffering from a painful erection and aching testicles. If he rolled over and entered his wife he found momentary relief, but was plagued afterward by a sense of profound disappointment, almost of disgust with himself.

Marriage, he concluded, was an arrangement like any other political arrangement. Driella provided him with important alliances and he had no reason to doubt she would in time give him sons. Such assets came at a price, but it was a price he must pay.

Compromise, he thought with a sense of irony. *The skill Murrough never mastered.*

When Driella began to ripen with a child, compromise seemed justified.

The birth of Donough's first live child, a boy he called Murchad, did not merit an entry in the annals. For that year Brother Declan wrote: "Branagan, a chieftain of Meath, was drowned in Lough Ennell, and Mac Conailligh, chief brehon of Malachi Mor, died, after the plundering of the shrine of Saint Ciaran by the both of them. The King of Leinster gained a victory over Sitric of Dublin at Delgany. Donough Mac Brian mediated between them and brought an end to dreadful slaughter."

Since abandoning Tara, Malachi had not summoned Donough to his banner. So Donough now sent a full report to the Ard Ri detailing his negotiations between the King of Leinster and the Dublin Danes, demonstrating that he was as skilled at bringing peace as at waging war. The unspoken but implicit addendum was: make me your successor.

Malachi did not respond.

The following summer found him leading an army against Sitric and the Dublin Danes at the Yellow Ford of Athboy, amid a shower of hailstones the size of apples.

Once more Donough Mac Brian had not been summoned.

Only a month later, Declan wrote, "The Age of Christ,

1022. Malachi Mor, High King of Tara, pillar of dignity, died on an island in Lough Ennell in the seventy-third year of his life. He relinquished his soul on the fourth of the Nones of September, after doing penance for his sins and receiving the body and blood of Christ. Masses, hymns, psalms, and canticles were sung throughout Ireland for the repose of his spirit."

Cathal Mac Maine directed his scribe to add, "Splendid though they were, the obsequies for Malachi Mor were a mere shadow compared to those for Brian Boru."

The Abbot of Kill Dalua had not attended either funeral, but he had Dalcassian honor to uphold.

Malachi was deeply mourned by his many adherents. Poets lauded his exceptional generosity. Donough confided to Carroll, "I am surprised to find myself genuinely grieved by his death. Malachi has been a part of my life, in one way or another, for as long as I can remember."

"I too mourn him," Carroll replied, "though perhaps for different reasons. He was of my generation; if he has walked over the rim of the world, I must shortly follow."

A fierce light leaped in Donough's eyes. "Not until you see me inaugurated Ard Ri!"

He thought it would be soon.

He was totally unprepared for the shock that followed.

The news was shouted across the countryside like an announcement of the end of the world. Thunderstruck, Donough saddled his fastest horse and galloped headlong to Kill Dalua to await formal confirmation.

The abbot was as taken aback as himself. "Malachi Mor has robbed the Dal Cais of their entitlement!" he complained.

But his anger was nothing compared to Donough's. "That wretched schemer must have made these plans long before he died. When I last saw him—and we shared a cup together—he already knew. He knew and said nothing and smiled at me like a fond uncle, Cathal! And to think I was mourning him! How did he manage to persuade them? Did he offer gold to Lismore to get the abbot to agree?"

Cathal was offended. "Impossible. A man of God?"

"This entire arrangement is impossible!" Donough vehemently protested. "He—*they*—cannot possibly be High King. How could two men hold one high kingship?"

The question was being repeated throughout Ireland in every noble household.

Assiduously searching Irish law, even the brehons were astonished to find nothing that could prevent the High King from naming dual successors if he chose. Brian Boru had endowed the office with unprecedented powers. In the last official act of his life, Malachi Mor used those powers to the fullest.

Henceforth Ireland was to be governed jointly by Cuan of the line of Lochlan, chief poet of Meath, and Corcran Cleireach, a renowned holy man and anchorite under the supervision of the Abbot of Lismore.

The title Ard Ri, however, was to be held in abeyance.

Tara would remain deserted.

Chapter Fifty-five

The explosion Cumara had expected came at last. Donough unleashed his rage.

While his mother was alive he would maintain a degree of amity with Sitric, but no one else was safe from his fury. He resurrected old Munster tribal feuds and initiated new ones. He flung himself from one battle into another with an energy that astonished, and eventually exhausted, his followers.

The Dalcassians' traditional rivals the Owenachts were his principal targets, but he also undertook raids into Ossory and Muskerry, bringing back hostages for whom he demanded a very high ransom.

Teigue was appalled. "I shall be blamed for this," he complained to his courtiers at Cashel. "The other provincial kings will think I'm encouraging him in preparation for invading their kingdoms."

"You might do," suggested a bored warrior hopefully. "You might reach beyond Munster and start laying claim to all of Ireland. There's plenty would support you."

"I have everything I want here," Teigue insisted when he saw the sudden fear in his wife's eyes.

The seed was planted, however.

In the dark of night he sat in his private chamber at Cashel and stared into the fire in the brazier, thinking of the high kingship. Brian's high kingship, suspended. Waiting.

Without saying anything to Maeve, he ordered his father's sword dug up and brought to him.

Donough resented the onset of winter that brought an end to battle season. If there were no wars to fight, he must retire to his stronghold and wait for spring; wait for winter's mud to solidify enough for marching upon once more.

Wait under the same roof with Driella. And Geoffrey. And his bitterness.

His second child was conceived that winter. Donough announced if it was a boy he would be called Lorcan, meaning "fierce." "Lorcan was the name of my father's grandfather," he explained when Geoffrey protested at such an un-Christian choice. "And what right have you to question the naming of my children?"

Feet wide apart, Geoffrey of the Fens stood his ground. His mouth opened as if he meant to say something—then he took a long look into Donough's eyes.

The mouth closed. The priest turned away.

Grimly, Donough endured the winter. He knew he was irritable and volatile, but his soul chafed as if he wore a hair shirt. Inactivity maddened him. Once or twice he took out the harp and tuned it, then put it back in its case unplayed.

There was no music inside him to express.

The days were long and the nights were longer. Like a fly trapped in amber, he felt hung up in life.

To pass the time he began inviting Lethgen to his hall. The loquacious cattle lord was content to carry on a conversation with only minimal replies from Donough and pretended to be unaware of his host's bad moods. Lethgen would have put up with a much worse temper for the sake of such a friendship. Donough would be Ard Ri yet, he had no doubt.

Besides, the Dalcassian was an unstinting host who always kept a vat of ale on hand.

Late one night when everyone else had fallen asleep, Donough and Lethgen were still matching one another cup for cup in drunkenly determined competition. They drank to Donough's son Murchad and to his unborn child; they drank to Lethgen's sons and daughters, and to everyone's cousins, and to Munster and Ireland and all the saints. When they had run out of anything else to toast, Donough said in a blurred voice, "I drink to my father's sword."

Lethgen belched. "A fine choice." He raised his cup. "To Brian in his tomb."

"The sword isn't in his tomb."

"No?" Lethgen put down the cup and peered owlishly at his host. "Where then?"

"My brother got possession of it some way. It's buried at Cashel."

"Tha's no place for a good sword. A sword that knows how to win wars. You should have that sword."

"I know," Donough replied morosely. "Teigue won't use it; he doesn't deserve it."

"You should have that sword. You should."

"I know."

"Yes indeed. My frien' Donough should have that sword. I will get that sword for him. I promise." Lethgen stared into his cup, dismayed to find it was empty again. "I promise," he repeated.

Donough refilled both their cups. When Lethgen finally tumbled off his bench and lay snoring on the straw that carpeted the floor, his host was still awake.

Anything was better than going to bed. He refilled his cup yet again and, swaying slightly, carried it to the door of the hall.

The stars were far away. His eyes would not focus properly; their individual lights became a shimmering blur. Only the moon was separate and distinct.

"Cera," Donough whispered.

He never allowed himself to think of her when he was sober.

Lethgen awoke in the cold gray dawn with a ferocious headache. He was halfway home before he recalled snatches of the conversation the night before. But once remembered, he did not forget. He was of the Gael; a promise was sacred.

Spring of the year 1023 came late. Lethgen's herds had suffered during the hard winter and their numbers were diminished. He hoped for a good breeding season, but his bulls were old and not as vigorous as he would have liked.

Hearing of a remarkable young bull down near Cashel, he set off to attempt some trading. Travel in Ireland was not as safe as it once had been, so Lethgen took with him an armed complement of Ely men.

"Let outlaws beware!" they told one another.

Unfortunately, even after several days' hard haggling the deal could not be done. The bull's owner proved intransigent. Lethgen was disappointed, but determined not to go home empty-handed.

* * *

Meanwhile Donough was beginning to respond to the change of seasons. The depression of the dark days lifted. He could not endure to be melancholy when the sun was radiant and the very air smelled green, so with an act of will he strove to be more pleasant—even to Geoffrey.

Relief was palpable in the fort.

Fergal also felt the sap rising in his veins. "It's time I took a wife for myself," he told Carroll.

"You've exhausted the local women?"

Fergal laughed. "Or they have exhausted me. But in truth, I feel a need for sons. I must find a woman suitable to marry a man of my rank. Bedding is one thing, marrying is another. And she should be a Dalcassian. These Ely females are fine and glossy, but they don't know any of the songs I know."

The old historian chuckled understandingly. "The sort of woman you want is best sought at Cashel. Where there is a rooster you find chicks; where there are kings you find princesses."

"If I go to Cashel, Donough will feel betrayed. You know how things are between Teigue and himself."

"Leave Donough to me," Carroll suggested.

Waiting until just the right moment, he broached the subject to Donough. "You have lost so much of your family, you should try to be on good terms with those who remain."

The explosion he half-expected did not come. "You think I should patch up my quarrel with Teigue?"

"I do, for many reasons. Not the least of them is the need to find an appropriate wife for our Fergal, and such women are most numerous at the king's court."

Though Donough did not smile, the grim line of his mouth softened. "I always did admire a good tactician, Carroll. You're offering me an excuse to visit my brother without looking as if I'm seeking something for myself."

Carroll's expression was one of perfect innocence. "What could you possibly be seeking for yourself?"

Donough took several days to consider. His rage had burnt itself out, and his expanding family reminded him of the importance of the family network. Perhaps the time had come to make amends. Kincora was still not his, but it was no longer as painful. Time and distance helped. He had his own home, his own life, even if they were not what he had dreamed.

"If we go to Cashel will you go with us?" he asked Carroll.

"Och, I'm too old. I'm done with traveling. You don't need me at your elbow, Donough, to give you words to say. You have the finest mind of all Brian's sons, and in spite of that hard shell you wear, I know there is a gentle man inside.

"Go to your brother and offer him the hand of friendship. If you are sincere, he will welcome you. Teigue cannot want this barrier between you any more than you do."

Preparing for the journey, Donough assembled casks of ale, piles of furs, bales of fine leathers to take as gifts to his brother. Once having made the mental commitment he was determined not to let pride stand in his way. He would make all the overtures; Teigue had only to accept.

He began to feel a sense of relief at shrugging off a burden he had carried far too long.

As he did not want Teigue to misunderstand the motives for his visit, he refrained from taking his army with him. Fergal and a score of others would accompany him, armed only with hunting spears and the ubiquitous Celtic short-sword every man carried at his belt.

Fergal questioned the decision. "You're taking a chance, Donough. We've been fighting half the tribes of Munster recently. What if one of them sees this as the perfect opportunity to ambush us?"

"We'll stay in Ely territory all the way to Cashel," Donough assured him. "And if we encounter outlaws, a score of our good men can overwhelm any band of mongrels."

"We can," Fergal agreed, heartened as always by his cousin's confidence.

Donough had a new horse—part of the ransom for the hostages of Ossory—which he meant to ride on the journey. A skittish brown colt with powerful hindquarters, the animal had tried to knock him off by running under a low branch the first time he rode it. The trip to Cashel would be a valuable training exercise because it was long enough to tire the colt and make it tractable.

Donough thought briefly of wearing his helmet, in case the horse tried to bash his head against another branch. Then, mindful of his determination to appear peaceful, he left the helmet behind.

As the party rode south he bantered amiably with his men. Delighted that he was more like his old self, they began to relax. Finally someone asked the question that had long been on everyone's mind: "Will you mount a challenge for the high kingship now?"

Donough shook his head. "Malachi was very clever. He knew I would not attempt to overthrow a poet and a holy man. Both are sacred in Ireland. As long as Cuan and Corcran are able to govern, the authority is theirs."

"But . . ."

"No buts. Let it be." Donough rode on in silence for a few heartbeats, then added, "For now."

The men with him exchanged meaningful glances and grinned.

In time Cashel rose before them from the plains of Tipperary. Donough reined in his horse. "King of Munster," he murmured to himself.

Only Fergal heard him. Urging his horse so close that his knee pressed against Donough's, he said, "If you are not going to be Ard Ri for now, why not be King of Munster?"

"If I will not challenge a poet and a holy man, what makes you think I would usurp my brother's title?"

"But do you not have the desire?"

Donough turned on his horse and looked at his cousin squarely. Responding to the shift in weight, the brown colt skittered sideways. "Desire? Let me tell you about desire. There are . . . things . . . I have wanted with such a passion I thought I would be torn apart. I never got any of them. Instead I have substitutes. Compromises."

"Half of what you have," Fergal told him, "would make most men very happy."

"Would it?" Donough's voice sounded strangely faraway. "They're welcome to it then. My cattle, my fort, my . . ." He paused, then gave a self-mocking laugh, "my wife. Though I suspect someone already has her."

Giving his horse a mighty kick, he rode forward at the gallop, and the company surged after him.

While Donough and his men approached Cashel from the north, Lethgen encamped on the south side of the limestone escarpment. There he made bold plans for theft.

Once deliberate law-breaking would have been unimaginable to him. But times had changed. The Irish had taken to plundering and pillaging with the enthusiasm of Vikings now that the power and majesty of Brian Boru no longer deterred them.

Lethgen's plan involved paying a formal visit to the King of Munster on the pretext of discussing the Munster cattle trade. Being polite to Teigue would be a necessary act of hypocrisy, for he felt Teigue had treated his friend Donough very badly. Lethgen was a man of abrupt emotions. He loved Donough. He hated Teigue.

While he kept the king occupied, his men circulated among the servants at Cashel asking questions. Lethgen, like Carroll before him, was aware that the lowly often know the most. Once he learned the location of the buried sword, Lethgen thought it should be a simple matter to dig it up by cover of night and carry the prize back to Donough.

But the theft, he discovered, would not be so simple after

all. When he met his men back at the camp, the spies reported, "The king keeps the sword with him now."

"Are you certain?"

"Absolutely. We are reliably informed he has secreted the weapon in a chest of clothing in his private chamber."

Lethgen's eyes gleamed. "Isn't that interesting? I do enjoy a challenge."

After fortifying himself with a considerable amount of ale, he paid a second visit to the king's hall. As before, he found the hall crowded with people seeking the king's judgment or support. Lethgen loitered among the crowd. He was not eager to speak with Teigue again, he was waiting for a different opportunity.

The moment came. No one was watching; he darted unnoticed through a doorway and down a passage described to him as leading to Teigue's private chamber.

He narrowly avoided being seen by Maeve, who, with her oldest son Turlough, a boy of some seven years, was just leaving the royal chamber. Lethgen flattened himself in an angle of the wall until they passed, then advanced on tiptoe into the room. His breathing sounded very loud in his own ears. He was filled with a sense of drunken daring.

A small fire crackled in a bronze brazier, casting enough light to reveal the carved wooden clothing chest at the foot of the king's bed. Holding his breath for fear the lid would creak, Lethgen opened the chest and began pawing through its contents.

The sword was at the very bottom. He found it by touch rather than sight and with an effort lifted it out.

Firelight gleamed on a weapon too large for any ordinary man to wield. The length of the blade and weight of the hilt astonished Lethgen. For a moment he could only stare, awed to realize he was holding in his hands—in his own hands!—the sword of Brian Boru.

"What are you doing with that!" cried an angry voice.

* * *

Upon reaching Cashel, Donough did not go directly to see Teigue. "I don't want to meet my brother until I've had time to bathe and make myself presentable," he explained to Fergal. "You should do the same, if you mean to make a good impression on the women."

Fergal agreed enthusiastically.

When they identified themselves, they were shown to a large guesting house at the foot of the Rock of Cashel. The top of the escarpment was too small to allow for a full complement of royal buildings. Only the great hall, the chapel, the private apartments, and an armory were there.

Everyone else must wait below, looking up.

When he was attired in fresh clothing and with his auburn hair still damp from the comb, Donough set out up the steep incline to the top of the Rock. He went on foot, with no escort and no weapon.

A massive double gate at the top of the incline barred the way to the interior, which was ringed with a wall of stone. One gate was ajar, but no sentry stood there. A roar of voices came from inside, punctuated by shouts and profanity.

Puzzled by the volume of noise, Donough stepped through the gateway. He was barely inside the walls when someone ran toward him, pursued by a crowd of shouting guards and a hail of spears.

Donough ducked instinctively.

The running man crashed into him, staggering them both. It was Lethgen.

"What . . ." Donough began, but Lethgen was thrusting something at him.

"Take this, I did it for you!" the cattle lord cried. He plunged past Donough, through the gate and down the incline. His pursuers pounded after him.

Looking down, Donough discovered he was holding the sword of Brian Boru.

Chapter Fifty-six

✠

My life ended that day. Or rather, any hope of the life I anticipated ended that day.

At first I could only gape dumbfounded at the weapon Lethgen had thrust upon me. I knew what it was, of course, though I never touched it before. Our father did not allow any of us to handle his sword, not even Murrough.

Just holding the hilt in my left hand gave me a strange feeling. For a moment the only thought in my head was astonishment to find it was not too large for me.

Then a guard grabbed me by the shoulders and shook me. "You!" he shouted into my face. "Did you have something to do with this?!"

"With what?" I pulled away from him. "Are you accusing me of something? I am Prince Donough, and I . . ."

He recognized me then, and a variety of emotions chased one another across his face. At last he simply said, "Come with me."

I was led through a great hall crowded with shrill, excited people who seemed to be trying to explain the unexplainable to each other by means of half-finished sentences and wild gestures. Beyond the hall a passage led to the king's chamber.

My brother lay on his back beside an overturned brazier.

Part of his clothing had caught fire and there was a stink of burnt cloth. Burns were not the problem, however.

A terrible wound in his chest poured blood.

I fell to my knees beside him. "Teigue! Teigue!"

He opened his eyes. Framed by their thick lashes, they were as soft and puzzled as a child's. With an effort he focused them on me. His mouth worked but no sound came out.

I heard a sob and glanced around. Maeve was leaning against the wall, holding her burned hands away from her body. It was she who had beat out the fire.

The boy Turlough shoved through a crowd at the doorway and stopped abruptly, staring at his father on the floor.

When I turned back to Teigue his lips were moving again. "You," he said, looking straight at me. "You."

His eyes closed and he seemed to go flat all at once.

With a pitiful cry, Maeve hurled herself past me and onto his body. Turlough ran to join her. The lad bent over his father and called his name several times, then glared at me with burning eyes. "You did this," he accused. "I heard him. You did this!"

"I did nothing," I protested. Tears were rolling down my face but I was hardly aware of them.

"You're carrying a sword!" Turlough cried, pointing.

Looking down, I discovered I still held the sword of Brian Boru in my hand. But there was no blood on the blade.

Though nothing made sense yet, I was relieved my father's weapon had not killed my brother.

Could the fatal wound have been made by a short-sword? I leaned forward to try to get a better look, to see if the blow had only penetrated or had gone all the way through. The mighty weapon I held was capable of cleaving a man in half.

But young Turlough blocked me with his own body. "Assassin!" he screamed at me.

Guards seized me then and dragged me out of the chamber, while I tried to point out to anyone who might listen that the sword I held was clean.

But no one wanted to hear me.

They threw me into a tiny chamber without a window, and I was left alone for a time I could not measure. There the full realization gradually dawned on me.

Teigue was dead. Murdered. My brother.

My last brother.

And they thought I did it.

"No!" I roared with all the power in my lungs. My cry reverberated in the stone chamber, deafening me.

Eventually they came for me. I was taken back to that terrible chamber, where Teigue now lay on the bed, his face covered by a blanket. Maeve sat beside him, keening. The chief brehon of Munster was in the room together with several other officials. Someone had had the sense to take Turlough away.

Questions were asked of me and I tried to answer. I must have been convincing; eventually I was allowed to ask some questions of my own.

"Lethgen of the Ely stabbed the king," I was told. "It may have been a thwarted theft. When you were seen with that sword in your hand everyone assumed you were involved."

"I was not! I knew nothing about this until I walked in the gate and he flung the sword at me!"

I honestly protested my innocence but already I was sick at heart. As clearly as if I had been an eyewitness, I saw what must have happened.

And knew I was indeed responsible.

When Maeve looked at me with reddened eyes, I think she knew too.

Officially, the brehons accepted my word. I was a prince of the Dal Cais; if I said I had not ordered the assassination, I must be believed. The unfortunate Lethgen had already been caught by the king's guards and slain on the spot without benefit of trial.

In my father's day he would have had a trial.

Chapter Fifty-seven

"God has bestowed a martyrdom upon me," bewailed Cathal Mac Maine, "by allowing me to live long enough to see this dark day. Teigue Mac Brian has been murdered amid terrible rumors that his own brother was somehow involved."

"Shall I put that in the annals?" inquired Brother Declan.

"Certainly not! Would you disgrace the Dal Cais?"

Declan refrained from recording the rumors in the Annals of Kill Dalua, but other annalists would be less generous.

No one would accuse Donough to his face, however.

It could be imprudent to accuse the King of Munster of murder.

Donough had been more surprised than anyone when Maeve sent for him the day after Teigue's death was shouted across Munster. The province was plunged into mourning. Masses were being said in every church and abbey. Together with his men, Donough was waiting to attend the king's final entombment.

He dreaded facing his brother's widow. Only his pride enabled him to meet her with his head up, though his face was bleak.

Hers was equally bleak. She had aged a decade overnight.

They gazed at each other in silence for a long moment, then with a cry Maeve flung herself into his arms.

Donough held the sobbing woman and patted her awkwardly, intensely aware of his maimed hand touching her.

"I'm sorry," he kept murmuring.

"I know." Her voice was muffled against his chest.

"I didn't order him killed, Maeve."

"I know that too. You never would have done that."

An integrity bred in his bones compelled him to say, "Yet I do feel responsible . . ."

She tore herself out of his arms and gazed up at him with frightening intensity. "Never say that. Never!"

"But . . ."

"Whatever burdens your conscience bears it must bear in silence from now on, Donough. Don't you understand?"

He hurt too much. He could not follow her thoughts.

Maeve bit her lip and tried again. "You are the senior prince of the Dal Cais now. My son Turlough is too young to be king, but the last thing any of the Dalcassians want is to relinquish the rule of Munster to the Owenachts again after all these years. The kingship has to stay in the clan O Brian.

"Therefore you must succeed Teigue."

Donough flinched as if she had struck him. "I cannot! Don't you see? People will consider it proof that I deliberately killed him for his title."

"Since it isn't true you have nothing to fear. This is what Teigue would have wanted, Donough, for the sake of our children and their children. The O Brian dynasty must continue."

"Through me?" he asked bitterly.

"Through you if need be. He loved you, for all your quarrels."

"I wish I could believe that."

She smiled sadly. "I tell you it is true."

Donough realized the effort this was costing her and was awed by her courage.

On the day of Teigue's entombment the chief brehon announced Donough Mac Brian was to be the next King of Munster.

He could not stay in his stronghold in Ely territory, because that would only fuel rumors of a conspiracy. Therefore his principal residence would have to be either at Cashel—or Kincora.

"I wanted Kincora with my whole soul," he admitted to Fergal. "And I wanted my father's sword. Now I have both, and I find I want neither. They cost too much."

Reluctantly, he decided to occupy Cashel. When Maeve had taken her children to their old home in the valley west of the Shannon, Donough ordered the murder chamber sealed. He had a new one built for himself a few paces beyond the tomb of another assassinated king—his own uncle, Mahon.

Upon Mahon's death, Brian Boru had succeeded him as King of Munster. Now the crown he had worn would be worn by Donough.

The irony was too close to the bone.

Fergal returned to Tipperary to escort Driella and the rest of Donough's household to Cashel. The Saxon woman was heavy with child and the journey was made very slowly. Geoffrey rode in the cart beside her, holding her hand.

Others were traveling to Cashel; the roads were black with people. Some came to express their loyalty, others out of morbid curiosity, eager to smack their lips at the sight of a king who had murdered his brother to gain a kingdom.

A king who was one of the high and mighty Dal Cais.

In spite of what he had said about being too old to travel any more, Carroll also returned to Cashel. He was immediately taken to Donough, whose appearance alarmed the old historian.

"You're as thin as a hazel wand!"

"Am I?" Donough shrugged indifferently.

"And your hair . . ."

"I know, it's turning gray. People have already pointed that out to me. Gleefully, some of them, as if it's no more than I deserve."

"You are guilty of no crime," Carroll said with certainty.

"Will history vindicate me then?"

"Ah." The other man stared down at the floor. "It depends on who tells the history."

"The Owenachts are doing everything they can to make sure their version is the one remembered. I suspect they will influence at least some of the annalists."

"Then you must live a life," Carroll replied, "which gives the lie to your accusers."

"I have lived such a life," Donough countered. "I've never done anything to make people think I could be guilty of fratricide. I've always done my best to live up to my father."

Carroll said softly, "Perhaps that's the problem."

"What do you mean?"

"You have taken too much on yourself. It was incredibly difficult for him. You started halfway up a ladder of which he had built every rung, then climbed from the bottom. Other people's expectations of Brian were never as demanding as his own."

"But he could do anything!"

Carroll laughed. "No, he couldn't. He was simply clever at making others think he could. He held us all spellbound and I suspect you've fallen victim to the same enchantment. I admired him as much as any man, but over the years I learned he was only human."

"He was more than human," Donough insisted doggedly.

The other man only shook his head. "You lack a historian's perspective. I tell you this frankly—I who loved him— Brian Boru has blighted the lives of his sons."

Donough did not want to hear.

On the day he was inaugurated King of Munster he made himself carry his father's sword.

All eyes were on him—and on that shining blade. He stood before his people with his head high and his face set in dauntless lines the oldest of them well remembered, and they cheered him. Even his enemies cheered him that day.

He received messages of congratulations from Malcolm of Scotland and Godwine of Wessex, and both sent gifts appropriate to a king. Malcolm wrote, "I trust you now have a considerable army at your disposal. Our struggles against various foes continue, and we would not take amiss the loan of some men-at-arms."

Donough promptly dispatched a contingent of Munstermen to Alba.

Earl Godwine's letter to his son-in-law was slightly different. "The death of Llywelyn, King of Wales, coincides with your own accession to kingship, thus reminding us that change is a law of nature. Canute retains the throne of England and is in full vigor, but I now have my first son, a big lusty boy whom we christened Harold Godwinesson. He is a splendid fellow, the image of me. My fond hope is to see him follow Canute on the throne. Should that opportunity present itself, I trust we may rely upon the support of a powerful ally in Ireland."

Powerful. Donough read the letter alone in his chamber, put it aside, took it up and read it again.

My power is only Earl Godwine's perception, he thought. *Unless someone tells him, he has no way of knowing what unstable footing I stand upon. What was it that Carroll said of my father? Ah yes—"Brian Boru was simply clever at making others think he could do anything."*

Donough summoned a scribe and wrote back to the earl, "At such time as you may require them, the full resources of my kingdom are at your disposal." He did not mention that he ruled over a divided Munster where fully half of the people, openly or secretly, thought him a fratricide. Nor did he mention that he had lost all hope of ever becoming Ard Ri . . . unless he acquired an exceptionally powerful ally himself by the time Cuan and Corcran were no longer able to rule.

He was still a young man, however. And there was always a chance Harold Godwinesson might someday gain the English throne. Godwine was an able player of the games of politics and power.

When the company of warriors from Munster arrived in Alba, Malcolm put them to good use in his renewed battle with the Northumbrians. He also heard a most interesting version of Donough's accession to the kingship.

"Blanaid," he remarked to his wife with considerable satisfaction, "the King of Munster is as canny as a Scot. He has wisely followed my example in eliminating obstacles."

"What are you talking about?"

"Your brother Donough had your brother Teigue killed for his kingship."

Blanaid gazed at her husband in horror.

Sitric Silkbeard believed the story, too, but he was not horrified. If anything he was admiring. He had learned a degree of caution when dealing with women, however, so did not suggest to his wife Emer that one of her brothers had murdered the other.

There was no point in telling Gormlaith, either. She no longer understood anything that was said to her.

She sat or lay mute in her chamber, trapped in a body too strong to die. The spirit her flesh imprisoned was like an extinguished flame.

Alone with her in the twilight, her big strong Scottish attendant sometimes held her hand.

The next year Cuan O Lochlan died unexpectedly, but the governorship of Ireland did not revert to high kingship. By the time anyone knew of the Cuan's death Corcran had appointed a new poet to serve in his place.

Tara remained deserted. Spiders spun cobwebs within its halls.

One battle season after another passed, gave way to winter, was renewed with the spring. Sitric's Dublin Danes sallied forth to plunder and pillage, but their enthusiasm for the sport was gradually diminishing. There was too much competition.

The joint governors of the Irish, poet and priest, were totally lacking in military experience and made little effort to enforce any degree of peace.

Donough Mac Brian, King of Munster, fought the wars that were necessary to a king, proving his right to rule by keeping his enemies intimidated.

At Cashel, Driella bore a third son to join Murchad and his

brother Lorcan. The new child was small and wizened; dark-visaged. Donough took one look at him and turned away.

Driella was watching him as she lay on the bed. Something like fear touched her plump, sweaty face. By now she had, inadvertently, acquired enough Irish to be able to ask, "What name for your son?"

Donough would not look at the infant again. "Call him anything you like," he said.

As he left the chamber he met Geoffrey of the Fens in the passageway. The two men locked eyes, a rare occurrence. The expression on the priest's face was guarded; anxious. Donough's left hand slipped to the hilt of the knife he wore at his belt.

What would my father do if this man had sired a child on his wife? Kill him, surely. Then send the body back to England in a box.

But the thought of England unexpectedly reminded Donough of Earl Godwine. As if someone were whispering them in his ear, he recalled the words Godwine had written about his own son Harold; words written with such glowing pride.

Sons, he found himself thinking. Fathers.

Donough drew a deep breath and extended his right hand. With infinite gentleness he rested the mutilated hand on the priest's shoulder. When he spoke his voice was kind.

"You have a son," he said.

Chapter Fifty-eight

The young apprentice scribe sat perched like a bony heron on his three-legged stool, quivering with the effort to look both humble and attentive. Brother Declan was explaining to him, "The keeping of the annals is a sacred duty. These records invoke the past for the sake of the future, that those who read them may avoid our sins and be inspired by our sacrifices."

It was the same speech Cathal had made to Declan many years before.

While the apprentice watched, trying not to squirm, Declan dipped his quill in his ink pot and carefully scribed, "The Age of Christ, 1027. Richard the Good, King of France, Duke of Normandy, and son of Richard the Fearless, died. After sweeping through Connacht and taking many hostages, Donough Mac Brian led the army of Munster into the tribeland of Ossory. There the Munstermen suffered a great slaughter. Among those who fell was Fergal, a noble son of Anluan, son of Kennedy. Great was the grief of the Dalcassians."

But no words on parchment could convey the full extent of Donough's loss when Fergal died.

Carroll had died two years previously, finally succumbing without complaint to a combination of old men's ills. Donough had mourned him, but the death was expected.

Fergal's was not. One minute they were fighting together, with Fergal as usual slightly behind his cousin, guarding his back. Then there was a sound like a thunk, hardly audible among the other sounds of battle. A weight crashed into Donough from behind.

He turned in time to catch his dying cousin in his arms. A spear protruded from Fergal's back, the shaft still quivering.

"You can't die!" protested Donough, who had seen countless men die in the same way and knew the wound was mortal.

Fergal squinted up at him. "I don't always have to follow your orders," he said hoarsely. "I'm a prince too." He tried to grin but coughed instead. Blood ran from the corner of his mouth and his bowels opened.

He was dead by the time Donough lowered him gently to the ground.

Fergal's sacrifice brought Donough no inspiration.

It was for nothing, he told himself as he accompanied the body back to Cashel. *I was trying to prove myself the warrior my father was, and what have I accomplished? Another skirmish, another battle, and none of them truly important, none of them worth a good man's life. Kill or be killed, and where's the glory in it? You die in your own stink.* He paused, struck by a disturbing sense of having heard those words before. But when? Who said them?

He could not recall.

The season was summer and every bush was vibrant with birdsong. The air was sweet, the earth was fertile, life was brimming all around them, precious and irreplaceable.

"Nothing is worth a life," Donough abruptly said aloud.

His men stared at him.

But the fighting did not end. Donough took hostages from Leinster and Meath and they harried his borders in retaliation. Meanwhile a disaffected Munster tribe refused to pay tribute to Cashel, Munster clans raided the cattle of other Munster clans, and the king was expected to act on behalf of countless petitioners. Act, or admit he was not strong enough to be king.

So Donough rode out from Cashel again and again. Sometimes he lost, sometimes he won. The battles all had a sameness, but they were a way of passing the days, a way of escaping from those things he did not wish to think about.

Driella called the baby Donalbane.

"That's no Irish name," Donough's courtiers grumbled. He refused to respond.

Since the child's birth he had not bedded his wife. He slept in another chamber, when he could sleep. There were many nights he passed stalking through the passageways of Cashel, a tall, grave man with hungry eyes.

His body still lusted, like some animal he could not tame.

But he would never touch Driella again. His restraint was not born out of anger at her betrayal; rather, he felt he had bequeathed her to Geoffrey the day Donalbane was born.

Bedding her now would be the betrayal.

He was almost glad he had no living confidantes. He could not have explained his decision in a way that would make sense to anyone else. He only knew he was living up to some inner standard of his own—even if it did not correspond to his image of his father.

There were other women. Donough was a virile man and there were always women who sought the honor of a king's embraces.

He did not feel anything for them, for which he was thankful. He was convinced they felt nothing for him either, imperfect, disfigured, as he was. Better that no emotions were involved, so sex became a straightforward transaction with each knowing the other's price.

But he hated the desolate melancholy that descended upon him afterward.

Sometimes when he could stand it no longer he sought distraction by riding north to inspect the garrison at Kincora. At the first sight of those timbered palisades, for just one moment he could be a boy again.

By chance he was there in 1028 when Cathal Mac Maine died.

Donough paid his final respects to the old abbot and attended his entombment within the walls of Kill Dalua. He was pleased to learn his friend, Brother Senan, was to succeed Cathal. They sat together in the abbot's chamber, reminiscing about its former occupant over cups of mead.

"Mind you," Senan remarked, "he was a dedicated Christian with a strong sense of purpose, even if I did not always agree with him."

Donough raised an eyebrow. "I was never aware the two of you quarreled."

"We did not quarrel; he was the abbot and I a mere

brother. But he knew I disapproved of his actions in the matter of the druid girl, for example."

Donough tensed. "What druid girl?"

"The one you sent for, the one he sent away."

Very carefully, Donough set down his cup. "Do you mean she came to me after all?"

"She did. The late abbot told her you refused to see her. He could not sanction your association with a pagan, you see, and therefore . . ."

Donough leaped to his feet. "She did not reject me because of this?" he roared, waving his right hand in the air.

The shocked monk stared up at him, appalled to realize just how big he was, how powerfully built; how furious. "You were misled," Senan whispered, half expecting from the look on his face that Donough would hit him.

He was weak with relief when the king ran from the chamber. With an unsteady hand, he took up Donough's abandoned cup and drained it.

At the same time, Sitric Silkbeard decided he had had enough. Since Clontarf his pleasure in life had been steadily eroded. He could not even look forward to Valhalla, because the chances of his dying in battle were very slim. He did not have enough warriors left to venture outside the walls of Dublin. The previous summer his Danes had been virtually destroyed by an army of Meathmen, and this spring his oldest son had been taken hostage by a prince of Brega who demanded as ransom twelve hundred cows, seven score British horses, and sixty ounces of white silver.

The plunderers were being plundered.

Now Sitric's wife Emer was in a terrible temper. Gormlaith had begun screaming at night and Emer demanded he get rid of her.

"What am I to do, set her adrift in the bay?"

"Or set her alight with a blazing torch, I don't care."

"I will do neither; she is my mother."

"Then send her to Donough," snarled Emer, "before I set fire to her myself."

When they were first married all those years ago, Sitric had been amused by the Irish temper of Brian Boru's daughter. He had laughingly referred to her as "my little lioness." The charm had soon worn thin, and ended forever on the day of Clontarf, when she had taunted him about his defeat and he struck her.

His face set in stubborn lines. "With every hand raised against me except Donough's, I cannot afford to break trust with him. I agreed to keep her here and keep her I shall. And if any harm comes to her through you, the same will be visited on you."

"But you have to do *something*!" Emer shrieked at him.

Sitric did something. He converted to Christianity. "If I cannot get into Valhalla," he explained to the bishop who baptized him, "I can at least lay siege to Heaven."

The bishop was dubious about the aging Viking's chances of entering Heaven, but wisely refrained from saying so. The conversion of Sitric Silkbeard was much to his credit.

After his baptism Sitric promptly departed on a pilgrimage to Rome, leaving his troubles far behind.

Donough had made a much shorter journey. From Kill Dalua he had ridden at breakneck speed, almost killing a horse under him, to Drumcullaun Lough. There it was a simple matter to locate the druid cabin among the oaks.

But once he drew rein and spancelled his horse so it would not wander off, he felt lost. What could he say to her after so long?

A worse thought struck him. What if she had another man?

He almost turned around and got back on his horse.

But he had never run from anything; he would not run now. With firm stride he walked to the closed door and banged on it with his one good fist.

In the silence that followed he could hear the hammering of his heart.

Someone moved inside; the door creaked on its hinges.

Cumara looked out at him in disbelief.

A few moments later Donough was inside, warming his hands by the fire. "My father's old friend Padraic gave me a home with his family," Cumara was explaining. "I've been here ever since, occupying myself with copying my father's biography of your father. But my health is poor, I think only their ancient wisdom keeps me alive."

"Where are the others—Padraic and his family?"

"Och, he himself died two winters ago, and his older daughter and two of his sons are married and gone. There's only Daman and Cera living here now with me."

"Cera." Donough braced himself. "Your wife?" he asked politely.

With a hollow laugh Cumara replied, "Not for lack of trying, but she won't have me. A wild one, our Cera. She won't have any man, she belongs only to herself."

Cumara was beginning to recover from his surprise. Squinting at Donough in the dim light, he thought he detected an expression of intense relief. Was the other so glad to find him, then? How gratifying! "Where are the rest of your men, my friend?" he asked aloud.

"I came alone."

"You couldn't! We heard you were made King of Munster; surely you go everywhere with an army now."

"I left them at Kincora," said Donough. "I allowed no one to come with me."

"Why not? You came to see me and wanted no one with you?"

"I did not even know you were here."

Cumara was taken aback. "Then I don't understand what . . . why . . ."

The door creaked open and daylight fell across Donough's face, giving Cumara a good look at his expression as Cera entered the cabin. Suddenly all the questions were answered.

She gazed at Donough in wonder. But when she started to speak, he sprang to his feet and crushed her so tightly against him Cera could say nothing at all.

"Ssshhh," he whispered into her hair. "Ssshhh."

He simply held her; a tall man enveloping a small woman in his embrace, letting their bodies speak for them with sensations more eloquent than words.

With a sad and wistful smile, Cumara arose and left the cabin.

Sometime later—much later—they spoke of that day at Kill Dalua when she had tried and failed to see him. "I thought you would not come to me because I was mutilated," Donough told her.

By way of answer she caught hold of his right arm and turned back the sleeve, exposing the discolored thumb and scarred, denuded palm. She held the ruined hand in the firelight so she could see it clearly, then bent her head and covered it with kisses.

Chapter Fifty-nine

When he took her back to Kincora with him she asked no questions. She was content to sit behind him with her arms wrapped around his waist and her cheek resting against the rough wool of his brat. From time to time she hummed. Her voice did not seem to enter his ears, but rather to inhabit them, as if it had always been part of him.

Upon reaching Kincora he took her at once to the king's chamber. His, now. His by right. "We will rest here for a few days," he told her, assuming she understood they would go on to Cashel afterward.

He was King of Munster; he belonged to his people. Cera was just for himself.

The first problem arose when he mentioned his plans to Senan, expecting congratulations for a mistake rectified.

Instead the new Abbot of Kill Dalua was dismayed. "You can't install a pagan woman at Cashel! I did not approve of the way the matter was handled, but I agree with the premise behind it. Thanks in large part to Cathal Mac Maine, there is now a strong movement to stamp out the old heathen ways in Ireland. For the King of Munster to make a favorite of a druid woman would be an open defiance of the Church.

"Bring her to me, Donough, that we may begin her conversion at once!"

But Cera had no intention of being converted. "I cannot change my spirit," she told Donough, "any more than you can grow a new hand. Does my spirit displease you so?"

"Everything about you pleases me," he replied truthfully. "Change nothing for me."

Once that decision was made, however, he must be circumspect about their relationship. He decided to take her to Cashel secretly and find her some unobtrusive place to live close to the Rock, yet away from the eyes of the Church.

When he told Cera his intentions she balked again. "I don't want to be hidden away like someone you're ashamed of! I want to live with you. I need to see your face beside me in the first light of morning and fall asleep in your arms at night."

"I have a wife," Donough tried to explain.

"Set her aside if you prefer me. Surely you would not insult her pride by keeping her in such a position. Apply to the brehons for a divorce and . . ."

"I cannot, Cera. You don't understand. I need her, or rather I need her connections. My position is tenuous at best and depends on other people's perceptions of my strength. If I end my relationship with King Canute, I may destroy forever my chance of becoming Ard Ri."

Her eyes locked with his. "You want to be Ard Ri?"

"My whole life has been directed toward that purpose."

"Do you want to be Ard Ri?" she repeated.

How clear her dark eyes were! How deeply they looked into his soul!

"I don't know," he said miserably.

He lay with her in the king's chamber at Kincora and wondered if his father had ever brought his druid to this room; this bed. Were their spirits watching from the shadows?

Then Cera's hands moved on his body and her mouth set fire to his flesh, and he forgot about his ghosts.

While she sat astride him, riding him, he gazed up in admiration at the underside of her breasts. Their lush ripeness was not obvious when she was clothed. Now they bounced with her movements. Cupping them in his palms, he bounced them higher and she laughed.

Cera's laughter rippled through her interior muscles. They clenched his penis rhythmically, provoking an orgasm so intense it hurt. Yet within moments he felt himself stiffening again, demanding more.

There was no limit to Cera's joyful giving.

She let him take her to Cashel with a shawl over her head to keep her face in shadow. She let him provide her with a hidden house—of warm timber, not cold stone like the structures atop the Rock—and there she waited each day for him to come to her.

For Donough she sacrificed her pride.

But in spite of her best efforts, she could not hide the pain it cost her. Sometimes in an unguarded moment he glimpsed anguish in her eyes and knew the depth of her love for him.

Donough vowed to himself that her sacrifice would not be in vain. He redoubled his efforts to put himself in a position where he might eventually make a successful claim on the high kingship.

Having proven himself as a warrior, he began endowing churches and monasteries. At the same time and with total ruthlessness he cleared Munster of the majority of its outlaws and made the roads reasonably safe.

Sometimes he felt he was fighting shadows. The deep forces of disintegration at work in Ireland could not be held back by any man.

Maeve came from her valley to inform Donough she had sent her oldest son to be fostered by Diarmait Mac Maelnambo, Prince of Leinster. "Turlough needs a noble father," she explained.

"I would gladly foster him. My brother's child . . ."

"Unthinkable. Even if I were willing, Turlough would never agree; he still holds you responsible for Teigue's death. No, it is better he grow to manhood as far from you as possible. Seeing you only keeps his anger alive.

"Besides," she added with a political shrewdness he had not expected of her, "someday he may have need of a strong alliance with Leinster."

He knew then that Maeve meant to see her son rule as King of Munster. Immediately Donough began grooming his own son Murchad to be a warrior prince; a king.

A year after Sitric Silkbeard returned from a protracted pilgrimage to Rome where he had been surprised to meet not a few fellow Vikings, Brother Declan's apprentice made his first entry in the Annals of Kill Dalua.

"The Age of Christ, 1030. Gormlaith, Princess of Leinster, mother of Sitric, King of Dublin, and of Donough, King of Munster, died. It was this Gormlaith who took three leaps which a woman shall never take again: To Dublin with Olaf, to Tara with Malachi, and to Kincora with Brian Boru."

Donough wept for her in private, and only Cera knew.

"If I ever have a daughter I shall name her Gormlaith," he vowed. But Cera did not dare give him children, though she ached to do so. A child would reveal their secret past any keeping; he would not be able to hide his joy and his pride.

With the passage of time their desire grew instead of diminishing. Coupling was richer, deeper, more inventive. Donough teased, "Surely such passion can't be natural!"

Soberly, Cera responded, "I would not employ druid sorcery for this. The only magic is in ourselves."

"Ourselves?"

Her grave expression softened into a smile. "Both of us. The magic is in both of us," she told him.

The following autumn an urgent message arrived from Alba.

"In spite of my efforts to conciliate him," Malcolm wrote, "Canute, King of England, has attacked Alba. He is marching north with a large army including a contingent of Danes recruited from Dublin. Therefore I call upon you to send me as many warriors as you can to hold Alba for my nephew Duncan."

The request rocked Donough. Assembling his wisest counselors, he explained the situation. "If I go to Malcolm's aid I find myself opposing Canute, thus making an enemy of the King of England. My wife is related to Canute," he added unnecessarily.

The chief brehon of Munster pointed out, "And your sister is wife to Malcolm. Which tie is stronger?"

There was too much advice altogether. Everyone had an opinion; none of them seemed to have an answer. At last Donough sent them all away.

Late in the day he found himself alone, leaning his elbows on the stone wall which encircled the top of the Rock of Cashel. A shorter man would have had to rest his chin on the same surface. Beyond lay Munster, glimmering in watery twilight.

Compromise. He considered his options. *Not possible in this situation.*

Avoidance. Pretend I never received Malcolm's letter. But avoidance is the coward's way and in the end it would cost me both of them, Malcolm and Canute.

Gazing fixedly into the night, Donough sought to think like his father.

Which is the more dangerous enemy? Canute, obviously. He has a larger army and more allies. If I am ever to gain Tara, it is Canute who can give me the advantage I need. Malcolm is an old man, a spent force. Canute is one of the Land Leapers. The future is with him.

In the same circumstances, Malcolm the savage pragmatist would probably do what Donough was about to do. But knowing that did not make him feel any better. He went to Cera and drank far too much ale.

The next day he wrote a long letter not to Malcolm, but to Blanaid, apologizing for his inability to send warriors "at this time." He related details of the various wars he was fighting and the number of men he could summon to his banner, giving an impression of a man already committed to the fullest, which was not untrue. Concluding with fond words for his sister, he sent the letter by swiftest messenger and waited.

No response came.

Donough never heard from his sister again.

Only later did it occur to him that siding with Malcolm would have freed him of the necessity of maintaining a marriage with Driella. But his decision was vindicated when Malcolm accepted Canute as overlord.

Donough had chosen the winning side, a decision he earnestly sought to square with his conscience.

In his battles both external and internal, Cera was his sanctuary. In the autumn of 1034 he went straight to her after learning the King of the Scots and the Picts had been

murdered at Glamis. As Malcolm had desired, the throne of
Alba passed to Duncan. And as was normal with kingship,
the succession was soon bitterly contested by Mac Beth of
Moray.

"Fortunately, that is one conflict which does not concern
me," Donough declared with some relief.

Then he resolutely put the matter out of his mind. When
he was sitting in Cera's small house, with his long legs
stretched out and her light weight in his lap, he could forget
there were such things as dynastic struggles. He could
forget . . . for a time.

But even the King of England was subject to the vagaries
of fortune. In 1035 Canute himself died unexpectedly,
causing a scramble for power. The next fifteen years was a
period of ineffectual kings and political turmoil until at last
Edward, known as the Confessor, ascended the throne—
and had Earl Godwine and his family expelled. They were
accused of plotting the new king's overthrow.

Donough read the earl's subsequent letter aloud to Cera.

"My trusted son-in-law,

"For the sake of your wife his sister, I beg you give refuge
to my son Harold. My family has been broken up and dis-
persed and our dangers multiply. I do not fear for myself,
for I am an old man and have not long to live, but Harold's
future is yet to come. Shelter him, I beg you, and give him
what support you can, for the sake of your wife my
daughter.

"Your servant, Godwine, formerly Earl of Wessex and
Kent."

"What do you think?" Donough asked when he finished.

Cera gave him a searching look. "I think you have always
regretted refusing Malcolm," she replied.

A letter sped to Godwine, assuring him his son Harold
would be welcome at Cashel.

Meanwhile the condition of Ireland sank into both a moral
and a physical depression. Battles broke out continually.

There seemed to be a hunger among men to rend and tear. No place was safe from plunder. While Donough marched east to retaliate against an attack by the Leinstermen, a warrior band from Connacht seized their opportunity and sacked the great monastic school of Clonmacnois.

At the same time the land was beset by natural calamities. Rain fell incessantly. Rivers flooded, cattle drowned, the earth oozed moisture like blood until crops rotted in the fields.

Although the Irish traditionally blamed bad kings for bad weather, the priests began saying it was God's punishment on the people for their wickedness.

Cera was amused by such claims. "Your Christ-men simply don't know how to placate their god," she told Donough.

"I suppose you could do better?"

She twinkled up at him. "I might."

But it was still raining when a weary and sodden Harold Godwinesson arrived at Cashel late in the summer of 1050. The young man was a strapping blond with the muscular grace of a warrior. Donough could see little resemblance between Harold and Driella, but nevertheless she fell upon her brother with glad cries and a babble of Saxon.

Donough thought with a pang of Blanaid, lost to him.

He did what he could to make the exiled Godwinesson comfortable while apologizing for the miserable weather. Harold was not interested in Irish misfortunes, however. In spite of exhaustion that left dark rings under his eyes, he stayed up most of the first night complaining about the injustice that had been done his family, who were now scattered from Flanders to Ireland. He was very bitter.

"They call old Edward a saintly man," he snarled. "I have another name for him."

Once Harold had rested from his journey his natural optimism began to emerge, however. He spoke of fulfilling his father's dream and replacing Edward the Confessor with a more virile king—himself. Soon he was brimming with the future.

I used to be like that, recalled Donough. *Hot and eager, ready for anything. In youth we are immortal, and it is always summer.*

He found himself caught up in Harold's enthusiasm and moved by the younger man's desire to fulfill Earl Godwine's dream.

Soon Donough was agreeing to supply him with warriors and arrange with the Norse of Waterford for ships to carry him and his men to the Isle of Wight, where his younger brothers were in hiding. With such reinforcements Harold could plan a return to England and a campaign to gain the throne.

Harold Godwinesson, King of England, Donough whispered to himself. *Indebted to me.*

Suddenly it all opened up again. Standing in the smoky great hall of Cashel, he envisioned himself under the clean, windswept sky at Tara, stepping onto the Stone of Fal.

That night in the privacy of his chamber he took out the highly polished metal mirror which had belonged to his mother. Upon her death her Scottish attendant had sent it to him; he kept it with his father's harp and sword.

For a long time he stared into the mirror's surface.

The face he saw reflected might almost have been that of Brian Boru. Seamed by a hard life and the passage of half a century, it was stern, grave. Commanding.

Ard Ri.

Audacity in war and competence in administration are not enough, the face in the mirror told him.

Donough nodded. By now he knew how to play the game.

He sent for the chief brehon and a scribe and worked late into the night. When he was so tired his brain felt like mud, he rode alone down the steep incline from Cashel, trusting his horse to know where to go. The animal followed a familiar pathway to a small house submerged in dense woods some distance from the Rock.

The woman who lived there had chosen a site where any view of Cashel was blocked. She could not bear to see where Donough lived with another woman.

Without ever being told when he would come, Cera knew the moment his horse set foot on the sloping road. She opened the door and stood waiting, framed by the firelight behind her.

Once he had thought she could not possibly comprehend his life. Now he lay in her arms and told her his secret thoughts, his most private plans, and she listened and understood.

When he rode away in the morning she stood in the doorway, following him with her eyes.

Requesting the chieftains and senior clergy of Munster to meet with him, Donough displayed for them a new aspect of his kingliness—an extensive knowledge of the usages of law.

In the Annals of Kill Dalua, Declan's successor wrote:

"The Year of Christ, 1051. At a convening of the wisest men in Munster, Donough Mac Brian presented and enacted new laws and restraints upon every form of injustice. In consequence, God has favored Ireland with a return to clement weather."

In the weeks that followed, old friends commended Donough and old enemies grudgingly paid him tribute.

"Your time has come," his allies insisted. "There has been no true Ard Ri since Malachi Mor, and the Irish are reduced to a pack of quarreling hounds. Assert your right to your father's high kingship. We will support you; all Munster will support you."

"I need more than Munster," Donough told them. "I have to have allies in the other provinces as well. Princes who recognize that their interests lie with mine; powerful clergy who can influence the people . . ."

"The Church will support you," he was assured.

Donough paid a visit to the Abbot of Kill Dalua. But when Senan asked him outright, "Is that druid still with you?" he would not lie.

"She is."

"Send her from you, Donough. You are far from being a young man and she is no longer a young woman; surely the fires have burned out. Only if you send her away can the Church give you the support you seek. But with Rome behind you, you may yet be Ard Ri of Ireland."

Chapter Sixty

Senan spoke the truth. Donough was not a young man, and there was more than a little gray in Cera's hair.

At Cashel whole days passed when Donough never saw Driella at all. She might be sewing in the grianan with her women, or kneeling in the chapel at her devotions. Then he would glimpse a fat, pleasant-faced woman pacing contentedly beside Geoffrey, who had gone quite bald. They were fond of strolling across the lawn together, talking in their common language that neither had ever forgotten.

When Donough nodded to Driella her answering smile was polite. They had discharged their duties to one another and both understood nothing more was required.

Driella had made a life for herself that suited her. She was luckier than most.

Donough wished her well.

Senan was expecting an answer about Cera, but he could

not give him the answer he wanted. "Surely the fires have burned out," Senan had said.

How little he knew.

I am a fly trapped in amber.

And still the seasons passed.

Murchad had grown into a sturdy, belligerent young man. Not as tall as Donough, he was nicknamed "Murchad of the Short Shield." He spoke confidently of the day he would follow his father as King of Munster.

In Leinster, Diarmait Mac Mael-nambo succeeded to the kingship. Within weeks of his inauguration Donough discovered he had an aggressive new rival. Diarmait's foster-son, Turlough Mac Teigue, took to the battlefield with him. They attacked Waterford, then together laid successful siege to Dublin.

Diarmait proclaimed himself King of Dublin and the Foreigners, exiling the sons of Sitric Silkbeard, who had died while on pilgrimage.

Diarmait and Turlough Mac Teigue made a formidable team.

Donough's followers clamored for him to strike them down before they became any stronger. "Diarmait means to gain a foothold in Munster," they warned, "by having young Turlough replace you as king here."

"Turlough has adherents in Munster already," Donough confided to Cera. "All of the Dalcassians do not support me; there is a faction which has never ceased to believe I murdered my brother. In a confrontation they would side with my nephew."

Under his feet he felt the shifts of power.

In England, Harold Godwine was maneuvering himself into position to replace the aged Edward the Confessor on the throne.

In Normandy, William, the bastard Duke, was considering a claim of his own to the kingship of England.

In Ireland, Leinster challenged Munster on one battlefield after another. Connacht and Ulster warred perpetually; occasionally Connacht sided with Leinster against Munster. In the absence of a strong High King to serve as a unifying force, Ireland's provincial kings savaged their neighbors.

"Assert your right to be Ard Ri, Father," demanded Murchad of the Short Shield. "I will then rule here at Cashel."

"Give up your druid," demanded the Church, "and Tara will be yours. With the support of Rome the Dalcassians will be forced to unify behind you."

He was a man; there were decisions he must make alone. Even Cera—particularly Cera—could not help him.

One chance, one chance, thundered like a drumbeat through him. *One final glorious chance to win it all!*

He was old, but not too old to fight. The years of life left to him could be made splendid with the realization of a dream. Donough had only to stretch out his hand.

Now, while there was still time.

Alone in his chamber at Cashel, he took up Gormlaith's mirror once more and gazed soberly at the face that looked back at him.

This time he was sure whose face it was.

On a brisk spring day Donough set out for Kill Dalua. As he neared the monastery he paused to admire a row of slender birch trees crowning a nearby hill like unlit candles, waiting for the flame of the sun.

No warrior escort accompanied the King of Munster. He was dressed in a simple tunic and a plain woolen brat. His face was serene, that of a man who had come to terms with himself at last.

After making him welcome with mead, the monks sent for their abbot. Senan expressed great pleasure at the visit.

"Have you finally come to bring me good news?" he asked hopefully.

"I have come to make a confession and an announcement."

"A confession?" Frowning, Senan tented his fingers. Was Donough going to admit to his brother's assassination after all? What should be the Church's response?

"From the day I learned that Cathal Mac Maine had kept Cera from me," said Donough, "I hated your predecessor and everything he stood for. In my heart I ceased to reverence his Church."

Senan was deeply shocked. "You've taken too many blows to the head over the years, you don't know what you're saying. I warn you, you put your mortal soul in danger!"

"I know exactly what I'm saying. I have done my duty—by Munster, my tribe, my family—even by the Church. I felt a hypocrite every time I laid a gift on the altar. Is that what Christ wanted of us? That we should become masters of hypocrisy?" Donough gave his head a small, sad shake.

"Now I am done with duty," he continued. "Before I die I shall seek absolution of my sins for the sake of my children. But before I die I intend to live, Senan. Live fully, without compromise."

"What are you talking about? Does this mean you agree to do everything necessary to achieve . . ."

"I have done everything necessary. I have already told Driella good-bye; this is my farewell to you. If Murchad wants to rule at Cashel he can fight for the right as kings have fought before. I leave it to him. Cera is waiting for me at Kincora."

The color drained from the abbot's face. "I don't understand."

"We're going away, Senan, to a quiet lakeshore where a man and woman can live in peace with whatever gods they worship. There we shall lie naked in the grass and celebrate together."

"You're talking blasphemy!"

Donough merely smiled. His gray eyes were full of light.

Holding his proud head high, he left Kill Dalua for the last time. As he passed between the gates their shadow fell briefly across his face, but then he stepped into the sun. He moved with an easy grace, like someone who had all the time in the world.

Rome, 1064

And so I walked away. Or rather, I rode away, with Cera behind me on the horse and the west wind in our faces. My father's ring was on my left hand; his harp was slung from the pommel of my saddle.

In my pack were the crown and sceptre that had been his as King of Munster.

His sword I left at Kincora.

Because it was Beltane we paused long enough to climb Crag Liath and leave an offering there, and I held my woman in my arms and gazed out across Munster. Lough Derg with the sun shining on the water gazed back at us like the blue eye of God.

Kincora lay below us. Never really mine.

We made a home for ourselves beside a quiet lake, a place inviolate, where I played the harp for her and no one spoke of war or kings. I grew a dense gray beard in which she plaited daisies.

We were not alone.

Sometimes I felt them watching us, that other king and his druid. My eyes would seek Cera's and she would nod, smiling.

I did not envy Brian his life, but I knew he envied mine.

When the time came and Cera went ahead of me into the Otherworld, I set out for Rome. I still knew how to play the game. By asking and receiving absolution from the Pope himself I hoped to expunge the stain clinging to my name. My descendants must not bear the burden of fratricide.

It was my last duty and one cannot totally escape one's duties.

I laid gifts upon the Pope's altar, various royal regalia I no longer wanted. What need ha s a man for gold when he has stood with his arm around his woman and watched the western sun gild an entire sea?

The Church proclaimed my soul clean.

What had not been done was thus undone, an irony I appreciated.

I have grown too weak to return to Ireland, so I have given instructions that my remaining possessions also pass to the Pope upon my death. They are final payment for his generosity. At the end of my life, the Church has not been unkind.

My only regret is that I shall not die at home and be put to rest beneath a tree with my Cera.

But she is with me, always.

And I . . . I am the son of Brian Boru.

I am the happiest man alive.

Author's Note

The history detailed in *Pride of Lions* is taken without revision from the chronicles of the time. The dynastic marriages by which the blood of Brian Boru entered the royal families of Scotland and England are documented, as are the events described.

In the years following 1014, Ireland went mad. With Brian's death the country quite literally lost its head, and the chaos that followed left Ireland vulnerable to any determined invader.

Malachi Mor was the last undisputed Ard Ri. Others would subsequently lay claim to the title, including Turlough Mac Teigue, who preferred to be known as Turlough O Brian. But he and five successors were at best "kings in opposition," never supported by more than a fraction of the people.

When the Normans invaded in 1170 the high kingship was soon permanently vacated, and the pattern of attempted conquest that would dominate the next eight hundred years of Irish history began.

Donough is buried in Rome; the reader may visit his tomb. Brian Boru's ring eventually made its way back to Ireland and, together with his sword, remained in the possession of the O'Brien family until the present century. As for the harp, a subsequent Pope presented it to King Henry II of England—the monarch under whom the Normans first invaded Ireland.

Donough would have appreciated the irony.

The druid Cera is fictional, but she and her lineage have roots in folkloric history. The Dalcassians of Munster have long believed in the existence of the guardian spirit called Aebhinn, who dwells on Crag Liath.

Although Donalbane disappeared from history, Donough's other children accounted for a number of progeny, as did the children of his brother Teigue. Through them the O'Brien dynasty continues to the present day.

The past belongs to those who shaped it; the future is ours to make.

A Partial Bibliography

Adamson, Ian. *The Cruthin*. Northern Ireland: Pretani Press, 1986.

Burke, Rev. Francis, trans. *Loch Ce and Its Annals*, Dublin: Hodges, Figgis & Co., 1895.

Byrne, Francis John. *Irish Kings and High-Kings*. New York: St. Martin's Press, 1973.

D'Alton, Rev. E. A. *History of Ireland*, Half-Volume I to the Year 1210. Dublin and Belfast: Gresham Publishing Co., n.d.

Ellis, Peter Beresford. *Macbeth, High King of Scotland*. Belfast: The Blackstaff Press, 1990.

Flood, J. M. *The Northmen in Ireland*, Dublin: Brown & Nolan Ltd., n.d.

Frost, James. *The History and Topography of the County of Clare*. Dublin: Mercier Press, 1978.

Gleeson, Rev. John. *History of the Ely O'Carroll Territory*. Kilkenny: Roberts Books Ltd., 1982.

Jones, Gwyn. *A History of the Vikings*. London: Oxford University Press, 1968.

Joyce, Patrick Weston. *History of Gaelic Ireland*. Dublin: The Educational Company of Ireland, 1924.

Joyce, Patrick Weston. *Social History of Ancient Ireland*, A, Vols. I and II. Dublin: The Educational Company of Ireland, 1913.

Kenney, James F. *Sources of Early History of Ireland*, Volume 1. New York: Columbia University Press, 1929.

Mac Airt, Sean, ed. and trans. *The Annals of Inisfallen*. Dublin: Dublin Institute for Advanced Studies, 1977.

Mackie, J. D. *A History of Scotland*. Middlesex, Eng.: Penguin Books, 1964.

Minahane, John. *The Christian Druids*. Dublin: Sanas Press, 1993.

Murphy, Rev. Dennis, trans. *The Annals of Clonmacnoise, to 1408*. Dublin: Dublin University Press, 1896.

Newman, Roger Chatterton. *Brian Boru, King of Ireland*. Dublin: Anvil Books, Ltd., 1983.

O Corrain, Donncha. *Ireland Before the Normans*, The Gill History of Ireland Series. Dublin: Gill & Macmillan, 1972.

O'Donoghue, John. *Historical Memoir of the O'Briens*. Dublin: Hodges, Smith, & Co., 1860.

O'Donovan, John, ed. and trans. *Annals of the Kingdom of Ireland—By the Four Masters*. Dublin: De Burca Rare Books reprint, 1990.

O Dwyer, Peter. *Celi De; Spiritual Reform in Ireland*. Dublin: Editions Tailliura, 1981.

Ritchie, Graham, and Anna Ritchie. *Scotland; Archaeology and Early History*. London: Thames & Hudson Ltd., 1981.

Stenton, Sir Frank. *Anglo-Saxon England*. London: Oxford University Press, 1971.

Stokes, Whitley, trans. *The Annals of Tigernach*, Volume 2. Wales: Llanerch Publishers, 1993.

Ua Clerigh, Arthur. *The History of Ireland to the Coming of Henry II*. London: T. Fisher Unwin, n.d.

White, P. *History of Clare and the Dalcassian Clans*. Dublin: M. H. Gill & Son, 1893.